ONLY MINE

S.K. ALLISON

ONE
WRENLEY

The rain's trying to tell me something.

It's been following me for three hundred miles, from New York City to this narrow coastal road where the GPS signal keeps dropping. *Not a coincidence*, I think, as droplets hammer against my windshield like tiny accusations.

Turn back, Wrenley. You don't belong here, either.

I haven't slept for more than four hours at a stretch in months. My eyes burn. My shoulders ache. The comments section of my life has been empty since I pulled the plug on everything two weeks ago, and I still check for notifications that will never come.

The wipers can barely keep up with the storm. I squeeze the steering wheel tighter as my headlights catch the reflective edges of a wrought-iron gate. This must be it. The address Celeste texted matches the elegant numbers mounted on stone pillars, barely visible through sheets of water.

I pull up to the intercom and press the call button.

Nothing happens.

I try again, holding it longer. Still nothing.

"Of course," I mutter, checking my phone. No service. Just great.

A small dirt road winds along the perimeter of the property. I carefully follow it, wipers fighting against the downpour, until I spot a service entrance with a smaller gate that's unlocked and hanging slightly ajar. I squeeze my car through the narrow opening until the property unfolds before me, glimpsed through flashes of lightning and my flickering headlights.

Cypress trees flank a winding driveway that leads to a sprawling stone house with dramatic windows. a palace in winter, a lake house in summer, a harvest manor in the fall, and my personal favorite, a garden paradise during spring. It adopts any fantasy a passerby could think up, simply by admiring it. Odds are, the owner of such a palatial dream doesn't have to fantasize about any of it, because they're living proof.

But I'm not here for the shapeshifting mansion. Celeste's directions mentioned a guesthouse somewhere to the east. I follow a smaller, offshoot path until my headlights illuminate a structure about a hundred yards from the main residence.

As I cut the engine and sit listening to rain drumming on the roof, my phone suddenly buzzes.

Excited to get service, I read the text immediately. It's from Celeste.

Arrived safely?

I type back: **No one answered the intercom. Found a side entrance.**

Three dots appear, then:

The key is under the blue pot by the guesthouse door. Make yourself at home!

I grab my duffel, resolving to grab my bigger suitcase

from the trunk when there's less downpour, and dash through the rain to the guesthouse's porch. The blue pot holds a plant that's definitely seen better days, and the entire thing tips over when I try to lift it, spilling wet soil across my already-soaked shoes. Perfect. I dig through the mud until my fingers close around a metal key, then wipe it on my jeans, leaving a dark streak across my thigh.

The lock sticks, because why wouldn't it? I jiggle the key, shoulder the door, and nearly fall face-first into the house when it finally gives.

Then I'm stopped cold by the sheer luxury of the interior. Vaulted ceilings with rough-hewn beams. An open kitchen and a stone fireplace that could roast an entire deer. Windows that frame the storm like it's performance art. It's the kind of space I would have once killed to feature on my platform, a rustic opulence without trying too hard, lived-in without being messy.

"This could work," I whisper, running a hand through my damp hair and turning slowly in one place.

For a moment, I just gape, dripping and disoriented. No notifications blowing up my phone. No emails demanding immediate response. No content to create, no comments to moderate, no endless performance of a life I no longer recognize.

Just me and the rain and a gorgeous new home.

I exhale for what feels like the first time in months.

My inner peace shatters when the back door slams open with enough force that I actually yelp, stumbling backward and knocking over a side table.

A man fills the frame, backlit by a flash of lightning that illuminates broad shoulders and a stance that suggests he's accustomed to being obeyed.

That burst of electricity reveals him in full: rain-slicked, dark hair, day-old stubble along a jawline that could cut glass, and eyes so startlingly blue, they seem to glow with their own internal fire. Rainwater tracks down his throat, disappearing beneath a Henley that clings to his chest in a way that makes my mouth go dry. His sleeves are pushed up, revealing forearms mapped with intricate tattoos that disappear beneath the fabric.

This is not a gardener or a caretaker. I know that immediately.

The overhead lights snap on, and I'm blinking into his incredible face. Another tattoo climbs the side of his neck, something botanical and delicate that contradicts everything else about him. His stubble is uneven, like he forgot to shave this morning, there's smudge of flour on his cheek, and—

Oh good, my fight or flight response chose "flirt."

Scrambling backward, I slam into the kitchen counter. My hand closes around a heavy cast-iron pan sitting on the stove.

I thrust the cookware forward with both hands. "Stay back. I'll throw it."

He stops prowling toward me, brows lifting. "You're threatening me with my own skillet?" His mouth twitches like he might actually smile, but the moment passes. "Careful. That pan's seen three generations. It's worth more than your car."

"*You* be careful. You're the one who burst in here like some kind of"—I release one hand to gesture wildly, and the cast-iron drops like an anchor, nearly pulling my shoulder out of its socket—"tattooed storm god!"

"I asked who the *hell* you are."

Through the tunnel of adrenaline, I finally hear the melody in his voice, low, accented, and unmistakably furious. It yanks me back to reality.

"Wrenley Morgan," I manage to say, lifting my chin

despite the water dripping from my hair and my heart bursting from my chest. "Celeste invited me. She said your guesthouse was available."

"Celeste," he repeats, the name sounding like a curse on his lips.

His eyes travel slowly down my body, taking in my soaked clothes, the way my white T-shirt clings to every curve. It's not a leer. It's an assessment, and somehow, that's worse. Heat crawls up my neck.

"She didn't tell you," I surmise.

"This is private property, Miss Morgan."

"Which I was invited to stay at."

"By my ex sister-in-law," he says, cheek muscles pulsing. "Who doesn't live here. She had no right."

"Okay, well, she failed to mention that part." I place the skillet on the counter. Carefully.. "Look, there's obviously been a misunderstanding. Celeste told me the homeowner was aware of this arrangement. That I could stay here for six weeks while—"

"Six weeks?" His eyebrows shoot up. "Absolutely the fuck not."

Blinking rapidly, I blubber, "I signed a contract."

This is a lie. I signed nothing. But this man makes me want to plant my feet. I bet no one stands up to him. Ever. He has that air about him.

"With whom? Because it wasn't with me."

"Sir—"

"Saint," he cuts in.

"What?"

"Everyone calls me Saint." His mouth twists like even he finds this ironic.

"Fine. Saint." The name feels strangely intimate on my tongue. "I don't want to cause problems. I just need..." My voice cracks embarrassingly. "I need somewhere quiet. To regroup. Celeste said you wouldn't mind."

I hug my arms across my chest, suddenly aware of how transparent I've become.

A muscle under his eye twitches. "I need you gone."

"Tonight? In this storm?" The thought of getting back in my car and finding a hotel in a town I don't know makes my stomach knot. "Please, I can leave first thing tomorrow."

"This isn't a negotiation." He takes another step toward me, as if he will personally escort me off the property, and I catch a whiff of something spicy and warm beneath the rain smell. I hold on to that instead of crumpling into a ball and keening with terror.

Don't. You've worked through this, Wrenley. You need to stay calm.

"Celeste has no right," he repeats, each word sharp as a knife. "No right to send strangers to my home. Near my daughter."

The last word makes his eyes flick toward the main house, and I follow his gaze. That's when I notice the small silhouette standing in the open doorway, a tiny figure in a yellow raincoat that's too big for her and quickly becoming soaked.

"Ivy?" he calls, his voice changing completely. "Ivy, go back inside!"

But the little girl doesn't listen. Instead, she hurls herself toward us, her bare feet splashing through puddles, a plastic flashlight clutched in one hand.

"She's going to slip," I murmur, stepping next to Saint instinctively.

He blocks my path with one arm as she reaches us. "Don't. You don't touch her."

Ivy pads inside, her feet leaving puddles. "You left the stove on. The pot bubbled over."

Saint mutters something in French that sounds distinctly unprintable.

The little girl, Ivy, studies me with unnerving focus. "You look like you fell in the ocean."

I laugh despite everything. "Close. Just driving through a biblical flood."

Saint says through clenched teeth, "This woman was just leaving."

"But it's raining." Ivy says this as if it settles everything. She approaches me without a trace of hesitation. "I'm Ivy. I'm five."

"Wrenley," I reply automatically. "I'm ... confused."

She smiles and pats my arm as if she understands.

Saint watches this exchange with visible disbelief. "Ivy, she can't stay here. She—"

"But Aunt Celeste said this lady needed somewhere quiet," Ivy says. "And you always tell me to help people when they need it."

I've never seen such a scary man look so thoroughly outmaneuvered by a five-year-old.

Ivy asks me, "We're having coq au vin, and Papa only makes it when he's really mad or really happy, and today, he's just regular mad about the rain, so it'll be extra good."

I don't know whether to laugh or cry. I'm soaking wet, terrified, exhausted, and standing before a man who clearly wants me gone. And his daughter is inviting me to dinner.

Saint makes a noise in his throat that sounds like frustrated surrender. "We need to call Celeste."

"Aunt Celeste just called. You missed it. We need to eat dinner now," Ivy counters with absolute certainty. "It's already seven thirty, and the sauce will separate if we wait."

She turns on her heel and marches toward the door, then pauses to look back at both of us.

"Seven minutes," she announces.

Ivy disappears into the rain, leaving Saint and me in a silence that feels combustible.

He stares at me, and I stare back, neither of us moving.

"Your daughter is persuasive," I say, desperate to break the tension.

"She doesn't talk to strangers. She hasn't shown interest in anyone new in years."

Oh. Well. I'm not sure how to handle that.

"I didn't come here to disrupt your life," I say. "I just needed somewhere to hide for a while."

His eyes sweep over me, taking in my damp clothes, my wearied face. "From what?"

The question stuns me with its directness. Nobody's asked me that. Not to my face. They all just assume breakdown, burnout, scandal.

"From myself," I answer honestly. "From expectations. From a life I built that doesn't fit anymore."

His expression shifts from drenched outrage to mild annoyance after my confession.

"You have one night," he finally says. "Because it's raining, and because my daughter has apparently decided you're staying for dinner. Tomorrow, we sort this out."

My shoulders sag in relief. "Thank you."

"Seven o'clock," he says, turning to leave. "And Miss Morgan? My home is private. My daughter is private. Whatever your reasons for hiding, don't make us part of your escape plan."

The door closes behind him with a decisive click.

As soon as I'm sure he's gone, I sag against the counter.

Some disappearing act this turned out to be. Less than an hour in Falcon Haven and I've already managed to threaten the owner with his own kitchenware and get myself invited to the world's most awkward dinner.

I check my watch: 6:05.

That gives me fifty-five minutes to transform from drowned rat to dinner guest.

Fifty-five minutes to prepare for a meal with a man who looks at me like I'm a problem he needs to eliminate.

Welcome to your fresh start, Wren. It's already a disaster.

TWO
SAINT

The rain hasn't stopped. Ivy's wet footprints are all over the foyer when I lock the door behind us and send her upstairs with a towel and my sharpest voice.

She doesn't flinch. She just looks at me like I missed something obvious.

"Miss Nora said she's quitting," Ivy announces casually as if informing me we're out of milk.

I freeze. "What?"

"She didn't like my unicorn mural."

I stare at her. "What unicorn mural?"

"The one I painted on her car. With the special paints from the art cabinet." Water drips from her pigtails as she gives me a defiant look.

Jesus Christ. Third nanny in six months that will walk, and this one will probably sue me for property damage. Just fucking wonderful.

"She's nice, Papa," Ivy says. Water drips from her pigtails.

"Who? Nora?"

11

"No, Miss Wrenley."

"Upstairs. Now." I point to emphasize the command, but my daughter just sighs, a sound far too world-weary for her five years.

"She needs to eat too, Daddy." Ivy's voice carries that stubborn note I recognize from the mirror. "And you always make too much anyway."

I glare at the ceiling. Fucking Celeste.

My phone buzzes with a voicemail from Nora I missed while dealing with our unexpected guest. I put it to my ear, if only to end the conversation with Ivy before she wins. "*Mr. Toussaint, I cannot and will not continue in this position. Your daughter has deliberately destroyed my vehicle with what appears to be industrial-grade paint. This goes beyond creative expression. I've contacted my insurance and will be in touch regarding damages. The psychological evaluation I suggested last month might be worth reconsidering.*"

I delete the message, picturing Nora's pristine white Honda now decorated with sparkling unicorns. Ivy's artistic talent is undeniable. Her impulse control, however...

"Go change," I order Ivy. "Now."

Ivy trudges upstairs, leaving twin trails of water behind her.

After wiping them up, I stalk back to the kitchen where my ruined coq au vin simmers, abandoned mid-stir. The sauce has separated, the chicken likely overcooked. Goddamn Celeste and her meddling. There was a time when I'd have sooner cut off my own finger than let a sauce break.

I grab my phone and stab at her contact, listening to it ring while I pull ingredients from the fridge. Butter. Shallots. Mushrooms. The knife hits the cutting board with satisfying precision as I dice the shallots into perfect, identical pieces.

Straight to voicemail.

"Celeste, call me back. Now. You can't just install random women in my guesthouse without—"

A text interrupts my message.

It's for your own good. She needs this. So do you.

I toss my phone onto the counter, nearly burning my forearm on the cast iron. "Fuck!"

After snatching a towel from the drawer and wiping my hands, I take three deep breaths.

Dinner is salvageable. Barely. I whisk in cold butter, watching the sauce come back together, glossy and rich. My hands move on autopilot, muscle memory from thousands of dinner services.

While I'm whisking, Ivy pads into the kitchen and straightens her place settings. Noticing, I turn and grab three plates from the cupboard to finish it, then pause, staring at my hands.

Why am I using the good plates? I only keep them for—

No one. I don't keep them for anyone these days.

The last time I cooked for someone besides Ivy and Celeste was one year ago. Some investor wanted to discuss reopening my Paris location. I sent him home with a signed NDA and a firm no.

Now there's a stranger in my guesthouse. A beautiful stranger with rain-soaked clothes and bright hazel eyes that seared right through me.

I'm not blind. I noticed her even while pissed off. Tall, curves in all the right places, that streak of pink in her blond hair almost the same shade as the peaks of her nipples showing through her damp white shirt...

Nope. Not going there.

Cloth napkins. Wineglass for me, water glasses for all. I catch myself polishing a water spot off Wrenley's glass and swear under my breath.

Through the window above the sink, I spot a glimpse of movement at the guesthouse. She's changed into dry clothes, a loose cream sweater that slips off one shoulder as she peers out at the rain. Even from here, I can trace the curve of her neck, the delicate line of her collarbone.

My body reacts before my brain can shut it down.

"Jesus Christ," I mutter, turning away before she can spot *me*.

This woman is trouble.

Tomorrow morning, she's gone. I'll help her pack if I have to. I don't care what Celeste thinks we "need." I don't need a house guest with eyes the color of a perfect autumn day and a body that reminds me of everything I've sworn off.

The clock reads 6:48. Ivy's bare feet slap against the hardwood as she races around. I turn, ready to scold her for not wearing socks, but the words die in my throat.

At some point between my whisking and now, she's changed into her "fancy" dress, the one with the tulle skirt she insisted on for her school picture. Her damp hair is out of her pigtails and brushed, and she's even attempted a crooked bow on the side.

The sight hits me like a sucker punch.

"Do I look pretty, Papa?" She twirls, the dress flaring around her knees.

"You look beautiful, *mon trésor*." My voice comes out rougher than intended. "But why...?"

"For dinner with Miss Wrenley!" She gives me an indulgent smile like I'm the slow one here. "It's a special 'casion."

Guilt sits in my stomach like a rock. One year since we've had anyone over. Twelve months of just the two of us sitting down for dinner.

"Papa, can I set out the candles, too?"

"No candles." I clear my throat. "Go wash your hands."

I plate the chicken, arranging it with the precision that once earned me Michelin stars. The sauce pools perfectly against the roasted fingerling potatoes. A sprinkle of fresh thyme. It's muscle memory, not effort.

"Papa, is it time yet?" Ivy yells from the powder room in the hallway.

"Almost." I check the plating one last time. "Did you wash your hands?"

She returns to the kitchen holding her hands up and showing off clean palms.

"Is Miss Wrenley going to sit next to me or you?" she asks.

"Does it matter?"

"Yes! I want to show her my bracelet and tell her about my book and introduce her to Mr. Pawsome and—"

There's a knock on the door to our back porch at exactly 7:00.

Merde. Of course she would be punctual. I was hoping she might chicken out.

Before I can stop her, Ivy bolts for the door, her tulle skirt flouncing. I take a steadying breath, wiping my hands on a kitchen towel, and follow at a more measured pace.

"I wore my fancy dress!" Ivy exclaims as a greeting. Her voice climbs an octave as she swings open the door.

"You look stunning," I hear Wrenley reply as I round the corner. "That's the prettiest dress I've seen in ages."

Ivy preens, twirling again while Wrenley crouches down to my daughter's level.

"Papa made chicken. It's the best chicken in the whole world. He cooks it in restaurants."

I gesture vaguely behind me. "Dinner's ready."

Wrenley straightens, finally meeting my eyes. "Thank you for the invitation. It smells amazing."

A cream sweater hangs loose on her frame, slipping off

one shoulder to reveal skin that looks impossibly soft. Her damp hair is pulled back in a messy knot, and without the rain plastering everything to her skin, she looks ... different. Softer. Flawless.

"It wasn't an invitation," I say, and it comes out like an accusation. "It was Ivy's idea."

An emotion close to hurt ripples across Wrenley's face, but she covers it with a smile. "Well, I appreciate it all the same."

Ivy grabs Wrenley's hand and pulls her toward the kitchen. "You can sit by me. Come on!"

I catch Wrenley's eye again as she's dragged past me.

"She's ... enthusiastic this evening," I say as an explanation.

"I can see that." A small smile plays at the corner of her mouth. "Must be genetic."

I scoff.

In the kitchen, Ivy positions Wrenley at the place setting at the end of the island, then climbs onto her own chair between us. I serve the plates with practiced efficiency.

"Wow," Wrenley breathes when I set her plate down. Her eyes widen, genuine appreciation washing over her face. "This looks like artwork."

"It's just dinner."

I pour myself a glass of burgundy before taking my seat, then notice where Wrenley's attention has gone.

"Are you old enough to drink?" I ask her.

She laughs softly. "I'm twenty-four. I'll be twenty-five in November," she adds almost defensively.

Wrenley picks up her fork, then hesitates. "This really does look incredible."

"You haven't tasted it yet."

I take a sip of wine, studying her over the rim of my glass. Young. Too young. But I find her a separate wineglass regardless. With the way she was drooling over mine and the night she's had, I'd say she needs it.

"Thank you," she says when I set a full glass in front of her.

"You're lucky. Papa doesn't share his wine," Ivy informs her while digging into her food. "He says it's older than dinosaurs."

I shoot Ivy a look. "Expensive. I said expensive."

Wrenley takes her first bite and closes her eyes. The small sound she makes hits me right in the gut. It's a noise of pure pleasure that belongs in my bedroom, not my kitchen.

"Oh my god," she murmurs.

I nod curtly, ignoring the unwelcome heat that spreads through me at her reaction. Most people respond to my food this way. It doesn't mean anything. I've been praised by critics worldwide, won awards, built an empire on my cooking. But there's something about the genuine surprise on her face that hits differently.

"Told you," Ivy says to her through a mouthful. "Sometimes people cry when they eat Papa's food."

"I believe it." Wrenley takes another bite, savoring it with the same quiet reverence. "I might cry myself."

"Please don't." I take a long sip of wine.

"Papa was on TV," Ivy announces, mouth full of potato. "But he doesn't do that anymore because he likes it here better."

"Don't talk with your mouth full," I say automatically.

Wrenley dabs her lips with her napkin. "So you were a chef?"

"He still is," Ivy corrects. "He has a restaurant in town. It's really fancy. You need a—what's it called, Papa?"

"Reservation."

"Yeah, that. You need one of those. And sometimes

famous people come, but Papa doesn't care if they're famous. He doesn't really come out to say hi to people."

I freeze, my wineglass halfway to my lips. "Ivy."

"What? You don't." She shrugs, sauce smeared on her chin.

I focus on slicing my chicken.

Ivy kicks her feet under the table. "Papa has stars."

"Stars?" Wrenley raises an eyebrow at me.

I don't look up from my plate. "Michelin. It doesn't matter."

"Three of them," Ivy announces proudly.

Wrenley's fork pauses halfway to her mouth. "Wait, that's *huge*. Congratulations."

I shrug, shoving enough food in my mouth so I don't have to continue the conversation.

"Papa doesn't like being famous anymore," Ivy stage-whispers, leaning toward Wrenley. "Not since Mama went to heaven."

An immediate and suffocating silence descends. My grip tightens on my fork until my knuckles whiten. Ivy continues eating as if she hasn't dropped a bomb on our perfectly civil dinner.

Wrenley's eyes dart to mine, questioning, uncertain.

"Enough chatter. Eat your dinner," I say to Ivy, my voice a low warning.

"What?" She looks genuinely confused. "Aunt Celeste says we should talk about Mama sometimes so we don't forget her."

I set down my fork with a careful *clink* against the china. "Aunt Celeste talks too much."

Wrenley takes a sip of wine, her throat working as she swallows.

"This chicken is incredible," she says, deliberately changing the subject. "What's in the sauce?"

"It's a trade secret," I answer, grateful for the redirect.

"Papa won't tell anyone his secret recipes," Ivy explains, sauce now on her cheek as well as her chin. "Not even me. And I'm his favorite person."

"That's because you'd sell them to the highest bidder," I say, reaching over to wipe her face with my napkin.

"Nuh-uh. I'd give them away for free." She grins. "And for candy."

A soft smile crosses Wrenley's face, and the tightness in my chest loosens just a fraction.

"How do you know Celeste?" I ask her.

Wrenley takes another bite and swallows. "She was a collab of mine. We met in Paris maybe a year ago and became friends."

Ivy says, "I talk to my grandma and grandpa every Sunday on the computer. They live in France. That's where Papa's from."

"Is that right?" Wrenley asks, glancing at me.

"Half right," I correct. "Born there, raised here after age ten, then went back to pursue my culinary career."

Ivy waves her fork. "Say something in French, Papa!"

"*Non.*"

"That doesn't count!" Ivy giggles, then turns to Wrenley. "He only speaks French when he's really mad."

"Or when little girls don't finish their dinner," I add pointedly in French.

Ivy rolls her eyes—a gesture she definitely picked up from Celeste—but returns to her food.

"So what did you do before you squatted in strangers' guesthouses?" I ask Wrenley.

"Papa!" Ivy scolds.

Wrenley's cheeks flush pink. She licks her lips. Big mistake, because that's where my focus goes. "I'm really sorry about the misunderstanding."

I take another sip of wine to distract myself from a plush, rose-colored mouth. "You didn't answer my question."

Wrenley tucks a loose strand of hair behind her ear. "I worked in content creation."

"Like on Instagram?" Ivy perks up.

My attention shoots to my daughter. "How do you know about Instagram?"

Ivy shrugs. "Aunt Celeste lets me see her phone sometimes. She follows lots of pretty ladies who tell her to get ready with them."

Wrenley nearly chokes on her wine.

"That's not exactly what I do," she starts.

"So you're an influencer," I say, the word tasting sour in my mouth.

A woman who makes her living telling people what to buy. Just what I need in my guesthouse.

Wrenley shifts in her seat. "I was. I'm taking a break."

"From influencing?" I can't keep the disdain from my voice.

She meets my gaze, not with insult, but something steadier. "From a lot of things."

Whatever sarcastic comment was forming on my tongue slithers back down my throat. There's weight behind her answer, a heaviness I recognize all too well.

"Miss Wrenley, do you want to read me a bedtime story?" Ivy pipes up, oblivious to the tension. "Papa always does the voices wrong."

"I do not."

"You do! You make the princess sound like a robot. You do a great dragon voice, though."

Wrenley's lips twitch. "I'd love to read you a story, Ivy, but only if your dad says it's okay."

I open my mouth to refuse. To tell my daughter we've already disrupted Miss Morgan's evening enough. To explain that bedtime is our time, one of the few sacred routines we've maintained since Celine died.

But Ivy's eyes, wide and hopeful, are on me.

How long has it been since she's asked for anything this simple? Since she's been this excited about bedtime?

"Fine," I say. "One story."

"Yes!" Ivy pumps her fist, nearly knocking over her water. "I'll go pick one out. The best one!"

She scrambles down from her chair and races toward the stairs.

"Walking feet!" I call after her, but she's already thundering up to her room.

Silence settles between Wrenley and me. She takes another sip of wine, realizes it's empty, then sets it back down. I also notice she's practically licked her plate clean.

Her attention darts around the kitchen, anywhere but at me. When she catches me looking, she ducks her head.

"Sorry," she says. "I was hungrier than I realized."

"Never apologize for finishing a dish. Would you like more?"

"Oh, I couldn't—"

I'm already reaching for her plate. "It's not a trick question."

"Then yes, please." A tentative smile plays at her lips. "It might be the best thing I've ever eaten."

I ladle more chicken and sauce onto her plate, adding extra potatoes. When I set it back in front of her, our fingers brush. The contact sends an unwelcome jolt up my arm.

She pulls back like I've burned her at the same time I

recoil, and both our wineglasses topple onto the marble counter with a piercing clang. The rest of my red spreads like a bloodstain between us.

Our hands collide again as she reaches for napkins and I grab a dish towel.

"I've got it."

"Let me help—"

"I said I've got it."

She withdraws, tucking her hands in her lap. I soak up the mess, tossing the ruined towel in the sink.

"I'm sorry," she says quietly.

"For what? Spilling wine or taking over my guesthouse?"

Her eyes meet mine, steady despite the flush on her cheeks. "Both, I guess."

I pour us each a fresh glass, sliding hers across the counter without making contact this time. "Drink your wine and finish your meal. I need to check on Ivy."

She nods, picking up her glass carefully.

I leave her in the kitchen, needing distance from whatever the hell just happened between us. The brush of her fingers shouldn't affect me. Nothing should affect me. I've spent three years making damn sure of it.

Upstairs, Ivy has emptied half her bookshelf onto her bed. Her room is a riot of color, the one area of the house where I let her personality run wild. Stuffed animals crowd her bed, books spill from shelves, and fairy lights twinkle along the ceiling.

"Papa! Help me pick! Should we read the one with the dragon or the one with the talking animals?"

"The dragons," I say automatically. "Always the dragons."

"But we read that one last night." She holds up a book

with a worn purple spine. "What about this one? It has a unicorn."

"You decide, *mon trésor*. It's your story time."

She bites her lip, weighing the options with the gravity of a Supreme Court Justice. "I think ... the unicorn. Because Miss Wrenley has pink hair like a unicorn's mane."

"Good choice."

"Papa?" Ivy's voice drops to a whisper. "Do you think Miss Wrenley likes us?"

The question catches me off guard. "Why does that matter?"

"Because I like her." She hugs the book to her chest. "And she has sad eyes like you do sometimes."

My throat tightens. For a long time, I didn't have to worry about Ivy noticing adult idiosyncrasies like grief and depression, but she's growing up so fast. It seems like yesterday she was crawling onto my lap and hanging off my ears. I don't know if I'm ready for the questions she will no doubt start asking.

"Where is Miss Wrenley?"

"Downstairs. Finishing her dinner."

"Can she tuck me in after the story?"

I pause on my way to the stairs. "Why would she do that?"

Ivy shrugs, her small shoulders rising and falling beneath her fancy dress. "I just thought it would be nice."

It takes all my self-control to keep the pain from affecting my expression. "Let's just see how the story goes."

My phone buzzes just as I reach the stairs, and it's a text from Celeste:

Nora called me. Unicorns on her car?? Seriously? 😂

Before I can respond, another message pops up: **Btw, how's it going with Wrenley? Ivy talking to her?**

And then: **Don't be mad, but Wrenley used to work with kids before the influencer thing. Creative types. Like Ivy.**

I stare at the messages, a creeping suspicion forming. The timing. The convenient solution to my childcare crisis appearing right as another nanny quits.

This wasn't a coincidence.

I look back at Ivy, hugging her unicorn book to her chest, more animated tonight than she's been in months.

It hits me then. My sister-in-law didn't just send a random friend to my guesthouse.

She sent me a fucking nanny.

THREE
WRENLEY

The first thing I do after returning to the guesthouse is search for *"Saint, the chef,"* on my phone, immediately regretting how little I knew about the man whose food I had practically orgasmed over.

Holy. Crap.

The search results yield dozens of articles. Most feature the same photo: a younger Saint, clean-shaven, his tattoos covered by a pristine white chef's coat. Nothing like the inked-up, scowling kitchen tyrant I'd just met.

"Michelin-starred at twenty-seven," I whisper, scrolling further. "James Beard finalist ... revolutionizing Parisian cuisine..."

He's smiling in one picture—*actually* smiling—standing next to a petite woman with Ivy's dark curls, a woman who looks a lot like ... no, is *identical* to...

I sit bolt upright, the springs in the couch protesting loudly. *Is that Celeste?*

It turns out it's not because the headline punches me in

the gut: **Chef Bernard "Saint" Toussaint Retreats from Culinary Spotlight Following Tragic Loss of Wife.**

Was Saint's wife Celeste's twin sister? She's never mentioned her, despite our many conversations. And Celeste is always so upbeat and positive. God, I hate when real people turn out to have actual complicated lives. It was so much easier when they were just characters on my feed.

I set my phone down, suddenly feeling like I've invaded something private. Which is ridiculous, considering these are public articles, but social media has made voyeurs of us all. We scroll through others' tragedies like entertainment, consuming their pain from the safety of our screens.

It doesn't stop my brain from scrolling, though. I met Celeste about a year ago, and the article is three years old, which would make Ivy about two when it happened…

Why am I even thinking about this? I came here for anonymity. I should be planning my exit strategy, not mulling over Toussaint family history.

It's just that something about the dinner has burrowed under my skin. Maybe it's because I recognize the haunted look in Saint's eyes like he's survived his own personal apocalypse. Or the way he watches Ivy, like she's both his greatest joy and deepest terror. I know that feeling. It's the one you get when you understand that happiness is temporary and the universe always collects its debts.

Forcing my head out of the clouds, I head to the bathroom. Its pale blue tiles and old-fashioned brass finishes feel like a sanctuary as I wash my face, avoiding my own reflection.

Old habits.

My hand drifts to the pink streak in my hair, fingers gently probing underneath where my hair is finally growing back, soft and fragile as a baby bird. Three months since I last pulled there. A personal record. At first, my followers thought it was just a quirky style change rather than a deliberate choice that started as a desperate cover-up. **#PinkHairDontCare.**

"Not tonight," I whisper to myself, forcing my hand away and reaching for my moisturizer instead.

My therapist would be proud. *Recognize the urge, redirect the energy.* Easy to say when you're not the one whose scalp tingles with the need to pull until it hurts, until the pressure inside your head finally releases.

I tug off my sweater, wincing as the fabric catches on the raw patches of skin across my left shoulder. The scratches aren't deep, but they're angry. In the bathroom's unforgiving light, they look worse than they feel. Some healing, while others are fresh from this afternoon's drive. Shirts with wide collars are my armor lately. Another calculated misdirection: one flawless shoulder revealed, while the other hides its hurt under fabric.

After I pull on a soft T-shirt, I slip into a four-poster bed with layers of sheets, comforters, and blankets, all a calming blue. I'm about to turn off the lamp when my phone buzzes, and I flinch reflexively before remembering I'd deleted all social apps a week ago. The memory of my last live stream still makes my stomach clench. I have to force myself out of the memory by checking the notification, and notice it's from Celeste.

How's the hideaway? Peaceful as promised?

I stare at Celeste's text for a long time, then type: **Your brother-in-law had no idea I was coming. Nearly burned his kitchen down when I showed up.**

Three dots appear immediately, then disappear, then reappear.

OMG, did I not tell him?? I SWEAR I texted him last week!

I can practically hear her voice, breathless with genuine horror but also somehow laughing. It's Celeste in a nutshell, her heart perpetually ten steps ahead of her organizational skills. It's part of what had us get along so well when we met.

The dots dance again.

Oh god, Wren, I'm the WORST. I was in Bali when we talked, and there was the yoga retreat drama with the fire ants, and then my phone fell into a rice paddy. But I meant to. Saint's such a dick sometimes, but he needs the help, and you need the space, and it was perfect in my head! He's not so bad once you get past the death glare. Promise. And Ivy's the best.

I have to smile despite myself. Only Celeste could forget to mention to Saint that she was sending a complete stranger to live on his property.

He didn't kick you out, did he?? Tell me you're not texting from your car in some gas station parking lot. I'll drive up his ass RIGHT NOW.

I decide to put her out of her misery.

I'm fine. Still in the guesthouse. But maybe call him?

Relief that I'm not mad at her pours through her response. **I'm so sorry about this! Calling him right now. Love you!!!**

Saint's about to get an earful from his sister-in-law, and I can't say I hate the idea. I'm trying not to think about the articles I'd found. About the tragedy lurking behind Saint's eyes. About the little girl who lost her mother so young.

Not my business. Not my problem. Not my life.

I repeat this like a mantra as I drift off to sleep.

Sleep comes in fits and starts, my dreams a jumble of tattooed hands ladling sauce and little girls with paint-splattered fingers. When morning light filters through gauzy curtains, I've already been awake for an hour, staring at the ceiling, tracing patterns in the plaster.

The open kitchen is small but well-equipped. I find coffee beans in the freezer—good, imported ones—and a French press beside the sink. While the kettle heats, I throw on a robe I found in the bedroom closet and step onto the porch, inhaling salt air that feels cleaner than anything I've breathed in months.

The storm that welcomed me to Falcon Haven has left everything glistening. Once my coffee's ready, I cradle the mug between both hands, letting the warmth seep into my fingers as I slip on my shoes and go back outside.

My shoes sink into the damp earth as I follow what appears to be a garden path. The air smells green and alive, like soil and flowers and pine. A sound catches my attention: birds calling to each other from the trees.

I pause beside a twisted apple tree, its branches heavy with small green fruit. My phone weighs down my robe's pocket, but I resist the urge to document this moment. No filters needed. No caption required. Just me, experiencing something without a phone in front of my face.

The path curves around a small pond where water lilies float like tiny islands. A wooden bench sits beneath a weeping willow, its slender branches swaying in the gentle breeze. I settle there, tucking one leg beneath me.

"Oh my god," I moan. "This is beautiful and I love it and I don't want to *leave*."

A little sparrow that landed nearby tilts its head, unimpressed with my emotional outburst.

Movement catches my eye, a flash of color beyond a

cluster of rosebushes. I leave my bench to investigate, coffee mug still in hand. As I round the corner, I nearly drop it.

Ivy kneels in the garden, surrounded by what looks like a rainbow explosion. Dozens of smooth river rocks are scattered around her, each painted in eye-searing colors. Her hands are stained purple and green, and there's a streak of neon pink across her cheek that matches my hair. She's wearing pajamas covered in dinosaurs, completely focused on the rock in her small hands.

She looks up, blue eyes widening when she spots me. For a moment, I expect her to bolt or yell for her dad.

Instead, she holds up her current masterpiece, a rock covered in swirls of blue and yellow that somehow form what might be a fish. Or possibly a planet.

"It's better when you mix the colors," she announces, as if continuing a conversation we'd been having all along.

"That's gorgeous," I say, genuinely impressed. "You have an eye for detail."

Ivy's eyebrows shoot up in surprise. "You can tell what it is?"

I study the rock more carefully. "It's a ... mermaid?"

She beams. "Yeah! Nobody ever gets it right."

Without invitation, I settle cross-legged beside her, careful to keep my borrowed robe from getting soaked. She scoots over, making room for me.

"You're very talented," I say.

"Nora says I make too many messes."

"Your nanny?"

Ivy rolls her eyes with such dramatic flair I have to bite back a smile. "She took away my paints yesterday."

"Ah. Because of the car incident," I say, recalling our conversation before reading her a story.

"*Before* the incident. That's why I broke into the cupboard and got the paints in the first place."

I pick up a small, smooth stone and turn it over in my hands. "May I?"

Ivy slides a palette of paints toward me. "You can use the good green. I mixed it myself."

"Thank you." I dip my finger into the moss-colored paint.

Ivy picks up another rock and slaps a glob of purple paint onto it. "I didn't ruin it. I made it pretty." She looks up at me through dark lashes. "It was a boring white car. I gave it unicorns."

"Unicorns?" I lean closer, genuinely interested. "With horns and everything?"

"And rainbows coming out of their butts!" She laughs riotously after saying this.

"Of course," I agree with a wide smile. "Rainbow farts are essential unicorn features."

Ivy's mouth drops open. She looks at me with wide eyes. Then she slaps her palms against her thighs and yells, "FARTS!" before she falls over laughing.

Her joy is so unexpected and delightful, my heart literally rises from the lightness of it.

Desperate to hear more, I say while dipping my finger in a puddle of blue paint, "Sometimes adults forget that art doesn't always have to stay on paper."

"That's what I said! But not with those words." She hands me a smooth, flat stone. "You can do this one, too."

I accept the stone with a smile.

"She screamed really loud," Ivy says matter-of-factly. "Papa had to give her money for the car wash. Then she said I was—" she pauses, clearly quoting, "—'impossible to manage' and 'deliberately destructive.'"

The hurt in her voice is unmistakable beneath the

bravado. I keep painting my rocks, giving her space to continue.

"I wanted to make her happy. She was always saying how much she missed her old car." Ivy's small fingers work methodically, adding intricate patterns to her mermaid. "I thought unicorns make everything better."

"That's because unicorns *do* make everything better—"

"IVY!"

The bellow slices through our peaceful moment like a chainsaw.

Saint charges across the garden, his face a thundercloud of fury. His hair sticks up at odd angles like he's been running his hands through it repeatedly, and he's in a wrinkled black T-shirt and sweatpants, as if he threw them on in a rush.

"Ivy!" he barks her name again. "I've been looking everywhere for you!"

He stops short when he sees me sitting cross-legged beside his daughter.

"What the hell is this?" His eyes narrow, flicking between Ivy and me.

"Papa!" Ivy jumps up, oblivious to his fury. "Look what Miss Wrenley and I made! She understands about unicorn butts!"

"Jesus Christ," Saint mutters, rubbing his hand over his face. "Do you have any idea—" He cuts himself off, jaw clenched so tight that all of his cheek muscles ripple. "You can't just disappear like that."

"I wasn't gone," Ivy protests. "I was right here."

"You weren't in your room when I checked. You weren't in the kitchen. You weren't—" He stops, seeming to realize I'm witnessing his parental meltdown.

"We're just painting rocks," I say, squaring my shoulders

despite the fact that I'm sitting on damp grass in a borrowed robe with paint-covered fingers. "She's been perfectly safe."

"I woke up and she was gone. Completely gone." His voice drops to a dangerous rumble. "Do you have any idea what that feels like?"

The raw fear beneath his anger is unmistakable.

"I'm sorry," I say, softening my tone. "She was already out here when I found her. I should've brought her back to the house."

Saint stares at me, and for a moment, I glimpse the sheer terror that comes with parenthood. The kind that turns rational people into frantic searchers of empty rooms.

"I'm sorry," I say again.

"No, I'm—" Saint stops himself, swallows hard. "I just woke up to her empty bed and..."

He doesn't finish the sentence, doesn't need to.

Ivy, oblivious to the adult undercurrents, tugs on her father's hand. "Papa, Miss Wrenley said my art doesn't have to stay on paper. She gets it."

Saint's eyes meet mine again, shining a gorgeous blue in the morning light. I have to stop myself from audibly gulping.

"Can she have breakfast with us?" Ivy asks. "Please? She likes my mermaids."

Saint hesitates, and I jump in to spare him. "Actually, I should probably—"

"Yes," he says, surprising me. "If Miss Morgan wants."

"Wrenley," I correct automatically. "Just Wrenley is fine."

"Wrenley, then."

The way he says my name sends a shiver through me that has nothing to do with the fact that I'm not wearing pants.

I should say no. I should retreat to the guesthouse, pack

my bags, and drive away from whatever this complicated situation is. Instead, I hear myself say, "I'd like that."

Ivy beams triumphantly and scampers toward the house, leaving colorful footprints in her wake.

When she's out of earshot, Saint runs a hand through his hair, studying me sidelong. "Usually her nanny is here at this time and I'm at the restaurant, but…"

"She quit," I say, standing and brushing grass off myself, but only managing to leave smears of paint on the robe. "Ivy told me a little bit about what happened."

His eyes narrow in further assessment. "Do you have kids?"

"No," I say, then bite my lip. "But I used to be a camp counselor for kindergartners."

Half-true. I shot a series of summer camp-themed videos for five-year-olds last year. Made them little friendship bracelets on camera. Got paid a ridiculous amount by a children's vitamin company. Close enough.

Saint glances toward the house, his expression puzzled. "Ivy doesn't warm up to people. Ever."

I shrug, uncomfortable with his attention being on me for so long, like he can spot every detail. "Kids like me. I don't talk down to them."

His shoulders slope, a barely perceptible softening around the edges. "You're covered in paint."

I look down at myself. "Occupational hazard of creativity."

"Come on," he says, turning toward the house. "You can wash up inside."

I follow him across the damp lawn, conscious of my bare legs beneath the robe and the bird's nest that my hair has surely become. How can a man on the brink of a meltdown and a tantrum still look so damned delicious? It makes me wonder if I'm still feeling the effects of my own breakdown two weeks ago.

Saint's phone buzzes in his pocket. He checks it, and his face darkens.

"Shit." He stares up toward the house. "I need to make some calls. The nanny agency says they're out of options, and I'm supposed to be prepping for the governor's dinner tonight."

"That's rough," I offer, genuinely sympathetic.

Saint's jaw works back and forth as he mulls over his situation.

"Papa!" Ivy's voice carries from the house. "The toaster's smoking again!"

Saint closes his eyes briefly.

"Coming!" he calls back, then fixes me with another unreadable look. "You don't have to join us if you don't want to."

"I want to," I say, surprising myself with how much I mean it.

He nods once, then turns and heads for the house. I follow a few steps behind, watching the way his muscles move under his shirt, trying not to stare too hard at the way those sweatpants cup his—

No. Absolutely not. I'm not here to ogle some stranger who just had a justifiable dad-panic. Even if he does have the kind of shoulders that could probably carry both a restaurant and a kindergartner at the same time.

Snap out of it.

I've never had particularly good taste and men, but even this is a new low for me.

The kitchen is a disaster zone when we walk in. Smoke billows from the toaster, strawberries are scattered all over the counter, and Ivy's standing on a chair waving a hand towel.

"I wanted to make you toast," she announces, completely unfazed by the potential fire hazard.

Saint moves with insane speed, unplugging the toaster and opening windows. He takes the smoking appliance to the sink and dumps the charred remains of what might have been bread into the garbage disposal.

"Ivy, what have I told you about using appliances without an adult?"

His voice borders on chilling, mixed with the realization that he doesn't want to terrify his child.

She shrugs, still standing on the chair. "I am an adult. I'm five."

"Five is not—" Saint stops, pinching the bridge of his nose. "Just … get off the chair. Please. I'll make breakfast."

His phone buzzes again. And again. He glances at it with a grimace.

"Do you need to take that?" I ask.

"It can wait."

The tightness around his mouth says otherwise.

"I can watch her for a minute," I offer. "If you need to make a call."

Saint looks at me, protective instincts struggling with practical necessity.

His phone buzzes again. He mutters something in French.

"Go," I say, waving him off. "I'll make sure no appliances catch fire in your absence."

"You sure?"

"Positive." I nod toward the hallway. "Deal with your restaurant crisis. We'll still be in your line of sight and I can figure out breakfast."

Saint hesitates, then gives Ivy a stern look. "Listen to Miss Wrenley. No climbing, no cooking, no escaping."

"No promises," Ivy singsongs.

He shoots me one last glance. The indecision on his face would be comical if it weren't so clearly painful for him. Then he disappears down the hall, answering his phone with a terse, "This better be important."

Ivy watches him leave, thankfully sitting on a chair at the countertop now. "He's gonna yell at somebody."

"Is he?" I ask, rinsing my hands before taking over the abandoned breakfast efforts.

She nods sagely. "When his voice gets all quiet like that, it means somebody's in big trouble."

"Good to know," I say, opening the refrigerator. "I'll avoid getting in trouble with your dad."

"Are you going to be my new nanny?" Ivy asks, swinging her legs from her perch.

The question hits me like a splash of cold water. I nearly drop the carton of eggs I've just pulled from the fridge.

"No, honey," I say, cracking an egg one-handed into a bowl. "I'm just passing through."

"Passing through where?" She tilts her head, reminding me of the sparrow from the garden.

"Life, I guess," I say, more to myself than to her. I add another egg to the bowl. "I was planning to leave today, actually."

"But you just got here." Her bottom lip juts out. "That's not fair."

"Life rarely is," I say, the words coming out more bitter than intended.

Wow, Wren. Way to dump your existential crisis on a kinder-gartner. Next, show her your therapy journal and really ruin her day.

Ivy's face falls instantly, her small shoulders slumping as she stares down at her paint-covered hands. "Everyone leaves."

Her matter-of-fact tone makes my heart twist. I set the whisk down and lean against the counter, facing her.

The sound of Saint's voice carries from down the hall. His low, intense vibrato switching fluidly between English and French.

From Ivy's grimace, I gather the conversation isn't going well.

"I was just visiting your guesthouse for a while," I explain, keeping my voice gentle. "I'm not actually here to be a nanny."

"Nora said I was a monster." Ivy picks at a spot of dried purple paint on her thumb. "Is that why you're leaving, too?"

"Hey," I say, moving closer and resting my elbows on the counter across from her. "You are absolutely not a monster. You're creative and smart and honest, which are all really good things to be."

Ivy's green eyes study me skeptically. "Papa says I'm 'spirited.'"

"That's a good word for it." I smile. "And I'm not leaving because of you. I'm leaving because that was always the plan."

"Plans can change," she says with a shrug, as if imparting ancient wisdom.

I rub my lips together, recognizing the dangerous waters I'm treading. The last thing I should do is give this child false hope about my sticking around, but the wounded look in her eyes makes my chest ache.

Saint's voice rises down the hall, though the words are muffled. Whatever crisis is unfolding at his restaurant, it doesn't sound like it's resolving quickly.

"How about we make pancakes?" I offer instead. "Do you like chocolate chips?"

"Only when I can make faces out of them," she says seriously.

"Well, obviously." I rummage through drawers until I find chocolate chips. "What kind of awful person makes pancakes without faces?"

Ivy snort-laughs, a hilariously undignified sound from such a small person. I find myself laughing too, genuinely, for what feels like the first time in months.

By the time Saint returns, Ivy and I have created a small army of pancake faces with varying expressions. There's Happy Pancake with a chocolate chip smile; Surprised Pancake with wide strawberry eyes and an O-shaped mouth; Sleepy Pancake with half-lidded banana slices; and the pièce de résistance: what Ivy has named "Pancake From The Bad Place."

This unholy creation features strawberry jam oozing from multiple "wounds," chocolate syrup tears of the damned, and a grotesque mouth formed from a slice of bacon curled into a snarl. The eyes are hollowed-out centers of kiwi slices that stare with an empty, soulless gaze.

"It's watching us," I whisper dramatically to Ivy, who giggles with unholy glee.

"If you eat it, you get its powers," she stage-whispers back.

"Or it possesses your soul," I suggest, and she nods enthusiastically like I've confirmed a long-held theory.

Movement redirects my attention as Saint stops in the doorway, phone still in hand, staring at the spectacle before him. The kitchen is a disaster zone of flour, eggshells, and every condiment from the fridge. Ivy's dinosaur pajamas now feature several new abstract designs in pancake batter and jam.

"What the hell happened to my kitchen?"

His voice is tightly leashed.

"Breakfast summoned a demon," I say, gesturing to Pancake From The Bad Place. "But we've contained the threat."

Saint stares at the creation with an expression that suggests he's questioning every decision that led to this moment. His eyes sweep over the chaos.

"We can clean it up," I offer, suddenly aware that I've essentially destroyed a professional chef's personal kitchen. While wearing a bathrobe and no pants.

He doesn't respond, just walks to the coffee maker and pours himself a cup with such precise movements it feels like he's counting each drop. The silence stretches, uncomfortable.

Ivy seems oblivious to the tension.

"Try this one, Papa," she says, stabbing a fork into our demonic creation and holding it out. "It gives you powers."

"Or steals your soul," I add helpfully, then immediately regret it when Saint's glare shifts to me.

"Not now, Ivy," he says, his voice clipped. He sets his phone on the counter, screen up. It immediately buzzes again.

"The restaurant's sous chef quit," he says abruptly. "That was the call."

"Is that bad?" I ask, immediately regretting the stupid question.

He gives me a look that could curdle milk. "No, it's fantastic news. I love scrambling to find a replacement before a VIP dinner."

"Oh," I say, not sure what else to add.

This isn't my problem. I should be packing, not standing here in a borrowed robe with flour in my hair.

"Papa," Ivy says, fixing him with an unnervingly adult stare. "Ask her."

"Ivy," he warns.

"Ask. Her." She crosses her arms, a tiny mirror of his stubborn stance.

Saint's nostrils flare slightly as he inhales. He looks at me, then away, his discomfort palpable. "My sister-in-law seems to think you're trustworthy."

I wait, sensing there's more.

"And I'm…" He pauses, the words clearly difficult. "I find myself in a difficult position."

"I noticed," I say dryly, then, before I can rethink it, decide to rescue him. "I could watch her. Just for today, until you can figure something out."

His head snaps up, eyes growing small with suspicion. "Why would you offer to do such a thing?"

Because your daughter sees rainbow unicorn farts and I haven't laughed like that in months. Because I recognize the drowning look in your eyes. Because maybe helping someone else will stop me from picking at my own wounds for a few hours. Because after spending three years of my life teaching strangers how to contour their noses, it feels weirdly good to do something that matters to an actual human being.

"Because I have nowhere else to be today," I say instead. "And Ivy's fun."

"I am very fun," Ivy agrees solemnly.

Saint studies me for a long moment, like he's trying to decode a particularly difficult recipe. "You have experience with kids?"

"Camp counselor," I remind him, sticking to my half-truth. "For kindergartners."

His phone buzzes again. He ignores it, still watching me. I

hope I'm not exuding the tingles cascading across my skin as obviously as I think I am.

"One day," he says finally. "Just until I can make other arrangements."

"One day," I agree.

"Fair warning, Ivy's ... energetic."

That's like describing a tornado as "a bit breezy."

"I noticed," I say dryly.

"And creative," he adds, with a pointed glance at the kitchen disaster.

"Also noticed."

He nods once, briskly, then downs the rest of his coffee. "I'll pay you, of course."

"That's not—"

"I insist." His tone leaves no room for argument.

"Fine."

"There's a list of emergency numbers on the fridge. My cell is at the top."

"Got it."

"No paint in the house," he adds. "No unicorn farts on any surfaces, including my car."

So cars are off-limits, but demon pancakes are apparently fine. Noted.

Ivy bounces in her chair, vibrating with excitement. "Can we make slime? And finish our rocks? And—"

"Ivy," Saint cuts her off, but his voice has softened slightly. "Go get dressed first."

She slides off her chair with a dramatic sigh that seems to come from the depths of her soul, then races from the room, her footsteps thundering on the stairs.

When she's gone, Saint turns back to me.

"I meant to say…" he stops, seeming to struggle with the words. "Thank you. For this morning. For watching her."

The begrudging gratitude makes me smile. "Go save your restaurant, Chef. We'll be fine."

He nods again, but hesitates at the doorway, looking back at me with an unreadable expression. "Celeste trusts you."

It's not exactly a ringing endorsement, but something about his grudging acceptance makes my shoulders relax for the first time since he stormed through the garden with pure wrath on his face. "Have a good day, Chef Toussaint."

His eyes linger on mine for a beat longer than necessary, and I don't look away, either. Then he's gone, calling for Ivy to hurry up.

I stand in the kitchen, surrounded by the remnants of pancake chaos, wondering what the hell I've just gotten myself into. I came here to disappear, not to become a temporary nanny to a pint-sized tornado.

One day, I assure myself. *What could possibly go wrong in one day?*

The universe, wisely, doesn't answer.

But I swear Pancake From The Bad Place gives me a knowing look as I move to clear the plates.

FOUR
WRENLEY

Saint's morning routine for Ivy involves seventeen steps, two checklists, and enough diligence to launch a space shuttle, all of which he explained to me in a rapid-fire text message that arrived precisely one minute after he left.

I'm relieved when Ivy chooses a simple purple dress, leggings, and none of the meltdowns the mom influencers I networked with often posted about.

"Time to brush your teeth and hair," I tell her, guiding her out of a room full of rainbows and into a marble bathroom.

"Papa makes me brush for exactly two minutes with the timer," Ivy informs me as she steps onto the footstool in front of the sink. She points at an old kitchen timer standing sentry to the right of the sink.

I stare at it, then pull out my phone. "Let's try something different today. We'll use a special tooth-brushing playlist."

Ivy's cheeks plump with a huge smile. "Really? Do I get to choose the song?"

"Sure. What are you thinking?"

"Baby Shark!" She bounces on her toes, and I struggle not to laugh at the earnestness in her small face.

"Perfect choice. Let me find it." I tap through my phone, locating the song that's haunted parents since its inception. "Ready?"

Ivy grabs her toothbrush, nodding as I press play.

What follows is two minutes and seventeen seconds of Ivy dancing while brushing, toothpaste foam occasionally escaping as she mimics shark movements with her free arm. I find myself swaying along, making exaggerated chomping motions that send her into giggles.

"Again!" she demands when the song ends.

"Nope, one song is perfect. Look at those sparkly teeth!" I hand her a small cup of water. "Rinse and spit, shark girl."

"Papa never lets me listen to music while brushing," Ivy confides after her spit misses the sink entirely.

"Well, your papa seems like he has lots of good systems in place," I say carefully. "But sometimes it's fun to try new things, right?"

She takes my hand when I help her down from the footstool. "I'm gonna make him play that song *every* time I brush my teeth now."

I cringe. *Oops.*

"Awesome. He'll love it."

For hair, I abandon Saint's detailed instructions about sectioning and detangler application. Instead, I position Ivy by the window where natural light streams in, because perfect lighting is second nature to me now, and demonstrate the "mermaid braid" I used in a tutorial that got over two million views.

She twirls, admiring her reflection.

"I bet you'll be the only mermaid in class today," I say.

"Really?"

"One hundred percent. Let's not be late, though. Your papa said we need to take his car today."

"Because my car seat is there," Ivy explains, skipping down the stairs with her mermaid braid swinging. "It's super complicated. Miss Nora always complained about it."

The keys Saint left on the counter feel unnaturally heavy in my palm. Probably because they're not just keys to a vehicle, they're the gateway to a $100,000 Range Rover Autobiography with custom everything, according to the text he sent with detailed operating instructions. The thing looks like it could transport the president through a war zone while serving champagne.

"Okay, backpack check," I kneel to Ivy's level in the foyer. "Lunch?"

"Check!" She points at the bento box peeking from her rainbow bag.

"Water bottle?"

"Check!"

"Folder for school papers?"

She hesitates. "Oops."

"Go grab it, quick like a bunny."

While she scampers off, I review Saint's car instructions again. The man sent a literal essay titled *Vehicle Operation Protocols*.

Who does that?

Saint does. That's who.

Outside, the black SUV gleams in the driveway like it's just gotten back from a car wash. Hell, it probably drove itself there this morning.

Ivy returns with her folder. We veer into the guesthouse so I can quickly change into jeans and a cropped tee, then head to the car.

"Let's go, shall we?" I lead Ivy down the driveway, keeping my grip on her small hand steady.

"Our car talks sometimes," Ivy informs me. "And it has stars in the ceiling."

"Fun," I say. "It probably makes your dad coffee and gives stock tips, too."

I press the key fob, and the Range Rover chirps a greeting that sounds like money. The door handles glide out from their flush position.

"*Very* fancy," I say to myself as we approach the rear. "Hop on in."

I almost recoil when I spot what's in the back. Ivy's car seat resembles a miniature throne with more straps and buckles than a straight-jacket.

"Miss Nora said bad words every time she had to put me in," Ivy confides, climbing up into her seat.

"I can see why." I study the contraption, trying to match it with step fourteen of Saint's text tutorial. "This thing looks like it could survive re-entry from space."

Five minutes later, I'm still wrestling with a harness that could secure a bull rider.

"Is it supposed to have this many ... everything?" I say more to myself, tugging at a strap that seems to have no beginning or end.

"Papa says it's the safest one in the world," Ivy says proudly, wiggling in her half-buckled throne.

"Of course it is." I blow a strand of hair from my face. "Your papa probably had it custom-made by a supervillain."

The buckle clicks, then immediately unclicks when Ivy shifts.

"Sorry." She giggles.

My nails find their way to my left shoulder before I can

stop myself. *Not now.* I force my hands back to the car seat, hyperaware of my hyper frustration.

"Stop squirming, sweetie."

My voice comes out sharper than intended.

Ivy freezes, her little face falling. "Miss Nora used to yell, too."

My heart cracks.

"I'd never yell at you, sweetheart. I'm just learning." I soften my tone, despite the sweat now forming at my hairline. "Maybe you can help me?"

Her face brightens.

"This part goes click," she points, "and then this part goes swoosh."

I follow her instructions, managing to secure one side before the other releases.

"For the *love of*—" I catch myself, forcing a bright smile. "For the love of learning new things."

A woman pushing a stroller slows as she passes the gate at the end of the driveway, openly staring through the iron bars at my struggle. She lingers, clearly hoping to witness a full meltdown. I turn my back to her, focusing on Ivy.

"Let's try one more time," I say, wiping sweat from my brow. My fingernails itch to dig into my shoulder, the familiar comfort beckoning.

"You have to press the red button while pulling the strap," Ivy explains, her little finger pointing at a nearly invisible button.

"Oh!" I exclaim, finally seeing what I'd missed. The secret button is practically invisible against the black fabric. "Why would they hide the most important part?"

I press the tiny red button while pulling the strap, and suddenly everything clicks into place. Literally. The harness tightens perfectly around Ivy's small frame.

"You did it!" Ivy claps her hands.

"We did it," I correct her with a big smile.

The woman with the stroller is still watching. She gives me a smug little smile before continuing her walk.

"Is it too tight?" I ask Ivy, ignoring my wounded pride.

"Nope! Perfect!"

She beams up at me, and I have to say, being the recipient of a five-year-old's praise is *so much* better than 100,000 likes.

When I close her door and circle to the driver's side, I catch my reflection. My pink streak sticks out at odd angles, there's a black smudge of mascara on my cheek, and my whole face is flushed. In my former life, I'd never have let anyone see me like this, with my hair frazzled, makeup smeared, and the frustration evident on my face. My followers had expected perfection, even when I was demonstrating "relatable struggles." The old Wrenley would have recorded seventeen takes before showing herself struggling with something this basic.

Well, Old Wrenley can't come to the phone anymore.

I stick my tongue out at my reflection, which Ivy catches. She copies me, and before I know it, we're in a full-on raspberry-blowing war.

I slide into the driver's seat, laughing, and nearly gasp at the dashboard that looks like a fighter jet control panel.

"Holy sh..." I catch myself. "Holy moly. Okay, now to find the ignition..."

"Voice acti-vaytion," Ivy pipes up from the back. "Papa says 'Start engine,' and it listens."

I clear my throat. "Start engine?"

Nothing happens.

"Maybe it doesn't like me," I say.

Ivy giggles. "You have to press the button on the steering wheel first."

"Right. Obviously." I locate a small button with a micro-phone icon. "Start engine."

The Range Rover purrs to life, dashboard lighting up like a Christmas tree.

"Now you say 'navigate to Little Acorns Elementary,'" Ivy instructs.

I follow her lead, and the navigation system displays our route on a screen that looks bigger than my first TV.

"You're really good at this," I tell Ivy as we back down the driveway.

"I've done it a lot."

She doesn't say it with a big, proud smile. Ivy stares out her window, her expression somber, and I wonder just how many nannies she's gone through since her mother passed.

And how many she became attached to who ended up leaving her.

It'll take twelve minutes exactly to get to the school, so I decide to distract Ivy by asking her to tell me everything she knows about Falcon Haven and all her favorite spots. She perks up immediately, pointing out landmarks like the book-store with the cat in the window, the ice cream shop that serves sprinkles shaped like dinosaurs, and the colorful public playground.

At the school drop-off line, I follow the procession of mini-vans and SUVs considerably less opulent than our ride. When I pull up, a woman in a yellow safety vest waves us forward with the skills of an air traffic controller. I park where indi-cated and help Ivy out of her fortress, which takes approxi-mately half the time of putting her in. Progress.

Another woman in a floral dress and sensible shoes comes up to us as I'm straightening Ivy's dress. Her smile is profes-sional, but her eyes are curious.

"Good morning, Ivy!" Her voice carries the extra cheer of

someone who spends her days with five-year-olds. "I don't believe we've met. I'm Miss Erin, Ivy's teacher."

"Wrenley." I extend my hand while using the other to subtly tug on the hem of my shirt to cover my belly button. There's something about being faced with a perfectly put-together woman when you're in loungewear. "Ivy's, uh, babysitter for the day."

"Saint didn't mention a personnel change." Her gaze skims over my pink streak, then down to my scuffed, used-to-be-white Chucks. "Not that he needs to, of course. We just have an open communication policy when it comes to Ivy."

The way she says *we* makes my belly button pull back into my spine. Erin doesn't use a possessive tone, and she's not being inappropriate with me, but it's just... familiar. Like she's letting me know that I'm a part of something I'm not invited into.

I glance around, wondering if I accidentally dropped Ivy off at a high school with all its drama, instead.

"This was a last-minute thing," I say, bringing my focus back to Ivy, who skips ahead. "She's been great."

Erin nods but stares pointedly at Ivy's swinging braid. "Ivy usually wears her hair in a simple ponytail. She does better without the visual stimulation."

I blink. "Oh. She asked for it. I thought it'd be fun."

"Of course." She gives me another smile, a little sharper. "But children also need guardrails. Especially after... everything."

Especially after everything.

That's the line that hooks behind my ribs. Not because Erin's wrong, but because it's the kind of truth that makes me feel immediately unqualified to even *exist* near someone like Ivy.

"It can be hard when you're unfamiliar with a child's triggers."

I stiffen.

She tilts her head like a well-meaning hospice nurse. "If you need help, I can walk you through what we've been doing. Ivy can be a lot for people who aren't trained."

My throat goes dry. I'm itching to tug at the edge of my shirt, at the skin beneath.

"Thank you," I say because it's all I can manage.

"We're just all protective of her. That's all." Erin gives a final smile that lands like a pat on the head. "I'm sure you understand."

"Sure."

"Well, it was lovely meeting you." Miss Erin checks her watch. "Time to line up, Ivy! The bell's about to ring."

Ivy does a complete U-turn without breaking her stride, then flings her arms around my waist in a surprise hug that knocks the air from my lungs. "Bye, Miss Wrenley!"

She doesn't let go, clinging to my waist a moment longer than necessary.

"I'll be here at pickup time," I assure her, squeezing her shoulders, and her hold loosens. "Front of the line, two thirty sharp."

Her face brightens as she spins and skips away to join the other kindergartners. Miss Erin lingers.

I pull out my phone. "I should let Saint know Ivy's settled."

"No need," Erin says. "I'll let him know everything went smoothly. Saint appreciates thorough updates. I know what he likes to read."

I frown at her back as she saunters away but manage to tap out a quick message before she can sink her claws into Saint.

Ivy dropped off. Mermaid braid was a hit. No apocalypse occurred.

I return to the driver's seat and rest my forehead against the steering wheel, taking some deep breaths before I drive off. I'd prepared myself for a change of routine when coming to Falcon Haven, but this morning's activities have skewed my predictions of what to expect so much that they're not even on the scale anymore.

Don't scratch. Don't pull. Just breathe.

Ivy's teacher clearly has a thing for Saint. Her territorial vibe was unmistakable, like a cat marking its territory with strategically placed urine. I don't blame her, though. Saint is insanely attractive in that brooding, tattooed chef way that makes women swoon.

And he's rich.

And he's a devoted father.

And he's tortured.

And he's my temporary boss.

Who thinks I'm a squatter on his property.

Shit. Seven more hours to go, and I'm already in way too deep.

FIVE
WRENLEY

The GPS on my phone announces that I've arrived at Falcon Haven's Main Street, though I could have figured that out myself from the sudden shift from winding country roads to a charming strip of weathered storefronts that look like they belong on a postcard. I ease Saint's car into a parking spot on the street, taking my time to check (and double-check) that I'm within the painted lines.

The last thing I need is to give Mr. Perfectionist another reason to scowl at me.

I don't feel comfortable just lounging in Saint's house, his guesthouse, or his property in general, so what better way to idle away the hours I have while Ivy is in school than to enjoy the quaint small town that I'll soon be leaving?

Falcon Haven has the storybook quality that social media filters strive to replicate, but fail to achieve. I walk by window boxes stubbornly clinging to the last of summer's flowers, a hardware store that probably sells fishing tackle alongside hammers, and a market called The Merc with wooden crates of apples displayed outside.

A silver-haired man sweeping outside his bookshop pauses, nods at me, then returns to his task. A woman walking her corgi smiles without slowing her pace. They see me, a newcomer in their town, but they don't stare. Don't approach. Don't pull out phones for sneaky photos.

My shoulders drop an inch, and my breathing eases.

I slow my pace without thinking when a blue-and-white-striped awning comes into view. *C'est Trois* is written above in fancy cursive lettering.

Saint's restaurant.

Though "restaurant" seems too ordinary a word compared to the chef behind it all.

I take five steps closer to the window, drawn by an invisible hand at the small of my back urging me forward. Through the spotless glass, I'm able to glimpse the inner workings of Saint's kingdom, with an open kitchen gleaming with copper and steel, and a line of white-coated staff moving around with stiff-backed confidence.

And there he is.

Saint stands out among his team, even though he's in white like the others. His broad shoulders are squared, his neck tattoos standing out against the crisp chef's coat as he bends over something on the counter.

His fingers move with surprising delicacy for such large hands, arranging what looks like paper-thin slices of ... something. His sheer focus radiates outward, creating a bubble of tense concentration that even I can feel through the glass.

He straightens, says something to a young man beside him who nods rapidly, then turns—

Our eyes lock.

My heart slams against my ribs. His expression shifts from concentration to recognition to something darker.

Panic floods my system. I drop to a crouch behind a row

of manicured boxwoods, the rough branches scratching my arms as I press myself against the bricks holding the plants.

"Smooth, Wrenley," I mutter to myself.

I press my forehead against my knees, my cheeks burning as I race through the possibilities of what's happening inside his head right now.

Maybe he thinks I'm spying on him. Perhaps he thinks I'm unstable. Maybe he thinks I'm exactly the kind of person who shouldn't be trusted with his daughter.

But I can tell you what he's *not* thinking. He's probably not thinking about how absolutely captivating he is while in his element, full of authority and confidence, yet careful and delicate in his handling of his creations.

I peek through the branches. The spot where Saint stood is empty, and I release a breath.

Maybe he didn't actually see me. Perhaps that look wasn't recognition, but just his normal resting scowl face. Maybe—

"Looking for something?"

I topple backward.

The deep voice above me sends me sprawling into the bushes. I tilt my head up to find Saint looming over me, one dark eyebrow raised, arms crossed over his chest. His chef's coat is unbuttoned at the top, revealing the edge of a tattoo that disappears beneath the fabric.

"I was just—" My voice cracks. "I dropped my ... um..."

"Your dignity?"

His mouth twitches at the corner.

I stand, brushing dirt from my knees, acutely aware of tiny scratches stinging my forearms and the relentless burn in my cheeks.

"I panicked. I didn't expect to see you, and then you looked at me, and I just ... reacted."

"By hiding."

"It's what I do when I'm caught off guard."

Saint stares at me for a beat too long, then shakes his head. "Stay out of trouble, Miss Morgan."

He turns to leave, his dismissal so abrupt that I'm left blinking in his wake.

"That's it?" I call after him. "No lecture about lurking? No 'stop spying on my restaurant'?"

He stops, shoulders tensing under his chef's coat. "I don't have time for—"

When he turns back, his eyes drop to my forearms. His expression shifts.

"You're bleeding."

"What?" I look down at the small scratches left by the boxwood branches. "Oh, it's nothing. Just a few scrapes."

He steps closer, taking my wrist in his hand. His touch is cool against my skin, professional rather than intimate, but my pulse jumps anyway. His fingers are callused, the hands of a chef who has known knives and fire.

"These need to be cleaned," he says. "Come inside."

"I'm fine, really."

"You're in charge of my daughter. I need you functional, not infected with whatever's in those bushes."

I roll my eyes. "Pretty sure boxwoods aren't harboring flesh-eating bacteria."

He releases my wrist and holds the restaurant door open. "Now."

"You know, most people just offer a Band-Aid and send you on your way," I say, stepping into the restaurant.

The air shifts into warm, rich scents that make my stomach clench in anticipation. Butter, herbs, sauces simmering, steam billowing, and the regular clatter of pots and pans as the staff moves around.

Saint leads me through the kitchen and past their curious glances. "I'm not most people."

I follow him into a small office tucked behind the kitchen. "Do you rescue all the women who fall into plants, or am I special?"

His jaw tightens as he pulls a first-aid kit from a cabinet. "I just don't like blood."

"You're a chef. You butcher things."

"That's different." He gestures to a chair. "Sit."

I perch on the edge, watching as he wets a cloth at a small sink.

He kneels in front of me, taking my arm with the same exactness I'd watched him plate food. His touch is clinical, but the proximity sets my skin buzzing.

"I didn't realize you had a medical degree along with the culinary one."

I just can't seem to keep my mouth shut around this man. I blame it on my nerves. And his insane gorgeousness.

His eyes flick up to mine. "I don't like smart-asses either."

"Yet here we are."

A ghost of a smile touches his lips before vanishing. He dabs antiseptic on the scratches, and the resulting sting makes me hiss.

"Hold still."

"I am. I'm not five."

"Could've fooled me, hiding in bushes."

His focus returns to my arm, his fingers gently cleaning the lines of red. I watch the dark ink peeking from his rolled sleeve, swirls and lines that hint at stories I don't know.

"You make a habit of surveillance?" he asks without raising his head.

"Only when people look like they might yell at me for accidentally existing in their line of sight."

I watch his hands, the controlled movements.

"These aren't deep," he murmurs, reaching for a small packet of antibiotic ointment. "But better safe." He rips it open with his teeth, squeezing a dab onto his finger before carefully applying it to the scratches. His touch is purposeful but so delicate, and I have to remind myself to breathe.

"So," I say, needing to fill the quiet. "C'est Trois. Clever name. The three of you?"

He pauses, his gaze still fixed on my arm. "Something like that."

Saint reaches for a box of bandages, selecting several small ones. As he moves to apply the first one near my elbow, the sleeve of my T-shirt rides up slightly. His fingers brush the edge of the older, deeper marks hidden beneath, the ones that map my shoulder like angry constellations. His hand stills. His head tilts, a question forming in his eyes as they drift upward.

"Does Ivy like it here?" I ask quickly, shifting my arm just enough to pull my sleeve back down. "The restaurant, I mean. Does she hang out in the kitchen?"

His attention snaps back to my face, the momentary curiosity replaced by his usual guarded expression. "Sometimes. When she has to." He presses the bandage firmly onto my skin. "She prefers the pastry station. Sugar."

"Ah, a girl after my own heart."

He finishes applying the bandages, his movements efficient and impersonal again. Saint rises, tossing the used cloth and wrappers into a small bin. "All done. Try to stay out of the shrubbery."

"No promises." I stand, flexing my fingers.

He leans back against his desk, crossing his arms again, studying me. It's an assessment that makes me feel like a particularly foreign ingredient he's trying to figure out.

"Thanks. For the first aid."

He shrugs. "Just needed you to be functional for Ivy."

"Right. Ivy." The reason I'm here. The reason he tolerates my presence. "Speaking of, her teacher seemed ... territorial this morning."

Saint goes still. "Miss Erin is dedicated."

"Dedicated enough to imply I was disrupting Ivy's carefully curated emotional regulation with a mermaid braid and a shark song?"

"Erin cares about Ivy."

"I care about Ivy, too," I say softly. "She hugged me goodbye like she was afraid I wouldn't come back."

A muscle jumps in Saint's cheek. He glances away, toward the small window overlooking a back alley. "Ivy gets attached easily."

"Or maybe she just needs someone who doesn't treat her like a porcelain doll about to shatter."

The words are out before I can stop them. I suck in a horrified breath. *Why* did I say that?

His head snaps back toward me, his eyes flashing. "You know nothing about what Ivy needs."

"I know she laughed today," I counter nervously, but hold his gaze. "Really laughed. Toothpaste foam and all."

He says nothing, just stares, the silence stretching between us, thick and hot.

"Are you hungry?" he finally asks, the change of subject abrupt.

"What?"

"Lunch. You're pale. You look like you need to eat."

It's not a question. It's a command steeped in reluctant hospitality.

"I wouldn't want to impose," I hedge, thrown off-balance again.

"Too late."

He walks past me, out of the office, and back toward the controlled chaos of the kitchen. "Keep up."

I hesitate for only a second before following him, drawn back into the orbit of this complicated, compelling man who seems determined to keep me at arm's length while simultaneously pulling me closer.

I trail him like a lost duckling, navigating around chefs carrying hot pans and stacks of plates. The kitchen hums with a focused energy, a symphony of sizzling, chopping, and quiet commands. Several pairs of eyes flick toward me, curious but quickly returning to their tasks under Saint's implicit command. Nobody speaks to me. Nobody needs to. His presence dictates the mood.

He stops at a small stainless steel counter near a prep station piled high with vibrant microgreens and edible flowers. He pulls over a tall stool. "Here."

I slide onto it, feeling ridiculously out of place amid the professional ballet. My simple jeans and T-shirt feel like a costume compared to their crisp whites.

Saint pulls a block of cheese, a rustic loaf of bread, and something green and leafy from a low refrigerator. His movements are easy and sure as he slices the bread with a long serrated knife and grates the cheese onto the slices.

"Grilled cheese?" I ask, watching him slide the open-faced sandwiches under a salamander broiler mounted above the counter.

He sends me an insulted crook of his brow. "Gruyère. Arugula. Pain de campagne."

Saint's attention goes back to the broiler.

He could have just pointed me toward the market down the street. He could have ignored me entirely after patching up my pathetic scratches. But he didn't. Saint brought me into his sanctuary, his domain, and now he's feeding me.

The cheese bubbles and browns. He slides the tray out, the aroma nutty and warm, then reaches for the arugula, tossing a handful lightly with a vinaigrette I didn't see him make, then places them on the sandwich.

He plates the sandwiches on simple white plates, adding a small pile of cornichons alongside mine. He slides the plate across the counter to me.

"Eat."

It's simple yet perfect. Miles beyond the sad salads I usually make for myself.

"Thank you," I say, my voice thicker than intended.

Saint leans against the counter opposite me, arms folded again, watching me expectantly. He doesn't get himself any food. He just watches like he's waiting for a verdict.

I lift half the sandwich to my lips. The bread crackles under my bite, the cheese oozes with a sharp tang, and the peppery arugula slices through the richness.

An involuntary sound, more elemental and euphoric than any moan I've ever uttered, bursts from my throat.

Cheese does that to me. Especially melted.

Saint freezes. His gaze snaps to my lips, then lifts to my eyes, the blue in them darkening like a sudden storm cloud. His knuckles turn white where his hands grip the edge of the stainless steel counter. For a fraction of a second, the air crackles, the professional distance dissolving into something spicy and unexpected.

The controlled chef disappears, and the man looks hungry for something else entirely.

Heat flares low in my belly, a direct response to the way his nostrils flare and how his chest seems to expand under the white coat.

A pan clatters loudly behind me. Someone clears their throat. The background hum of the kitchen falters, the rhythm disrupted.

I risk a glance sideways. Two line cooks exchange a wide-eyed look before quickly turning back to their stations. Even the young man Saint had spoken to earlier pauses mid-chop, his knife hovering over a pile of herbs. They saw it. They felt it too.

My cheeks flame hotter than the broiler.

Oh God. Did I really just make that noise? Over a sandwich? In front of him and his entire staff? I want to melt into the stool, disappear behind the microgreens. I quickly take another bite, chewing with far more fervor than necessary, staring intently at the pattern on the white plate.

Saint pushes off the counter, the movement sharp and almost violent. He spins toward the pastry station.

"Pierre! Are those tart shells blind-baked yet?"

His voice is rougher than before and very clipped.

"Oui, Chef!" Pierre calls back, startled by the sudden command.

Saint doesn't look back at me. He strides toward the main cooking line, running a hand over the back of his neck, his shoulders rigid. He points at something in a sauté pan, barking an order in rapid French that I don't understand, but the cook jumps to obey.

C'est Trois snaps back into its focused rhythm, but the air still feels peppery and charged.

I force myself to take another bite, then another, needing to finish and escape the echo of that mortifying sound and the fire still lingering in Saint's wake.

Saint doesn't return. He keeps his back to me, immersing himself in the work.

I'm left alone on my stool, eating the best damn sandwich

of my life in the middle of a world-class kitchen, feeling more confused and strangely cared for than ever.

When I finish, I slide the plate away discreetly, unsure of the protocol.

Saint glances back, nods once as if confirming I completed the task, then returns to his work. No further words are exchanged. I slip off the stool, feeling the familiar urge to make myself small and invisible.

"Thanks again," I say quietly to his back.

He doesn't turn around, just lifts a hand in a half wave of acknowledgment. I find my own way out, pushing through the doors back onto the quaint street, the scent of herbs and butter clinging to my clothes, the taste of peppery arugula lingering on my tongue, and the weight of his attentiveness settling somewhere deep inside me.

SIX
WRENLEY

The school pickup line is shorter this time.

I spot Ivy immediately, her mermaid braid slightly looser now, leaning against the brick wall with her head down while all the other kids talk animatedly with each other.

Miss Erin stands nearby, clipboard in hand. She sees the Range Rover and her professional smile thins almost imperceptibly.

No words are exchanged with me this afternoon, just a curt nod as I step out and open the passenger door in preparation for buckling Ivy into her space-age car seat.

"Miss Wrenley!" Ivy looks up and launches herself at me, wrapping her arms around my legs. "Guess what? We painted!"

"Awesome! Did you paint a shark?" I smooth her hair back.

She pulls back suddenly. "You have boo-boo stickers like me!"

"I had a disagreement with a rosebush," I say, not entirely a lie.

"Did you win?"

"Not really."

Ivy pats my arm sympathetically. "Bushes are sneaky fighters."

I bite back a smile. "So, what did you paint?"

"I painted Papa's restaurant. Miss Erin said it was very detailed."

I glance at Miss Erin, who offers a tight-lipped smile that doesn't reach her eyes.

"Ivy is quite the artist," she says.

"Ready to go, Picasso?" I take Ivy's hand and her backpack.

"Can we get ice cream?" she asks as I buckle her in, the process marginally faster this time.

"Maybe after we check in at home," I hedge.

Saint's car and Saint's child are both my responsibility. The thought of deviating from getting both safely home makes my palms sweat.

"Papa never lets me get ice cream on a school day," Ivy says matter-of-factly.

"Well, maybe today is special," I say, catching her eye in the rearview mirror as I slide into the driver's seat.

Her grin is instantaneous.

We drive toward the edge of town, Ivy chattering about paint colors and playground drama. As we turn onto the quieter road leading to Saint's property, she points toward a small roadside farm stand. "They have flowers!"

"They do," I agree, slowing slightly.

"Can we get some? Papa never gets flowers for our house."

"We'll see," I murmur, glancing at the stand, then back at the road.

Maybe a small bouquet wouldn't hurt. It might be nice to add a splash of color to the monochrome kitchen.

In that split second of distraction, checking the rearview mirror to see Ivy's hopeful face, the car ahead of me brakes abruptly. A squirrel darts across the road. My foot slams on the brake, but it's too late. Our heavy SUV connects with the other car's bumper with a sickening crunch of metal and plastic.

Not hard. Just ... enough. My heart leaps into my throat.

"Whoa!" Ivy gasps from the back.

"Ivy? Are you okay?" I twist around, frantic.

She looks startled, wide-eyed, but nods. "Yeah. What happened?"

"Just a little bump," I say, my voice shaking.

Oh God. Saint's car. His precious, insanely expensive car.

The driver of the car ahead, an older woman with tight gray curls, is already getting out, her face pinched with irritation.

I take a deep breath and unbuckle my seat belt. "Stay right here, okay? Don't move."

I get out, legs trembling. The damage isn't catastrophic, but it's definitely noticeable. The front bumper has a deep scratch and a small dent. Her rear bumper is similarly scraped, with maybe a cracked taillight.

"Look what you did!" the woman accuses, hands on her hips.

"I am so sorry," I stammer. "You stopped so suddenly..."

"A squirrel ran out! You should pay attention!"

"I know, I'm sorry. Are you alright?"

"I'm fine, but my car isn't!"

We exchange insurance information in an agonizingly

slow process. The woman eyes the Range Rover, then me, her gaze lingering on my pink streak and bandaged arms. I can feel her judgment like a physical weight. By the time we're done, my hands are shaking so badly I can barely sign my name on the information slip she demands.

Back in the car, I grip the steering wheel, trying to calm my racing heart.

"Is the car broken?" Ivy asks quietly from the back.

"No, sweetie. Just a little dent. Everyone is okay. That's what matters."

But my stomach churns. What will Saint say? He'll kill me. He'll fire me. He'll throw me out of the guesthouse.

At that exact time, my phone decides to buzz, and of course it's a text from Saint.

The governor's running behind, which means I am, too. Won't be home until late. Maybe 2 a.m. Make sure Ivy eats.

Relief washes over me, quickly followed by renewed dread. It buys me time, but the reckoning is only delayed.

"Okay," I say, forcing cheer into my voice. "Change of plans. How about we go home, make an awesome dinner, and then we talk about flowers tomorrow?"

Ivy, sensing the shift in my mood, just nods solemnly.

Does she know? Does she sense the tidal wave of panic crashing inside me? Of course she does. Kids always know.

Pulling into Saint's long driveway feels like entering the lion's den. I park the Range Rover carefully, positioning it so the damaged front end isn't immediately visible from the main house entrance. A pathetic attempt at concealment, I know. He'll see it the second he walks outside.

"Home sweet home." I force a smile as I unbuckle Ivy.

She slides out without comment. Inside, the house feels too big, too quiet.

Making dinner becomes a necessary distraction. I find

chicken breasts and pasta, deciding on a simple lemon-herb chicken pasta dish. Ivy pulls her little step stool up to the counter, appointing herself Chief Herb Chopper.

"Careful with the knife," I instruct, handing her a small, relatively dull paring knife and a bunch of parsley.

"Papa lets me use the big knives," she says, concentrating fiercely on her task.

"Does he now?" I raise an eyebrow, dicing onions nearby.

"Only when he's watching super close. He says knife skills are important."

She meticulously saws through a parsley stem. My hands tremble slightly as I assist her.

"Are you cold, Miss Wrenley?" Ivy peers up at me.

"A little," I lie.

As the pasta boils and the chicken sizzles, I arrange the cooked components on our plates.

Instead of just piling it on, I swirl the pasta, nestle the sliced chicken beside it, drizzle the sauce artfully, and shower it with Ivy's painstakingly chopped parsley and lemon zest. Old habits.

"Wow," Ivy breathes, looking at her plate. "It looks like the pictures in Papa's cookbooks."

"Does it?" I try to sound casual, but a warmth spreads through my chest. "Just trying to make it look as good as it tastes."

We eat at the huge dining table, the two of us feeling small in the grand room.

"Will Papa be mad about the car?" Ivy asks softly, not meeting my eyes.

"I hope not, sweetie. It was an accident. And nobody got hurt."

My voice sounds thin, unconvincing even to my own ears.

"He doesn't like accidents," she whispers. "He yelled real loud at Miss Nora when she scraped the wheel on the curb."

Great. Just great. My stomach clenches tighter. Scraped wheel versus crunched bumper. I'm doomed.

"Well, hopefully, he'll understand," I say, trying to project confidence I don't feel.

We finish dinner, and the conversation shifts to lighter topics, such as school subjects, favorite colors, and the merits of different dinosaur shapes for sprinkles.

The easy normalcy is a balm, but the dread beneath remains, a low hum under the surface.

Bath time is uneventful, filled with bubbles and splashing. We skip the shark song tonight. As I tuck Ivy into her bed, surrounded by rainbows and stuffed animals, she grabs my hand.

"Don't leave?" she asks, her blue eyes shining.

"I'm not going anywhere," I assure her, settling into the rocking chair beside her bed. "I'll stay until you fall asleep."

I stay for a long time, watching her peaceful face, the knot in my stomach tightening with every tick of the clock downstairs.

This little girl deserves consistency, deserves someone who doesn't bring chaos and car accidents into her life. Maybe Miss Erin was right.

Finally, I slip out, leaving her door cracked just enough for the hallway light to spill in.

Downstairs, the house is silent again. I wander into the living room, sinking onto the plush sofa.

My phone screen shows 9:17 p.m. Hours to go. Hours of waiting for the sound of tires on gravel, for the heavy tread of his boots on the porch, for the explosion I know is coming.

I find the familiar spot on my left shoulder, tracing the raised skin through my T-shirt. The urge to scratch, to pull, is almost overwhelming. I curl my hands into fists, digging my nails into my palms instead.

Breathe. Just breathe.

To give myself something to do, I clean the kitchen, wiping away stray bits of herbs and cheese, the mundane task a welcome distraction. But once the counters are clean and the dishwasher is humming, there's nothing left to do but wait.

I get up, pace the room, straightening pillows that don't need straightening, adjusting picture frames on the mantelpiece. Photos of Ivy, laughing. Photos of Saint and Ivy, with him looking softer and younger.

I pace, check the time, try to read, fail. Anxiety coils tighter and tighter in my stomach. Every creak of the house sounds like Saint returning.

Finally, headlights sweep across the guesthouse window. It's 2:17 a.m. My breath catches.

I watch from the window as he parks the sleek gray Jaguar he drove this morning next to the Range Rover. He gets out slowly, his weariness evident even from a distance. He runs a hand through his hair, then stops dead, his gaze fixed on the front of the SUV.

Even in the low porch light, I see his posture change. He goes utterly still for a second, then stalks toward the Range Rover, his movements jerky and unnatural.

He drops to a crouch, examining the dent.

I should go out there. I should explain. But fear roots me to the spot.

He straightens abruptly and strides toward the main house, slamming the door open so hard it bangs against the wall.

"Wrenley!" His voice cracks through the house, sharp and jagged.

It's not anger. It's something deeper and more intrinsic.

My feet finally move, carrying me out of the living room and into the foyer.

I find him at the bottom of the staircase, his face pale, eyes wild. He hasn't even taken off his jacket.

"The car," he grits out, his hands clenched into fists at his sides. "What happened to the car?"

"Saint, I—"

"Where's Ivy?" He cuts me off, his voice dangerously unsteady. "Is she alright? Did something happen?"

He pushes past me, heading up.

"She's fine! Saint, she's asleep. Nothing happened to her."

I hurry after him.

"It was just a tiny fender bender. Barely a scratch. Everyone is okay."

He ignores me, taking the stairs two at a time.

Saint bursts into Ivy's room. I follow, hovering in the doorway, heart pounding.

He goes straight to her bed, his hand hovering over her small sleeping form, checking her breathing. Saint smooths her hair back from her face, his touch gentle, his own breath coming in ragged gasps. He sinks onto the edge of her bed, burying his face in his hands for a moment. The tension radiating off him is suffocating.

When he looks up, his eyes find mine in the dim light filtering from the hallway. The sheer terror in them steals my breath.

It's then I realize it's not about the car. It was never about the car.

He doesn't say anything. Just stares at me, the accusation, the fear, the unprocessed grief of three years ago laid bare in his gaze.

Then he turns back to Ivy, pulling her blanket higher around her shoulders.

The dismissal is absolute.

I back away slowly, retreating down the stairs with the image of his tortured expression seared into my mind. The front door feels miles away.

Back in the suffocating quiet of the guesthouse, the carefully constructed walls I maintain around my own pain crumble.

The shaking starts in my hands, spreading up my arms.

Saint's reaction, the utter agony ... it triggered that darkness deep inside me.

That familiar, ugly urge claws its way up my throat.

My fingers find my scalp, twisting strands of hair around them, pulling until the sharp sting offers a sweet release.

It's not enough.

My nails dig into the skin of my shoulder, scraping over the old scars, seeking the sharp, grounding pain that momentarily drowns out the noise in my head.

Breathe. Just breathe.

But the air won't come, trapped behind the frantic rhythm of my heart.

A silent scream builds inside me, a pressure cooker with no escape valve, except for the one I inflict upon myself.

<h1 style="text-align:center">SEVEN
SAINT</h1>

The smell of burning rubber and gasoline clings to the edges of my consciousness, a phantom scent that jolted me awake long before the weak dawn light.

I lie there, staring at the ceiling, the image of my mangled car replaying behind my eyelids.

My wife.

Not the SUV Wrenley managed to dent, but Celine's little blue Fiat, crumpled like a discarded sheet of paper.

The same icy panic I'd felt last night at the sight of the damaged Range Rover swells my throat now, hot and suffocating.

It's always the same. Any accident, any *hint* of one, and I'm back there on that rain-slicked road, the world tilting.

I throw the covers back, the need to move, to do something, overriding my exhaustion. The governor was demanding as expected, his family even more so, but I've cooked for many picky eaters, especially the unnecessarily annoying ones, without batting an eye. But the one variable that wasn't accounted for was my daughter in the arms of a virtual stranger, her safety balanced against Wrenley's experience, which is slim to none.

Wrenley has Celeste's blessing, which goes a long way when it comes to my small circle of loyal friends and family, but as anyone who's experienced a loss knows, there's no one, absolutely *no one*, who can be trusted with the little heart beating outside of my chest aside from me.

Yet I can't stop working. Because if I stop, I think, and I remember, which is the exact situation I find myself in now.

Coffee. Ivy's breakfast. Routine. These anchors keep me from drifting completely.

I dress in the near dark in a T-shirt and well-worn jeans, and head for the kitchen deliberately early. I'll tell Wrenley this morning. Firmly. Her services are no longer required.

Ivy would adjust, of course. She has to. But this revolving door of nannies, this constant, low thrum of disorder Wrenley seemed to drag in with her, is not sustainable.

I need control over my realm, and Wrenley Morgan, with her sad eyes and pink-streaked hair, is a variable I cannot manage.

When I come downstairs to the kitchen, however, it's not empty.

Wrenley stands at the island, already dressed, earbuds in, humming to a beat only she can hear. She's in tight yoga pants that fit like a second skin, perfectly outlining an ass so round it could've been grown at a peach farm.

I don't realize I've been staring until my eyes burn, and I have to blink. My gaze drags up over the curve of her waist and the gentle sway of her ponytail as she bounces on her toes, completely unaware she's waking me up in ways my two morning espressos could never.

I subtly adjust myself, grateful she's facing away. Because

if I had to see the way her tits move in that fitted workout top —fuck me. She'd know. There'd be no hiding it.

I'm attracted to her.

Not just some passing, inconvenient awareness.

I want my hands on her ass. On her breasts. On every goddamn part of her.

No.

Fuck.

Leaning against the doorway, I watch her assemble something on the counter between her dance moves and notice a small, worn suitcase and a duffel bag sitting by the back door, a silent testament to her intention to leave.

Good. Makes this easier.

I push off the doorframe, opening my mouth to speak, the carefully rehearsed words ready, but they catch in my throat.

On the counter, Ivy's lunchbox lies open. Her ham and cheese sandwich is cut into the shape of a goddamn star. Carrot sticks are arranged like rays of a sun around a small container of hummus, and a cluster of grapes sits next to a tiny, folded note with what looks like a crudely drawn shark on it.

Moving next to Wrenley, I pick up the note. Inside, in neat print, it says: *Have a fin-tastic day, Shark Girl!*

A muscle under my eye twitches. I fold the note up and put it back.

This ... this is not the work of someone just going through the motions. This is care. The kind of thoughtful detail I, in my grief-stricken haze and demanding schedule, rarely manage anymore. I can make sandwiches, obviously. But a star-shaped one with a shark note? That's a language I'd forgotten how to speak and time I didn't allow myself.

Wrenley turns, a half-eaten apple in her hand, and screams.

Her apple thuds to the floor, rolling under the kick plate of a cabinet. Wrenley yanks out her earbuds, one hand flying to her chest, her eyes wide and wild.

"You—you scared the shit out of me! I didn't hear you come in. I thought you were ... I don't know, a giant bear with a vendetta."

A giant bear. With tattoos, apparently. I look pointedly at her suitcase by the porch's door.

"Planning a quick getaway before the bearpocolypse?"

She follows my gaze, the blush deepening. "Something like that. I figured after last night… the car…"

She worries her lower lip. The air in the kitchen, moments before filled with her quiet, pleasant singing, now crackles with an awkward tension.

I cross my arms, leaning back against the counter, the image of the star-shaped sandwich fighting with the fresh memory of Celine's crumpled Fiat.

"The car is just metal, Wrenley. It can be fixed."

The words sound hollow even to me. Last night, the sight of that dent had ripped open a wound I keep trying to stitch shut.

Wrenley nods, her gaze dropping to the floor. She looks like she didn't sleep either. There are faint shadows beneath her eyes. "Well, good. Because I really am sorry about that."

I don't elaborate. I don't mention my own terror, and the way the sight of it had sent me spiraling. I just look at the meticulously prepared lunch that Wrenley wasn't obligated to prepare.

"Ivy will appreciate this," I say.

Wrenley's eyes light up, the darkness under them seeming to disappear instantly under her genuine hope. "You think so? She seems the type to like shapes. And notes. It'll make the carrots less offensive."

"Hmph."

I need coffee. Now. I move toward the machine, turning my back on her, on the suitcase, on the fucking star-shaped sandwich that's currently derailing my entire plan.

She bends to retrieve her apple, turning to throw it in the garbage bin, her movements subdued now that the music is gone.

Good. This is my opening. Tell her it's not working out. Tell her Ivy needs consistency, and she isn't it. But the words taste like burned coffee.

The cutesy lunch.

The goddamn shark note.

"About last night," I say. Wrenley flinches, her shoulders coming up to her ears.

What is with that? Any sudden movements and the girl spooks like an abused horse.

"Look, Saint, I get it," she says quickly, her voice suddenly brittle. "I screwed up with the car. I'm a terrible nanny. I'm probably setting Ivy back years in therapy. My suitcase is packed. I'll just finish making Ivy's lunch and then I'll be out of your hair. I'll even pay for the bumper."

She says it all in a rush, a shield of rapid-fire words.

I stare at her.

Wrenley flushes under my scrutiny.

The vulnerable admission, hidden under the sarcasm, throws me off. I hadn't expected her to be so prepared for dismissal.

Or so hard on herself.

"I've had it rehearsed since approximately 2:18 a.m.," she admits, then takes a bite from a new apple, chewing with a defiant sort of energy.

"You're not a terrible nanny," I say, my voice kinder than I intend. I turn back to the coffee machine, focusing on the familiar ritual of grinding beans and filling the carafe. It gives my hands something to do, a focal point other than her earnest, anxious face. "You dented a car. It happens."

Wrenley says nothing. I can feel her watching me, probably waiting for the other shoe to drop, the part where I tell her to get the fuck out, anyway.

This is my opening to do it. More politely, of course. The girl doesn't deserve a curt dismissal, just as she didn't deserve my unexpected wrath last night.

"The thing is," I say, busying myself by grabbing a couple of mugs from the upper cupboard. "Ivy's attached to you. Temporarily."

The thought of another tearful goodbye for Ivy, another adjustment, makes my gut clench. "She enjoys a person who understands her artistic level."

I risk a glance. Wrenley is very still, her apple forgotten in her hand. She's shifted slightly, putting a little more distance between us, her posture wary.

"My last nanny quit without notice. The one before her lasted three months." I spin with a full mug of coffee and hand it to her, forcing myself to meet her wide-eyed, beautiful gaze. "Ivy's still recovering from her mother's death. She doesn't need another person walking in and out of her life on a whim."

"It's not my intention—" Wrenley stops herself, then glances at her suitcase. "That's fair."

The coffee machine gurgles behind me. Wrenley carefully folds the lunchbox closed, her fingers lingering on the clasp.

"Are you asking me to stay? As her nanny?"

"Two weeks." I say it fast before I can second-guess myself. "Give me two weeks to find someone permanent. Someone qualified."

The words surprise me as much as they do her, but after

reading an email early this morning from the nanny agency stating that their best employee has just accepted a job, and I'd have to wait a few weeks for an adequate replacement, I'm desperate.

"That's not in my usual job description." Wrenley tilts her head, studying me. "My references are mostly TikTok comments."

She takes a tentative sip of the coffee, her eyes still wary over the rim of the mug. "I like Ivy. A lot. But I don't have any formal training, Saint. No early childhood education degrees, no CPR certification beyond what I learned for a boating license years ago."

Jesus, I am regretting this by the second.

"You have a boating license?" I ask.

Wrenley offers a small, self-deprecating smile. "Long story. Point is, I'm not exactly nanny material on paper."

"This is by no means permanent. Ivy doesn't care about your résumé. She cares that you taught her a mermaid braid and aren't afraid to be silly with her. For two weeks, that's enough."

I loathe how desperate it sounds. How much it exposes the gaping hole in our lives.

"Ivy needs someone who sees her," I continue, "And you seem to embrace her differences. The agency is backed up. This buys me time."

Wrenley sets the mug down. "And what do I get out of extending my babysitting gig? Besides the pleasure of your sunny company?"

"What do you want?" I ask, wary.

Wrenley looks out the window toward the guesthouse, then back at me. "Space. Privacy. I came here to get away from everything, and from the little bit that I saw yesterday, I love this town."

"You can stay rent-free," I blurt, cursing inwardly. I'm usually a much better negotiator than this.

"I don't usually take hand-outs, but while I'm taking care of your daughter, that seems fair. I don't need you to pay me."

"Retiring early, are you?"

Her face shutters. Wrenley shifts her weight. "I have enough saved away to get by."

I don't know why I asked that. Or why I feel a distinct clenching behind my ribs after noticing her answering expression. I have no qualms making a person shrivel where they stand when they don't meet my expectations, but with Wrenley, it doesn't feel like a dressing down. It feels like I've kicked a puppy.

"And after two weeks?" I ask.

She shrugs, a studied casualness. "After two weeks, I'll have figured out my next move. And you'll have found Mary Poppins 2.0."

The coffee maker finishes brewing a second cup. I reach for it, needing its familiar, habitual buzz right about now.

"Keep her safe," I say. "Stick to her routines as much as possible. And if anything, anything at all seems off, you call me. Immediately."

Wrenley's expression sobers. "I understand what's at stake, Saint. Ivy will be in good hands."

Something in her tone makes me believe her. Not trust her —I don't trust anyone with Ivy—but I believe that she grasps the gravity of what I'm asking.

"Good," I say, taking a long swallow of coffee, the heat doing little to warm the knot in my stomach.

A ghost of a smile plays on her lips, but it doesn't quite reach her eyes. There's a weariness there that mirrors my own, a fragility she tries to hide beneath a layer of quick wit.

"Just keep her happy," I amend, the words feeling foreign on my tongue.

Before she can respond, the telltale thud of small feet hitting the stairs reaches my ears.

"Papa?" Ivy's sleepy voice calls out, followed by a loud yawn.

She shuffles into the kitchen, rubbing her eyes, her dark hair a wild halo around her head. Her gaze lands on Wrenley, then on the suitcase still by the door.

A flicker of confusion, then anxiety, crosses her small face.

"Miss Wrenley? You're still here?" she asks, her voice small.

Wrenley's expression softens instantly. She crouches down to Ivy's level. "Morning, Ivy. Of course I'm still here."

Ivy's face breaks into a wide, relieved grin. She launches herself at Wrenley, wrapping her arms around her neck in a fierce hug.

Wrenley catches her easily, her earlier tension dissolving as she returns the embrace and laughs when she almost topples over.

I watch them, a complicated ache in my chest.

This is why.

This small, adorable child is the reason I'm letting this pink-haired, apple-dropping, car-denting woman stay in my house, in my life, for two more weeks.

"I'll see you after school, *mon trésor*," I say to Ivy, walking over and kissing the top of her head.

As I head for the door, I'm aware of Wrenley watching me go and of her suitcase still by the door. I use it as a tangible reminder that she was ready to leave.

That she still will, eventually.

EIGHT
WRENLEY

The weight of a five-year-old's hug is surprisingly effective at keeping a packed suitcase exactly where it is.

Ivy's arms are a warm vise around my neck, her small body pressed so tightly against mine I can feel the fast thump of her heart, or maybe it's mine.

Saint's footsteps recede, the click of the back door soft but final. He's gone, leaving behind the lingering aroma of dark coffee and cologne, the type of morning hit that makes me inhale deeply.

It's the kind of scent that doesn't announce itself with a shout. Instead, it settles into the background, a subtle, woody spice that draws you in without you realizing why. It's entirely too appealing for a man who communicates primarily through grunts and glares.

Why that particular brand of broken, grumpy, and utterly captivating man pulls at something deep inside me, I can't explain. It's not logical. I came to Falcon Haven seeking quiet, anonymity, a respite from emotional storms, not to stand in the path of a Category 5 human.

Yet, maybe it's the way his gruffness occasionally cracks, revealing glimpses of the aching grief and fierce love warring within him, like that moment in his office when he'd tended to my scratches with such unexpected gentleness. Or how he looks at his daughter with a tenderness that could melt glaciers.

There's no artifice, no carefully constructed charm with him. What you see is what you get, even if what you get is a scowl and a sarcastic remark. After years of swimming in the shallow end of performative online personalities, his grounded, unfiltered presence is bracing. Like a shot of straight espresso instead of a saccharine latte.

"Are you really, really staying?" Ivy mumbles into my shoulder, her voice thick with leftover sleep and a touch of lingering worry.

"Really, really," I confirm, loosening my arms just enough to look at her. Her blue eyes, so like her father's in their intensity but softer, search mine. "For a little while, anyway. Two whole weeks."

I push aside the inconvenient truth that Saint, in all his tattooed glory, is starting to feel less like a temporary boss and more like a very complicated craving.

She beams. "I'm glad you're not leaving. Now you can paint with me every day!"

"We'll see about *every* day," I say, ruffling her already wild hair. "But today is definitely a painting day. After we get home from school."

She giggles and slides off my lap, heading for the low cupboard containing her cereal boxes with the unerring focus of a heat-seeking missile.

While Ivy crunches her way through a mountain of

brightly colored O's, she outlines her plans for our next fourteen days. They involve a lot of glitter, opening a potential mud pie bakery, and teaching me all the words to a song about a llama who wears pajamas.

The thought of doing all this with Ivy is unexpectedly endearing. Two weeks. It's a breath, a pause button on my life, yet not a full stop. The relief that flooded me when Saint asked me to stay, however reluctantly, felt far too significant for a temporary gig. It felt like being thrown a lifeline when I hadn't noticed how badly I was drowning.

"Earth to Miss Wrenley!" Ivy waves a spoon in front of my face. "Are you thinking about Papa's cranky morning face? You look like you are, 'cause you're making the same face."

"Something like that," I admit, my cheeks warming. "Let's get you dressed."

The morning routine is smoother this time, less about deciphering Saint's seventeen-step manifesto and more about Ivy's enthusiastic narration of her dream about a talking raccoon who wanted to borrow her sparkly shoes. We had a different song for teeth-brushing this time, a pop tune about believing in yourself that Ivy sang at the top of her lungs, and another, slightly more complex braid that winds around the crown of her head that earns me an impressed, "Wow!"

The drive to Little Acorns Elementary is blessedly uneventful. No rogue squirrels, no sudden stops, no new additions to the Range Rover's growing collection of character marks.

I pull into the drop-off line with the practiced ease of a seasoned parent, which is laughable, but I'll take the small victories. Ivy scrambles out after I reach behind and unclasp the buckles of her car seat, backpack already halfway off her shoulder.

"Bye, Miss Wrenley!"

"In a while, crocodile!" I call back, watching her skip toward the school entrance.

While she's in school, I plan to really explore the downtown. The morning chill has burned off, leaving behind a perfect September day, the kind that makes you want to buy a pumpkin spice something, even if you don't particularly like pumpkin spice.

I could just record a few clips. For myself. No one needs to see them. A visual diary.

But the thought of hitting record brings a familiar prickle of anxiety. The lens, even on my phone, feels like an eye, and I've had enough eyes on me to last a lifetime. Falcon Haven is my escape, my anonymous haven. Documenting it, even for my own private collection, feels like a betrayal of its quaintness, a crack in the sanctuary walls.

Still, the urge to capture it—to bottle this feeling of peace and simple beauty—is strong. What if I forget? What if the sharp edges of this memory dull over time?

As if it knows I'm thinking of it, my phone buzzes in my purse. Pulling it out on a sigh, I read the notification. It's an email from my agent.

Subject: Still alive? 😊

Wren,

Heard you'd gone off-grid. Hope you're not holed up in a cabin somewhere writing a manifesto. Or worse, knitting. Listen, funny thing. Was chatting with a contact, and guess whose name popped up, practically vibrating with untapped potential? Bernard Toussaint. Apparently, your

new neck of the woods is his reclusive kingdom. The man's a culinary unicorn, darling. Brooding, brilliant, and tragically widowed. Basically, catnip for the masses. Just a thought, but if you were ever considering a gentle re-entry like a 'finding myself in a small town with a hot, emotionally unavailable chef' arc could be gold. Pure, unadulterated, monetizable gold. People are starving for authenticity, and what's more authentic than a fallen influencer finding solace (and maybe love?) among the heirloom tomatoes? Unless, of course, you're still not feeling up to... well, you know. Facing the world. After everything. No pressure, obviously. But the algorithm waits for no one, kiddo. Let me know if you're ready to rise from the ashes, phoenix-style.

Just marinate on it for me. It's all I ask.

XOXO, Brenda

My stomach plummets. Brenda Chu. Of course. She has a bloodhound's nose for opportunity and the subtlety of a sledgehammer.

The casual mention of Saint and the way she framed him as a potential "arc" makes my skin crawl. She doesn't know I'm nannying for him. My agent just sees an angle, a story to spin, another chance to package a life for consumption.

Not to mention the casual, dismissive "after everything," she added, as if that encompasses the complete meltdown my millions of followers witnessed.

As if the public implosion—the weeks I couldn't leave my apartment, the feeling of a million eyes dissecting my every mistake—was just a minor hiccup, a temporary setback in the content creation game.

The phone feels slick in my hand.

I shove it back into my purse, the screen dark, but Brenda's words resonate, bright and intrusive, in the quiet car.

Marinate on it.

I'd rather marinate in a vat of actual acid.

A loud, prolonged honk sounds out behind me, making me jump out of my skin. I'm about to apologize profusely and drive off when a shadow falls over my open window.

"You're holding up the car line. Wrenley, was it?"

"Miss Erin." I give her a close-lipped smile.

Her floral dress today is a symphony in muted pinks and greens, and her voice is as crisp as her ironed collar. Her gaze flicks over the Range Rover, lingering for a moment on the front bumper, though the new dent isn't visible from this angle.

Erin says, "Mr. Toussaint asked me to keep an extra eye on Ivy today. He was concerned over yesterday's incident."

The way she says "incident" makes it sound like I'd driven the SUV into a fireworks factory. My knuckles whiten on the steering wheel.

Brenda's email, Erin's condescending tone … it's a one-two punch to my already frayed nerves.

"Saint was concerned about Ivy, yes," I say, keeping my voice even. "As he should be. She's his daughter."

"He and I had a long chat this morning about ensuring her environment remains stable. He values my input, especially when it comes to new influences."

Her gaze flicks to my pink streak, then back to my face.

The implication isn't lost on me: *You, flighty girl with your pink hair and dented cars, are not what Ivy, or Saint, needs.*

"Well, I'm glad Saint has such a dedicated professional he can confide in," I reply, my own smile just as saccharine. "Accidents happen. Luckily, it's just metal and easily fixed. Unlike, say, a chronically judgmental attitude. That's much harder to buff out."

Erin's smile falters for a millisecond before snapping back into place. "Mr. Toussaint relies on those of us who provide a more consistent, grounded influence in Ivy's life. He and I have been discussing potential long-term solutions for Ivy's care. Someone with the right qualifications."

"How proactive," I say, offering her my own version of a bright, meaningless smile. "It's always good to have a plan B. Or C. Or, in some cases, all the way to Z. Have a wonderful day, Miss Erin."

As I drive off, I offer a cheerful little wave that I hope conveys utter indifference to her territorial display. But the image of Saint calling her personal cell, saying her name, confiding in her, stings more than I want to admit.

My nails find their way to my shoulder, rubbing at it through my sweater's fabric. The skin there burns from the phantom sensation of yesterday's nails digging deep, seeking an anchor in the storm of Brenda's opportunism and Erin's smug superiority.

That familiar, ugly whisper starts in the back of my mind, promising relief from the pressure building behind my ribs.

Just a little. No one will know.

My breath hitches. I force both hands to the wheel, clenching the cold leather.

No. I will not let them drive me back to that. But I do need air that doesn't taste of judgment and something to look at besides the inside of Saint's ridiculously expensive SUV.

My foot presses the accelerator a little harder than necessary. I drive not toward Saint's secluded property, but back toward the heart of Falcon Haven, the quaint storefronts a blur through my stinging eyes. I need a distraction, something immediate and benign.

There.

A flash of cheerful yellow and white.

Libby Jude's.

The sign, painted in a whimsical script, depicts a steaming coffee cup and a slice of pie. It looks like the kind of place where problems are solved with buttermilk pancakes and a sympathetic ear, neither of which I'm looking for, but the facade is soothing.

The image of Saint confiding in Erin, the two of them discussing *my* suitability, plays on a loop.

I pull the Range Rover into a parking spot directly in front, the engine's quiet hum a counterpoint to the frantic thrumming in my veins.

For a moment, I just sit, staring at the café's welcoming windows, the urge to rake my nails across my skin a live creature under my sweater.

Maybe a strong coffee and the clatter of other people's lives will be enough to drown out my own demons. It's a flimsy shield, but it's all I have right now. I kill the engine, take a shaky breath, and force myself out of the car.

The bell above the door of Libby Jude's chimes a cheerful, almost musical greeting as I step inside. I walk into warmth, thick with the comforting scent of baked goods, roasted coffee, and something vaguely cinnamon-y. It's a hug in olfactory form.

Behind a counter laden with glass-domed cakes and oversized cookies, a woman with kind brown eyes and a cascade of warm brown hair pulled back loosely from her face looks up from where she's wiping down the espresso machine. She wears a simple apron over a chambray shirt, and her smile is genuine, crinkling the corners of her eyes.

"Morning! Come on in. What can I get for you?"

Her voice is as welcoming as the atmosphere, an absolute melody after the discordant notes of my morning.

This must be Libby Jude. Or maybe just Jude. Or Libby.

"Just coffee, please," I manage, my voice still a little shaky. "Black."

"Coming right up." She turns to the gleaming machine, her movements efficient and graceful.

"Stressful morning?" she asks over her shoulder, her tone casual, inviting.

I almost laugh. "Is it that obvious?"

She glances back, her smile softening with sincere empathy. "Only to someone who's had a few of their own."

She finishes pulling the shot, the rich aroma filling the small space between us. "I'm Noa, by the way."

"Wrenley."

"Pretty name." She pours the coffee into a sturdy mug, then slides it across the counter. "On the house. You look like you need it."

I stare at her, then at the coffee. "Oh, I… I can't. Thank you, but—"

"Nonsense." Noa waves me off. "Consider it a welcome-to-Falcon-Haven-even-if-you're-having-a-terrible-day gift. Besides"—her eyes twinkle—"anyone brave enough to drive Saint's monster truck deserves a free coffee. Or maybe a medal."

My jaw drops slightly. "You know Saint?"

"Know him?" Noa chuckles, a warm, genuine sound.

Oh. It suddenly makes sense. Noa would be the perfect love interest for that man. She's gorgeous, genuine, and makes irresistible baked goods.

This is the kind of woman who belongs in Saint's life. Grounded, talented, radiating a quiet strength that complements his storm.

When my stomach sinks at the realization, I'm not even surprised anymore even though I'm not sure what to identify this feeling as. Envy? Jealousy? Sadness? Loneliness?

"He practically made Libby Jude's happen. Helped me pursue my one true passion when he opened C'est Trois here. Taught me everything I know about pastry and most of what I know about not taking crap from anyone." Noa's expression turns fond. "He's a pain in the ass, but he's family."

The knot in my stomach tightens, a familiar ache. It's not just envy, it's the sharp pang of realizing how utterly out of my depth I am. I'm a temporary placeholder, a two-week solution, while women like Noa are the sturdy, hand-built furniture of his world.

"So you're not Libby Jude?" I ask, grasping for something, anything, to say that isn't *So were you and the grumpy chef with the soul-searing eyes ever an item?"*

Noa laughs, shaking her head as she wipes a stray coffee ground from the counter. "Libby Jude is a combination of my husband's and my mothers' names." She leans forward, her expression kind. "You okay, Wrenley? You look like you've seen a ghost."

Or like I've just experienced a relief that is so off-balance, I'm not sure what to do with it. *Why* should I care that Noa has a husband and is therefore not on the market for Saint?

"Just ... processing," I say, taking a grateful sip of the coffee. It's strong, rich, and undeniably good. "Small town. Everyone knows everyone, huh?"

"Pretty much," Noa agrees. "Especially when 'everyone' includes a six-foot-four tattooed chef who glares at people for a living but secretly has a heart of gold. Or, you know, slightly tarnished bronze. Saint's life is… well, it's a frequent topic. Especially when it involves someone new. Don't worry," she adds after noting the blush creeping along my cheeks. "Around here, 'new' just means we haven't figured out your favorite pie flavor yet."

Her gaze is curious, but not prying. Friendly.

"I'm not sure I have one. Still in the exploration phase," I say.

Of Falcon Haven, of Saint, of this strange new chapter in my life.

Noa's smile widens. "Well, when you're ready to commit, I make a mean apple crumble. It's Saint's favorite, actually, though he'd rather die than admit it."

I try to picture Saint enjoying something so wholesome. It's another crack in his fortress, a tiny detail that makes him infuriatingly more likable.

The bell above the door jingles, its cheerful sound slicing through the air, and—

No. Way.

I don't have to turn around to know.

The inviting atmosphere shifts, charged with the static before a lightning hit, the scent of his cologne cutting through the sweet bakery smells of cinnamon and sugar.

"Speak of the devil," Noa says, her voice warm and easy. "We were just talking about you."

Noa gestures toward me. And even though I keep my attention on my coffee, I can feel his eyes on me. My skin buzzes like the lightning's getting closer to striking me where I stand.

Slowly and reluctantly, I lift my head. Saint comes up next to me, his bright gaze locked on mine. He doesn't smile. He doesn't scowl. He just looks with that evaluating stare that makes me feel like he can see every stupid, anxious thought scrolling through my mind.

Then his gaze flicks down to the pastry case and the slice of apple crumble Noa had referenced, before returning to me.

He takes a step closer, not to Noa, but toward me and the small space I occupy at the counter. "Find anything you like yet, Wrenley?"

NINE
WRENLEY

My heart does a little flip-flop at what Saint probably thinks is an innocuous question. It's ridiculous, this fluttery reaction to a man who considers smiling to be a strenuous activity.

"I'm still browsing," I say, my voice a little too breathless for a casual pastry inspection.

My gaze skitters from his intense blue eyes to the apple crumble. "But you guys are right. That one looks promising."

Promising? What am I, a food critic now?

Noa, bless her observant, probably smirking soul, chimes in. "There's only one slice left. Usually I reserve it for Saint, but since you were first in line…"

Oh no.

My eyes widen. "Oh. No. Absolutely not. I couldn't. That's practically grand larceny in the Toussaint penal code, isn't it?"

I glance at Saint, expecting a thundercloud, but find something far more unsettling: a flicker of amusement in his eyes and the barest hint of a grin playing on his lips.

He leans an arm on the counter, bringing him closer. Too close. The scent of him, cooking smoke and that subtle, woody spice, wraps around me.

"Grand larceny?" he repeats, his voice a low rumble that vibrates right through me. "You have no idea, Wrenley. Crumble theft is a particularly heinous crime in Falcon Haven. Punishable by ... well, we'd have to consult the ancient town charter. It involves public shaming, possibly."

Noa chuckles, wiping down an already spotless part of the counter. "He's kidding. Mostly. Though he does get a little possessive over that last slice."

Noa slides the warm slice onto a plate with a spatula, then places it between us. "I'll let you two work it out while I restock the muffins in the back."

Noa winks at me—*winks* at me—before disappearing through the kitchen's double doors.

I practically shove the air in the direction of the crumble. "You have it. Please. It's all yours."

My stomach rumbles with the loss, and I swear Saint hears it because he pushes off the counter and picks up a fork from the nearby container.

His fingers are long, calloused, and tattooed between each knuckle. The same fingers that had so gently bandaged my arm now wield a dessert fork like a weapon.

Saint stabs the fork into the crumble, expertly capturing a perfect bite, laden with apple and buttery topping. Then he extends it toward my mouth.

"Go on," he murmurs, his voice dropping to a husky whisper that seems to thrum through the floorboards. "Steal my crumble, Wrenley."

My eyes lock with his. The air in the small café suddenly feels thick and hot as every background noise fades into a distant hum. His expression is unreadable, but there's a glint in his eyes, a subtle shift that makes my pulse hammer.

Slowly, because my limbs feel like they're moving through honey, I lean forward.

My lips part, brushing against the cool metal of the fork as he gently settles it on my tongue.

The crumble is warm, sweet, the cinnamon a gentle spice. It melts. I melt. This is divine.

"Good?" he asks, his attention fixed on my mouth.

My cheeks are on fire. I snatch up the other fork, needing to do something with my hands. "It's very good."

"Just very good?" Saint stands close enough that I can feel his breath on my lips. "If you said that about one of my dishes, I'd kick you out of the kitchen."

Before I can process what's happening, he lifts another bite to my lips. "Try it again. Properly this time. Close your eyes."

My eyes do the exact goddamn opposite. "What?"

"You heard me. Do it."

He leaves no room for argument, but his tone is edged with something that isn't annoyance for once.

I hesitate, then slowly let my eyelids drift shut. The world narrows to the scent of cinnamon, apples, and Saint.

"Now," he murmurs, his voice closer, "you don't just attack it with your teeth. You let it linger. Feel the warmth on your tongue first, then the way the apple gives, the texture. Let it coat your tongue before you even think about swallowing."

He's talking about the apple crumble. He is. But the way he's describing this moment is like he's giving instructions for a far more intimate moment, like if I were on my knees and he was unzipping his pants...

Mind out of the GUTTER, Wrenley! This is your boss now. And you're in a public place. Have some decency.

My brain has the right idea, but my body doesn't want to hear it. My thighs clench together, containing the ache.

The fork touches my lips again. I part them, a shiver tracing down my spine as he carefully places the bite inside. This time, I follow his instructions, the crumble a slow explosion of flavor and sensation, the buttery topping melting, the apples soft and tangy. It's ridiculously, obscenely good.

And the way he described it...

My eyes fly open as I swallow, a small, mortified sound escaping me. "Oh my god. That's your crumble. You're the one who makes it, aren't you? I just ate your crumble. Twice."

Saint's mouth quirks. He sets the fork down on the plate, then leans back and crosses his arms. "Technically, Noa and I have joint custody. We created it together when she was a student in my cooking class."

My brows jump, and I blurt, "You taught people? Willingly? And you didn't make them cry?"

"I taught a local class for one summer when I first opened C'est Trois to bring in business. Never again."

Saint's probably referring to the teaching, but my brain, traitor that it is, is stuck on the other kind of instruction he'd just delivered, the one that had my thighs clenching and my stomach doing a nervous, fluttery jig. The man weaponizes dessert.

And I, apparently, am a willing casualty.

His gaze drops to my mouth again, a slow, deliberate trail that makes me have to remember to breathe. "You have a little... right there."

Saint reaches out, his thumb brushing the corner of my lips. His touch is like fire, and it fucking *brands* me.

"Oh." My voice is a whisper. I feel like I've just run a marathon. "Thanks."

He doesn't pull his hand away immediately. His thumb lingers for a fraction of a second too long, his blue eyes holding mine captive. The air crackles again.

Add walking electrical storm to his résumé, too.

"You should probably," I stammer, gesturing vaguely toward the door, "get back to your restaurant things. Chef duties. Important stuff."

My brain has officially shriveled.

"Probably," he agrees, but he doesn't move. His gaze is still on my mouth, as if he's memorizing the shape of it.

I need to escape. Now. Before I do something monumentally stupid, like ask him to feed me the rest of the crumble.

Or kiss me.

"Well, this has been … crumbly," I say, then clamp my mouth shut at the *horror* of what I just said. "I, um, I have to go."

I grab my purse, nearly knocking over my coffee cup. Smooth. So smooth. Saint raises an eyebrow, a hint of that earlier amusement back in his eyes. I practically flee Libby Jude's, the cheerful bell above the door mocking my clumsy retreat.

Outside, the crisp autumn air is a shock to my heated skin. I gulp it down, leaning against the cool metal of the Range Rover, trying to get my pulse under control.

What in the actual hell was that? It felt like foreplay. Hot, intense, cinnamon-dusted foreplay.

I need a distraction. A big one. I drive a few blocks, my hands still trembling slightly, and park near the town green, a picturesque square with a gazebo and ancient oak trees. Grabbing the book I'd optimistically brought, I find an empty bench beneath one of the oaks, its leaves a riot of red and gold. The words on the page blur. My mind keeps replaying Saint's thumb on my lips.

Giving up on reading, I pull out my phone. Maybe a mindless scroll through social media will help. But Brenda's email still casts a shadow, and I've banned myself from accessing socials for at least a week. Instead, my thumb hovers over the camera icon. The sunlight filters through the leaves, dappling the grass, and the gazebo looks like something out of a movie.

It's all so perfect. Too gorgeous not to capture.

I'll record just a few clips. For me to look back on.

I tap the record button.

The familiar weight of the phone feels steady in my hand. I pan slowly, capturing the way the light catches the vibrant leaves, the intricate ironwork of the gazebo, and the distant steeple of a church. It's purely mechanical at first, framing shots and adjusting focus, as the muscle memory of a thousand videos takes over.

A dog walker ambles past, his golden retriever sniffing enthusiastically at the base of a lamppost. A group of children chase a stray soccer ball across the green, their laughter bright and unrestrained. Another clip of the charming, colorful storefronts across the street, the old-fashioned lampposts.

The beauty of Falcon Haven, unfiltered and unassuming, pulls me forward. I take another clip, then another, the small act of framing these moments a tiny harbor in the swirling mess of my emotions.

Saint's face, the taste of his passion on my tongue, the heat of his touch against my skin... it all recedes, just a little, with each frame I save.

TEN
SAINT

I recognize Ivy's footsteps even above the precise rhythm of knives against cutting boards and pans sizzling on the line. My daughter has arrived at C'est Trois.

A sprig of thyme is pinched between my fingers when I glance up just as the back door swings open. Ivy bursts in, a small blur of purple and pink.

"Papa!"

Ivy's voice cuts through the kitchen's controlled din. She makes a beeline for me, narrowly avoiding a busboy laden with dirty dishes. I catch her before she cannonballs into my temporary sous chef, instinctively halting her by her small shoulders and kneeling to her level.

"Careful, *petit chou*. This isn't a playground."

Wrenley hovers by the door, her hands clasped in front of her. She looks like she expects me to eject them both.

"Ivy insisted," Wrenley says, her voice quiet but clear over the clatter. "She wanted to show me where you work."

I push to my feet, scooping Ivy along the way. "So this is

your first official tour, then? Not counting any unscheduled reconnaissance missions through the shrubbery?"

Wrenley's cheeks flush a delightful shade of pink that nearly matches her hair streak. Her eyes dart to Ivy, then back to me, wide and a little panicked. "Ivy was very persuasive. And I, um, certainly wouldn't object to another… demonstration of your skills."

Her eyes dart away, then back to mine, a flicker of remembrance, maybe, in their hazel depths.

That damn apple crumble. It's my own fault, really.

I'd walked into Noa's planning to grab a coffee and maybe talk to her about the new produce delivery, but then I saw Wrenley. Standing there, looking lost and lovely, and my carefully constructed morning routine went to shit.

I hadn't planned to fucking hand-feed her, to watch her lips part for me, and to feel the jolt that followed when she'd moaned. It was supposed to be a simple peace offering, a way to smooth over my earlier gruffness.

The urge to lean in, to taste her instead of the crumble, had been a visceral punch to the gut. It was reckless. Stupid. I'm her employer. She's Ivy's nanny. There are lines. Boundaries that I, of all people, should respect.

But I'm pulled toward her anyway, undeniable and inconvenient. It's more than just the curve of her mouth or the way her eyes flash with intelligence. It's the fragility I sense beneath the quick wit, the darkness that sometimes clouds her expression. A wound, deep and hidden, that resonates with my own. I can recognize the landscape of carefully managed pain.

It makes me want to … what? Protect her? That's ridiculous. I barely know the woman. Yet for some reason, I want to know the shape of her sorrow and its cause.

"Well," I say, my voice grittier than intended as I set Ivy

down. "Since you're here, you might as well watch early dinner service. Ivy's always loved doing it."

I point at a countertop far off to one side. We use it occasionally for those who want to book the "chef's table," where they can watch us cook while they dine.

A personal nightmare for me, but we're able to charge triple the cost for it.

"You know the drill, *mon trésor.* Don't touch anything sharp. Or hot. Or expensive."

Wrenley's lips curve. "So, basically, don't touch anything."

"Exactly," I say, guiding them toward the small, elevated counter that offers a panoramic view of the line. "Best seats in the house, if you like watching people sweat."

Ivy scrambles onto one of the high stools, thrilled at being behind the scenes.

Wrenley follows, her gaze sweeping over the organized chaos of gleaming stainless steel, copper pots, and white-coated chefs moving with practiced speed.

"Behave, my sweet," I say to Ivy, then move to Wrenley. "Ivy's been my harshest critic since she could talk."

Ivy puffs out her chest. "I have high standards."

I tousle her hair, then turn back to the line, barking an order for the sea bass that makes Wrenley jump.

As I supervise, I do everything in my power to focus on the only other love of my life: creating masterpiece dishes. But, since my morning routine went sideways, it comes as no surprise that my afternoon one is quickly following. My attention keeps straying to two bright spots of color in my monochrome world.

At some point, I hear Ivy as she tugs on Wrenley's hand.

"Come see! Papa lets me smell the herbs!"

She drags Wrenley toward a small collection of potted

herbs near the prep station—fresh basil, rosemary, mint—their scents mingling with the richer aromas of the kitchen.

"This one smells like pizza!" Ivy proclaims, gently rubbing an oregano leaf between her fingers and holding it up for Wrenley to sniff.

Wrenley leans down, inhaling deeply.

"You're right. And this one"—she touches a sprig of mint — "smells like sunshine and sweet tea."

Ivy giggles. "Papa says it smells like mojitos."

Wrenley's eyes meet mine over Ivy's head, a small, surprised smile playing on her lips, like she enjoyed learning that I'm capable of humor.

I grunt, turning away to inspect a tray of confit duck legs one of my line cooks presents. But I'm acutely aware of them, of Wrenley's patient attention as Ivy points out each herb, her voice animated. Wrenley's focus on Ivy is absolute. She doesn't glance at her phone or look bored. She asks questions, her head tilted, her expression genuinely engaged.

It's a scene I've witnessed before, not with any former nanny, but with Celine, her laughter taking over the environment as she taught Ivy the language of flavors.

That memory is a sharp, unexpected pang, until an unlikely warmth curls in my chest, fighting the memory's icy grip.

An unexpected thawing.

Celine's ghost is still here, but it's quieter. Muted by the sight of Ivy's unrestrained joy, by the genuine kindness in Wrenley's eyes as she listens to my daughter explain the difference between thyme and marjoram with the dignity of a seasoned botanist.

Ivy is, for the first time in a long time, truly connecting with someone new.

"Can we show Miss Wrenley your special place, Papa?"

Ivy asks, her eyes bright with excitement, pulling me from my thoughts. "The one behind the restaurant?"

My special place. Celine's herb garden. The small patch of earth we'd cultivated together, first in Paris, then here, when I planted a living memorial to her love for fresh ingredients, for life.

I almost refuse. The thought of Wrenley there, in that space so intimately tied to Celine, feels like an intrusion.

But then I see Ivy's face, alight with anticipation, and Wrenley's curious, gentle gaze.

"Alright," I say. "But be careful. Some of those plants are delicate."

Like memories, I think.

Like hearts.

Ivy's small hand slips into Wrenley's, and she pulls her toward the back exit, her purple dress a vibrant splash against the muted tones of the alley.

Despite demands for my attention, I follow at a distance.

The garden isn't much to look at, just a few raised beds tucked into a sun-drenched corner behind the restaurant, shielded by a weathered wooden fence. But every plant, every stone, is imbued with Celine. Her laughter, the smudge of dirt on her cheek, the way she'd talk to the herbs as if they were her confidants.

I lean against the rough brick wall, observing.

Ivy, with a newfound sense of importance, points at each plant. "Maman loved planting lavender. She said it smelled like sleepy dreams."

Wrenley crouches down beside her. She doesn't offer platitudes or try to steer the conversation. Wrenley just listens, her warm eyes fixed on Ivy, absorbing every word.

"And this one," Ivy continues, her small finger brushing

against a rosemary bush, "Maman said it was for remembering."

Wrenley reaches out, her fingers gently touching a rosemary needle.

"She sounds like she made everything beautiful," Wrenley says, her voice quiet and imbued with a sincerity that resonates deeper than I expect.

Something in the careful way Wrenley holds herself, in the quiet respect she affords this sacred space and Ivy's memories, chips away at another layer of the ice around my heart.

Wrenley doesn't try to fill the silence or offer empty condolences. She simply bears witness, and in doing so, she lightens a burden I hadn't realized I was still forcing Ivy to carry alone.

I can't hear everything they say, just fragments carried on the breeze. Ivy points at the lemon verbena, the delicate chervil, and the purple sage. She's reciting the names, the uses, the little anecdotes I'd shared with her over the years, words I'd spoken to keep Celine's memory alive for her.

Then Wrenley's head lifts.

She scans the edge of the garden and finds me. Our eyes connect. The air stills.

The kitchen noise, the distant traffic, even Ivy's voice recedes to a dull hum. It's just us, separated by ten feet of fragrant earth.

Her expression is open and unguarded. There's a question in her eyes, something soft and searching that bypasses all my defenses.

The pull toward her is a physical thing, a tightening in my chest, a sudden, sharp awareness of her scent, subtly tropical.

I should look away. I need to retreat.

This is too much, too fast. But I can't. Her lips part slightly, as if she's about to speak, but no words come.

I'm getting the same feeling I did at Noa's restaurant, but amplified, stripped bare.

Ivy tugs on Wrenley's sleeve, demanding her attention for a ladybug discovery, and the spell breaks. Wrenley's focus drops back to my daughter, a faint blush rising on her cheeks.

I push off the wall, the movement abrupt.

Turning my back on them, on the sudden, disorienting warmth that had begun to seep into the frozen corners of my heart, I stride back into the kitchen. The clatter of pans and the sizzle of food are a welcome cacophony, a shield against the quiet vulnerability I'd just witnessed.

And felt.

ELEVEN
WRENLEY

I jolt awake with Saint's name on my lips, the dream version of him (all heat and hands and forgotten boundaries) fading into the darkness of the guesthouse.

Did I just have a sex dream?

Oh, I absolutely did.

I can still feel his weight as he pressed me into the mattress. My skin tingles where his dream-hands roamed, where his mouth explored. It had been vivid, overwhelmingly so. Not just the act itself, though that had been... thorough. It was the details, the ones my waking mind has apparently cataloged with unsettling precision.

Like the way his dark hair fell across his forehead when he peeled my nightshirt off. The surprising softness of his lips and the rough scrape of his stubble against my inner thigh.

And the tattoos.

In the dream, his chef's coat had been discarded, his T-shirt joining it on the floor, revealing the full expanse of ink that usually disappeared beneath fabric. Swirls of black and gray covered his chest, wrapping around his ribs, disappearing lower. My dream-fingers had traced those lines.

I suck in a breath when I remember the silk of his tongue and the way he tasted me like I was the finest delicacy, a dish he'd been starving for. He'd murmured things against my skin in French, words I didn't understand but felt at the center of my heart, his voice a gravelly scrape against my skin, setting my nerves endings on fire.

"Oh my god."

I press the heels of my hands into my eyes, trying to banish the images and sensations. But they linger, a blush spreading from my chest to my hairline and a desperate, throbbing ache at my core.

I have to take care of it. Otherwise, I'll be writhing around in this bed for the next few hours until dawn and tangling the sheets around myself more than they already are.

My hand slides down my body and over the cotton of my oversized shirt, the fabric catching on my peaked nipples. Then lower, between my legs, where I find the slick evidence of just how much this dream wrecked me.

His hands replace mine in my head, his day-old scruff, the scrape of his teeth. My hips lift to meet the pressure of my palm and I bite my lip to keep from crying out his name.

"Close your eyes. You heard me. Do it."

I murmur a reply. "Saint.."

"Now, let it linger. Feel the warmth on your tongue first …. Let it coat your tongue before you even think about swallowing."

In my head, I scream. *SAINT.*

He falls to his knees. Palms my ass. Moans into my pussy when he presses his mouth against it…

I'm conjuring images of him so overwhelming and relentless that I come apart, shuddering, his name turning into a whispered gasp on my lips.

Afterward, I lie there, panting.

I've known the man for less than a week. He's my boss. He's a grieving widower. He's emotionally unavailable. He's … perfect.

No.

Not perfect.

Complicated. Troubled. Tortured in a way that calls to my own scars, my own need for distraction.

I throw an arm over my eyes in an attempt to block out the lingering heat, the sound of his voice when he worships me, and the way my body *still* hums with want.

Rolling onto my side, I pull the covers higher, a sigh escaping my lips.

It was just a dream. A very, very effective dream. But still.

A low rumble, almost subliminal, vibrates through the floorboards of the guesthouse.

Hair falls into my face when I push up to my elbows, frowning.

It sounded distant, like a truck on a far-off highway.

Before I can process it, an earsplitting CRACK shatters the quiet, so loud and sudden it's like the sky itself ripped open directly above me.

My body jerks violently, a strangled yelp tearing from my throat. My heart catapults into my windpipe, choking me.

Thunder. That's all it is.

But this isn't the rolling city thunder that I found to be pleasant white noise while sleeping in my apartment in Brooklyn. No, this is the kind that announces its arrival with the fury of a vengeful god.

Another flash illuminates the small room in stark, ghostly white, followed by a deafening boom that rattles the window-panes in their frames. Rain begins to lash against the glass, driven by a wind that howls like a banshee around the eaves of the little house.

The guesthouse, moments ago a cozy sanctuary, now feels like Dorothy's before she was launched into Oz.

Familiar tendrils of panic start to spread into my chest. The lights flicker once, twice, then plunge the room into absolute blackness.

"No. No, no, no."

My denial's swallowed by the roar of the storm. I'm in absolute darkness. It presses in on me, suffocating.

Fingers fly to my scalp, twisting a thick strand of hair until my scalp screams in protest. The small, sharp pain is a pinprick of focus in the overwhelming black.

Another crack of thunder, closer this time, and the floor beneath me seems to tremble.

I scramble out of bed, tangling myself in the sheets, my bare feet hitting the cold wooden floor.

My hands fly to my shoulder, nails digging through the thin cotton of my shirt, seeking an anchor.

The sound of splintering wood and a door almost swinging off its hinges has me swiveling toward it in time to see a dark shape filling the doorway, silhouetted for a horrifying instant against a flash of lightning.

A scream rips from my lungs, bloody and animalistic. I stumble back, tripping over my own feet, my hands flying up to shield my face.

"Wrenley!"

Saint's harsh command cuts through the thunder's rage. He's inside in two strides, wind and rain swirling behind him and instantly soaking the floor. Saint's bare chest is slick with rain, and that eternal part of me that will always appreciate the male form regardless of circumstance wriggles with glee when she realizes that dream-Saint and real-Saint match up pretty good.

Relief, so potent it makes my knees buckle, washes over me, immediately followed by a fresh wave of adrenaline-fueled terror at his violent entrance.

"Jesus, Saint! You nearly gave me *another* heart attack!" I gasp out in ragged spurts.

My shoulder throbs where my nails had been.

He's across the small room in three long strides, reaching for me in the dark.

When his fingers close around my arm, he says, "The power's out in the main house, too. But it's much safer there. You're coming with me."

"I … okay," I manage, my teeth chattering.

"Grab something warm. Quickly."

I fumble around in the dark for the oversized, button-down cardigan I'd left on the sofa chair. But I'm clumsy and shaking too hard to find the sleeves.

Saint makes an impatient sound, then his hands are on mine, guiding my arms into the cardigan.

His fingers brush my skin as he tugs the sleeve into place, and a jolt entirely separate from the storm shoots through me.

It's a direct echo of my dream, and I have to force myself to swallow.

"You're trembling," he states.

"This storm, it's a bit much," I reply through clenched teeth to keep them from chattering harder.

He lingers at my neck when he fastens the cardigan's top button, that small comfort causing me to question even needing clothes during this emergency.

"Better?" His voice is low and almost on par with the building thunder.

I manage a nod.

"Good. We need to move. Now."

Saint doesn't wait for my verbal reply. His hand slides from my shoulder down my arm, his grip firm and reassuring before engulfing my own.

"Stay with me."

The door groans open again as he pulls it, the wind snatching at it and trying to rip it from his grasp.

Saint steps out into the maelstrom, pulling me with him. The rain is a solid wall of water, instantly plastering my hair to my face, my thin shirt clinging to my upper thighs. The wind howls, tearing at us.

Lightning splits the sky again, illuminating the churning chaos around us, the trees thrashing like tormented spirits.

I stumble on the slick grass, my bare feet searching for purchase, a small cry escaping me. Saint stops, his body a shield against the worst of the wind.

"Can you make it?" he yells over the roar.

"I—I can't see—"

Before I can finish, he makes a low sound, something between a growl and a curse. Then, with a swiftness that steals my breath, he releases my hand only to scoop me up into his arms.

My scream is swallowed by the wind as I'm lifted, my body colliding with his hard, wet chest. I instinctively wrap my arms around his neck, clinging to him as he strides through the tempest. I press my face against his shoulder, the scent of rain and his skin filling my senses, his heart thudding a powerful, steady rhythm beneath my ear.

Saint moves over the slick ground with surprising agility, navigating as if he could see in the dark. It's like I weigh nothing to him, but I'm clinging to him like he's the only fixed point in a collapsing world.

The back door of the main house bursts open under his

shoulder, and then we're inside, the relative quiet of the kitchen a sudden, shocking contrast to the storm's fury.

He sets me down. My legs are so embarrassingly unsteady that I lean against the closed door, gulping air. Rain drips from my hair and pools around my feet.

Saint is already moving, grabbing a thick towel from a drawer.

"Here." He wraps it around my shoulders after I peel off my cardigan, his fingers brushing my neck again, sending another jolt through my system. "Dry off."

"You're soaked too," I manage to say.

I reach for another towel, intending to hand it to him, but he's already turning away, heading toward the living room.

"Fireplace," he calls back. "We need light. And warmth."

I follow, clutching the towel around me, shivering.

The kitchen is dark, but the living room is even blacker, though I can hear him moving around. A clink of metal, then the rasp of a match.

A small flame flickers to life, casting dancing shadows on his face as he kneels before the hearth, coaxing the kindling until the fire catches and pushes back the oppressive darkness.

Only after he adds more logs and the warm light illuminates him more fully do I truly see him.

Water streams down his bare chest and arms. His briefs are soaked through, molding to his muscled thighs and very toned ass. But setting aside his gorgeous, well-endowed body, I realize he hadn't bothered with a shirt, pants, or *shoes* before running outside to find me.

Me.

That naked truth hits me with the force of another thunderclap, but this one resonates deep in my chest, a strange, warm ache.

"You didn't even grab a shirt," I whisper.

He hears me over the crackling fire and stops, his hand tangled in the wet hair on his head. Saint looks down, as if just noticing he's bare-chested and dripping, and every ridge of him under his briefs is on display. "There wasn't time."

"You could have been struck by lightning," I say lamely, because I'm so overwhelmed by the fact that this man ran out in a dangerous storm for me.

Saint lifts his gaze to mine before he looks away, toward the growing blaze. "The main house is renovated, but the guesthouse is old. I didn't want you trapped in there alone."

This entire time he hasn't shivered, hasn't complained. Hasn't even paused to consider his own comfort or safety until I was wrapped in thick terrycloth and a growing sense of bewildered gratitude.

"Is Ivy okay?"

"She has a white-noise machine that rivals the sound of a pod of a thousand whales. She's sleeping through this like a baby."

He finally turns, grabbing another towel from a linen closet I hadn't noticed tucked beside the fireplace. He scrubs it roughly over his hair, then his chest and arms, the movements brisk. Water still slicks his skin, gooseflesh rising on his arms despite the growing warmth from the fire.

I'm holding the spare towel I'd grabbed earlier, the one I'd almost offered him. It suddenly feels rough in my shaking hands. "Saint."

He turns, one eyebrow raised in question.

"You're going to catch your death."

I pad closer, into his space. The heat from the fire warms one side of me and the chill from his wet skin cools the other. I lift the towel, my intentions clear.

Saint's eyes follow the movement, then meet mine again.

He doesn't move to take it, nor does he stop me when I press it against his cheek. My knuckles brush against his temple.

He stills.

I work the towel over to his other cheek, then over his shoulders, absorbing some of the rain, the friction a small, inadequate offering against the cold that must be seeping into his bones.

Using the towel, I skim over the hard planes of his chest, tracing the edge of a chef's knife tattoo that disappears under his arm. His ink is extra dark in the firelight, intricate and thick.

"You have a lot of tattoos," I murmur, the towel slowing, my hand lingering perhaps a little too long over a swirl of ink near his hip-bone.

Saint's chest rises and falls with steady breaths, but his eyes won't leave my face. "Each one means something."

"I bet they do."

My attention drops to the waistband of his soaked briefs, then back up to his eyes.

Big mistake.

"Wrenley."

My name comes out raspier than usual, more like a warning than a command. His fingers close over my wrist, stopping my downward trajectory. The towel falls, landing softly on the rug between us.

"You're ... still wet," I say.

What a stupid thing to say out loud. An obvious thing.

"Am I?"

His hand skims from my wrist to cover mine where it rests against his skin. He's warm, calloused, engulfing my entire hand and pressing my palm more firmly against him. The contact is electric, a direct current bypassing all my caution. Then the memory of my dream, of his hands and mouth on my body, floods back with dizzying accuracy.

"Your shirt is practically see-through," he counters.

I look down. He's right. The thin cotton, soaked and clinging, leaves absolutely nothing to the imagination. My nipples are hard, dark pebbles against the pale fabric. The curve of my stomach, the swell of my hips, the shadow between my thighs—all on display.

"Oh." The word is a puff of air.

His thumb strokes the back of my hand, a slow, sensual movement that sends tremors down my spine.

"Are you going to pretend you weren't about to dry off my dick?"

My eyes snap to his face, wide with mortification and a confusing thrill. "What? I was—I was patting you down with a towel!"

His gaze drops to my mouth, then lower, lingering on the damp fabric clinging to my breasts. "Or were you just curious about what else matches your dream?"

My stomach plummets.

He knows. How can he possibly know?

"I don't know what you're talking about."

"Liar."

He crowds me, backing me toward the hearth until the heat of the fire scorches my calves.

"You screamed my name loud enough for me to hear it from my balcony before the thunder drowned you out."

"No," I deny, my voice too high-pitched to contain any truth. "You must've heard wrong. A bird, or an owl, or some farm animal nearby. It could be anything—wait, what were you doing on your balcony in your underwear?"

"Couldn't sleep."

Saint doesn't elaborate, and his unreadable expression doesn't betray why he couldn't fall sleep.

I'm trapped. Trapped between the fire and the storm in his eyes.

"I..."

Excuses fail me.

He squeezes my hand still plastered against his chest, where his heart beats faster. "Tell me about the dream, Wrenley."

Saint's free hand comes up, his fingers tracing the line of my jaw, then dipping to the hollow of my throat where my pulse hammers a frantic rhythm. "Was I good to you?"

My mind races. The heat from the fire, the heat from his body, the heat from my own blush, it's all melding into one molten wave of lava.

"You were ... present," I finally say.

"Oh, well that needs correcting." His thumb brushes against my pulse point again. "When I fuck a woman, I'm not just 'present.' I become her everything, and she becomes mine. I devour her."

I gulp. "Okay, well, you were ... you seemed to know what you were doing."

Saint's mouth curves. He's enjoying this. The bastard. He's enjoying my utter mortification.

"Did I make you come, Wrenley?"

The storm outside answers with a furious gust of wind that rattles the windows, as if scandalized on my behalf.

My mouth opens, but no sound emerges. His fingers slide from my throat, pausing just above the swell of my breast.

"Did I?" he asks again, his voice softer, almost a caress, but no less demanding.

My nipples ache beneath the thin cotton, betraying me. He

leans closer, his breath warm against my ear. "Use your words, *chérie*."

"Yes," I whisper, the admission a surrender. "You did."

"Good."

He finally, *finally* skims lower, brushing the side of my breast.

A gasp escapes me. "Saint…"

"Tell me more," he urges, his voice a dark velvet rasp against my skin. "What else did I do in this dream of yours?"

"You … you kissed me."

He goes still. Raises his head, then angles it so his nose brushes against my cheekbone.

Then his mouth finds mine.

It's not a gentle exploration like in the dream, but a claiming. Hard, hot, demanding. His tongue sweeps in, tasting of rain and smoke, and I meet him stroke for stroke, a desperate hunger clawing through me as soon as his lips claimed mine.

The storm outside rages, but it's nothing compared to the hurricane he ignites within me.

My hands fly up, tangling in his damp hair, pulling him closer and arching into him.

His other arm snakes around my waist, crushing me against his hard, wet body. I can feel every ridge, every muscle, until the undeniable evidence of his arousal presses against my stomach.

Saint groans into my mouth, and I can feel it all the way to my bones. One hand leaves my breast, sliding down my back, over my hip, cupping my ass and lifting me, tilting me against him. My legs instinctively wrap around his waist, my soaked shirt riding up, baring me to the air and the heat of his skin.

"Saint," I heave out when I manage to tear my mouth from his. "This is…"

I'm unable to name the reckless energy ricocheting between us.

"Inevitable," he finishes for me.

He holds me by the hip, fingers digging through the thin, damp cotton. His other hand cradles my head, his thumb stroking my cheekbone. Saint leans back just enough to look at me, really look at me.

"Tell me I was gentle in your dream."

His lips brush mine with each word.

"You were," I say through hitched breaths.

"That's good." His eyes turn hooded. "Because I'm not gentle in real life."

Saint finds the hem of my nightgown, sliding his hand along the curve of my thigh beneath the fabric and sending a fresh, throbbing ache through me.

I gasp, my hips instinctively arching closer, seeking more of that forbidden contact.

"Saint," I breathe, my voice shaky, lost.

"Tell me to stop," he murmurs, his lips against my throat, his stubble a delicious friction against my sensitized skin. His fingers inch higher, exploring, claiming. "Tell me this isn't what you want."

But the denial won't form. All I can do is cling to him. My body is alive with a need so potent, it eclipses everything else.

All the reasons that this could be a terrible idea fade, drowned out by the roaring in my blood and the undeniable truth that I want this.

I want him.

TWELVE
WRENLEY

Saint trails a line of fire down my jaw, my throat.

"You feel good," he rasps, his lips finding the frantic pulse at the base of my neck. "So fucking good."

I arch against him, a whimper escaping as he slides higher up my thigh, pushing the soaked cotton of my nightgown with it.

His fingers are rough, firm, branding my skin.

"Oh, god," I breathe, my head falling back against the warm stone of the mantelpiece.

The fire crackles, the storm rages, but all I feel is him, all I smell is rain and smoke and him. His arousal is a hard, insistent pressure against my core.

"You're so wet for me," he murmurs, his lips now at my collarbone, his voice a dark caress. He reaches the apex of my thighs, brushing against the curls there, then dips lower.

I choke on a breath as he finds my clit, swollen and aching.

"Is this what you want?"

He circles it once, twice, the pressure exquisite. My hips buck against his hand.

"Yes," I manage. "Please."

"Say my name again."

His thumb presses down, a direct hit.

"Saint!"

He groans, his mouth finding mine again, swallowing my cries as he moves his fingers, a relentless rhythm that mirrors the storm's fury.

The world narrows to this: to his touch, his taste, to the fire at my back and the inferno he's building inside me.

My nails dig into his shoulders, not for balance, but to ground myself to the only solid thing in a universe that had tilted on its axis. He kisses me, deepening it and tangling his tongue with mine, the taste of him a drug I'm going to crave more of with each passing second.

"More?" he asks against my lips, his own breath coming in harsh pants that match mine.

I can only nod, a helpless gesture. His thumb finds that spot again, the epicenter of the earthquake, and presses.

Hard.

Arching off the mantelpiece, my body tenses, tighter and tighter. The pleasure is a sharp, sweet agony of unbearable velocity. The room spins, firelight blurring into streaks of orange and gold.

I'm unraveling, coming apart at his touch, and the only sound in the world is his name, torn from my throat as the first wave hits, a convulsive shudder that rocks me from head to toe.

Saint holds me through it, his mouth fused to mine, his fingers buried inside me until the aftershocks subside, leaving me boneless and heaving against him.

He lowers me slowly, his hands sliding from my hips, his gaze locked on mine. Firelight flickers across his face but isn't able to chase away the harsh lines of his jaw or the shadows beneath his eyes.

For one dumb millisecond, I think he's going to kiss me again and pull me back into that vortex of heat and sensation.

Instead, he retreats, taking one step back, then another, the growing space between us suddenly feeling vast and cold despite the roaring fire.

Saint's hands clench at his sides. "Fuck." He shakes his head. "This isn't—we can't. I can't do this."

His abruptness is like a physical blow. My body, still humming and pliant from his touch, registers the rejection before my mind does.

Saint notices. He turns away, running a hand through his hair, his back rigid. "This was a mistake."

Each word is a perfectly aimed arrow. I wrap my arms around myself, the damp shirt inefficient armor. The heat in my cheeks turns to a burning shame.

"A mistake," I echo.

Saint doesn't look at me. "I shouldn't have. I'm not..."

He trails off.

He's not what? Not available? Not interested? Not capable of separating sex from the ghosts that clearly haunt him?

The storm outside seems to quiet as if holding its breath, leaving only the crackle of the fire and the thick silence of his regret.

And my dream, my beautiful, perfect dream, shatters into a million pieces.

"Right," I say, my voice a fragile thread.

My skin still burns where he touched me, where his mouth had been. It now feels like a brand of humiliation.

Lowering, I pick up my discarded cardigan, a useless

gesture. The cold seeping into the room isn't just from the storm. But before I can pull the sodden cardigan around myself, Saint's sharp question freezes me.

"What happened?"

My blood runs cold. I yank the cardigan around me, desperate to cover the puckered, angry skin he'd glimpsed on my shoulder because of my wide collar.

"What are you talking about?" I ask.

"Your shoulder."

He advances, his eyes turning to flint as he targets my left shoulder. "Those marks. Don't tell me it's from falling into the fucking bushes."

I can't breathe. Shame, hot and brutal, swells my throat. "It's nothing. It's old."

"Old how?" His voice lowers in warning. "Who did it, Wrenley?"

"No one," I insist.

The implication that he thinks someone else had hurt me, that these scars were a testament to violence inflicted by another, is almost worse than the truth.

"It's not what you think. Please, Saint, just drop it."

He ignores my plea, his gaze unwavering and accusatory. "If someone laid a hand on you—"

"It's not like that!"

Tears prick my eyes, blurring the image of his rigid stance, the condemnation etched on his face. The weight of his scrutiny on top of the storm, the dream, his rejection, is too much.

"Then what is it?"

He crowds me again, but this time it's not desire radiating from him. It's cold, hard fury.

A sob escapes me. "I can't ... I can't talk about it."

I turn away, hugging myself tighter, the damp fabric cold and sticky against my body.

He spins me back to face him, the sudden movement sending a fresh wave of dizziness through me.

"Do you think I'm going to let you hide away until you tell me who put those marks on your skin? Is that why you came to this town? To escape someone?"

"It's not—"

"Don't lie to me." He gives my arm a small, impatient shake. "I've seen injuries, Wrenley. Those aren't accidental. Did he hit you? Burn you?" His voice drops to a dangerous level. "Because if someone hurt you, I will find them."

The possessive fury in his tone, the assumption that I'm a victim of someone else's cruelty, is a fresh stab of humiliation.

He thinks I was broken by another. Not broken by myself.

"You don't understand," I whisper, the fight draining out of me and replaced by a bone-deep weariness.

Saint loosens his hold, but his gaze pins me in place. "Then make me understand. Who is he?"

He's so sure. So utterly convinced. And the truth feels like a shard of glass lodged in my throat, impossible to speak but impossible to swallow.

"Please," I choke out. "Leave me alone. Just show me a guest room where I can stay until Ivy wakes up."

Saint doesn't reply. The only sound is the dying crackle of the fire and the distant rumble of the retreating storm.

But nor does he move.

His eyes, those piercing blue jewels, are still fixed on my shoulder, as if he can burn through the thin fabric of the cardigan and see the truth I'm so desperate to hide.

Then he blinks.

"The room at the end of the hall," he says finally, his voice flat. "There are spare clothes of Celeste's in the drawers."

Saint turns his back to me then, staring into the fire. The dismissal is as complete as his earlier rejection.

I nod, a jerky, puppet-like movement, and stumble toward the hallway, each step an agony. The plush runner beneath my bare feet feels like sandpaper. Tears finally fall, hot and silent.

And he doesn't watch me go.

THIRTEEN
WRENLEY

The red stain won't fucking come out.

My knuckles are raw against the nubby fabric of my favorite cream cardigan, the one that feels like a hug. I scrub harder, the water and stain remover useless against the stubborn crimson bloom.

It's not even a big stain. Just a small, accusing circle near the collar, a souvenir from me worrying my shoulder raw during another sleepless night. But it's there, a mar on the perfect softness, a visible imperfection I can't erase no matter how much force I apply.

Three days. Seventy-two hours of tiptoeing around Saint. When we do run into each other, polite, excruciatingly brief exchanges about Ivy's schedule and meals are about all we can conjure up. He hasn't mentioned the night of the storm, or what happened by the fire, or the gouges he saw on my shoulder.

He just studies me sometimes when he thinks I don't notice, even though my thoughts seem to be on him *all the damn time.*

If it weren't for Ivy, I'd have taken my suitcase and bolted. But Ivy is a pocketful of sunshine in this perpetual twilight. Her laughter, endless questions, and quests for the strangest art textiles are a welcome distraction. Her small, paint-stained hand in mine is a link to the real world.

Ivy's enthusiasm for everything is infectious, and despite the tension between me and Saint, I find myself smiling more than I have in months. She's been home from school every afternoon this week, our time together filled with paint, glitter, and the occasional foray into the kitchen to scrounge up snacks.

It's Friday now, and I'm not sure what the weekend will entail. If I'm watching Ivy or if Saint will take over. If I'll have to see him. If I'll have to avoid him.

I hold my sweater up to the light. The stain is still there. It always will be. I throw it in the sink and grab a clean chambray shirt to put on instead.

Ivy's school day is shorter on Fridays, and when I pick her up, she announces that she wants to paint tree trunks in the back garden of their house. I tell her it's a great idea. The afternoon is already looking up, because Miss Erin isn't in charge of the pickup line. It's another teacher today.

Besides, painting trees isn't the worst way to spend a Friday.

"Look, Miss Wrenley!"

Ivy steps aside to showcase the dripping rainbow on one of the larger oak trees. Her fingers are stained with the same colors, and her nose is streaked with green.

"Beautiful," I say. "You're going to have the most artistic garden in all of Falcon Haven."

She wanders away from the tree and closer to the garden's border, inspecting a small bush. "Is two weeks a long time?"

I blink at the subject change, considering I was just wondering what she planned to do to a blackberry bush.

Since I'm not sure where this is going, I hedge, "Kind of. Why?"

"Because that's how long you're staying. Right?"

My ribs seem to close in around my heart. "We still have a whole week to go, sweetie."

Ivy's brow furrows with a seriousness that makes her look older than five. "I don't want you to go."

"Oh, Ivy."

I crouch down, wiping the green streak from her nose.

"Just stay forever."

She says it as if it's the simplest solution in the world, with a small, determined voice.

"I wish I could."

"Papa can make you stay. He makes everyone do stuff."

I laugh, though it comes out more like a strangled breath. "He's very good at that, isn't he?"

"Uh-huh." Ivy nods. She leans in, whispering loudly, "He likes you."

My wheeze turns into a cough.

"Does not," I manage, my voice a squeak.

"Does too," she insists. "He looks at you like ... like this."

She scrunches her face into a very serious expression, crossing her arms. I can't help but laugh.

"That's his cranky face, Ivy. He looks at everyone like that."

"Not you," she says, then skips off to inspect her next tree.

Ivy's wrong. She has to be. Yet the small, hopeful part of me that still wants to believe in the impossible—that he could care, that I could be enough—is louder than I'm comfortable with.

Ivy finishes another tree, the bright stripes more chaotic

than the last. When the sky begins to turn a dusky pink, I tell her it's time for us to go into the house. She heads toward it without complaint, her bare feet leaving a trail of colorful footprints in the grass.

I follow, and once inside, I wipe her hands and face (and feet) with a damp cloth, the water turning a murky brown in the farmer's sink.

Ivy chatters about her plans for the weekend, some of which involve convincing her father to let her paint the main house.

"Maybe he'll let us paint the guesthouse first," I say in a conspiratorial whisper.

"Maybe!" Ivy chirps. "After dinner, can we paint the doghouse? It's left over from the people who lived here before. We don't have a dog, but we could get one. Or a cat. Or a rabbit."

"Let's ask your papa about a ferret. He'd love it," I say. "But first, we need to eat."

I make her favorite: peanut butter and banana sandwiches with a side of strawberries and tomatoes. We eat them on the floor, Ivy's idea, with a thick blanket spread in front of the fireplace and a stack of picture books beside us.

She stretches out on her stomach, her chin propped on her hands, and listens to me read, interrupting every few pages to ask why a cookie would need to go to school.

I'm halfway through our fourth book when I notice she's gone quiet. I glance over, and she's fast asleep, her dark hair curling over her eyes, her mouth slightly open.

Carefully, I gather her into my arms and carry her up to her room and tuck her in.

The house is quiet, the only sound the creak of the floorboards as I make my way back downstairs. I pause in the kitchen, staring out the window at the guesthouse. The thought of returning to its emptiness tonight makes my stomach twist. I grab my phone from the counter, hesitating.

Ivy's words—*He likes you*—are on repeat in my mind.

But they're quickly drowned out by the memory of Saint's voice, flat and final: *This was a mistake.*

I can't keep doing this to myself. Wishing for something that can never be.

The front door swings open, and Saint's sudden presence fills the room. I hadn't heard his car. He stands there, his hair tousled by the wind, but his expression is a void I don't dare step into.

"Wrenley."

"Saint."

The air between us stretches, taut and uncomfortable.

"Ivy's down," I say, just to fill the space. "She had a great day."

One corner of his mouth twitches. "I saw the trees."

"Sorry if I overstepped. I promise the paint is washable, environmentally friendly, biodegradable, all that stuff."

More silence. Not tense, exactly, but charged. Like the air before a summer storm.

"She wants to paint the doghouse next," I say, trying to sound light. "I told her we'd have to ask you first."

"Let her," Saint says, his voice softer than I expect. "It'll keep her from painting the walls inside."

"Smart man," I reply, tucking my hair behind my ear. My fingers itch to tug. "Well, since you're home, I'll get out of your way."

His eyes don't leave mine. "Are you hungry?"

Saint doesn't wait for an answer, just crosses to the fridge.

"Saint, you don't have to—"

"Sit." He nods toward the kitchen island.

I hesitate, caught between the urge to flee and the pull of

getting another amazing meal from him. But the thought of sitting across from Saint, sharing food, sharing space, is terrifying in equal measure.

I take a deep breath and sink into one of the stools.

"I've been experimenting with something new. I'd like your opinion."

Saint's back is to me, so it's impossible to read any body language behind his words.

"Sure." Then, because I'm a glutton for awkward moments, I say, "I'd hate for you to make a mistake."

His shoulders stiffen. It's subtle, a small shift, but I see it.

"Wrenley." My name is a rough exhale. "I didn't mean…"

"I know."

I say it quickly before he can finish even though I'm the one who started it.

Saint moves fast, his attention on the ingredients he pulls from the fridge. The kitchen fills with the smell of fresh herbs and something citrusy. He focuses on a container full of something pink, an avocado, and something orange and shiny.

He's silent again, but this time it's not the silence of the past three days. It's a language I'm beginning to understand. Saint cooks when he can't say what he wants to say.

I watch, captivated as he cuts the pink flesh—salmon—into thin strips. The sight of his inked hands handling something so delicate makes me want to bite my lip and lean closer. He moves with the same attention to detail he had when he'd bandaged my arm. When he'd kissed me by the fire.

When Saint plates the dish, it's a work of art. Strips of salmon, cured and almost translucent, curl around themselves, nestled beside thin slices of avocado. They're arranged like a mosaic, and dotted with tiny orange pearls, like caviar.

It's bright and beautiful, like a sunrise on a plate.

He slides it in front of me, a small, careful offering.

"I'm trying a new cure," he says. "Passion fruit. Yuzu. Mango. Thought you might like it."

I pick up a fork, my heart thudding in my chest. The food is vibrant, unexpected, and I know, deep down, that this is more than just a meal.

The flavors burst in my mouth. Sweet, tangy, a hint of salt. It's exquisite, and even though I should expect it by now, I can't help the small sound that escapes me.

Saint's eyes darken, a flicker of molten fire crossing his face. Muscles in his cheeks pop before he blinks once and says, "Wine?"

"Please," I say, my pulse a quick, uneven beat.

He pours two glasses, the white wine catching the light and flickering against the gleaming countertop. Saint hands one to me, his fingers grazing mine, sending a familiar, frustrating jolt through my system.

"Thanks," I say, my voice a little shaky, my heart a lot shaky.

He watches me take another bite, the cured salmon melting on my tongue. The tiny pearls of roe pop with a satisfying brininess.

Saint takes a sip of his wine, his eyes never leaving my face. He leans against the counter. "I wasn't sure you'd like it."

"Why? Because it's not peanut butter and bananas?"

He almost smiles again.

"It's perfect," I say, feeling the warmth of the wine, the food, his attention.

Saint's shoulders relax as if my reaction has lifted a weight. "I'll remember that."

He refills my glass, his fingers grazing mine against the stem, lingering this time. "Ivy's happy with you."

I look down at my plate, at the delicate arrangement of flavors and colors. "She's not the only one."

The wine is crisp, cutting through the rich flavors of the salmon. And Saint still won't take his eyes off me.

I feel like I'm the one who's been cured with sweetness and ready to melt on his tongue.

"Is this a one-time thing?" I ask, my voice tentative. "Or will you be experimenting more?"

He lifts the wineglass to his lips, fully aware of my double meaning. "That depends."

"On what?"

"On whether you want to stay."

My heart skips. No, it doesn't just skip. It lurches sideways, cramming itself against my ribs like it's trying to escape through a space in its cage of bone.

"Ivy wants me to," I say softly. "But I don't know if—"

"If I want you to?" Saint finishes for me, his voice gruffer than before. "I told you. Ivy's attached."

I pick at the edge of the salmon, the fork trembling slightly in my hand. "And you?"

He doesn't answer right away. Instead, he moves around the island. I catch the scent of his cologne mixed with wine and lemon. He's close enough that I notice how his jaw shadows his neck.

"I'm attached," he finally says. "Too much. Too fast."

The air turns thick as honey in my lungs. I stop knowing how to breathe because breathing means accepting this is real and not a dream.

"You didn't seem attached three nights ago."

"Because I panicked." He cups my chin, forcing me to stay on his eyes. "You're not a mistake, Wrenley."

The knot in my chest loosens, just a little.

Saint releases my chin, his fingers trailing down my neck before stroking a loose strand of hair back from my face. "But I'm not sure I can be what you need."

A chill creeps in, and I reach for my wine, needing something to hold on to to keep my hands busy.

Saint's voice is firm, but edged with hesitation. "I'm not easy. And I've already put you through too much."

"So is this you trying to protect me?"

The familiar sting of rejection pierces my stomach.

"Trying not to fuck it up," he corrects. "I don't want to hurt you, Wrenley."

He already has. But I don't say it. I can't, because saying it allowed means admitting I've already let him in enough to draw blood from my heart.

"Then don't fuck it up," I say instead, reaching for him, my fingers brushing his bare forearm. "I want to stay, Saint."

He looks at me, really looks, and for a moment, I think I've gotten through. That this time he won't retreat.

Then his expression shifts. "I talked to Erin."

Air is knocked from my lungs. I shake my head, dislodging the confusion his statement brings. "Miss Erin, from Ivy's school?"

He nods. "She offered to help with Ivy before and after school while I wait for a permanent replacement."

A hollow laugh escapes before I can stop it, falling apart inside my chest and rattling against my ribs. "Of course she did."

Saint's jaw tightens. "She's highly qualified. Certified in child development, education, and care. I'd be a fool not to consider it."

A shard of ice drops into my stomach. Its cold spreads outward until my fingertips go numb around the wineglass.

"Qualified," I repeat. "Right."

The exquisite salmon, the shared wine, his admission of being "attached"—it all curdles in my stomach, turning into a bitter, mocking joke. Saint wasn't asking me to stay. He was… what? Softening the blow? Offering a consolation prize before delivering the final verdict? My hand, still holding the wineglass, trembles so violently I have to set it down before I drop it. The delicate clink against the stone countertop sounds unnaturally loud in the sudden, suffocating silence.

"She's good with Ivy," Saint continues, his gaze steady, oblivious, or perhaps indifferent, to the devastation he's just wrought. "She understands her needs from a professional standpoint."

Consistency. Professional. Qualified.

He's choosing the sensible option, the one that makes sense on paper, the one that doesn't involve messy emotions or women with questionable pasts and pink-streaked hair. He's choosing Erin. The man who just admitted he was attached to me, who kissed me senseless by the fire, is now calmly explaining why another woman is a better fit.

I can't meet his eyes. I can't let him see how thoroughly his words have gutted me.

"So when is Erin taking over?" I ask through a thickening throat.

Saint frowns, a crease appearing between his brows. "Not taking over. I thought it would free you up as well. You didn't come to this town to be a nanny. I essentially blackmailed you into it so you'd have a place to stay while you figured out other lodging."

Saint's being reasonable and logical. He's offering a solution to a problem he thinks I have. He doesn't see that *he* is the problem. Or rather, my stupid, persistent feelings for him are. And for his daughter.

"Erin, with her degrees and her professional standpoint, is a much better long-term investment than the flighty influencer who dents your cars and has meltdowns during thunderstorms."

My voice is dangerously quiet, each word carefully enunciated to mask the tremor threatening to break through. He's not offering me an out. He's showing me the door, albeit politely, with a side of cured salmon.

Saint's expression darkens, a shadow of confusion obscuring his features.

"That's not what I meant."

"No, it's fine," I interrupt, pushing back from the island, the beautiful plate of food suddenly nauseating. "It makes perfect sense. Ivy needs stability. Someone reliable."

"Wrenley."

"You don't need to explain." I force a brittle smile. "You're right. I didn't come here to be a nanny. And it's good that Erin stepped up."

I need to get out of here before he sees the cracks. Yes, he's offering me my original wish on a silver platter, but why does it feel like a severance package?

Saint's giving me the freedom I thought I wanted, but taking away the one thing—the two people—who had begun to make that freedom feel less like a vast, empty expanse and more like a space I could actually inhabit.

"Next week, it's off the table, then?" I manage to ask.

I accidentally meet his stare and notice a flash of emotion in his eyes. I hope to god it's not pity. "Erin can start Monday."

Nodding, I say, "I'll be out by tomorrow morning. Just please, let me say goodbye to Ivy."

Saint's expression falls. "Of course."

My feet move, carrying me toward the back door to the

guesthouse, the only sanctuary I have left, however tempo-rary. Each step is a monumental effort, like wading through concrete.

"Wrenley, wait."

Saint's voice follows me, but it's distant, like he's calling from the other side of a canyon. I'm already at the door, my hand on the cool metal of the knob, a desperate need to escape writhing around inside me.

Inside, I don't turn on the lights. I don't want to see my reflection, the inevitable tear tracks, the stupid hope that had been so clearly written on my face just minutes ago.

He's attached. Too much. Too fast.

Liar.

Or maybe just an asshole.

I collapse onto the small sofa, my chambray shirt clinging to my damp skin. But I don't scrape. I don't scratch, or pull, or break skin.

My fingers hover over the screen of my phone, then I force myself to type out a message before I lose my nerve.

Hey, Brenda. I've been marinating.

I hit send, then drop the phone onto the cushions, a sunken feeling settling in my chest.

FOURTEEN
SAINT

My coffee burns my tongue, but it's nothing compared to the heat that shoots through me when Wrenley stumbles into my kitchen in nothing but pajama shorts and a threadbare T-shirt that leaves too little to my imagination.

I should've locked the back door.

For many reasons, since Ivy is the one leading Wrenley inside.

My daughter's hair is a rat's nest, her feet are bare and filthy, and her small face is alight with a triumphant grin that tells me this was a premeditated mission.

"Papa!" Ivy chirps. "Miss Wrenley's awake!"

Wrenley, who looks like she's been dragged through a hedge backward and then dressed by a confused pixie, blinks at me, her eyes wide and still clouded with sleep, the pink streak in her hair a bright slash against her pale face.

Her shirt drapes over the peaks of her nipples. My gaze snags there for a beat too long.

"I, uh," Wrenley stammers, crossing her arms over her breasts. "Ivy was very... persuasive. At my door. Then climbing onto my bed. Very early."

I purse my lips, containing the annoyed grumble. My daughter, the miniature escape artist, decided to bypass the stairs and make a pre-dawn raid on the guesthouse.

Explains why the house was so quiet while I prepared pancakes for our Saturday morning ritual.

"Miss Wrenley, why are your eyes puffy?" Ivy asks, abandoning Wrenley's side to circle her. "Were you crying?"

Wrenley's cheeks turn a deep scarlet, and she laughs louder than usual, then rakes a hand through her hair and replies, "No, sweetie. Just sleepy."

"Oh." Ivy considers this. "Papa's eyes look weird too. And he's using the wrong spatula."

I glance down. She's right. I'm using the fish spatula instead of the pancake turner. Christ.

Last night has affected me more than it should. I've fired plenty of nannies since moving here, and none of them had me questioning my sanity or my kitchen utensils.

"Maybe we should let Miss Wrenley go back to the guesthouse," I say, still facing the stove.

"Why? Papa made extra pancakes," Ivy announces, tugging Wrenley toward the table. "He always makes too many."

I don't. I make exactly seven. Three for me and four for Ivy who insists on slicing and arranging them into towers she demolishes with theatrical glee. The batter bowl sits empty by the stove.

Wrenley's bare feet hesitate on my kitchen tile. Her toes curl against the cold. "I should get back. Get dressed."

"You're here. Eat."

It's not a request. It's a clumsy attempt to rewind the clock, to erase the hurt I see etched around her mouth, even if it's just for the duration of a stack of pancakes. She finally lifts her head, her eyes meeting mine for a fleeting second, and the openness there is a punch to the gut.

Wrenley's fingers find the hem of her shirt, twisting the fabric. The gesture pulls the material taut across her chest, and I force my gaze to the window. To the coffee maker. To anywhere else.

"Just one, then," Wrenley murmurs, finally. "If it's no trouble."

Oh, it's fucking trouble.

Her presence is a constant, low-grade disruption. A beautiful, unwelcome sunrise in a world of gray.

I slide pancakes onto plates. Three plates. My hands move on autopilot while my brain screams at the stupidity of prolonging this while Wrenley leads Ivy to the sink to wash their hands.

"Saturdays are for pancakes and horses," Ivy says as Wrenley holds the soap. "We're going to Rome's Ranch, right, Papa? You promised."

Wrenley's eyes clash with mine over the faucet. The question there is clear: *Does she know?*

I give the slightest shake of my head. No. Ivy doesn't know Wrenley's supposed to leave this morning. Taking Ivy to the ranch was supposed to fill the gaping hole Wrenley would leave behind and act as a distraction while I told Ivy that Wrenley would no longer be watching her.

"What? I just want to see the horses." Ivy turns to Wrenley. "You like horses, right?"

"Ivy." I need her to stop talking. Need to think. Need Wrenley to stop looking at me the way she is.

"Papa?" Ivy presses, her sweet voice pulling me back. "You said we could go. Wrenley should come, too."

I should say no. Keep things clean and simple. Send Wrenley to the guesthouse to pack and stick to the plan.

The refusal sticks in my throat when I meet Ivy's expectant face. It's been so long since she's lit up like this with someone who isn't me or her mother.

Wrenley shifts her weight as she dries both their hands with a small towel.

"I can stay here," she offers quietly. "You two should go have fun."

"No!" Ivy protests. "Miss Wrenley has to come too. She's never seen the horses!"

Wrenley's eyes find mine again. Her shoulders are braced for rejection, steeling herself against another dismissal.

"You want to see horses?" I ask her on a sigh.

She blinks, surprised by the question. "I ... yes. I love horses."

"You do?" Ivy gasps with delight. "Because some of them are secret unicorns, right?"

Wrenley's laugh is soft and genuine. "Absolutely. The magic ones hide their horns when humans are watching."

The cage around my heart nearly cracks open at the sight of Wrenley playing along with Ivy's fantasy. Not dismissing or correcting her, but joining her in that sacred space of childhood, where anything is possible.

"Fine," I concede, and it nearly chokes me to death. "You can come."

Ivy squeals, bouncing on her toes. Wrenley's eyes widen, her lips parting in surprise at my surrender.

"But," I add quickly, pointing the spatula at my daughter, "you need to get dressed first."

Ivy nods excitedly.

Wrenley settles at the island beside Ivy, her movements cautious, like she's navigating a minefield. Which, in a way, she is. I've practically pushed her out, then invited her back in for breakfast and a ranch visit.

What the fuck am I doing?

Extending this goodbye is cruel to all of us. It's giving Ivy false hope. It's giving an uncomfortable spice in my chest that I *really* don't like because I keep having to clear my damn throat.

Ivy chatters through breakfast, oblivious to the current running between Wrenley and me. Each time our eyes meet, electricity pulses through the room. When Wrenley's fork slips from her fingers, clattering against her plate, I know she feels it too.

"These are amazing," she says.

"They're special pancakes," Ivy explains seriously. "Papa puts vanilla in them. And fairy dust."

"I can taste it," Wrenley replies, taking another bite. Her tongue darts out to catch a drop of syrup on her lower lip, and my body responds with an immediacy that's both inappropriate and undeniable.

I push back from the counter. "I'll get the car ready."

I need air. Space. Distance from the soft curves under that threadbare shirt and the way Wrenley looks at my daughter like she's a miracle.

"I should get dressed." Wrenley rises as well.

Ivy glances between the two new bookends on either side of her.

"Yes. Go," I say to Wrenley harsher than intended. "We leave in twenty minutes."

Her eyes narrow slightly at my tone, but she nods and

slips out the back door. The sight of the muscles undulating under the skin of her bare legs makes my mouth go dry.

The moment she's gone, Ivy turns to me, arms folded in front of her in a gesture so reminiscent of her mother that my breath stalls.

"You're being mean again, Papa."

"Eat your pancakes," I mutter, pushing her plate closer.

"You like Miss Wrenley," she accuses as she drowns her stack in more syrup. "But you're scared."

I nearly choke on my coffee. "What? I'm not scared of anything."

Ivy rolls her eyes with the dramatic flair of someone three times her age.

Rather than remaining stunned, I arch a suspicious brow at my daughter.

"Miss Wrenley makes you have feelings," Ivy says, methodically dismantling her pancake tower. "That's why your face gets all scrunchy when she's around."

"My face does not get scrunchy," I reply, appalled.

Ivy demonstrates what she means, furrowing her brow and pursing her lips in an expression that's uncomfortably accurate.

"Finish your breakfast," I say with a dismissive wave that is in *no* way a surrender to my daughter. "And then go brush your teeth and find shoes. Real shoes, not those sparkly monstrosities that fall off every three steps."

Outside, the morning is crisp, autumn settling firmly into the bones of Falcon Haven. I stand by the Range Rover, keys dangling from my fingers, and try to breathe through the rigidity of my posture.

This is so fucking dumb. One last adventure before the inevitable goodbye. One more memory for Ivy to mourn when Wrenley leaves.

For me to mourn.

It's for the best.

"I'm ready!" Ivy announces, skipping down the porch steps in her favorite purple cowboy boots.

Wrenley follows, now dressed in tight jeans and a cream sweater, her hair tamed into a loose braid, the pink streak woven through it.

She's beautiful. Effortlessly so.

"I brought Ivy's jacket," she says, holding up the small purple jacket. "It's supposed to get windy."

"Thanks," I say, appreciating her forethought.

Our fingers brush when I take the coat from her, a spark of warmth shocking the cool morning air.

I pretend I don't feel it, turning my attention to helping Ivy into her seat while Wrenley slides into the passenger side.

The SUV feels suddenly smaller when I get in, Wrenley's floral, vanilla scent filling the confined space and expanding in my lungs with deadly accuracy.

I adjust the rearview mirror, catching Ivy's grin in the reflection.

We pull away from the house, the tires crunching over the gravel drive. I keep my eyes fixed on the road ahead and clench the wheel at 10 and 2, despite never being in the habit of doing so.

Wrenley's profile in my peripheral vision is a constant distraction. The curve of her cheek and the fullness of her mouth, the line of her jaw, her angles and curves are more mesmerizing than any landscape offered outside these windows.

"Miss Wrenley, did you know horses can sleep standing up?" Ivy's voice cuts through the silence from the back seat.

"I did know that," Wrenley replies, turning to look at her. "Pretty amazing, right?"

"Rome says they have special legs that lock so they don't fall over."

The road narrows as we leave the outskirts of town, winding through fields where morning mist still clings to the grass. Weathered fence posts line the roadside, some leaning at precarious angles after years of withstanding storms.

"Is Rome the owner?" Wrenley asks.

"He's Papa's best friend," Ivy declares before I can answer. "He has tattoos too, but not as many as Papa."

I catch Wrenley's glance at my forearms where my ink peeks from beneath my rolled sleeves.

"I didn't know your Papa had a best friend," Wrenley says, a teasing smile tugging at her lips.

"Talon Ranch is the biggest one around here," I say, finally breaking my silence while also avoiding the question. "Been in his family for generations."

The road curves sharply, and a vista opens before us of rolling hills dotted with black-and-white cattle and the distant glimmer of the Atlantic visible on the horizon. The landscape unfolds like a painting, all blues and the burned-off colors of summer beneath the clear morning sky.

"It's beautiful," Wrenley murmurs, leaning forward.

"Wait till you see the horses!" Ivy exclaims. "Rome has seven of them. My favorite is Scribbles. She's beige with all kinds of white dots on her."

"Does Scribbles let you ride her?" Wrenley asks.

"Uh-huh! Rome lets me go fast too. Not like Papa, who says 'slow down' all the time."

I frown into the rearview mirror. "That's because Rome is irresponsible."

"That's not what you said when he fixed your car that time," Ivy counters, her voice saccharine sweet.

Wrenley's lips quirk, and she turns to look out the window, hiding what I suspect is a full-wattage smile. My stomach does a strange flip at the shy, quiet tuck of her chin as she tries to hide it.

Christ, I'd trade my best knife set to know what's running through her head right now. Is she thinking about how pathetic I am, getting verbally outmaneuvered by a five-year-old? Or worse, is she filing this away as another reason she's better off leaving? My brain's like a lovesick teenager trying to decode if that smile means something, when I'm the idiot who made sure it can't.

After one hard blink, I turn my attention to the weathered barns as we pass, stone walls draped in wild roses, and glimpses of the ocean between stands of pine. *Anything* but Wrenley Morgan.

A massive red barn appears on the horizon, its weathered face burnished gold in the morning light. We pull up a long gravel drive flanked by split-rail fencing, where horses graze in the distance.

"We're here!" Ivy squeals, already fumbling with her seat belt before I've fully stopped the car.

"Easy," I remind her, putting the SUV in park.

The farmhouse door swings open before we've even gotten out, and Rome strides across the yard toward us. He's six-foot-three of sun-weathered skin and easy confidence with chestnut hair cropped close on the sides but longer on top. The sleeve of tattoos running down his right arm is visible beneath his rolled thermal shirt.

"Well, look what the storm blew in," Rome calls out, his voice carrying across the yard.

Ivy is out of her seat in seconds, flying across the gravel. "Uncle Rome!"

He catches her mid-leap, swinging her high. "There's my favorite artist! Come to paint my horses again?"

"No! Just to ride them!"

Rome sets her down and turns his attention to me, his grin widening when he spots Wrenley climbing out of the passenger seat. His eyebrows shoot up, a question in them that makes my molars clench.

"And who might this be?" he asks, though his knowing smile tells me he's already pieced it together from our brief phone conversations.

"This is Miss Wrenley," Ivy announces before I can speak. "She's my nanny, and she makes the best braids, and she's never seen Scribbles!"

Rome extends his free hand to Wrenley. "Roman Miles, but most people call me Rome. Owner of this dusty patch of heaven and unfortunate friend to the grumpiest chef on the Eastern Seaboard."

Wrenley's laugh is genuine as she takes his hand. "Wrenley Morgan. Temporary nanny to said chef's daughter."

Her eyes flick to mine, a shadow passing over her features.

"Temporary," I echo, mostly as a reminder to myself. "Very temporary."

Rome's eyebrow arches as he looks between us, his intuition picking up on the undercurrents like he always does.

"That so?" He sets Ivy down, who immediately tugs on Wrenley's hand.

"Can we see the horses now? Please?"

"Of course," Rome says, ruffling Ivy's hair. "Why don't you and Miss Wrenley head down to the paddock? I need to talk to your papa for a minute."

Ivy pulls Wrenley toward the wooden fence where several horses graze in the distance. Wrenley glances back at me but allows herself to be led away.

"Temporary, huh?" Rome asks the moment they're out of earshot.

"Shut up," I mutter, watching Wrenley's cream sweater grow smaller as Ivy leads her into the paddock.

Rome says with a low whistle, "Very mature response."

"She's leaving today. This is..." I gesture vaguely at the ranch. "A goodbye."

Rome crosses his arms, the muscles of his forearms flexing beneath his faded thermal. "Funny kind of goodbye. Usually those happen at the door, not thirty miles away at a horse ranch."

"Ivy wanted her to come."

"And Saint Toussaint always does exactly what his daughter wants." Rome's tone is dry as the dust beneath our boots. "That why you've got that stick up your ass this morning?"

I glare at him. "Aren't you supposed to be shoveling horseshit or something?"

Rome laughs, a deep, easy sound that has always irritated me. "Three years of friendship and that's the best you've got? You're slipping."

We watch as Ivy points excitedly at a dappled mare near the fence. Wrenley leans down, listening intently to whatever my daughter is saying, her hand resting protectively on Ivy's shoulder.

"She's good with her," Rome observes.

"She's unqualified."

"She seems pretty damn qualified at making Ivy smile."

I don't answer. Can't answer. Because he's right, and it's ripping me up inside.

Rome sighs, running a hand through his hair. "Look, I don't know what's going on between you two, but that woman isn't looking at Ivy like she's counting down the minutes until she can leave."

"It's complicated."

"With you? Never would have guessed." Rome claps me on the shoulder. "Come on. Let's go watch your daughter show off her riding skills before you scowl so hard your face gets stuck that way."

We make our way toward the paddock, Rome's cowboy boots kicking up small clouds of dust with each step. Ahead, Ivy is pressed against the wooden fence, Wrenley beside her, both of them watching as a speckled horse trots along the perimeter.

"That's Scribbles," Ivy announces as we approach. "Isn't she the prettiest horse ever?"

"She's gorgeous," Wrenley agrees, her voice warm with genuine appreciation.

"One of the gentlest mares I've ever trained. Perfect for little riders." Rome winks at Ivy. "Want to saddle up, kiddo?"

Ivy bounces on her toes. "Yes, please!"

Rome whistles sharply, and Scribbles's ears prick forward. She turns, trotting toward us.

"She knows me!" Ivy squeals, straining against the fence.

Rome unlatches the gate. "Easy now. Let her come to you, remember?"

Ivy stills immediately, her small body vibrating with contained excitement as she holds out a flat palm. Scribbles stretches her velvet nose forward, snuffling Ivy's hand before giving it a gentle bump.

"Horses never forget a friend," Rome says as he leads the mare through the gate. "Especially one who sneaks them sugar cubes."

Ivy giggles, guilty and delighted. "Only sometimes."

I catch Wrenley's gaze over Ivy's head. The look in her eyes—a quiet joy, a sense of belonging—makes that mysterious spice rise, forcing me to clear my throat.

She belongs here at this moment, the autumn sun highlighting the gold in her hair, her cheeks flushed with the crisp air. The sight of her, so natural beside my daughter, hits me with an unexpected punch.

"Want to pet her?" Rome asks Wrenley, noticing her hesitation.

"Can I?"

"She won't bite," Rome says. "Unlike some people around here."

Wrenley's eyes flare at Rome's humor, but then she smiles, a real one that transforms her face and sends a bolt of heat straight to the groin.

"Go on," Rome encourages. "Right between the eyes. She loves that."

Wrenley stretches out her hand, palm flat like Ivy's had been. Scribbles leans into her touch immediately, and a look of pure glee crosses Wrenley's face.

"Oh! She's so soft," she breathes, stroking the white blaze that runs down the mare's face.

"Ready to saddle up?" Rome asks Ivy, who's practically levitating with anticipation.

"Yes!"

"I'll get her tacked while you three head to the arena," Rome says, leading Scribbles toward the barn. "And Saint, try not to terrify Miss Wrenley with your charming personality before we return."

I scowl at his retreating back while Ivy tugs Wrenley toward a fenced ring nearby, chattering about how fast she can make Scribbles go.

"She means trot," I clarify, falling into step beside them. "Not gallop."

"I can go super fast," Ivy insists. "Rome lets me."

"Rome also once broke his collarbone trying to ride a mechanical bull while holding a plate of nachos," I mutter. "His judgment is questionable."

FIFTEEN
WRENLEY

The smell hits me first: hay and leather and something earthy that immediately tells me I'm out of my element. Talon Ranch sprawls before us, all wooden fences and dusty paths, and I'm acutely aware that my sneakers are the wrong shade of white for this place.

"Miss Wrenley, look!" Ivy grabs my arm, dragging me toward the barn. The girl likes to lead. "That's where Scribbles lives!"

Saint follows, hands shoved in the pockets of his jeans. He's been quiet since we left his house. Quieter than usual, which is saying something. Every time I catch his eye, he looks away, like he's remembering this is my last day, if it can even be considered that. What is this morning to him? Am I an unwanted interloper, or does he want me here?

I just never know with him.

Inside the barn, Rome greets us with an easy smile that's nothing like Saint's rare, guarded ones. He's all golden skin and confidence, the kind of guy who probably never overthinks anything.

He scoops Ivy up, making her squeal. "Scribbles is set to go. Ready to ride?"

"Yes! But Miss Wrenley needs gear too. She's never been on a horse." Ivy announces this like it's a scandal.

Rome's eyebrows lift as he sets Ivy down. "City girl?"

"Guilty." I tuck a loose strand of hair behind my ear.

"Well, we'll fix that." His grin widens. "Let's get you sorted."

Saint shifts somewhere behind me. I can feel his presence like a phantom behind me, watching as Rome guides us deeper into the barn where riding helmets and boots line the walls.

"You should be about a size seven," Rome says, studying my feet with a practiced eye. He pulls a pair of worn leather riding boots from a shelf. "These belonged to my sister before she moved to Colorado. Should fit you just fine."

I take the boots, surprised by their weight. They're beautiful, the leather soft from years of use.

"Thank you," I say, sitting on a nearby bench to slip them on.

"Miss Wrenley needs a helmet too!" Ivy declares, already trying on a black one that swallows her small head.

"Safety first," Rome agrees, selecting a navy helmet from the wall. "Can't have Saint losing his favorite nanny to a tumble."

Saint makes a noise somewhere between a cough and a grunt. When I glance up, his mouth is a thin line, eyes fixed on something fascinating on the barn wall.

The boots fit perfectly, though I feel clumsy standing in them.

Rome adjusts the strap under Ivy's chin. She stands perfectly still, clearly familiar with the routine.

"Your turn," Rome says to me, walking over and handing me the navy helmet.

Our hands touch during the exchange, and I'm acutely aware of Saint watching us from the corner of the barn. When I turn, helmet in hand, his jawline looks carved from stone, his eyes tracking Rome's every movement with unmistakable possessiveness over me.

"What?" Rome asks, noticing Saint's expression.

"Nothing," Saint says, his tone flat as pavement.

Rome shrugs and turns back to me. "Let me help you with that."

"I'll help her," Saint says suddenly, stepping forward so suddenly that stalks of hay snap under his boots.

The barn quiets. Even Ivy stops fidgeting.

Saint takes the helmet from my hands.

"Turn around," he instructs, his voice low.

I comply, my heart racing as he positions the helmet on my head. His breath stirs the fine hairs at my nape as he adjusts the straps, his movements careful and precise.

"Too tight?" he asks, his voice close to my ear.

I shake my head, not trusting my voice to get through all the goosebumps he's caused.

"Words, Wrenley."

"It's fine," I croak.

When I turn back around, Rome's watching us with undisguised interest. Ivy looks between us, too, with a wide grin.

"Right," Rome says, clapping his hands together. "Let's get you ladies on some horses."

Ivy races ahead to the arena, leaving me walking between the two men. Our footsteps are the only sound until Rome asks, "Wrenley. Cool name. Where'd it come from?"

"Oh." I laugh, surprised by the question. "My mother was

obsessed with birds. Our house was filled with feeders and identification books. She used to drag my father on these weekend bird-watching expeditions." I smile at the familiar story. "One morning, they spotted a Carolina wren building a nest in the maple tree outside their bedroom window. That same afternoon, my mom found out she was pregnant with me."

I adjust the riding helmet, feeling its unfamiliar weight. "My dad wanted to name me Carolina, but Mom thought Wrenley sounded more unique. Less like a state, more like a mythical creature. You know, half human, half bird."

Rome nods appreciatively even though I might've just said the most nerdy girl sentence this cowboy has ever heard.

I glance sideways and catch Saint's face transforming. The hard lines around his mouth soften with a warmth that wasn't there before. He stares at me longer than necessary, studying me with new interest.

"That's..." Saint begins, then stops. "I didn't know that about you."

"You never asked," I reply, holding his gaze.

Unintentionally, my response is weighted with all the things about me he might have learned if circumstances were different. If he weren't sending me away. If I weren't leaving.

Rome clears his throat. "Well, let's see if you've got any natural talent with horses, Carolina Wren."

I break eye contact with Saint, my heart beating too fast.

"Actually, would it be okay if I recorded some of this?" I ask, pulling my phone from my pocket. "Your ranch is beautiful, and I'd love to have some memories of today."

The word "memories" slows my steps. It's a reminder that after today, memories are all I'll have.

Rome nods easily. "Film whatever you like. Just keep a safe distance from the horses until you're comfortable."

"Thanks." I unlock my phone, grateful for the distraction. "I promise I won't post anything online. This is just for me."

Saint's head tilts slightly at this comment, but he says nothing as we approach the corral where Ivy waits, her face alight with joy.

I lift my phone, framing the shot of Ivy's small form against the backdrop of rolling hills. Through the screen, everything looks more manageable somehow, like a perfect, contained moment I can revisit later when the ache of leaving this place, these people, becomes too much.

Saint's eyes are still on me, watching as I frame the first shot.

"Wrenley, you coming?" Rome calls, lifting Ivy onto Scribbles's saddle.

I lower my phone, tucking it into my back pocket.

The horses are much larger up close, powerful creatures with muscles rippling under glossy coats. A chestnut mare with a white star on her forehead watches me with liquid brown eyes that seem just as skeptical.

"That's Penny," Rome says, noticing my attention. "Gentlest horse in the stable after Scribbles. Perfect for a first-timer."

My mouth goes dry. "I'm actually riding?"

"Scared?" Saint asks.

When I turn, he's right beside me, one arm resting on the fence rail.

"Cautious," I correct, lifting my chin. "There's a difference."

The corner of his mouth twitches. "Not much of one."

"I'll help you," Rome offers, leading Penny toward the mounting block. "It's like riding a bike, except the bike has a mind of its own and weighs a thousand pounds."

"That's comforting," I mutter, but follow him anyway.

Ivy's circling the arena on Scribbles, her small hands confidently holding the reins. "Look at me, Miss Wrenley!"

"I see you! You're doing great!" I call back, my voice steadier than I feel.

I'm getting on a horse. I'm gonna ride a horse. I'm not gonna die.

Rome pats Penny's neck. "Left foot in the stirrup, grab the saddle horn, and swing your right leg over."

I hesitate, suddenly aware of how ridiculous I must look in borrowed boots and helmet, with Saint witnessing the most city-girl stereotype there ever was.

But why do I care what Saint sees? Does his opinion matter all that much?

Yes. Because he *matters.*

Ugh. I wish my mind knew how to stop talking.

"I'll help," Rome offers, extending his hand.

Before I can take it, Saint steps forward. "I've got her."

His hands circle my waist, warm and steady through my sweater. I freeze, the contact sending bolts of energy racing up my spine.

"Foot in the stirrup," Saint murmurs, his breath tickling my ear. "I won't let you fall."

I obey, placing my left foot in the metal stirrup. His grip tightens as I push off the ground, helping me swing my right leg over Penny's broad back. In the span of a second, I'm suspended between earth and sky, held aloft by Saint's strength alone.

I'm on a horse. I'm on a fucking horse.

"I'm on a horse!" I whoop. "I'm sitting on an animal!"

Ivy cheers excitedly in response, and under her exclamations, Saint's laughter rings out. *Laughter.* Like he's enjoying the feat as much as I am.

When I look over at him, his eyes are soft, his hands slow

clapping for me. "Good job. Now you really are half animal, half girl."

For the next twenty minutes, Saint walks beside Penny while I learn the basics. His hand rests on the horse's neck, steadying her, but I'm hyperaware it's really me he's paying attention to.

"Heels down," he instructs. "Grip with your thighs, not your knees."

Every instruction feels loaded, his commands doing things to my concentration.

"Papa never helps anyone ride," Ivy calls out as Scribbles passes us. "Not even Miss Erin, and she asked twice!"

Rome snorts from where he's leaning against the fence. "That right?"

Saint works his jaw. "Ivy, eyes forward."

"I am!" She circles back around. "Miss Wrenley, you're doing really good. Papa keeps staring at you like when he tastes a new sauce and can't figure out the secret ingredient."

My face burns. Saint mutters something under his breath that sounds suspiciously like a curse.

"Kids," Rome says with a wide grin. "They see everything."

"Can we do the trail now?" Ivy asks. "Please? The one by the creek?"

"That's a bit advanced for beginners," Saint starts.

"I can handle it," I interrupt, surprising myself. The truth is, I'm starting to enjoy this. The rhythm of Penny's walk, the sun on my face ... the way Saint hasn't left my side.

Our eyes meet. Snag. He frowns and looks away first.

"Fine," he says quietly. "But we go slow."

Rome pushes off from the fence. "Why don't you grab Dante?" he tells Saint. "I'll watch Ivy and Carolina Wren."

"Don't call her that."

Rome halts mid-step. "What now?"

"The bird thing. Don't."

"You mean the bird she's named after?" Rome glances between Saint and me, grinning now.

Saint frowns. "Just use her name."

"I am using her name. Technically."

"Rome," Saint warns.

"Wrenley, you care if I call you Carolina Wren?"

Before I can answer, Saint cuts in, "She doesn't need a nickname from you."

Rome cocks a brow. "From me specifically?"

He looks between us again, and I can see the moment it clicks. My heart does this stupid little flip because Saint is being territorial over me, even if it's just a nickname. Even if it doesn't change anything between us.

"Well I'll be damned, Saint. Didn't realize you were taking applications for nickname privileges."

I press my lips together to keep from grinning like an idiot. This possessive side of Saint shouldn't make me feel giddy, but here we are. Too bad it's just his protective instincts and not actual feelings.

It could be wishful thinking, but I swear Saint's expression darkens as he has to walk away from me and stroll toward the stables.

While he's gone, I grip the reins like a lifeline and refuse to move, much to Ivy's entertainment. Rome offers to lead Penny around, but I shoo him away, telling him to focus on Ivy instead. I'm happy with Penny staying still and munching on the grass growing around the fence posts. In fact, I take the time to set up my phone, nestling it near the front of the saddle to capture a close-up of Penny.

While I'm futzing with my phone, another horse's snort

catches my attention, and I raise my head to note Saint's return and—

Oh my god.

He's wearing a cowboy hat. His button-down shirt is loose around the collar, showcasing a V of tanned muscle and inked skin. Saint holds the reins one-handed as the horse trots toward us.

I nearly fall off Penny.

"What?" he asks, drawing Dante to a stop beside me with such smooth sexiness, my mouth goes dry.

"Nothing." My voice comes out strangled. "Just. The hat."

"Sun's bright on the trail." He adjusts the brim, the gesture so casually masculine I have to look away. "Rome keeps spares in the tack room."

The worn brown Stetson transforms him completely. Gone is the controlled chef in his pristine kitchen. This version of Saint looks dangerous. Capable. Like he could pin me against a barn wall and—

"Miss Wrenley, you're all red!" Ivy observes cheerfully. "Did you get sunburned already?"

"Must have," I say.

Saint's eyes crinkle under the shade of his hat, and I swear he knows exactly what I was thinking. The corner of his mouth lifts in the barest hint of a smirk.

"Ready?" he asks.

I nod, not trusting myself to speak.

He guides Dante closer, close enough that our knees brush. "Remember what I said. Heels down." His gaze drops to my legs. "Grip with your thighs."

Jesus Christ.

"Are we going or what?" Ivy calls, already halfway to the trail entrance.

Saint doesn't move. Neither do I. We're trapped in this

charged moment, the horses shifting beneath us, and all I can think about is how good he looks in that hat. How his hands look holding the reins. How I want to knock that Stetson off his head and run my fingers through his hair and hear him murmur all the dirty things he wants to do to me.

"Wrenley."

My name on his lips is a warning. Or maybe a plea.

"We should go," I breathe.

"We should."

Neither of us moves.

"Well, I guess Ivy's taking the lead," Rome drawls, grabbing Scribbles's reins and walking alongside, notably a good distance away from us.

Saint clicks his tongue, and Dante starts moving. To my pleasurable surprise, Penny does, too, and keeps pace alongside Dante.

The trail narrows once we enter the trees, forcing Saint to ride closer. Our legs brush occasionally, each contact sending sparks through my borrowed boots.

"You're a natural," he says quietly, so Ivy and Rome won't hear.

"Liar."

"I don't lie." His voice drops lower. "You're doing beautifully."

The compliment steals my breath. This is the most he's spoken to me all morning, and I'm pathetically desperate for more.

"Why did you—" I start, then stop.

"Why did I what?"

"Help me. Instead of letting Rome do it."

He's quiet for so long I think he won't answer.

"I didn't like his hands on you."

The admission has me rolling my lips together so I don't

blurt out something stupid like, *the only hands I want on my body are yours*. I have to swallow a few times before rediscovering my vocal cords.

"Saint."

"I shouldn't say that to you. I know." His knuckles are white on the reins. "Because of Monday. And Erin." He cuts himself off, glancing at Ivy.

"Then why?"

"Because I'm a fucking idiot," he says simply.

"Papa, look! A butterfly!"

Ivy's voice drifts back, followed by Rome's patient response about staying centered in the saddle.

The trail curves ahead, and Saint's knee presses against mine as the horses navigate the turn. He doesn't pull away.

"Your phone's recording," he observes, nodding to where I've propped it against the saddle horn.

"Is that okay? I just wanted..." I trail off, embarrassed.

"Wanted what?"

"To remember this." The sound of my voice is more faded than I'd like. "For when I'm gone."

His jaw works. "Don't."

"Don't what?"

"Talk about leaving. Not today."

"You're the one who—"

"I know what I said." His tone is unsettled. "Doesn't mean I want to think about it."

Penny stumbles slightly on a root, and Saint's hand instantly shoots out, steadying me with a grip on my elbow. The touch burns through my sweater.

"Sorry," I breathe, though I'm not sure what I'm apologizing for.

"Stop apologizing." He doesn't let go. "And stop looking at me like that."

"Like what?"

"Like you want me to do something stupid."

My heart hammers against my ribs. "What kind of stupid?"

His eyes darken. The hand on my elbow slides up to my shoulder, and for one suspended moment, I think he might actually pull me off Penny and onto his horse. The thought makes me dizzy.

"Miss Wrenley! Papa! You're going too slow!" Ivy's complaint breaks the spell.

Saint releases me like I've burned him. "Coming."

We catch up to find Rome and Ivy stopped by a small creek. Ivy's practically electric with excitement.

"Can we let the horses drink? Please?"

"Sure thing," Rome says, but he's watching us with knowing eyes. "Why don't you two dismount for a minute? Stretch your legs. I'll keep an eye on Ivy."

I should protest that I don't know how to get down, but Saint's already off Dante, reaching up for me. His hands span my waist, and I let myself slide down, my body dragging against his the entire way.

We stand frozen, his hands still on me, my palms flat against his chest. Under the hat's brim, his eyes are molten.

"This is a bad idea," he mutters.

"The worst," I agree.

"Papa, why are you hugging Miss Wrenley?" Ivy's voice carries clear across the water.

We spring apart, and I nearly trip over a rock. Saint steadies me again, cursing under his breath.

"Just helping her down," he calls back.

Rome coughs something that sounds suspiciously like, "Bullshit."

If I thought my face was red before, it's probably a nice

puce color now as I put distance between us, pretending to be fascinated by the creek. The water babbles over smooth stones, and I focus on that instead of the way my body aches to be touched by Saint without the annoyance of clothes.

Needing something to do with my hands, I pluck my phone from Penny's saddle. Through the screen, I frame a shot of Ivy on Scribbles and Rome holding the reins as the horse drinks. The afternoon light filters through the leaves, creating a dappled pattern across the water.

"She adores you."

I jump. Saint's moved beside me, close enough that I catch the scent of leather and that cologne that's been driving me crazy ever since I met him.

"I adore her too," I admit.

"That's the problem."

The words are so quiet, I almost miss them.

"Saint..."

"I hired someone else because I couldn't stop thinking about you." The confession comes out scalded, like it's been burned out of him. "Thought distance would fix it."

My heart stops. "Did it?"

He turns to look at me, and the open hunger in his eyes makes my knees weak. "What do you think?"

"Papa! My legs are tired!" Ivy's voice breaks through the moment. "Can we go back now?"

Saint blinks. Then he steps away, taking the warmth with him.

"Oui, *mon trésor*. We can head back."

During the return journey, Saint and I listen to Ivy chattering about horses while deliberately avoiding talking to each other, but she's clearly wearing down, her voice getting drowsier. By the time we reach the barn, she's slumped in the saddle.

"Someone had too much excitement," Rome observes, helping her down.

"I'm not tired," Ivy protests, then yawns so wide we can see her molars.

Saint dismounts and reaches for her, but she's already winding her arms around my legs.

"Can Miss Wrenley put me to bed tonight?" she mumbles against my pants.

The question gives us all pause. We all know what tonight means. What tomorrow brings.

"I—" I start.

"Please?" Ivy looks up with those eyes that are so like her father's. "You can read me the unicorn book."

Saint's face is inscrutable. "If Miss Wrenley wants to."

"Of course I want to," I say softly.

Rome coughs. "I'll take care of the horses. You guys get the little one home."

Saint nods, scooping up Ivy, who immediately burrows into his shoulder. I follow them to the SUV, my legs unsteady from more than the riding.

The drive home is quiet except for Ivy's soft snores. I sneak glances at Saint, catching him doing the same. His hands grip the steering wheel a lot like they did coming here, the tendons of his forearms standing out.

"That thing you said," I whisper. "About not being able to stop thinking about me."

"Not now." His voice is strained. "Please. Not with her in the car."

I bite my lip, then turn to watch the landscape blur past. My body still feels electrified from every touch, every loaded look. The space between us in the car feels vast and microscopic at the same time.

When we pull into his driveway, the sun is starting to set.

Saint carries Ivy inside while I trail behind, unsure of my place in this domestic scene.

"Bath first," he says, starting up the stairs. "She smells like horse."

"I can do it," I offer. "If you want to start dinner."

"Wrenley." He pauses on the landing. Ivy is dead weight in his arms. "After she's asleep, we need to talk."

The promise—or threat—of that conversation makes my stomach flip.

"Okay," I breathe.

He disappears into Ivy's room, and I lean against the wall, trying to steady my racing heart. Tonight. After weeks of tension, of almosts and not-quites, something's finally going to break.

I just don't know if it'll be us coming together or falling apart.

SIXTEEN
WRENLEY

The guesthouse door closes behind me with a soft click that sounds like finality.

I lean against it, chest heaving like I've run a marathon instead of just tucking in a five-year-old. Ivy had requested three stories after somehow becoming re-energized in the bathtub, her little fingers playing with my hair as I read about brave unicorns and midnight adventures. She'd fallen asleep mid-sentence, one hand clutching my wrist.

"Don't go," she'd mumbled in her sleep.

Now, in the quiet of my temporary home, those words resonate.

My riding clothes smell like hay and horse and Saint's cologne from when he'd steadied me. I should shower. I should pack. Miss Erin starts the day after tomorrow, and I need to be ready to leave.

Instead, I stand frozen, replaying every one of Saint's looks, every touch that lingered on my skin.

"After she's asleep, we need to talk."

Once I'm showered and changed, I check my phone. It's

been thirty minutes since I left the main house. Is that enough time? Too much? God, why am I analyzing this like a teenager?

A knock makes me jump. Three short raps that somehow sound decisive and uncertain at once.

My heart's in my throat as I open the door.

Saint stands on my small porch, hands shoved in his pockets. He's changed out of the ranch clothes, back in dark jeans and a Henley that clings in all the right places. No more cowboy hat, but my body remembers exactly how he looked wearing it.

"Hi," I breathe.

"Can I come in?"

I step aside wordlessly. He enters, bringing that dangerous energy that's been simmering between us all day. The guesthouse suddenly feels impossibly small.

"You wanted to talk," I prompt when he just stands there, tension radiating from every line of his body. "I know you probably don't want to leave Ivy alone too long, so…?"

"That's not what I want." His voice is curt, honest. Saint pulls his phone from his back pocket and shows me the image of Ivy sleeping peacefully in bed. "And I'm monitoring her, so we don't need to rush."

"Then what did you want to talk about?"

"You know what I want." He turns to face me fully, and the pure hunger in his expression makes me forget how to exhale. "The question is, what do you want. Because if you tell me to leave right now, I will. I'll walk out, and on Monday, Erin takes your place, and we pretend none of this happened."

I close my mouth, but the sheer want swelling my throat also peels apart my lips. "And if I don't tell you to leave?"

He takes a step closer. "Then I'm going to do what I've

wanted to do since you trespassed on my property and tried to throw a skillet at me."

My pulse thunders in my ears. "Which is?"

Another step. He's close enough now that I have to tilt my head back to maintain eye contact. "Everything, Wrenley. I want everything."

"That's not fair." My voice comes out breathier than intended. "You're the one who hired someone else. You're the one who—"

"I know." His hand comes up, fingers ghosting along my jaw. "I'm an idiot. A complete fuck. I thought if I could just get you out of my house, I could stop this." He breaks off, thumb tracing my bottom lip. "But then you walked into my kitchen this morning in those damn shorts, and Rome put his hands on you, and I realized I'd rather set myself on fire than watch you leave."

"Saint—"

"Tell me to go." His other hand finds my waist, pulling me against him until I can feel every ridge of him pressing against my stomach. "Tell me this is a bad idea. Tell me you don't feel this too."

"I can't." The admission breaks free on a whisper. "I've tried. God, I've tried. But I can't stop wanting you."

He makes a sound low in his throat. "Thank Christ."

Saint's mouth crashes down on mine, and it's nothing like I imagined. It's desperate, consuming, a week of pent-up desire unleashed in a single kiss. I gasp against his lips, and he takes advantage, stroking me with his tongue until all I can taste is him.

My fingers tangle in his hair, tugging until he groans. He walks me backward until I hit the wall, his body caging me in.

"I've wanted this for so long," he mutters against my

throat, pressing hot kisses to my pulse point. "Do you have any idea what you've done to me? Walking around my house, looking at me with those eyes?"

"Me?" I laugh breathlessly, arching as he finds a sensitive spot. "You're the one who—oh god—who keeps finding excuses to touch me. Who stares at me like…"

"Like I want to lick you clean?" He pulls back, eyes dark with promise. "Because I do. I want my tongue on every inch of you. Want to find out what sounds you make when I—"

"Stop talking." I yank him back down. "Show me."

Saint lifts me like I weigh nothing, my legs wrapping around his waist automatically.

He's already moving, kissing me senseless as he navigates the small hallway. When he sets me on the bed, I try to pull him down with me, but he resists.

"Wait." He's breathing hard, hair messed from my fingers. "If we do this…"

"Are you seriously trying to talk me out of this now?"

"No." He leans down, bracing his hands on either side of me. "I'm trying to tell you this can't fix anything. Erin still starts on Monday."

My heart sinks, but I lift my chin. "I'm well aware."

"Are you?" He traces my cheekbone. "Because I need you to understand. I can't offer you what a normal man can. One your age. But I don't know what this is between us. I just know I can't watch you leave town without…"

"Without what?"

"Without knowing what you taste like everywhere." His eyes burn into mine. "Without hearing you come apart under me. Without having this, even if it's just once."

His blunt honesty should hurt. But instead, it sets me on fire. Because at least he's not lying. At least he's not pretending this is something it's not.

"I'm not asking for promises," I whisper. "I'm not even asking you to figure out what this is tonight."

"Then what are you asking for?"

I pull him down until our lips are seconds apart. "I'm asking you to stop overthinking and just be with me. Tomorrow will still be complicated. The new nanny will still come. But right now? Right now, I just want you."

He groans, capturing my mouth in a kiss that's all desperation and adrenaline. "You have no idea how much I've needed to hear that."

"So stop talking," I repeat against his lips, reaching for his shirt. "Off. Now."

His mouth claims mine again as I tug his shirt upward, desperate to feel his skin against my palms. Saint breaks the kiss just long enough to rip the Henley over his head, revealing the full canvas of ink that I've only glimpsed between shadows. Dark lines swirl across his chest, down his ribs, disappearing beneath his waistband. I trace a finger along a constellation of stars etched under one pec.

"Beautiful," I whisper.

"Your turn," he growls, his hands finding the hem of my shirt.

I lift my arms, letting him pull it off.

Saint drags his teeth across his lower lip when he sees my white bra. Nothing fancy, but the want in his eyes makes me feel like I'm wearing the finest lingerie.

"Christ, look at you," he murmurs, trailing his fingers down my sternum.

His hand pauses at my shoulder, thumb ghosting over the raised lines we've both been pretending don't exist. The scars that led to our fight, to my walls slamming up, to his frustrated silence. His eyes flick to mine, a question there.

"Don't," I whisper. "Not tonight."

Something passes over his face. It could be anger at whoever marked me, frustration at my secrets, or his want despite it all. Probably all three.

His mouth tightens.

"Saint." I catch his face between my palms. "Please. Just—don't ask. Not now."

He studies me for a long moment. Then he leans down, pressing the softest kiss to my shoulder, right over the worst of the scarring. The tenderness of it makes my eyes burn.

"Okay," he rasps. "Not tonight."

His mouth continues its path, kissing along my collarbone and down to the edge of my bra. Each touch feels like a promise that my secrets can stay buried for now, and that he wants me anyway, damaged parts and all.

"But Wrenley?" He looks up at me, eyes clouded with possession. "One day you're going to tell me who did this to you."

It's not a question. I nod, unable to speak past the lump in my throat.

"Good." He rises to kiss me again, fiercer this time. "Because right now, all I want is to make you forget everything but my name."

My skin pebbles under his touch. When his thumb brushes over my nipple through the thin cotton, I arch into his hand with a gasp.

"Sensitive," he notes, a wicked gleam appearing in his eyes. "I wonder where else..."

Saint lowers his head, replacing his thumb with his mouth, drawing the peak into wet heat through the fabric. The sensation shoots straight between my legs, and I whimper, clutching his shoulders.

"Saint, please—"

He reaches behind me, unclasping my bra with practiced

ease. When it falls away, he sits back on his heels, just looking.

"You're staring," I whisper.

"I'm memorizing," he corrects.

But then his mouth is on my breast again, hot and insistent, and thinking becomes impossible. His tongue circles my nipple while his fingers tease the other, and I'm writhing beneath him, desperate for more friction.

"Too many clothes," I rasp, reaching for his belt.

Saint captures my wrists, pinning them above my head with one large hand. "Patience."

"I've been patient for too long," I protest.

His laugh is dark velvet against my skin. "Then you can be patient a little longer."

With his free hand, he works open the button of my jeans, sliding the zipper down with agonizing slowness. My hips lift instinctively, seeking his touch.

"So eager," he murmurs, pressing his mouth to my stomach. "I like that."

He releases my wrists to tug my jeans down my legs, taking my underwear with them. And then I'm naked beneath him, exposed to his hungry gaze.

"Fuck, you're perfect," he breathes, his hands sliding up my thighs.

I reach for him again, needing to feel him. "Your turn. Fair's fair."

Saint stands, unbuckling his belt while never breaking eye contact. I push up on my elbows to watch, the metallic rasp of his zipper loud in the quiet.

When he pushes his jeans down, the outline of his cock against his black briefs makes saliva pool in my mouth.

"See something you like?" he asks, the corner of his mouth lifting.

"You know I do."

He kneels between my legs, spreading them wider. Saint's eyes gleam through the night as he lowers his mouth to my inner thigh, pressing hot, open-mouthed kisses that trail higher with each touch. I moan when his stubble grazes the sensitive skin there.

"I've thought about this non-fucking-stop," Saint murmurs against my flesh.

When his tongue finally strokes through my folds, I cry out. He hums with satisfaction, the vibration intensifying the pleasure as he explores me with deliberate, torturous skill.

"Fuck, you taste even better than I imagined," he groans, his hands gripping my thighs to hold me open for his mouth.

I thread my fingers through his dark hair, holding him against me as he finds my clit and circles it with his tongue. The pressure builds low in my belly, coiling tighter with each expert flick.

"Saint," I gasp when he slides two fingers inside me. The stretch is delicious, his calloused fingertips curling to find that perfect spot that makes stars explode behind my eyelids.

He works me tenaciously, his mouth never leaving my center as his fingers pump in a rhythm designed to drive me wild. I'm trembling, hovering on the edge, my thighs beginning to shake.

"Let go," he commands. "Come for me, Wrenley."

The sound of my name on his lips while he eats me out pushes me over. I shatter, waves of pleasure crashing through me as I cry out his name. Saint doesn't stop, drawing out my orgasm until I'm gasping, turning into an oversensitive puddle.

When he finally raises his head, his mouth is glistening with evidence of my pleasure. The sight is so erotic I whimper.

"That's one," he says, his voice rough as he wipes his mouth with the back of his hand. "I want to see at least two more before we're done."

He rises to his knees, finally pushing his briefs down to free his cock. The size of him makes my jaw drop.

"You're staring," he says, echoing my earlier words with a smirk.

"I'm memorizing," I reply, reaching for him like a kid in a candy store.

My fingers wrap around his length, feeling the velvet-soft skin over steel hardness. Saint's breath hisses between his teeth as I stroke him, his eyes darkening to midnight.

"Condom," he manages, voice strained.

"Not before I lick you first."

But I take the time to drink in the sight of him, thick and hard, the head glistening. Saint's fingers thread through my hair as I take him into my mouth, his breath audibly catching when my tongue swirls around the sensitive tip.

"Jesus, Wrenley," he groans, his hips jerking slightly.

I take him deeper, hollowing my cheeks as I work him with my hand and mouth together. The weight of him on my tongue, the salt-sweet taste, the way his muscles tense with each movement quickly becomes my new addiction. His exhales turn ragged when I find a rhythm that has him cursing in French.

When I glance up, Saint's watching me with an intensity that makes my core throb. His jaw is clenched, the tendons in his neck standing out as he fights for control.

"Stop," he finally growls, gently pulling me off him. "I'm not finishing like that. Not our first time."

He flips me onto my back in one smooth motion, his body covering mine. The weight of him is delicious, his skin hot against mine.

"Condom," he repeats, reaching for his discarded jeans.

I watch as he tears the packet open with his teeth, rolling it down his length. Then he's positioning himself between my thighs, the blunt head of his cock pressing against my entrance.

"Say it again," he demands. "Tell me you want this."

I give him a deep, consuming kiss as my answer, hoping I steal both his breath and his sanity. I feel him at my entrance, teasing, the barest hint of pressure.

He pushes in, just the tip, then pulls back, making me moan.

"Saint, don't be mean…"

His answer is to lift my ass for a better angle and keep stretching me with a slow, purposeful thrust that has us both groaning into each other's mouths.

The initial burn gives way to exquisite fullness as he sinks deeper, filling me completely. He stills when he's fully seated, giving me time to adjust to his size.

"Fuck," he hisses, forehead dropping to mine. "You feel like heaven."

I wrap my legs around his waist, pulling him deeper. "Move. Please. I'm going insane."

He silences me with a kiss that's all ownership as he loses control and goes full throttle. Saint's hands pin mine above my head as he builds a rhythm that has me stuttering his name.

"Look at me," Saint commands, his voice thick with need. "I want to see your face when you come around my cock."

His order sends heat flooding through me. I meet his gaze, drowning in the blue fire of his eyes as he drives into me harder, faster. The coil of pleasure tightens again, impossibly intense after my first orgasm.

When his thumb finds my clit, circling in perfectly timed

circles to match his thrusts, I'm lost. The pressure builds impossibly fast, every nerve ending alight with sensation as he drives me toward the edge.

"That's it," he growls when my walls begin to flutter around him. "Give in to me."

The orgasm hits like lightning, more intense than the first, tearing a scream from my throat as pleasure pulses through every inch of my body. Saint doesn't slow, fucking me through it, his jaw cutting through his skin as he watches me come apart beneath him.

"So fucking beautiful," he rasps, his rhythm faltering as my body squeezes him.

He flips us suddenly, bringing me on top without breaking our connection. The new angle seats him impossibly deeper, drawing a shocked gasp from my lips.

"Ride me," Saint commands, his hands gripping my hips.

I plant my palms on his chest, the ink beneath my fingers slick with sweat as I begin to move. His eyes eat me up, tracking the bounce of my breasts, the place where our bodies join. The power of being above him, of controlling his pleasure, is my *next* new addiction.

"Look at you," he murmurs, one hand sliding up to cup my breast, pinching my nipple until I cry out. "A fucking natural rider."

His words fuel something primal in me. I roll my hips faster, chasing that building pressure again. Saint's fingers dig into my flesh hard enough to bruise, guiding my movements as he thrusts up to meet each downstroke.

"That's it," he encourages, his voice strained.

"I can't—" I gasp, overwhelmed by sensation.

"You can," Saint insists, his hips snapping up harder. "One more. Give me one more."

He sits up suddenly, wrapping an arm around my waist to

hold me against him as he takes control. The change in position has him hitting a spot that makes dynamite go off inside me.

I shatter a third time, my nails digging into his shoulders as I sob his name. This orgasm is different, deeper, more consuming, radiating outward until even my fingertips tingle with it.

Saint follows me over the edge with a guttural groan, his hips jerking erratically as he empties himself. I feel each pulse of his release even through the condom, his body shuddering beneath mine as he buries his face in my neck.

We stay tangled together, breathing hard, neither willing to break the spell. His weight against me feels perfect, necessary.

Saint kisses me softly, then pulls out and shifts us until we're lying down, pulling me against his chest. I can feel his heartbeat, still racing.

I start to pull away, aware that he has to get back to the main house and wanting to make this easy for him, but his arm locks around me, keeping me pressed against him.

"Don't," he says roughly. "I'm not—I'm not good at this part."

"I'm not asking for explanations," I say softly. "Or declarations. Or anything, really."

Saint doesn't answer. His hold tightens instead until my head returns to resting against his chest.

"Five more minutes," he murmurs into my hair.

I smile against his skin. "Five more minutes."

Neither of us mentions tomorrow again.

wake in my own bed, alone, with Wrenley's tropical perfume still clinging to my skin.

The clock reads 5:47 a.m. I'd slipped out of the guesthouse around midnight, after she'd fallen asleep curled against my chest. Leaving her had felt wrong, but leaving Ivy alone in the main house would have been worse. Then I'd had the absurd thought to lift Wrenley into my arms and carry her back to my bed with me, but thankfully, better judgment reminded me how fucking stupid that was.

Now I lie here, staring at the ceiling, my body aching in ways that confirm last night wasn't some fever dream. Wrenley beneath me, around me, calling my name like she needed me to breathe.

Fuck. What have I done?

I should regret it. Should be planning damage control. Erin starts tomorrow and I've just complicated everything by sleeping with the woman who just wanted a quaint small town to escape to for a while and instead got herself ensnared by the town's brooding chef.

All I can think about is going back to the guesthouse. Waking her properly. Seeing if she tastes as sweet in the morning light as she did in the dark.

I'm so fucked.

By six, I give up on sleep. Ivy won't be up for another hour. I pull on sweatpants and a T-shirt, then head to the kitchen. Cooking has always been how I process. My hands know what to do even when my mind is being an idiot.

I'm halfway through mixing batter when I hear the back door open. My heart jump-starts against my ribs.

Wrenley stands in my kitchen doorway, wearing those goddamned hot pink pajama shorts and thin top, her hair a beautiful disaster. The morning light turns her gold at the edges.

"Hi," she says softly.

"Hi."

We stare at each other across the space where everything started. Where she wandered in that first night for a simple dinner that changed everything.

"I was just..." She gestures vaguely toward the door she just walked through. "Going to shower and change, then leave, but I saw the light on and didn't want to go without saying goodbye."

"Stay." The request escapes before I can stop it. "For breakfast. I'm making—" I look down at the bowl in my hands, realizing I've been operating on autopilot. "French toast, apparently."

She hesitates in the doorway, arms wrapped around herself. "I don't think that's a good idea."

"Why not?" I set the bowl down, trying to read her face. Last night, she was open and exposed. This morning, she's all walls.

It's unsettling to see my own defense mechanism reflected back at me.

She takes a breath. "Because we both know what last night was."

"It's just breakfast, Wrenley. Not a marriage proposal."

She flinches at my tone, and I hate myself for it. But this is easier than whatever the fuck happened to me last night. Easier than admitting I watched her sleep for an hour before forcing myself to leave.

"Fine." She moves to the counter but doesn't sit. "Erin starts tomorrow."

"I'm aware."

"So this..." She gestures back and forth between us. "It doesn't change anything."

I set the bowl down with too much force. "I remember what I said."

"Do you?"

"Crystal clear. You needed to get it out of your system. Mission accomplished."

Her sharp intake of breath tells me I've hit the mark. Good. Better to be the asshole than the pathetic fuck who almost begged her to stay ten seconds ago.

"Papa?" Ivy's voice drifts down the stairs.

"Go," I say without looking at Wrenley. "Out the back."

For once, she doesn't argue. The door clicks shut just as Ivy's footsteps hit the kitchen tiles.

"Morning, baby."

"Are you making French toast?" She climbs onto her stool, then looks around. "Where's Miss Wrenley?"

"Not here."

"But she always—"

"Not today, Ivy."

My daughter studies me with those eyes that see too much. "You're using your mad voice."

"I'm not mad."

"Yes you are. You're whisking angry."

I look down at the bowl, realizing I've been attacking the batter like it personally offended me.

"I'm not mad," I repeat, forcing myself to slow down.

"Did you and Miss Wrenley have a fight?"

"No."

Yes. Maybe. I don't fucking know what that was.

"Then why'd she leave without breakfast?" Ivy's voice gets smaller. "Is it 'cause Miss Erin is coming tomorrow?"

I plate the French toast with mechanical care. "Eat your breakfast."

"I don't want Miss Erin."

"Ivy."

"She smells like too much perfume, and she talks to me like I'm a baby." She stabs her French toast. "And she looks at you weird."

"What do you mean, weird?"

"Like how Madison's mom looks at you during school pickup. All smiley and giggly." Ivy makes a disgusted face. "It's gross."

Christ. I mean, I'd noticed. I just didn't care enough to deal with it.

"Miss Erin is qualified."

"Miss Wrenley sings songs and knows about art and doesn't care when I get dirty." Ivy's eyes fill with tears. "Why can't she stay?"

Because I'm an idiot. Because I hired someone else instead of dealing with the fact that Wrenley makes me feel things I swore I was done feeling. Because last night I had her beneath me, around me, and this morning, I let her walk away thinking it meant nothing.

"It's complicated, *mon trésor.*"

"I hate complicated." She pushes her plate away. "I'm not hungry."

"You need to eat."

"No." She slides off her stool. "I'm going to my room."

"Ivy."

"I want Miss Wrenley!"

I dump both plates in the trash, appetite gone. Through the kitchen window, the guesthouse sits quiet, morning light catching on its windows and preventing me from seeing inside.

Do I even want to? Is she still there? Packing her things into those mismatched suitcases she arrived with? Where will she go after she leaves here?

My phone buzzes. It's a text from Erin confirming she'll arrive at six tomorrow morning. Professional. Punctual. Qualified.

Everything Wrenley isn't supposed to be for this job.

Except, Wrenley was never just the nanny, was she? Not from that first morning when she stumbled into my kitchen with that random pink streak in her hair and startled deer eyes, cracking something open inside me I thought was dead. Something I'd buried with Celine and promised myself I'd never risk again.

I pour coffee with hands that want to punch something, the familiar ritual doing nothing to bring calm. A burn on my palm from a few days ago when I was distracted—thinking about Wrenley—reminds me of what happens when I lose control in the kitchen.

When I let myself feel too much, care too much, want too much.

Upstairs, Ivy's crying shifts from angry to heartbroken, the sound yanking my heart straight out of my chest.

Fuck.

I take the stairs two at a time, coffee abandoned on the counter. Ivy's door is closed, her sobs muffled but steady. I knock softly.

"Go away!"

"Baby, please."

"I said go away! You ruined everything!"

I lean my forehead against her door, listening to my daughter fall apart because of the choices I made.

The smart choices.

The safe choices.

Choices that were supposed to protect us both.

My phone vibrates again.

Rome: **Ivy left her riding gloves here. Want me to drop them by?**

I stare at the text, remembering yesterday. How Wrenley looked on that horse, tentative at first, then confident. How she laughed when Penny tried to eat her hair. How she fit against me when I helped her down, like she was meant to be there.

Through the hallway's window, I catch movement below. Wrenley's car pulls away from the guesthouse, heading toward town. Not headed toward the highway.

Okay, so she's not leaving permanently. Not yet. Just ... leaving.

That fact sparks a tiny light in the dark concave of my chest.

"Papa?" Ivy's voice comes through the door, smaller now. "Is Miss Wrenley really not coming back?"

I close my eyes. "Miss Erin starts tomorrow."

"That's not what I asked."

My too smart daughter. Always seeing through the bull-shit, just like her mother would have.

"I don't know, baby."

The crying starts again, quieter this time. Defeated. It's so much worse than the anger.

I head back downstairs, needing to move, to cook, to do something with my hands before I do something I can't take back, like drive to town and tell Wrenley that last night meant everything. That I've been slowly falling for her since she walked into my life. That Ivy isn't the only one who needs her.

Instead, I take Ivy to a playdate to cheer her up and start prep for dinner service at my restaurant. Three hours early, but who's counting? I dice onions with unnecessary force. The knife's rhythm is usually meditative, but now it's just marking time.

How long before Wrenley finds somewhere else to go or leaves town entirely? A week? Two? How long before I run into her at the Merc or Libby Jude's and we have to pretend we're strangers who never shared a bed, who never—

The knife slips. Not enough to cut, but enough to remind me why I don't cook angry. Why I built walls in the first place.

And why I never should have let Wrenley Morgan through them.

EIGHTEEN
WRENLEY

My hands won't stop shaking on the steering wheel.

I make it three blocks from Saint's house before I have to pull over, my breathing too threadbare to drive safely. The morning sun streams through the windshield, cheerful and bright, mocking the disaster I've made of everything.

You knew this would happen, I tell myself. *You knew better than to get involved.*

But knowing and doing are two different things, and last night I did everything I'd sworn I wouldn't. Let him touch me. Let him inside me. Not just my body, but through all the caution I'd built, all the better sense I'd acquired, since the incident six months ago. Since everything fell apart in front of twenty million people.

I rest my forehead against the wheel, trying to steady my box breathing. *In through the nose, out through the mouth.* The technique my therapist taught me feels useless now, when I can still smell him on my skin. Still feel his hands on my waist, his mouth on my—

Stop.

As soon as I find somewhere to settle down, I'll call my therapist. Talk this out. *Figure* this out.

I force myself to drive, to focus on the road leading into downtown Falcon Haven. The town is just waking up. Shop owners are flipping signs from Closed to Open as the morning light paints everything golden. A week ago, this place saved me. The quiet. The anonymity. The blessed absence of cameras and recognition and people who think they know me because they watched me shatter on their phones.

My stomach growls, reminding me I fled before breakfast. Before Saint's French toast and his questions and that look in his eyes that made me want a life I can't have.

Libby Jude's comes into view, and I find available street parking right in front of it.

The bell above the door chimes as I enter, and the scent of bacon and fresh-baked muffins wraps around me like a hug.

"Well, look what the cat dragged in," Noa calls from behind the counter. She takes in my rumpled appearance of yesterday's jeans, hastily finger-combed hair, and probably visible beard burn on my neck.

"Rough night or rough morning?"

"Both," I admit, sliding onto one of the three vinyl barstools at the counter.

"Coffee, please. And..." I scan the menu board, looking for something completely unlike my usual healthy fare. "The chicken fried steak. Extra gravy."

Noa's eyebrows climb. "At seven in the morning?"

"Yup."

She pours my coffee, then leans against the counter. "Want to talk about it?"

"Not really." I wrap my hands around the mug, letting the warmth seep into my palms. "But thank you."

"No problem." She writes my order on her pad and disappears into the kitchen briefly. When she returns, she starts wiping down the already clean counter. "You've been here about a week now, right?"

"Just over, yeah."

"How are you finding it?"

"It's beautiful," I say, and mean it. "It's so quiet I can hear birds in the morning. In Brooklyn, all I heard was helicopters and sirens. And people actually make eye contact here when they pass on the sidewalk."

Noa releases a quiet laugh, her brown eyes sparkling. "You sound like my husband. The eye contact thing throws a lot of city people. He still forgets to wave back sometimes."

"Your husband's from New York?" I lean forward, interested. "How did he end up here?"

"He came here for family, stayed for me. Though we took the scenic route to figure things out. Small towns have a way of forcing you to face what you're running from."

My stomach tightens. "What do you mean?"

"Small town, big feelings. Nowhere to run." She tops off my coffee. "We have a three-year-old now who terrorizes the café every time we bring him in."

The kitchen bell dings, and she retrieves my plate, setting the massive chicken fried steak in front of me.

"This looks like a heart attack on a plate," I say.

"Comfort food usually does." She watches me cut into it. "So are you still watching Ivy?"

I pause mid-bite. "Actually, no. Saint found someone more

qualified." As soon as I realize I sound more bitter than I aimed for, I amend, "Which makes total sense."

"Ah."

Noa turns to fiddle with the intricate coffee machine, giving me space.

"It's the right decision." Apparently, I've decided to double down. "Ivy needs someone with experience, who knows what they're doing. Not someone who just stumbled into it."

"And how does Ivy feel about that?"

My throat closes. "I'd be lying if I said it didn't suck for both of us. But … I never came here to be a nanny."

"Hmm." Noa's tone is carefully neutral. "So what's next for you? Have you explored much yet?"

"A little. Yesterday at Talon Ranch was incredible. All that open space, no crowds. Just horses and sky." I pause. "Though honestly, I haven't really walked around downtown. I keep meaning to explore the shops, maybe hike some trails, but..."

But I've been caught up in Saint's world instead. Breakfast with Ivy. Dinner at their table. Living in their guesthouse like I'm part of something I'm not.

I take another bite, buying time. "I actually came here to figure out what's next. I needed a break and to clear my head. Instead, I spent the whole week playing house with them."

I'm not sure what it is about Noa that's made me vomit honesty like this, but her kindness and nonjudgmental ear are things I've really missed. When was the last time I had that? Before I became an influencer, definitely. I lost a lot of friends when my life became about content and I started documenting everything instead of living it. Turned every girls' night into a photo shoot, every brunch into content. Some friends loved being part of it, others pulled back. By the time

I realized I needed better boundaries, my circle had gotten smaller without me noticing. They tried to tell me I was losing myself, and by the time I realized they were right, they'd already stopped calling.

My phone buzzes on the counter. Brenda's name fills the screen. **Wren, we need to discuss your contracts NOW.**

"Everything okay?" Noa asks, noticing me tense.

"Work," I say on a sigh, setting my phone on the counter face down. "I've been dodging calls, but…"

"But?"

"But I can't hide forever." I take another bite of delicious comfort. "My job follows me everywhere, and I came here to get away from it."

Noa's quiet for a moment. "You know, when things feel overwhelming, sometimes you just need your own space to think. No pressure, but there's an apartment above the bookstore. The owner's been trying to rent it out. Marcus is pretty flexible on terms."

"An apartment?" The idea of my own space, somewhere that isn't Saint's guesthouse but isn't leaving Falcon Haven either, unties the knot in my chest.

"Two rooms, lots of light. The radiator's noisy, but the location's perfect. You could walk everywhere, really explore the town you came here to see."

"How do you know the owner?"

"Small town." She smiles. "Want me to see if he can show it today?"

"Please." I nod eagerly. "That would be amazing."

Noa pulls out her phone, texts rapidly, then looks up with a smile. "Marcus says he can meet you there in an hour. It's literally just across the street and two doors down."

"Thank you," I say, meaning it from the bottom of my heart. The idea of somewhere neutral, somewhere that isn't charged with memories of Saint's hands and Ivy's laughter, feels like the lifeline I desperately need.

My phone buzzes again. Brenda's face appears on my screen, this time for an actual call. I can't avoid her forever.

"I should take this," I say, reaching for my wallet.

Noa waves me off. "Go ahead. Your food will be here when you're done."

I step outside onto the sidewalk, the morning sun warming my shoulders as I answer.

"Hey, Brenda."

"Eight days, Wrenley. Eight days of minimal contact." Her voice is tight with professional restraint. "Do you have any idea what I've been dealing with? Sponsors are threatening to pull contracts. Your legal team is having kittens."

I lean against the brick wall of the café, closing my eyes. "I know. I'm sorry."

"Sorry doesn't pay your bills or mine. Look, I've managed to hold them off, but we need to discuss your options. You said you marinated. Does that mean you like the idea of getting to know the gorgeous Mr. Toussaint?"

Oh, if only she knew.

"I can't go back to posting like nothing happened," I hedge instead of answering. "I just can't, Brenda."

There's a pause, then her tone softens slightly. "I'm not asking you to pretend the attack didn't happen, Wren. Or your breakdown after. But it's been a few weeks since your last post, the one that went, you know … viral. People are worried after seeing you like that, but they're also starting to forget. If you're going to come back, now's the time."

My fingers instinctively rise to my shoulder, where the worst of it burns. However, the terror of that night, the help-lessness as hands grabbed me in the dark of my hotel room, and the sound of my own screaming when security finally arrived…

I'd always had a problem pulling, cutting, and scratching. But it was under control. Hidden. Until that night.

"I don't know if I can," I whisper.

"You have three major contracts you need to fulfill. Unless you want to be sued into oblivion, we need a plan." Brenda's voice is gentle but firm. "But we can modify. Small steps. No live streams for now. No events."

My mind churns, calculating options. "What if … what if I documented my temporary, small-town life? Nothing personal. Just scenery. No actual locations. The town square. No faces, no names. I already have a few saved videos to start with."

Brenda sighs. "That could work for the lifestyle brand, but the cosmetics line and the athleisure contract…"

"I'll figure something out. I can take long-range photos of myself with a timer."

"They want close-ups," Brenda says quietly. "Which is why you haven't posted anything since—"

"I know." I cut her off sharper than intended. A woman walking by with her dog glances over, and I lower my voice. "But I also know what happens if I breach the contract."

"Wren." Brenda's tone shifts, becoming the voice of the woman who's been my advocate for three years, not just my agent. "Talk to me. Really tell me what you can do. Because what happened in that hotel room … and then when you tried to go live to let your followers know you were okay, but you couldn't stop shaking … honey, that wasn't just a bad day. That was trauma."

Trauma. Such a clinical term for the way I claw at myself when I'm alone in the dark. For the way I check locks three times now. For the scars on my shoulder that Saint kissed so gently last night.

"I can't talk about it on camera," I whisper. "I can't have millions of people watching me fall apart again."

"Then don't. We'll work around it." Her voice is firm now, back in problem-solving mode. "Okay, so small-town content. Nature shots. Oh! Maybe some cooking if you're up for it. People love that cozy, domestic stuff. No personal details, no locations that could identify where you are."

"And the contracts?"

"I'll renegotiate. Tell them you're taking a wellness break and focusing on mental health. It's trendy now. Brands eat that authenticity up."

I almost laugh at the irony. My authentic breakdown went viral, and now we're going to package my recovery for consumption, too.

"Okay," I say finally. "I'll call you tomorrow with a content schedule."

I end the call before she can probe further.

When I return to my seat, the chicken fried steak has gone cold, but I eat it anyway. The grease and salt feel appropriate for my current emotional state.

"Better?" Noa asks.

"Clearer, anyway." I take a long sip of lukewarm coffee. "Thank you for listening. And for the apartment lead."

"That's what neighbors do." She smiles. "And Wrenley? Whatever brought you here, whatever you're running from, this town has a way of helping people figure things out. Give it time."

An hour later, I'm standing in front of Cornerstone Books, a narrow three-story building with forest-green shutters and window boxes full of late-season mums after receiving the grand tour, which took all of ten minutes.

"I'll take it," I say to Marcus.
Marcus hands me the keys.

onday morning arrives like a hangover I didn't earn.

Erin shows up at six sharp, wheeling a teacher's tote behind her and wearing a smile that's trying too hard.

She's everything I thought I needed. She's Ivy's preschool teacher, already knows Ivy's routine, and has glowing references from every parent in town.

She's also wearing enough perfume to choke a horse.

"Good morning, Mr. Toussaint!" Her voice hits a pitch that makes my teeth ache. "I'm so excited to start this journey with you and Ivy!"

Journey. Christ.

"It's just Saint," I tell her for the millionth time since we've met. "Ivy's upstairs. She's..." I pause, searching for the right word. Devastated? Betrayed? "Adjusting."

"Of course! Transitions can be challenging for little ones. I have several techniques for managing attachment disruption."

Attachment disruption.

Is that what we're calling it when I ripped away the one person who made my daughter laugh?

"She likes her eggs scrambled, not too dry," I say instead of what I'm thinking. "No foods touching on the plate. She's particular about how her entrée is organized."

"I've reviewed all the notes you sent." Erin pulls out a fucking tablet. "I've actually created a structured routine that should optimize her development while maintaining consistency."

Optimize.

"My five-year-old isn't a restaurant operation."

"Oh—not at all! I just meant that children form attachments *fast*, especially motherless ones who've had rotating caretakers, and I'm taking all of that into account to make sure she's all right after … what was her name? Some kind of bird, right? I'm sure she might've given Ivy some bad habits."

"Wrenley." My voice drops to a temperature that usually sends line cooks scrambling. "Her name is Wrenley."

Erin's smile falters. "Right. Well, I'm sure she did her best, but it's difficult to manage an exuberant child like Ivy without proper training."

"She made my daughter happy."

I let that hang in the air, simple, damning, and expectant.

"Papa?" Ivy appears on the stairs in her pajamas, clutching her favorite plushy unicorn, Mr. Pawesome. "Is Miss Wrenley coming back today?"

The hope in her voice guts me.

"Miss Erin's here to help with mornings now, remember? Then she'll take you to school."

"I don't want her." Ivy wrinkles her nose. "She smells weird."

"It's not nice to say those things out loud, Ivy," Erin scolds.

"Like the candle store that makes you sneeze," Ivy continues unabashed. She backs up a step, then repeats, "I want Miss Wrenley."

"Wrenley was never meant to be your nanny, *mon trésor*. We've talked about this."

At length. For hours last night.

Erin's smile stays in place. "Are you ready to pick out clothes for school? We could wear your butterfly shirt!"

Ivy looks at her like she's violated something sacred. "I *hate* butterflies."

"No, you do not." I fold my arms, losing patience. "Apologize to Miss Erin right now."

Ivy turns and runs back upstairs.

"That's perfectly normal," Erin assures me, though I didn't ask. "She's just testing boundaries."

"Right." I grab my keys, already late for prep. "I need to get to the restaurant."

"Don't worry about a thing! We'll have a wonderful morning and be at school right on time!"

I leave before I say something I'll regret, Ivy's muffled crying following me out the door.

C'est Trois's kitchen is already humming when I arrive. Eddie, my new sous chef, has the prep cooks started on basics, but he takes one look at my face and wisely doesn't comment on my mood.

"Special's already on the board," he says. "Duck confit with cherry reduction."

"Fine." I tie on my apron with sharp movements. "Where are we on the Henderson anniversary order?"

"Chocolate soufflé's ready to go. Just needs your final touch."

I nod, falling into the rhythm of knife work. This, at least, makes sense. Blade meets board, ingredients transform, and order emerges from a complete mess. No complications. No pink-haired women who smell like sun-soaked vacations and make me forget why feeling nothing is safer.

"I heard that new girl in town, Wrenley something, moved into the apartment above Cornerstone Books."

My knife slips enough to send a carrot rolling across the board.

"It's not often we see a new face that's not an annoying tourist," the garde manger continues. A young guy with plenty of pimples. "And she's hot."

"*So* fucking hot," the saucier chimes in.

"You've seen her content?"

"Wait, what?"

"Dude! She's on social media. She's like an influencer or some shit. Has two million followers. Or I should say, had. Have you seen the video that went viral?"

"What are you talking about?"

They're huddled by the cold station, thinking I'm absorbed in my prep. The lunch rush hasn't hit yet, that twenty-minute window when discipline loosens slightly. They've got a phone out between them, heads bent together like teen boys.

"Here, look." The garde manger angles his phone. "This was from three weeks ago. Twenty million views."

I should cut them off at the knees right fucking now. There's no gossip in my kitchen, and there sure as fuck is no idle talk about Wrenley Morgan. But their revelations don't come as a surprise.

Of course I'd done my research on Wrenley before letting her near Ivy. Found her social media, saw the follower count and the sponsored posts. She had two million people watching her curated life. I'd scrolled back through months of content with her bright smiles, perfect outfits, and multiple "latest hot spot" posts.

Then nothing. Six months of radio silence until three weeks ago.

But when I'd clicked on that most recent post, it was gone. *This content is no longer available.* The comments below were turned off. Whatever had happened three weeks ago, she'd scrubbed it clean.

I'd screenshot her profile, done a background check, and verified she had no criminal record. That was enough due diligence for a temporary fix while I found a real nanny, and with Celeste's assurance that Wrenley's online drama was long finished, I'd trusted my gut.

Except now my garde manger has it pulled up on his phone.

"My girlfriend screen-recorded it before Wrenley deleted everything. She saves all the influencer drama."

"Jesus, is she crying?"

"Full breakdown, man. She was trying to film a 'life update.' Look."

The phone's volume is too high. Another indication that I should make these idiots shit their pants for their insubordination before this goes any further. But I don't move because curiosity doesn't just kill cats.

Wrenley's voice fills my kitchen in a shaking, guttural tone I've never heard come out of her mouth.

"I know everyone's been asking where I've been for months. I'm sorry. I'm so fucking sorry." Her voice is thick with tears. "I tried to come back. Tried to be normal. But I…"

A sob cuts through. The sound ignites a wildfire in my throat, and my head shoots up, staring holes into the staff huddled around the phone.

"In Miami, some guy got my hotel key. Paid off a desk clerk. Two thousand dollars to get into my room." Her breath comes in gasps. "I woke up to him straddling me. His hands in my hair. His tongue—"

My knife drives into the cutting board with enough force to split wood.

"When I screamed, he wrapped his hands around my throat. Told me I'd been teasing him for three years. That every good morning video was meant for him. That I owed him for all the times he defended me in the comments section."

The rage building inside me is volcanic. Murderous.

"Hotel security found us because I triggered the fire alarm. Broke a wine bottle over his head first. But he'd already—" Her voice cracks. "Fifteen minutes. That's how long he was in my room before I woke up. Taking photos. Touching me. Collecting souvenirs."

"Holy fuck," someone whispers.

"It took months of therapy, but I thought I could push through. So I turned on the camera one day. I tried to film again. But I just froze. Because behind every username, every avatar, every 'love you bestie' comment, could be another him. When I looked at the camera, all I could see were the thousands of strangers who thought they owned pieces of me, too."

The prep counter's metal edge cuts into my palms. I'm leaning on it hard enough to break through skin.

"The police asked what I was wearing in my videos. If I'd been 'suggestive.' The detective, while taking photos of the bruises on my neck, said, 'Well, you do put yourself out there.'" Wrenley's voice empties. "As if posting makeup tutorials meant I consented to a stranger trying to rape me."

"What the fuck," someone breathes.

"My safety was sold for money. And when they caught him, his lawyer argued I'd been 'inviting attention.' That my videos were 'intimate invitations.'"

The paring knife slips. My thumb's bleeding before I register the cut.

"The comments were worse. 'What did she expect?' 'She made herself a target.' 'Play stupid games, win stupid prizes.' Two million people watched me build a career, then told me I deserved to be violated for it."

My bleeding thumb throbs in time with my heartbeat. The pain is nothing.

"So here's what 'asking for it' looks like at 3 a.m. When I wake up feeling his weight on me, when I can't breathe, I dig my nails in until skin splits. See these trenches in my chest? That's from reading comments about how I should be grateful he didn't do worse."

My jaw locks so hard my teeth ache. Blood from my hand drips steadily onto the cutting board.

"This bald spot above my ear? From the night someone DM'd my old account to prove how easy I was to find. Pulled out a fistful of hair because at least that was my choice. My pain. My control."

A broken sound escapes her throat.

"At least when I hurt myself, it's someone who actually wants me to survive doing it. That's more than I can say for the rest of you who are enjoying my trauma."

I'm moving before I realize it. The prep table flips with a

crash that shakes the entire kitchen. Plates shatter. *Mise en place* goes flying while I roar, "GET OUT."

"Chef?"

I grab the nearest pan and hurl it across the kitchen. It hits the wall with a crash that makes everyone jump.

"I said GET THE FUCK OUT."

They run. Actually run. The kitchen empties in ten seconds flat.

I stand there, chest heaving, seeing it all differently now. The way she'd frozen while a scream wrecked her throat when I burst into the guesthouse to get her out of the storm. How she'd shut down when I noticed the scars on her shoulder. The panic in her eyes when I asked who hurt her.

She'd hurt herself.

And when she finally found peace—in my home, with my daughter, in my bed—I took that away, too.

I'm no better than every other person who's failed to protect her.

Pacing the kitchen, I find an abandoned knife at another prep station. I grab it, needing something to do.

The knife goes into a cutting board. Again. Again. The wood splits further with each strike.

For months, she's been carrying this. Months of jumping at shadows, of cutting herself to feel alive, of apologizing for surviving.

Then she came here. Let Ivy hug her. Let me touch her. Started to smile again.

Until I proved she was right not to trust anyone.

"FUCK."

The word tears from my throat as I grab the entire cutting board and send it flying. It hits the dish pit with a spectacular crash.

Eddie appears in the doorway, takes one look at my face,

and backs away slowly, hands raised. "Was it the wrong time for me to take a ciggie break?"

"I'm closing lunch service," I tell him.

"I can see that."

"Anyone who has a problem with that can find another job."

Eddie doesn't move from the doorway. "You want to tell me what's going on?"

"No."

He surveys the destruction. "I'll call the Henderson party. Tell them we had an equipment failure."

I start to untie my apron, but I force myself to stop. To think.

Every instinct screams to go to Wrenley. To fix this. To prove she's safe here.

But that's what I want. Not what she needs.

She came here to disappear. To heal without an audience. And what would I be doing if I showed up at her door right now? Adding to the list of people who won't leave her alone.

"I need to pick up Ivy," I say instead.

"It's barely noon."

"I need my daughter."

Eddie nods slowly. "What about the kitchen?"

I look around. Shattered plates. Overturned prep. My blood on the cutting board. "Clean it up. We'll open for dinner."

I leave through the back, stepping into an alley that suddenly feels too bright. Too normal. Like the world should have shifted after what I just heard.

My phone buzzes, and it's a text from Erin. **Ivy had a rough morning, but she's doing better now! We're working on letters!**

Attached is a photo of my daughter at her desk, face turned away from the camera.

Ivy's not doing better. She's just stopped fighting.

I pocket the phone and start walking.

TWENTY
WRENLEY

'**ve** spent the morning arranging my three pieces of furniture: bed, chair, questionable desk from a yard sale, and pretending this new apartment feels like home.

My phone's propped against the window while I film the rearranging (my second one this week), narrating something about "small-town rhythms" that sounds peaceful enough.

It took twenty-seven takes to get my voice steady enough to record a voice-over. Hopefully, my followers won't be able to tell. I'm confident that the nicer, loyal ones will heart the post and comment about how happy I look and how brave I am for starting over. No one needs to know that I've been walking the long way around town to avoid a certain restaurant, or that I tested my ring light at 3 a.m. when sleep wouldn't come.

The bookstore's cat, Ralph, wandered up earlier and made himself at home on my unmade bed. I captured a pic of that, too, to post in addition to the video content.

Ralph's orange fur looks like a sunrise against my pale blue sheets. He's become my first friend in this apartment, appearing each morning to weave through my legs and demand attention before slinking back downstairs to his official bookstore duties.

"You're not supposed to be up here," I tell him, scratching under his chin. "But I won't tell if you don't."

He purrs in response, utterly unconcerned with boundaries or social media contracts or the fact that I keep looking out my window toward the road that leads to Saint's restaurant.

I check my phone, and there are already five comments on the new post. My thumb hovers over the notification, but I force myself *not* to read them. Not yet.

Baby steps, like Brenda said.

The apartment above Cornerstone Books is exactly what I needed. Cozy, private, with tall windows that catch the setting sun.

Marcus charges me a laughably low rent, and the location lets me pretend I'm establishing a routine. Coffee from Libby Jude's. Fresh produce from the farmers' market. Afternoon walks along Main Street, where I nod at shopkeepers who've started recognizing me.

Five days of this new normal. Five days since I left the guesthouse.

Five days without seeing either Saint or Ivy.

That part hurts most of all. I've caught myself reaching for my phone a dozen times to text Saint and ask how she's doing with Erin. Is she still fighting the transition? Is she painting trees? Has she convinced anyone to get her a ferret yet?

But what would I even say? *Hey, just checking if your daughter still misses me as much as I miss her. Oh, and how's that qualified nanny working out after our meaningless hookup?*

"This is pathetic," I mutter, setting my phone down.

Ralph meows in agreement.

I need to get out of this apartment and do something productive besides filming myself arranging throw pillows.

Falcon Haven is full of picturesque spots I haven't explored yet. The gazebo in the town square. The covered bridge just outside of town. The nature trail that winds along the creek. Perfect backdrops for casual, non-threatening content that won't trigger my anxiety or breach any contracts.

I throw on a blue sweater and my most comfortable pair of ripped jeans, grab my phone, and head downstairs. The bookstore is quiet this morning, just Marcus reorganizing a display and one elderly customer browsing the mystery section.

"Morning, Wrenley," Marcus calls. "Ralph abandon his post again?"

"Afraid so. He's claimed my bed as his new territory."

Marcus chuckles. "Let me know if he becomes a nuisance."

"Never," I promise, pausing at the door. "Hey, is there a walking trail nearby? Something scenic but not too strenuous?"

"Maple Creek Trail starts about three blocks east. Can't miss it. Beautiful this time of year."

"Thanks, Marcus." I duck out the door and head east, exhaling in a way that would make my online yoga instructor proud when the cool autumn air kisses my cheeks.

This is good for me. It's exactly why I came to Falcon Haven in the first place. Saint was just a … an interlude. A sexy one. An irresistible one.

An *unobtainable* one.

The trail appears exactly where Marcus said it would, marked by a weathered wooden sign. Fallen leaves crunch beneath my sneakers as I follow the winding path deeper into the woods. The canopy above shifts from green to gold to fiery red, creating a kaleidoscope effect when sunlight filters through.

Perfect for content. I lift my phone, framing a shot of the tunnel of trees ahead, then add a voice-over about finding peace in nature. It sounds almost convincing, even to me.

I'm twenty minutes into the hike when I reach a small wooden bridge spanning Maple Creek. The water below rushes over smooth stones, creating a soothing soundtrack. I lean against the railing, my muscles relaxing for the first time in days.

My phone buzzes. Brenda again, this time with a screenshot of my latest post's engagement numbers. They're climbing, but nowhere near what they used to be. The message below reads: **Good start. Ready to show your face yet?**

I ignore it, slipping the phone back into my pocket.

Farther down the trail, I find a small clearing with a fallen log. I position my phone on a nearby stump, setting the timer for a long-range shot of me looking contemplatively into the distance.

The camera clicks three times before I hear footsteps on the trail behind me.

I turn, expecting to see another hiker, but my breath catches when I spot a familiar small figure in purple boots picking her way carefully over the roots.

"Miss Wrenley!" Ivy's voice carries across the clearing, bright with joy and disbelief.

My heart stops. She's alone, which can't be right. I scan the trail behind her, but there's no sign of an adult.

"Ivy?" I'm already moving toward her, my stomach clenching with worry. "Sweetie, where's your dad? Where's Miss Erin?"

"I runned away," she announces, like it's the most reasonable thing in the world. "Miss Erin was being mean, and I told her I was going to the bathroom, but I went outside instead."

Oh god. "Ivy, how did you find this trail? How long have you been walking?"

She shrugs. "I asked Mr. Marcus where you went, and he told me about maple tree paths. It wasn't very far."

My mind races. Saint must be frantic. The school must have called him. And here's his five-year-old daughter, alone in the woods because she ran away from school.

"We need to call your papa right now," I say, backtracking enough to grab my phone off the log. "He's probably so worried—"

"No!" Ivy wraps around my thigh with surprising strength. "Please don't call him yet. I missed you so much, Miss Wrenley. Miss Erin doesn't know anything. She tried to make me eat eggs with cheese, and she said my unicorn drawings were 'unrealistic.'"

Her little face crumples, and my heart breaks all over again. I crouch down to her level, smoothing her wind-tangled hair.

"Oh, honey. I've missed you too. So much. But running away isn't safe. Your papa must be terrified."

"He doesn't care," she says, voice small and defeated. "He likes Miss Erin better. She talks to him about 'devopmental milestones' and uses big words."

The pain in her voice guts me. I pull her into a hug, breathing in her familiar scent of strawberry shampoo and playground mulch.

"That's not true, Ivy. Your papa loves you more than anything in the world."

"Then why did he make you leave?"

Oh, man. How do I explain adult complications to a five-year-old? How do I tell her that sometimes people make smart choices that still can hurt everyone involved?

"It's complicated, sweetie. Sometimes grown-ups make choices that seem right but feel wrong."

Ivy assesses me with her little perceptive face. She's so direct that it makes me want to avert my eyes.

"I missed you so much. Papa's being extra grumpy, and he burned the toast three times yesterday, and he keeps staring at his phone like it might blow up."

My chest tightens at the image of Saint struggling just as much as I am. But I push that thought away. I can't let myself hope that his difficulty means anything beyond parental stress.

"We still need to call him," I say gently. "He's probably calling the police right now."

Ivy's bottom lip trembles. "Can't we just stay here for a little bit? Please? I promise I'll go back, but I haven't seen you in forever, and Miss Erin said you probably forgot about me."

The casual cruelty of that comment makes my teeth clank together. What kind of person tells a grieving child that someone who loves her has forgotten her?

"Ivy, listen to me." I cup her small face in my hands. "I could never, ever forget about you. You're one of the most important people in my whole world."

Her expression brightens. "Really?"

"Really. But that's exactly why we need to get you back safely. Because people who love each other don't let each other worry."

My pulse picks up when I find Saint's contact, then turns into a hammer when I press the green button and put the phone to my ear.

It rings once before he answers.

"Wrenley?" he rasps. "Please tell me you've seen Ivy."

"I have her," I say quickly. "She's safe. She's with me."

The sound that escapes him is one of pure relief, mixed with something that might be a sob. "Thank Christ. Where are you?"

"Maple Creek Trail. About half a mile in, at the wooden bridge."

"Don't move. I'm coming to get her."

"Saint, wait—"

But he's already hung up.

I slide the phone back into my pocket and sit on the fallen log, pulling Ivy onto my lap. She burrows against me like she's trying to absorb my essence through her skin.

"Is Papa mad?" she asks in a quiet voice.

"He's scared," I assure her, "and maybe a little panicky."

"Are you mad at me?"

"Never." I press a kiss to the top of her head. "But you can't run away again, okay? It's dangerous."

Ivy sighs dramatically. "Grown-up rules are stupid."

Heavy, rapid footsteps on the trail cut our conversation short. My heart lurches into my throat as Saint thunders around the bend, moving with a single-minded focus that makes my pulse trip.

He looks like hell. Dark shadows cup his eyes and his jaw sports several days of stubble. His clothes are rumpled like he slept in them—or didn't sleep at all. The sleeves of his button-down are rolled haphazardly, revealing the tattoos I traced with my fingertips four nights ago.

Ivy stiffens in my arms, pressing closer to me.

"Papa's really mad," she whispers.

Saint reaches us in four long strides, dropping to his knees in front of us. "Ivy. Don't you *ever*—"

His voice breaks, and he pulls her from my lap into a crushing embrace.

Saint buries his face in her hair, his shoulders trembling once before he locks them rigid again.

I rise to my feet, suddenly unsure what to do with my hands. Saint's eyes finally lift to mine over Ivy's head, and for one unguarded moment, he lets me see everything. His relief, exhaustion, and a shine that might be tears before he blinks, and the shutters come down.

"Miss Wrenley didn't know I was coming," Ivy says. "Don't be mad at her."

Saint sets Ivy down but keeps his hand firmly on her shoulder. "Go wait by that big oak tree. I need to talk to Miss Wrenley."

"But—"

"Now, Ivy."

She throws me one last worried glance before trudging to the tree, just far enough away that she can't hear us but close enough that Saint can watch her.

The moment she's out of earshot, Saint turns to me, tension vibrating through every fiber of his body.

"She could have been kidnapped. Hit by a car. Fallen into the creek." His voice is low, controlled, but with an undercurrent of something volcanic. "Do you have any idea what it was like getting that call from the school?"

"I can imagine," I say quietly.

"No, you can't." He runs a hand through his hair, which is already standing on end like he's been doing that all morning. "She's never run away before. Not once. Then suddenly she disappears from school to find you."

The accusation lands like a slap. "Are you blaming me for this?"

"I'm—" He cuts himself off, jaw working. "No. I'm not."

We stand facing each other, the rushing creek providing white noise for all the things we're not saying.

"I just..." Saint looks away, his profile sharp against the backdrop of autumn trees. "I spent two hours thinking I'd lost her."

The open fear in his voice makes my heart throb. I want to touch him, to offer comfort, but the distance between us feels wider than the creek.

"She said Erin told her I'd forgotten about her," I say softly.

Saint's head snaps back to me. "What?"

"Among other things. Apparently, she's also critiquing Ivy's art.'"

A muscle jumps under his eye. "I'll handle that."

"She misses me, Saint." I wrap my arms around myself, suddenly cold despite my sweater. "And I miss her."

His eyes search mine so thoroughly, I feel like my soul was just examined. "Just her?"

The question, those two simple words, sends a tingle all the way from my head to my toes.

"No," I admit, holding his gaze. "Not just her."

Saint takes a half step toward me. "Wrenley..."

"Papa!" Ivy calls from her tree. "Can Miss Wrenley come back with us? Please?"

Saint's expression shutters again, professional mask sliding back into place. "We need to get you back to school, Ivy."

"But it's almost lunchtime! Can't we have lunch with Miss Wrenley instead?"

I see the refusal forming on his lips and jump in before he can crush her. "I should get back anyway. I have some work to do."

"What kind of work?" Ivy skips back to us. "Can I help?"

"Maybe next time," I say to her with a forced smile.

Saint's eyes flick to my phone, still clutched in my hand.

There's a shift in his expression, a darkening, a kind of recognition that makes my stomach drop.

"Are you back to making content for your followers?" he asks quietly.

I freeze. "How did you know?"

"Papa knows everything," Ivy announces, oblivious to the sudden tension. "He's magic."

Saint's gaze doesn't waver from mine.

"Not everything," he says, and there's an implication in his tone that makes me wonder exactly what he knows—or thinks he knows—about me.

"I should go," I repeat, taking a step back.

"Wrenley." Saint's voice stops me. "Thank you. For calling. For keeping her safe."

"Always," I say, meaning it more than he could know.

Ivy lunges forward, wrapping her arms around my waist in a fierce hug. "Promise you won't forget me?"

I crouch down, meeting her at eye level. "I could never forget you, Ivy Toussaint. Not in a million years."

She nods solemnly, then whispers, "Papa misses you, too. He just won't say it."

Saint's sharp intake of breath tells me he heard her whisper. When I straighten, his face is carved from stone, but an unnamed pain ripples behind his eyes.

"Ivy. Time to go."

She deflates but obeys, slipping her small hand into his. I turn to leave, needing distance before I do something ridiculous like beg him to let me back into their lives.

"Wrenley."

I pause but don't turn around. Can't. Not when his voice sounds like gravel and yearning, a tone he reserves just for me.

"The apartment above the bookstore. Is it ... are you comfortable there?"

The question catches me off guard. I glance over my shoulder. Neither he nor Ivy has moved.

"It's nice," I say.

"The radiator in that building is ancient. Marcus should have—" He stops himself, cheek muscles popping against his stubble. "Never mind."

"He's giving me a great deal on the place." I shift my feet. "How did you know where I'm living?"

A ghost of a smile touches his lips. "Small town."

"Right." I take another step away. "I really should get going."

"You look good."

The observation stops me cold. "So do you."

Saint would look good half drowned and covered in dead fish. He'd look amazing dressed in a paper bag. Even now, when he's exhausted, rumpled, and looking like he's been subsisting on rage and coffee, he's devastating. The stubble just makes him look more dangerous. The wrinkled shirt draws attention to his shoulders and the way the fabric pulls when he moves. And those shadows under his eyes? They just make me want to drag him to bed.

For sleep. Obviously. Just sleep.

"Papa, you're staring again," Ivy observes.

Heat creeps up my neck.

Saint blinks, the moment fracturing. "Come on, *mon trèsor*. Let's get you fed."

I glance at Ivy, whose face has fallen. "Maybe I could walk you both back to town? Make sure she doesn't stage another escape attempt?"

Ivy brightens immediately. "Yes! And you can tell me about your new apartment! Does it have good hiding spots?"

"Ivy," Saint warns.

"What? I'm just asking for future reference."

Ivy slips between us, grabbing my hand with her left and Saint's with her right. "This is perfect! Just like before!"

Saint and I carefully don't look at each other as we start walking, Ivy chattering about everything she's done in the past five days. Each detail is a small knife—how she tried to make cookies with Miss Erin, but they turned out "crunchy in the wrong way," how she painted a picture of me, but Miss Erin said it was "nice but maybe focus on something else now."

"She sounds..." I search for a neutral word. "Structured."

"She has a degree in early childhood development." Saint's voice is carefully neutral.

"I'm sure that's very helpful."

"It is."

"Good."

"Great."

"Papa, you're doing the thing where you say words but mean other words," Ivy observes.

Saint's mouth twitches. "I don't do that."

"You literally do it all the time," I say before I can stop myself.

His eyes meet mine over Ivy's head, and for a second, I see affection flash through them. "Maybe you just think you know what I mean."

"Maybe I do."

"Maybe you're wrong."

"Maybe I'm not."

"Are you two going to kiss?" Ivy asks helpfully. "Because that would fix everything."

TWENTY-ONE
SAINT

vy's words splash into my face like cold water. Pink creeps up Wrenley's face.

"Kisses don't fix everything, baby," I say, my voice tight.

"They fixed it when Sleeping Beauty was asleep," Ivy counters. "And when the frog was a frog. And when—"

"Those are fairy tales."

The words come out harsher than they should.

Ivy's face falls. "Oh."

Wrenley squeezes her hand. "But hugs help a lot. Can I have one of those?"

Ivy launches herself at Wrenley with the enthusiasm of someone who's been starved for affection. Wrenley catches her easily, lifting her off the ground in a spinning hug that makes Ivy giggle.

The sound punches through my ribs. I haven't heard that particular laugh in five days. The one that's pure joy, uninhibited and bright. I'm struck by how natural they look together.

How right. Wrenley's eyes drift shut as she holds my daughter.

"Better?" Wrenley asks, opening her eyes with a smile and setting Ivy down.

"Much better." Ivy beams up at her. "Papa needs one too. He's been extra cranky since you left."

"I'm standing right here," I mutter.

"That's why I said it loud enough for you to hear," Ivy replies pertly.

Wrenley stares at me, chewing on her lower lip. The sight has me wanting to bite her lip for her, and maybe run my tongue along it after.

I should snap out of it. Retreat. Maintain the distance I've worked so hard to create.

Instead, I move closer.

"Saint."

My name on her tongue is the barest of sounds.

Her arms come around me tentatively, like she's afraid I'll bolt. When I don't, they tighten around my waist, pulling me into her warmth.

My hands span the narrow width of her back. She's so much smaller than I remember, more fragile.

One of my hands ends up tangling in her hair, bringing her closer. I let myself sink into the hug for just a moment, plunging into the sweet scent of her hair, the way she fits against me like she was made for this exact space.

Like the past five days of pretending I didn't need this exact feeling were a complete waste of time.

"This is nice," Ivy announces from somewhere near our knees. "Now Papa doesn't look like he wants to punch trees anymore."

Wrenley's laugh vibrates against my chest.

But she pulls back first, her cheeks flushed. "We should keep going."

The walk continues with Ivy filling up most of the space between us. She also breaks the charged silence by chatting about everything from squirrel behavior to cloud shapes, though my attention keeps drifting to Wrenley. The way she moves beside me. How she automatically shortens her stride to match Ivy's. The soft smile that appears whenever my daughter says something particularly ridiculous.

But whenever Wrenley's phone vibrates in her back pocket, her entire body goes rigid. The first few times, she pulled it out, glanced at the screen, then silenced it before shoving it back into her jeans. This time, there's something in the way her shoulders hunch forward before she lifts her head, scanning the perimeter while she clenches her phone.

Alarm bells go off in my head.

"Everything okay?" I ask as we approach the town square.

"Fine." Her smile doesn't reach her eyes. "Just work stuff."

A car backfires somewhere down the street, and Wrenley flinches so hard she nearly crumples to the ground. My hand shoots out to steady her, but she's already pulled away, composing herself with visible effort.

"Is that where you live now?" Ivy points at the upper windows of Cornerstone Books.

"That's right," Wrenley confirms, but her attention is divided. She glances over her shoulder, scanning the street behind us.

"Can we see it?" Ivy bounces on her toes. "Please?"

"Another time," I tell her without taking my focus off Wrenley. "I'm not about to reward you for running off, *mon trésor*."

"Fiiiiiiiine."

While Ivy examines a particularly interesting rock on the sidewalk, I ask Wrenley quietly, "Are you sure you're all right?"

Wrenley nods while rubbing her lips together.

She's lying. I've seen this look before, on the sous chef who worked for me in Paris after he was mugged. Hyper-vigilance.

"You don't have to tell me what's going on," I say, keeping my voice low enough that Ivy can't hear, "but don't lie to me either."

Wrenley's eyes snap to mine, wide and startled. The truth sends shock waves of raw fear across her face before she masks it with a half-smile.

"Sorry. Just jumpy lately." She tucks her phone deeper into her pocket, fingers lingering there like she expects it to bite her if she moves away too fast. "Comes with the territory."

I pretend ignorance. "What territory?"

She hesitates, and I can almost translate the internal debate playing across her features.

Her phone buzzes again. This time, she doesn't even check it. She just presses her lips together so hard they turn white.

"Wrenley." I step into her space. "What happened in Miami?"

Her entire body goes still.

"Papa, look!" Ivy interrupts, holding up a leaf shaped like a perfect heart. "It's a love leaf! Miss Wrenley, you should keep it!"

Wrenley accepts the gift with a trembling hand and a mega-watt smile. "Thank you, sweetie."

"Why don't you come by the restaurant tonight?" The words tumble out before I can catch them. "For dinner."

Wrenley's eyes return to mine, wary and uncertain.

"Please, Miss Wrenley?" Ivy abandons her nature hunt to tug at Wrenley's heart. "Papa makes the best pasta on Thursdays."

"It's just dinner," I add, trying to keep my voice casual when there's nothing casual about this invitation. "No expectations."

A lie. I have a thousand expectations, most of them involving answers to questions I shouldn't ask.

"All right," she says finally, "What time?"

"Seven?" I suggest. "After the early rush."

Wrenley's phone buzzes again, drawing my attention to the way her grip tightens around it. Her eyes dart toward the bookstore, then back to me.

"Seven works," she says, but her voice lacks conviction.

"Are you sleeping okay?" I ask without thinking. "Your light was on at 3 a.m. last night again."

Wrenley freezes. "How would you know that?"

Shit. I rub the back of my neck. "Uh, the window of my back office faces the bookstore."

At her concentrated stare, I add, "I'm usually there until two or three. The kitchen needs cleaning after service, and there's always paperwork."

"And you can't help checking on me?" she asks. I'm relieved when it's followed by a slight uptick to her mouth.

"I just want you to know you're safe," I confess before I can second-guess it. She looks like she needs someone to say it to her.

And mean it.

Ivy looks between us, curiosity blooming on her face.

"Safe," Wrenley repeats, like she's testing the word for authenticity. "That's..." She swallows hard. "Thank you."

Her simple gratitude ignites a ferocity in my chest usually

reserved for Ivy. It makes me want to hunt down whoever caused her to be this scared in a cozy small town.

"Miss Wrenley has a cat in her apartment," Ivy announces, clearly bored with our adult conversation. "Marcus told me. His name is Ralph, and he's orange."

"He's the bookstore cat," Wrenley clarifies, grateful for the subject change. "I pretty much pay the rent to him, not Marcus."

"Can I meet him tonight? After dinner?"

"Ivy," I warn.

"What? You said no rewards for running away. You didn't say anything about after-dinner visits to cats."

I fight a smile. My daughter, the lawyer. "We'll see."

Wrenley's phone buzzes yet again. This time, her face drains of all color as she glances at the screen.

"I should go," she says, her tone deceptively light.

Ivy wraps her arms around Wrenley's waist one more time. "Don't forget about dinner!"

"I won't." Wrenley extracts herself form Ivy's grip and backs toward the bookstore. "Promise."

I watch her retreat, noting how she keeps glancing around, scanning faces, checking corners. She doesn't turn her back fully until she reaches the bookstore door, and even then, she looks over her shoulder one last time before disappearing inside.

"Papa, is Miss Wrenley okay?"

Ivy's question mirrors my own thoughts.

"I don't know," I admit, keeping my eyes on the now-empty doorway. "But we're going to make sure she will be."

TWENTY-TWO
WRENLEY

Ralph watches blandly when I check my door lock three times.

"What?" I ask the orange cat sprawled on my bed. "I'm being thorough."

The cat offers a noncommittal yawn, stretching languidly across my pillow.

My phone vibrates on the nightstand, startling me. It's probably Brenda again, checking on the new content schedule I promised. Or maybe Saint, confirming dinner plans. My fingers twitch with the hope it's the latter.

But I know it's worse than that.

I shouldn't have checked my notifications while walking the trail with Ivy and Saint. But Saint's sudden, towering presence with sky-blue eyes that know too much and his arms wrapping around me, the ropes of his tendons and tattoos holding me against him like I'll never have anything to worry about again, forced me to find a distraction.

And so I did what I promised my therapist I wouldn't do.

My promise of no engagement, no scrolling, no obsessing over responses went out the goddamn window.

I chose the most innocuous post to check. The one with Ralph sleeping on my bed, captioned "Small-town life comes with built-in companions. #NewBeginnings #FreshStart."

Most comments were harmless.

So cute! Love this for you! That orange boy is everything!

But then I saw it.

Pink looks better in your hair than blue did. Though I miss the way you'd twist it around your finger when you talked to me through the camera. I miss watching you sleep, princess.

I'm shocked my legs didn't give out when I read it. I'm proud of how I handled myself in front of Saint and Ivy even though it took all my energy to keep it together until I climbed up the stairs to my apartment.

I deleted the comment instantly, of course, but it doesn't matter. He's out. He's seen my new content. He's found me again despite the multiple court orders telling him to fuck all the way off.

My chest constricts as I sink onto the edge of the bed. How? I've been so careful. No location tags, no identifiable landmarks. Nothing to connect me to Falcon Haven.

Yet somehow, he knows about my pink streak. Knows I've changed it.

But it might not be him. It could be a troll, fully aware of my situation and using it for clout. Trolls study influencers like specimens, learning our histories, our traumas, and crafting messages designed to destabilize us. It's sick, but it's not necessarily him.

Ralph pads over and butts his head against my elbow, purring.

"You're right," I tell him, scratching behind his ears. "I'm spiraling."

I should call the jail and make sure he's still there. Or call Brenda and ask her to check for me. Get off social media entirely, find a new job, a new country.

God, I used to *love* what I did. I found joy in everything that came with becoming an influencer: the planning, the editing, the content, the connections, and yes, the PR packages were never unwelcome. I couldn't imagine doing anything else. Not to mention what it did for my social anxiety and how I blossomed when I realized I could build a career around something I was naturally good at despite how much I fumbled through face-to-face conversations. I found confidence. I found happiness. I found *belonging*.

My hands won't stop shaking. The screen illuminates again, showing a text from Saint.

Still on for 7?

I stare at the message, my throat closing. I should cancel. Pack my things. Run again.

But I'm so tired of running.

I tap out a reply: **Yes. See you then.**

Ralph meows, clearly judging my life choices.

"It's just dinner," I tell him, though my heart pounds like I'm confessing to murder. "I'll be in public. Surrounded by people. He'll be busy in the kitchen."

My phone vibrates again with a notification from Instagram. I swipe it away without looking, then power off the device completely.

I need a shower. I need to wash off the trail dust and the sensation of Saint's arms around me and the lingering fear that someone dangerous knows where I am.

The bathroom is tiny, but the water pressure is surprisingly good. I stand under the hot spray for a long time, letting it sluice over my skin, trying to wash away the residue of fear.

It doesn't work.

The comment is seared into my brain, a brand mark over the fragile serenity I'd started to build.

Pink looks better.

I miss watching you sleep, princess.

I scrub at my hair with too much force, the pink a mocking reminder of my attempt to reclaim some part of myself.

After toweling off, I stare at my reflection. The woman looking back is a mess. Dark circles under her eyes, a tremor in her lips she can't quite control.

This is not the picture of a woman about to have a casual dinner date. But I promised Ivy. I promised Saint. And a small, treacherous part of me wants to go. Wants to sit in the warm glow of C'est Trois and see Saint in his element.

I choose a simple black dress and spend too long on my makeup. Ralph watches me from the doorway, his green eyes unnervingly perceptive.

"Don't look at me like that," I tell him, stepping into the new suede cowboy boots I bought yesterday. "I'm fine."

He blinks slowly, unconvinced.

Grabbing my keys and a small clutch, I take a deep breath. The lock clicks behind me, a small sound in the quiet of the stairwell.

One foot in front of the other. That's all it takes.

The walk to C'est Trois is only a few blocks, but every shadow seems to lengthen, every passerby feels like a potential threat. By the time I reach the restaurant, my palms are sweating.

The front windows glow gold, condensation fuzzing the edges of the glass. Inside, the tables are half full. I hover on the sidewalk, half lit by the interior, half hidden by the shadow of the awning. My reflection stares back: tall, a little haunted, armed with lipstick.

Saint clocks me through the glass before I make it to the door. He looks up from a conversation with a server, his head tilting a fraction.

In that second, the world slows. That impossible blue collides with my gaze, and I'm unmoored, tossed back into last week's perfection: his body pinning mine to the mattress, his mouth on my scars. Holding me in place.

Saint is the first to compose himself, but I can tell that my appearance has knocked his evening off its axis.

C'est Trois is warm and bright inside, and the host stand is operated by the same blonde from my last visit. She spots me when I walk in, pasting on a smile and asking, "Table for...?"

"Toussaint."

The name sticks against the back of my throat.

Her gaze flicks over my outfit and hair. "Right. He said you'd be joining him. This way."

She leads me past the open kitchen, where Saint stands at the pass. He's in chef blacks tonight, sleeves rolled, arms tense with veins cresting under his tattoos.

When the hostess says, "Your guest is here, sir," he looks up.

His blue pulls me under again.

Saint gestures me into the kitchen. "Right on time. Ivy's waiting at the private table in here."

It takes a minute to process that he's inviting me into the heart of his domain. Willingly.

I'd expected a quiet table in the corner, maybe his subtle wave from the kitchen, but not this. Not the heat, the clang, the rush of a dinner shift in progress. Not the wall of noise and scented steam and the sudden, total attention of every cook on the line as the boss's "guest" trails in wearing a dress that now feels absurdly fancy for the occasion.

Saint's kitchen is a different ecosystem than the dining room, and he moves through it with the animal grace of someone who isn't thinking about motion at all. Someone who is, in fact, the sole gravitational force in the room.

The VIP table sits in an alcove at the back of the kitchen, a polished cherry wood table for four gleaming under a single copper pendant light, while the rest of the kitchen blazes under industrial fluorescents. A white linen tablecloth, crystal glasses, and heavy silverware create the impression of a dining room luxury, but with the unmistakable thrill of being behind the velvet rope.

Ivy waves frantically from her seat, half standing on her chair until Saint gives her a look that settles her back down. I notice a small placard on the table: RESERVED.

"The chef's table," Saint says, pulling out a chair for me. "Usually booked months in advance."

"Or years, depending on who you are," calls another chef without looking up from the salmon he's plating.

"Mayor Dillinger's still mad about tonight," adds another cook, eyebrows waggling suggestively in my direction.

Saint's jaw tightens. "Focus on your stations."

"You denied the mayor?" I ask, sliding into my seat.

Saint stays close enough to catch his scent, smoke and salt, appearing at my elbow. "I told him we were fully committed."

The word "committed" does something stupid to my pulse. I reach for my water glass to have something to do other than melt.

My phone vibrates against my hip in my purse. The sound is barely audible over the kitchen noise, but I feel it. Once. Twice. Three times in quick succession.

"You good?" Saint asks, catching my slight frown.

"Fine."

But the buzzing continues. Insistent. Too many for Brenda. Too aggressive for anyone who has my number with my permission.

Saint's eyes narrow, cataloging my expression with the same care he applies to a delicate sauce. He slides into the seat across from me.

"Miss Wrenley looks like a princess," Ivy declares, bouncing slightly in her seat. She's wearing a blue dress with mismatched socks, one striped, one polka-dotted.

"You're shaking," he says to me quietly.

"Am I?" I force a laugh. "Just hungry. I haven't eaten since breakfast."

Which consisted of a handful of trail mix.

A server appears with bread and a tiny dish of sea-salted butter. Ivy dives in like she's been fasting for days. I focus on buttering a roll, hoping the ritual will steady my hands, but the trembling only gets worse. Saint's gaze drills into me, more relentless than the kitchen's heat.

"Wine?" the server asks, voice pitched to a hush. "Chef selected a white for the first course."

Saint nods. "Thank you, Mags."

The wine is poured. I clutch the glass, letting condensation chill my fingers, but it does nothing to slow the boiling under my skin.

Ivy's feet swing below her chair. "Miss Wrenley, guess what I drew in art today?"

"What?"

She grins. "A cat superhero who saves everybody from mean people. Her name is Captain Ralph."

Saint's attention flicks to Ivy long enough to give her an indulgent quirk of his mouth, then right back to me.

"You're not eating," he says, so low only I can hear.

The kitchen is a wall of noise and light behind us: the percussion of pans, the hiss of oil, and the overlapping, urgent language of a line under pressure.

I force myself to focus and be present, but the phone keeps going. My skin crawls with a familiar dread.

"Your phone's having a party," Ivy observes.

"It's probably work." I fish it out, planning to silence it, but the preview on the screen stops my blood.

Pink looks better than blue, but I miss watching you twist it around your finger when you...

No. No, no, no.

My vision starts to tunnel.

"Miss Wrenley?" Ivy's voice sounds far away. "You look sick."

I stand too fast. The chair tips. Saint pushes to his feet.

"Bathroom," I croak out, already moving.

But my legs aren't working right. The kitchen tilts. Too many faces, too many strangers, any one of them could be *him*.

I make it to the bathroom, barely. Lock the door. Slide down the wall.

My chest constricts. Can't breathe. Can't think. The walls are too close, and he's out there somewhere, watching, waiting—

I can't get enough air. I press my face against my knees, palms over my ears, but the phone keeps vibrating, little seismic shudders against my thigh. I want to throw it, smash it, flush it, but my hands won't unclench.

A knock on the door nearly stops my heart.

"Wrenley?"

Saint's voice is muffled but unmistakable, deep and sharp with worry.

I want to answer, but my throat is a pinhole. The only sound I can make is a wheeze.

I scrunch my eyes shut and try to remember what my therapist said—*slow inhale, hold, slow exhale*—but the world narrows to buzzing and Saint's voice and the memory of a stranger's hands on my skin.

"Wrenley." The knob rattles. "Say something."

Nothing comes out of my throat, though I try. Not even a squeak. I can't. I can't move, can't speak, can't do anything but drown in the riptide of my panic.

"If you don't answer, I'm coming in."

Please, no.

I don't want this. I don't want to be the girl who needs rescuing. I don't want to be a burden or a story or another fucking problem for him to solve. I want to get up, splash water on my face, and walk out like none of this ever happened.

There's a pause, then a heavy thud. Then another. The hinges shudder, paint cracking at the seams.

"Chef, you can't—"

A woman's voice from outside, maybe the server, maybe the manager.

"Move," Saint orders. He doesn't shout, but the force of it vibrates through the floor.

The door shudders in its frame, then bursts open with a splintering sound. Saint fills the doorway, wild and unholy and more terrifying than the demon he was accused of being by every critic who ever set foot in this kitchen.

TWENTY-THREE
WRENLEY

Saint is terrifying to look at for anyone who's not me. The relief of seeing him is so vast that I want to weep.

Even though I hate that he sees me like this. With my mascara running and my arms clamped around my knees, my chest spasming in shallow, useless breaths.

But Saint doesn't hesitate. He kneels, crowding into my small, tile-bound world.

The close-up sight of him, fierce and bloodless with worry, does the impossible. It jars me loose, just enough for my lungs to drag in a ragged, scraping inhale.

"Wrenley."

I shake my head, nails digging into my shins.

"Look at me."

He moves closer, so close I can feel the heat of him, the scent of smoke and basil and char surrounding me.

"You're safe. Hear me?" His voice is a rasp, so rough it could sand down steel. "No one's going to touch you. Not in my house."

I squeeze my eyes shut and nod, but the images keep coming: hands around my throat, the weight of a body pinning me to the bed.

Saint's hand settles on my back, warm and steady, not moving except for the pressure of his palm. He doesn't try to haul me up. Doesn't say anything more. He stays with me in the silence, his thumb tracing slow, hypnotic circles through the fabric of my dress. I try to match my breathing to his. In, out. In, out. The rhythm is clumsy at first, but then his hand slides to the nape of my neck, grounding me. I cling to his wrist like a lifeline.

"Good," he murmurs. "You're okay."

I want to tell him I'm sorry that I ruined dinner, that I'm an embarrassment, but all I can do is swallow air.

He crouches closer, his knees bracketing mine.

"That's it," he says, and I realize he's cradling my head to his chest, using his own heartbeat as the metronome. "Again."

I breathe. I shake. I breathe again.

My phone buzzes on the tile.

Saint snatches it up and glances at the screen. His entire body goes still.

I watch his face change as he reads. Watch as the controlled chef transforms into something else entirely.

When his eyes meet mine, they're nearly black.

"Who is this?"

The question is deceptively quiet.

"He's—" The words stick. "Someone who—"

"Your attacker." Not a question. Saint's pieced it together. "The one who hurt you. Who's supposed to be locked up."

I nod, mute.

Saint's lips flatten to a line so thin it could slice through atoms. He lifts my quaking body in a single smooth motion, arms locked strong around me, and for a second, I think he might actually barrel through the wall with his rage alone.

Instead, he pivots and carries me down the back hall, away from the kitchen. Away from the eyes of line cooks and managers and servers with phone cameras.

He sets me gently onto a prep table behind walk-in doors, then crowds the space in front of me, blocking out everything but the pulse of heat between our bodies and the white tile behind his shoulder.

Saint flicks through the phone, scrolling, reading. Every few seconds, his thumb pauses, the muscle in his jaw ticking like a bomb. I want to tell him to stop, that there's no point, that it will only make it worse. But the pleas are stuck somewhere behind my teeth.

"He's not supposed to have any access to the internet," I say with a shaking voice. "He shouldn't even be able to comment, let alone create new accounts."

Saint's eyes snap to mine. "When's the last time you checked your DMs?"

"I … I don't. My agent screens them." The confession tastes like blood. I've been hiding behind Brenda and the buffer of two different social media managers for a few weeks now.

"It's not just the comments," Saint mutters.

My hands shake just thinking about what he might've uncovered. There are videos saved on my account, ones held as potential evidence instead of deleted. I wonder if Saints found the video that was sent to me by my attacker, which included a still frame of my own face in the preview. Not a recent one. It was a screen grab from a year ago, taken from a live Q&A I did for a lipstick launch. My mouth is open mid-sentence. My hair is platinum then, no pink, just wild and loose.

The video was silent. It's me, looking into the camera, smiling and talking, but with the sound removed. The effect is eerie, like watching a puppet version of myself. A steady, slow zoom closes in on my lipsticked mouth. Then, abruptly, the video cuts to a photograph of my face, my mouth circled in red: *love how your mouth trembles when you don't know what to say.*

Saint's thumb moves with fast swipes, opening apps, switching screens. He's logged out of my Instagram and locked my phone before I can even see what he's doing.

"Why are you still on this fucking thing?"

He sets the phone on the table with the screen facing down.

"My therapist calls it controlled exposure. I'm sorry," I say again, voice scraped raw. "I didn't mean to ruin dinner."

Saint makes a noise that's almost a laugh, but there's nothing amused in it. "You didn't ruin anything. You did scare the shit out of me, though."

He's close enough now that I spot a faint nick on his chin from a razor, the fluttering pulse in his throat.

I want to crawl under the stainless steel and never come out. Instead, I reach for my phone, but Saint beats me to it, holding it out of reach.

"Abso-fucking-lutely not," he says, voice like a slammed door.

"I'm not a child," I snap, and immediately regret how shrill I sound. "Give it back."

"You're not thinking straight."

"Neither are you. You can't take away my phone like I'm your rebellious daughter—"

"I don't care about your goddamn phone. I care about *you.*"

He's so matter-of-fact that I almost laugh, but my body is

still fighting for air. The adrenaline comes in aftershocks, waves that leave me limp. Saint softens, just a fraction. He sits beside me on the prep table, forearms across his knees.

"Did you know," he says, "that every time Ivy so much as coughs, I lose two years off my life? That when she fell off the monkey bars and split her chin last year, I nearly threw up on the playground?"

I shake my head.

"I've never been so scared," he says, "as I was when I got that call from the school today. Unless you count the ten minutes just now, standing outside that bathroom, listening to you not be able to breathe."

I want to tell him that my panic attacks aren't voluntary. That he can't possibly understand what it's like to live in a body that betrays you every time you think you're safe. Maybe he does, in his own way. Maybe that's why I can't stop coming back to him, why I crave the cold burn of his attention like a drug I know is going to kill me.

But for the first time since coming to Falcon Haven, I'm not thinking about the next panic attack or how to apologize for my existence. I'm just listening.

Saint rubs his palms together, the friction loud in the hush. "I'm intense. I know I am. But I'm not going to let this happen to you again. Not here, not ever."

He's silent for a long time, and I don't dare break it. The kitchen beyond the walk-in is a muted roar, the world's volume dialed down to just the two of us and the thump of my heartbeat in my ears. He stares at the wall for so long I wonder if I've broken him.

"My wife died because I chose work over her," he says quietly. "Did you know that?"

I can only shake my head again.

"Celine used to do this thing. She'd get anxious about

dumb shit, like whether she left the iron plugged in or if Ivy's pajamas were warm enough. I'd listen, but I never actually heard her. Not really. I was always thinking about work, about the next menu, the next step." He scrapes a hand over his face. "One night, she called, asked if I could pick her up from some charity event. I said no. Too busy. Told her to call a car or drive herself. She never made it home. Black ice, two miles from the house."

His voice goes so flat I almost miss the tremor in it. "I told myself it was bad luck. That I couldn't have changed anything. But the truth is, she was calling because she was scared to drive in the dark. She just wanted someone to say she'd be okay."

I can't look at him. My chest aches so fiercely that it steals my voice. I know this isn't about me, not really, but the weight of his confession presses me into the chair.

"Ivy was two. She doesn't remember her mother, not really. But every time she wakes up from a nightmare, she calls for her. Not me. Her mother."

Saint rubs his palms against his thighs, tattoos shifting.

"I've spent the last three years making sure nothing like that ever happens again. No surprises. No fuckups. No distractions." He inspects his hands, the callused knuckles, the ragged half-moons of his nails. "I thought if I just stayed in control, I could keep everyone safe. But that's not how it works, is it?"

"Unfortunately not."

"You're coming home with me tonight."

I laugh, but it's not a sound so much as a breath expelled in disbelief. "Is that your solution? Kidnap me?"

Saint stands, blocking the prep room door with his entire body. "You think I'm joking?"

"You're not actually going to shove me in the trunk of your car, are you?"

He shrugs, a dangerous tilt to his mouth. "You wanna test me?"

I want to argue, to throw up a boundary just to see if I still can, but the truth is, the idea of being alone in my apartment tonight terrifies me. Even with Ralph, even with the triple locks. Even with the lights on.

The last time fear burrowed this deep, it took three days to stop the shakes.

Saint doesn't even wait for the protest. He stands and offers his hand. I take it, and the steadiness of his warm, dry palm is enough to make my knees work again. He doesn't let go, just leads me through the kitchen, ignoring the gossamer hush that falls over the line as we pass.

He detours to the VIP table where Ivy sits with Mags, her chin propped on her fists.

She looks up at our entrance, worry creasing her brow. "Miss Wrenley! Are you okay? Did you barf?"

I kneel beside her chair and smooth a hand over her hair, feigning composure. "I'm okay. I just needed a minute."

Mags eyes all three of us. "Everything all right?"

"Can we get the rest boxed?" Saint asks her. "And dessert, to go."

She nods, already in motion. "I'll pack up some of Ivy's favorites for you, too."

Saint dips his chin in thanks to Mags, then gently shepherds me toward the back exit, bypassing the main dining room and the sight lines of any remaining guests.

The night air is brutal after the heat of the kitchen, but it wakes me up. My boots scrape the gravel of the lot behind C'est Trois. Saint's hand never leaves my elbow, guiding with quiet insistence. Ivy skips ahead to the car, reciting her wish list of ice cream toppings.

Saint opens the passenger door for me, waits until I'm settled, then he tucks a blanket from the back seat around my lap.

"It's clean," he says, misreading my startled glance. "For emergencies. Ivy runs cold."

I wish I could say something and explain my gratitude, embarrassment, and confusion at being so completely and forcibly cared for. The words won't come, so I just sit there, the blanket tucked around my knees, and watch Saint as he buckles Ivy into her car seat, runs back in to grab our food, then settles into the driver's side, the engine catching with a deep-throated rumble.

During the drive to Saint's house, I aim my gaze out the window, watching the town fold up for the night, every porch light a tiny beacon in the dark.

Saint's hands stay anchored on the steering wheel, but I feel him watching me at every stoplight. I don't know what he's waiting for. Maybe for me to break again. Maybe for me to run.

When we pull into his driveway, the headlights sweep over the familiar porch. The same blue ceramic planter, the same scuffed doormat. I half expect to see my suitcase on the stoop, a silent reminder of the boundaries I once set for myself.

The silence in the car is so thick I could eat it. Ivy, who's usually a fountain of words, has gone quiet in the back seat.

Saint kills the engine. The headlights die, leaving us in the dark, the only light coming from the porch. It's a blue dusk, the color of Saint's eyes in a storm.

He gets out without a word, then circles to unbuckle Ivy. I hear the soft click of the harness, her sleepy whine as he lifts her. She wraps her arms around his neck, face buried in his shoulder, and I can't help but think how safe she must feel there.

Saint waits for me to get out. I do, the blanket slipping from my lap, and he grabs it before it can hit the ground. He doesn't hand it back, just drapes it over my shoulders, his hands lingering for a second too long. The heat of him seeps through the fabric, and I'm suddenly aware that my heart has doubled its pace.

We walk up the steps together, Ivy heavy in his arms, her breathing slow and even. I follow them inside, the door closing softly behind me.

Inside, Saint moves with efficiency. He carries Ivy to her room, tucking her in with a ritual that's all muscle and gentleness. I hover in the entryway, feeling like a ghost in my own skin, until he reappears and jerks his chin toward the kitchen.

"Sit," he says, and it's less a command than a fact of nature.

I obey, sliding onto a barstool at the island while he unpacks the take-out containers.

The kitchen is warm, the overhead light haloing Saint's head and making him look less like a villain and more like someone who could save you from one.

He lines up the boxes, then glances at me, his gaze so sharp it nearly slices through the air. "You need to eat."

"I'm not really hungry."

"Eat anyway."

He sets a plate in front of me and watches, arms folded across his chest, until I pick up a fork and take a bite.

The food is excellent, but my stomach is a clenched fist. Saint doesn't eat, just leans against the counter, eyes pinned to my face. I swallow a mouthful of pasta, then push the plate away. "You're staring."

He doesn't look away. "You're still shaking."

"Am not," I say, but the fork wobbles in my grip. "But I am tired. Is the bed in the guesthouse still available?"

"You're not staying in the guesthouse."

"Saint—"

"You're not. I don't care if you have a hundred locks and a gun taped under the mattress. I'm not letting you out of my sight until I know you're safe."

I want to argue. I want to tell him that nothing short of a meteor strike could keep me from my own bed, that I'm not some damsel for him to rescue. But I remember the way my body folded in on itself in the restaurant bathroom. Remember the taste of panic, the helplessness. And I'm so tired.

"Fine," I say, pushing the plate away. "I'll sleep on your couch."

Saint's mouth twitches, not quite a smile. "You'll sleep in my bed."

"You can't decide that for me."

He leans in, hands braced on the edge of the counter. "I can, and I am. You want a vote? Fine. It's two against one. Ivy would chain you to the bed if I let her."

I can't help it. A laugh escapes, fragile but real.

"I'll take the couch," he says, but the arrogance in his eyes tells me he's lying.

The air between us contracts to a single, sparking thread. He moves to the fridge, pulls out a bottle of water, and slides it across the island.

I take a sip, cold water sluicing through the heat in my chest. Saint's eyes track the movement.

He circles the island, coming to stand directly across from me.

He's so close. The space between us is measured in heartbeats, not inches. If I leaned forward, my forehead would brush the column of his throat. I want to press my face there, to disappear into the scent of him and let the world fall away.

Instead, I say, "I'm fine."

Saint's gaze drags up, pinning me. "You're not."

I want to deny it, but he's right. I'm not fine. I'm a shape made of terror and adrenaline and leftover want, stitched together by the barest thread of self-control. I'm also starving for him, in that way that feels like humiliation and fantasy all at once.

Saint's hand comes up, slow and careful. I flinch before I can stop myself.

Not because I think he'll hurt me, but because I'm so desperate that even the anticipation of his touch is enough to make my skin vibrate.

Saint doesn't make contact, just lets his hand hover near my cheek, patient and devastating.

"Wrenley."

The way he says my name almost makes me moan.

"You want me to stop, say so now."

I shake my head because it's too much. Too much holding back, too much pretending this is anything but the *only* thing that I want.

He closes the distance, his palm cupping my jaw, thumb tracing the seam of my mouth like he's memorizing the shape of it.

My lips part on instinct, and he leans in, the heat of his breath fusing with mine.

His kiss is nothing like I expect. There's no carefulness, no slow build. He kisses like a man who has run out of time, like he's been dying for this and knows it might be the last.

My hands find his shirt, knotting in the fabric.

His tongue parts my lips with a purpose so unambiguous

I whimper. I've kissed men before, but never like this, with the sense that I might actually be consumed from the inside out.

Saint's hand knots in my hair, angling my face, deepening the kiss until I gasp. The sound only fuels him. I feel him everywhere—in the heat of his breath, the grip of his hand on my hip, and the way his thigh wedges between my knees. I am a bonfire, and he's the wind.

When he finally breaks the kiss, I'm panting. My dress is rucked high on my thighs, my skin fevered.

Saint stares at me, pupils blown wide.

His voice is shredded when he speaks. "Tell me to stop."

"No," I say, and it comes out like an order.

He lifts me onto the island in a single motion, knocking aside a bowl of lemons.

Saint's hands are everywhere at once. My waist, my ass, sliding up my back and down again, like he's mapping out a territory he already owns but wants to reconquer just for the pleasure of it. His mouth moves from my lips to my jaw, then down my neck, biting hard enough to leave a mark.

I gasp and dig my nails into his biceps, the muscles flexing under my grip.

Saint's palms slide under the hem of my dress and part my thighs until the only thing separating him from me is the damp cotton of my underwear.

He bites my lip and pulls, just enough to make me gasp. "You want to be in control? Go ahead. Tell me what you want."

"Touch me," I say, voice trembling but clear. "Now."

He grins, wolfish, then obliges.

Saint hooks my panties, yanking them aside, and the brush of cold air makes me realize how soaked I am for him.

He drags two fingers along my slit, and I nearly vault off

the counter at his touch. Then he brings them to his mouth and licks them clean. "You taste like pure sugar."

Saint knows exactly what I need, how to circle my clit until I'm gasping with his thumb while never breaking eye contact. The heat in his gaze is so ferocious I feel it everywhere, even in the places he's not touching.

I try to say his name, but it comes out as a breathy whimper. He seems to like that, because his fingers increase their pressure, circling and stroking until my knees clamp his hips and my hands fist his shirt so hard the buttons threaten to pop.

He doesn't stop. Not when my head falls back, not when I start to beg, and not when I grind my hips against his hand in a way that would have embarrassed me in any other universe. He just keeps working me, pushing me higher until I shatter, my body arching off the island in a silent scream. The tremors go on forever, my only anchor the grip of his arm around my waist.

He waits for me to come down, then kisses the corner of my mouth.

"That's one," he murmurs.

He lets me catch my breath for exactly three seconds before hauling me off the island and onto his lap, settling me astride him on the barstool.

Saint's cock is a steel rod under me, an impossible ridge through his pants, and I grind down without shame. The friction is everything I've been craving, and Saint's growl vibrates up through his chest into mine.

He gathers the skirt of my dress in his fists, yanking it up to my waist. My thighs splay wide around him, shameless and hungry, and I rock against him in a rhythm that's part need, part challenge. I want to see how long he'll let me take the lead.

Not long, apparently.

He clamps his hands around my hips, pinning me in place, and bites my shoulder through the fabric of my dress.

"You're going to make me come in my pants like a fucking teenager," he rasps.

"Maybe I want you to," I whisper, reaching between us to palm him through the black fabric.

He's thick and hot, even restrained, and the knowledge that it's *me* doing this to him makes me bold.

I drag my palm up and down his length, slow at first, then harder, until he's panting into the hollow of my neck.

He lifts his hips to meet my strokes, his teeth scraping my collarbone. "I'm about to lose it."

"That's the idea," I reply.

Saint stands suddenly, lifting me with him. My legs wrap tight around his waist, and I cling to his shoulders as he carries me down the hall. We crash into the wall, and he holds me there, his mouth devouring mine.

He breaks away only long enough to rip the dress over my head, leaving me bare except for my bra and the panties already shoved aside. His eyes blaze as he takes me in, pupils swallowing blue.

He shoves his own pants down with one hand, freeing himself, and the sight of him, thick, flushed, and slick at the tip, makes me bite my lip.

Saint holds me suspended, his cock pressed against my entrance, not sliding in, just there, so close I could sob.

"Tell me to stop," he says again, voice so guttural I barely recognize it.

My answer is a curse and a plea tangled together. "Just fuck me, Saint."

He groans like he's been waiting all his life for that sentence, and then he drives into me in a single, deep stroke that makes my vision go white. I have never, ever been this full. Saint stretches me to the edge of pain and beyond until it's just pleasure. I'm nothing but sensation, an open circuit, every nerve ending exposed and lit.

He fucks me like I'm the only thing keeping him alive. Like if he stops, we'll both cease to exist. The hallway vibrates with every slam of my back against the drywall. It should hurt, but I want more. I want to be bruised by him, marked by him, ruined for anyone else.

His hands slip under my thighs, hiking my legs higher, opening me even wider, and the new angle makes me see stars.

"Harder," I gasp, and he laughs, a savage, incredulous sound.

"Careful what you ask for, *cherie*."

He pistons into me, brutally, and my head snaps back. The world narrows to his cock fucking me open, the scrape of his stubble on my neck, the burn of his hands on my skin.

"Look at me," he growls, and I do, and the sight of his face undone, hair wild, eyes black, jaw clenched in savage focus, makes me come again, even harder than the first time.

He fucks me through it, never stopping, finding my wrists and pinning them above my head as I clench and sob and shatter. Every thrust is a dare for me to survive this much intensity.

I want to say his name, but all that comes out is a broken sound that used be be language.

He clamps his mouth over mine, swallowing my cries while my legs are jelly, my arms useless. Saint holds me up, impaling me again and again.

Saint moves his mouth to my ear, breath hot. "You feel that? How tight you are? How fucking perfect?"

He slows, finally, sweat running down his temples, his

breath carving the space between us. I'm so full I can't even move. He lets go of my wrists and brings my hands to his face.

"You okay?" he rasps, and the question is so at odds with the way he just annihilated me that I start to laugh, then cry, then laugh again.

"Not done," I manage, and I mean it. I want more. I want all of him.

Saint hauls me off the wall and into the nearest room. It's his bedroom, sheets still unmade from this morning, the windows black mirrors. He tosses me onto the mattress and follows, crawling up my body like a predator, his eyes locked on mine. No smile now, just a taut line of restraint about to snap.

He yanks my bra down, not bothering with the clasp, exposing my breasts to the cool air and his hot mouth. He sucks one nipple, then the other, biting hard enough to make me shout while his hand nestles between my thighs, fingers plunging, finding the spot that makes me arch and claw at his shoulders.

Far from done, Saint flips me onto my stomach, and I gasp as he braces my hips, pulling my ass into the air. He drags my ruined panties down and off, then spreads me open, all the way, making a low sound of approval.

He eats me from behind, tongue and teeth and fingers until I'm nearly sobbing for him to fuck me again. Saint licks me through the aftershocks, then thrusts his tongue inside, and when I come again, it's a silent, body-racking quake that leaves me slack on the sheets.

When he rears up, I feel the head of his cock tease between my folds before he sinks back into me, deeper than before. The force ripples up my spine, and I bite the pillow to keep from screaming. He pistons in and out, his hands tight on my hips, until he holds me there, impaled, while his hand wraps around my throat—not choking, just holding, just making sure I can't escape the sensation of being completely, totally possessed.

"Can you take more?" he asks, panting.

"Yes," I gasp, and it's not even a question.

Saint rides me through it, his grunts getting rougher, his rhythm faltering. He pulls out at the last second and strokes himself once, twice, before coming in hot streaks across my ass and lower back. Weight presses me into the mattress when Saint collapses on top of me, his breath sawing in and out.

There's a second, maybe two, when the only sound is the thump of his heart against my spine. I stay perfectly still, afraid to ruin the moment.

Pressing his face into my hair, Saint inhales so deep I feel it all the way down my back. His voice, when it comes, is a rumble against my skin.

"You're safe."

He says it like a vow. Like he's reminding the universe.

I nod, though we both know safety is a moving target.

Saint rolls off me, pulling me against him. I think he's going to say something. That he'll launch into an apology, or a lecture, or a monologue about how this was a mistake.

But instead, he just asks, "Are you cold?"

I shake my head. "I'm good."

His heart still races, pounding against my cheek.

After a while, I whisper, "You still smell like basil."

Saint snorts. "You smell like coconut and sex."

His hand smooths over my hair, softer than I thought possible from a man with fingers burned from years of kitchen wars.

I keep waiting for the shame to settle in, the old, familiar recoil in my chest that says, *You don't deserve this*. But it doesn't come. Not even when Saint props himself up, looks down at me with a reverence I've never seen from him before, and traces my jaw with a knuckle.

It's then that I realize how screwed I am. Another, small part of my chest opens, widening the hole in the idea that Saint could just be a friend with benefits. Or a boss with benefits. Or even just a hot guy with benefits.

Because looking at him now, a traitorous voice in my head tells me that he could be different. That he could accept me for all my flaws, and none of it would matter.

Oh yes.

I'm well and truly fucked.

TWENTY-FOUR
WRENLEY

Three weeks later, I'm professionally lying to myself.

"Just dropping off a book I saw at Cornerstone that I think Ivy will love," I tell my reflection, applying lipstick I definitely don't need for a book run.

The same excuse I used yesterday for the apple crumble Noa makes that Saint loves. And Tuesday's urgent need to return Ivy's hair ribbon she left at my apartment when she was playing with Ralph.

I've propped my phone against the bathroom mirror, recording as I blend concealer over the beard burn Saint left on my neck last night. In his kitchen. Against the Sub-Zero fridge. While Ivy napped upstairs, he whispered filthy promises about what he'd do if we had more time.

"Morning routine in small-town life," I narrate cheerfully, angling my body to hide the evidence. "Sometimes using a bunch of products to create a 'natural' look is just necessary, you know what I mean? God forbid a girl wants to be in her unfiltered filter era."

The comments are already flooding in.

Girl, WHERE have you been hiding?

That glow, though!

Small town agrees with you, bestie!

Twenty-seven thousand views in six hours. My follower count is climbing steadily back toward two million. Brands are sliding into my DMs with partnership offers I can finally stomach again.

I'm almost back to who I was. Almost.

Except the Wrenley from before didn't know what Saint's hands felt like twisted in her hair. Didn't time her entire day around stolen moments in walk-in coolers and hidden corners. Didn't lie awake replaying the sound he makes when he comes, low and hot against my throat.

"It was so great spending time with you guys this morning. Now I'm off to run errands," I tell my audience, shutting off the camera.

Another lie. I'm off to accidentally run into Saint during the Friday lunch prep lull, when Erin takes Ivy to her music class and we have exactly forty-three minutes to pretend we're not completely fucked.

My phone buzzes. Brenda.

These numbers are insane! Whatever you're doing, keep at it. Also cleared my schedule next week. Surprise visit! Can't wait to see this cute town you're hiding in.

My stomach drops. Brenda. Here. Where I've been carefully cropping Saint out of frame while wearing his shirt. Where the entire town has started referring to me as "Saint's girl" when they think I'm not listening.

At least the attacker situation was resolved. Turned out to be some sick trolls who'd found police records from the original case, not him. He's still locked up. Noa had her lawyer best friend trace the IP addresses, and it turned out to be just some bored teenagers in Denmark getting their kicks from scaring me.

"Pathetic little shits," Saint had muttered when we found out, but the relief in his eyes was unmistakable.

Now our only danger is self-inflicted. This thing between us that neither of us will name but can't seem to stop.

This is fine. Everything is fine.

I grab Ivy's book—my flimsy excuse—and head out into the October morning, pretending I'm not counting the minutes until I see him again.

The restaurant is a blast furnace of noise and motion, but Saint's kitchen exists in its own climate, hyper-focused and hot. I slip through the back, past the dish pit, ignoring the line cook's knowing smirk.

Saint's at the pass, orchestrating with his usual economy of motion, but I can tell he's noticed me before I even clear the walk-in. There's a shift in his stance, a barely perceptible roll of his tattooed forearm as he wipes down a plate edge, and then he's nodding at Eddie to cover the line.

He stalks toward me, apron low on his hips, and the sheer focus on his face makes my pulse skitter. I barely have time to brandish the book and say, "I brought the new Bear and Bean —" before he's in my space, crowding me back into the walk-in, the door hissing shut behind us with a pneumatic exhale.

"You're late." He crowds me against a rack of parbaked tart shells. "I don't tolerate tardiness from anyone."

"It's 11:07," I say, but my voice is already shot.

He kisses me so hard my skull thunks against the metal. Cold air hits my legs as he hikes my skirt up to my hips, pushing his thigh between mine while his tongue fucks my mouth like he owns the air I breathe.

I don't even get a warning before he breaks the kiss, and

Saint pins my wrists above my head, the metal shelf's edge digging into my spine. "Seven minutes late."

My body turns traitor so fast that I drop the book. "You're being dramatic."

He grins, a dangerous tilt. "You want dramatic?" His hands slide under my sweater, bunching it at my ribs. Cold air prickles my stomach, but his palms are furnace-hot, callused from knife work and rougher than they have any right to be.

He's not gentle. He never is. That's the point.

Saint palms my breast, thumb circling until my nipple is a hard peak. "Do you like knowing I'm thinking about what you look like naked every fucking second I'm away from you?"

I nod, because language is suddenly very difficult.

He parts my legs with his thigh using a slow, implacable pressure.

"I have ten minutes until the next check-in," he says, nipping my neck. "So if you're going to be a brat, you better be fast."

His hand slips below the waistband of my skirt and my tights. He finds the damp heat between my legs and chokes out a sound I've heard countless times, but it never fails to turn me on.

"God, you're soaked," he says, pleased, but with an edge that says he's only going to make it worse. "Were you wet the entire time you walked here?"

"Saint," I gasp, but that's all I get before he slides two fingers inside, curling until I see bursts of white behind my eyes. He works me open, his palm grinding upward, and the shelf rattles behind my head when I arch into him.

He keeps my wrists pinned high, thumb stroking the

inside of my wrist, a tiny gesture as he fucks his fingers deeper.

"You're not going to make a sound," he murmurs, and the command is so cold and so hot at the same time that my mouth snaps shut. "You want Eddie to hear you? The whole fucking line?"

I shake my head, but I'm already close to losing it, my body jerking against his unforgiving strokes.

Saint kisses the corner of my mouth, then slides lower, biting my jaw, my neck, until he finds the spot that makes my toes curl.

"You're going to come for me," he says, "and then you're going to walk out of here and pretend you didn't almost scream my name and beg for my dick."

I want to make him work for it, but my body betrays me. I'm already so close, my thighs shaking, my chest heaving, nipples brushing against the rough fabric of his chef's coat. I try to hold out, but Saint has mapped every inch of me now. He knows exactly how to make me unravel.

He pulls his fingers out and drops to his knees, hiking my skirt higher and pushing my tights and underwear down past my knees.

Saint's tongue is on me, flat and insistent, licking a stripe up my center that makes my knees buckle. He braces my ass with both hands, fingers digging in hard enough to bruise, and fuck if I don't want the marks later.

I have to bite the crook of my arm to keep from crying out.

His stubble rasps against the inside of my thighs, a raw burn that makes everything sharper. He glances up once, eyes gone midnight, and the look on his face is pure fucking worship, none of the control he wears outside this freezer.

Saint tongues me slow, savoring, until I'm shaking so hard I almost topple the entire rack. He groans when I fist his hair, the vibration traveling straight through my bones. When he slides his fingers back inside, tongue circling my clit, it's over. My body seizes, every muscle locked, but I'm silent, just the ragged staccato of my breath and the metallic clatter of the shelving as I come on his hand and mouth.

Saint stands, wipes his mouth with the back of his hand, and kisses me hard, letting me taste myself.

"That's my *bonne fille*," he says.

I sag against the shelf, boneless, as he tugs my panties and tights all the way off. He's hard, straining against his black chef's pants, and doesn't even bother with pretense.

He unzips, pulls himself free, and lifts me by the waist until my ass is wedged on a lower shelf.

I barely manage to brace my feet on a crate before he lines up and pushes inside, no warning, no easing, just a single hard thrust that spears every last thought out of my skull. Saint's so big and the angle so punishing that it knocks the wind from me, but I want more.

Hands on my hips control the pace. Saint pulls me forward so my forehead rests on his shoulder, and I can smell his skin, the sweat and spice of him, and I want to stay here forever, impaled on his cock, hidden from the world in this cold, fluorescent-lit box.

"Don't move," he mutters, but it's pointless. I'm already locked in place, speared and trembling, my body his to do with as he pleases. He fucks me slow at first, savoring, then faster, rough enough that I have to bite the seam of his coat to keep from wailing. The shelf rattles. A jar of preserved lemons teeters and falls, thumping to the floor.

I giggle, delirious, and he bites my ear hard enough to leave a mark.

"Quiet," he growls, but he's smiling, the bastard.

He pulls out, just enough to make me whimper, then

slams back in, filling me to the hilt. Over and over, until the cold is gone and I'm nothing but heat, nothing but slick, desperate need. My second orgasm builds fast, a pulse in my spine, my legs shaking so bad I nearly lose my footing on the crate.

Every thrust knocks loose the last of my self-control. I come, and it's volcanic, clamping down on him and squeezing so hard, Saint jerks his hips and hisses a string of curses in French, biting my shoulder to keep his own voice down.

He slams in once, twice, and I feel the hot pulse of him as he finishes, buried to the hilt, his whole body vibrating with the effort to stay silent.

We stay tangled like that, both of us panting clouds into the air.

Then he grins, still breathless, and kisses me, slow and deep.

"You're trouble," he murmurs, still inside me, still holding me up like a rag doll.

"You're the one who pulled me in here," I say, but my voice is fuzzy, blissed out.

He pulls out gently, tucks himself away, and helps me stand, steadying me when my knees give out.

Saint licks his thumb and wipes a smudge of mascara from under my eye, grinning like an ass.

"You're a menace," he says. "You're going to get me fired from my own restaurant."

"You're the *boss* of your own restaurant," I retort.

He snorts and tugs my skirt down, but there's pride in the way he smooths my hair, straightening what he mussed. "Come eat something before you pass out."

I try to look dignified with my tights balled in his fist and the taste of him still on my tongue.

The kitchen is a loud engine that runs the restaurant, but Saint slices through it with a glance, steering me to the storage closet off the pastry station. He grabs a clean apron, snaps it around my waist with a practiced flick, and after we both wash our hands, he sets a stool in front of the prep table.

"You could just let me go home," I tease, hopping onto the stool and swinging my legs. There's a delicious, worked-over ache between my thighs when I sit.

"You're not going anywhere until you've eaten."

Saint pulls a loaf of sourdough off a rack and sets to slicing it, then grabs a tub of the whipped honey butter Ivy loves. "You didn't have breakfast, did you?"

I don't answer because he already knows.

A moment passes where I'm sure he wants to say something real, but he just slides the plate toward me. "Eat."

"I have a weird request," I say, picking at the bread to buy time. "But you have to promise not to make fun of me."

Saint leans in, resting both arms on the stainless prep table, eyebrows raised. "I don't promise anything. But you have my attention."

I nibble a corner of sourdough, then roll my eyes at myself. "I want to make a video. Of you making me lunch. No names, no faces. I promise."

His mouth quirks, equal parts challenge and disbelief. "You want to film me?"

"Just your hands," I repeat, realizing how weird it sounds when I say it out loud. "People are obsessed with food prep videos. It's… soothing. And your hands are, um. Photogenic. I'm starting to get more confident posting again, and I'd love to do this."

Saint glances down at his own knuckles, which are battered and tattooed and currently dusted with flour. "You want my hands to be internet famous."

"Don't act like you don't know you have the hands of a dark kitchen god," I say, and he laughs, a real one this time, low and warm. "Plus, I want to show people what actual skill looks like. Not those TikTok hacks where someone microwaves a cup of ramen and calls it lunch."

Saint considers this, then shrugs. "Fine. What are we making?"

"Dealer's choice," I say, suddenly nervous. "But it has to look good on camera. And, uh, you have to let me direct you."

He gives me a look that could curdle milk. "You're going to direct me in my own kitchen?"

"Don't worry. I'll be gentle."

Saint gives a slow, sexy smile. "Set up your shot, then."

I get up, still feeling the aftershocks of a thorough fuck in my thighs, and prop my phone against a flour canister so it frames the work surface. I flick to video mode, but don't hit record yet.

"Okay, stand right there," I say, pointing a few feet to his right.

He smirks, but does as told, baring strong forearms with the faintest bloom of red where my nails caught him earlier. The sight is so distracting I nearly forget to tell him what to do next.

Shaking myself out of it, I step behind him and guide his hands into the center of the frame. "This is where you'll prep everything, so the camera can see you. What are you going to make?"

"Carbonara," he says.

Naturally.

Saint moves around me, making sure to brush up against my tender nipples before grabbing eggs, pancetta, and a wedge of pecorino from the fridge, setting them down in whatever order makes the most sense to him. I see the switch flip in his head: the Saint who dominates a kitchen, who can fillet a fish in thirty seconds flat and break a line cook's spirit in less. His hands move so fast I have to adjust the camera angle to keep up.

He notices.

"You want me to go slow?" Saint asks with so much innuendo my underwear is instantly wet again.

"Painfully slow," I manage to say, then press record.

I pan the camera to follow, catching the sinew of his hands, the flex of his wrist, the faint twitch in his thumb whenever he's about to break his own rules and speed up.

Edging closer, trying not to let my voice betray how much I want to climb him right now. "Crack the eggs. Separate the yolks. Go *slow*."

He obeys, but only to mock me, exaggerating every move. He cracks an egg one-handed, letting the white slip through his fingers in a slow-motion ooze. Then he holds the yolk in his palm so the camera can drink in the slick gold.

"Happy?" he asks.

"Not yet," I say in all seriousness, and then circle around him, eyeing the angle, my own reflection ghosting in the spotless steel.

Saint holds the yolk between thumb and forefinger, pinching just hard enough that the gold membrane bulges at the seam. I zoom in as he bursts it, the liquid sun spilling down in slow, gorgeous ribbons.

"Dammit, you're a natural for the camera," I say. "Is there anything you're not good at?"

"Not a thing," he says, but there's laughter over the arrogance.

He breaks two more eggs, each one with a little more

showmanship, and then stops to look at me sidelong, shirt stretching across his back. "What's next, boss?"

"I don't know. This is your recipe. I have no idea how to cook carbonara, I just know how to eat it."

My stomach rumbles in agreement.

"Ah, but you're the director. I don't do anything without your say-so."

Uh. What?

This bastard is testing me. He's well aware that I don't know the first thing about cooking.

"Okay, um…" I start to bluff. "Can you do it where you let the cheese rain down in slow motion? People are obsessed with cheese pulls and cheese snow. It's a thing."

He scoffs. "Cheese snow. Christ. We're not at the cheese yet," he adds patiently. Too patiently. "What comes after eggs?"

"The … pasta"

"No."

"The meat?"

"Getting warmer. But what do I do with the pancetta?"

I squint at the ingredients like they'll tell me their secrets. "Cook it?"

"Brilliant. In what?"

"Oil?"

His jaw ticks. "Pancetta renders its own fat."

"Right. That."

"So I put it in the pan…"

"Yes?"

"When?" he asks.

"Now?"

"Is the pan hot?"

"I don't know, you're the one cooking!"

"You're the director." His patience is fraying beautifully. "Should I heat the pan first?"

"Obviously."

"Obviously." He turns on the burner with more force than necessary. "And while that's heating?"

"You ... wait?"

A vein in his temple throbs. "Or I could prep the—"

"Pasta! You prep the pasta."

"By?" He draws out the word.

"Putting it in water?"

"What kind of water?"

"The wet kind?"

"Wrenley."

"Boiling! Boiling water. I knew that."

"Did you?" He's gripping the counter's edge and trying not to lose it. *Oh, I love this so much.* "And when do I add the eggs to the pasta?"

"After it's cooked?"

"Temperature?"

"Hot?"

"No. Christ, no." He abandons all pretense of letting me direct. "You add the eggs off heat, or they scramble. The residual warmth cooks them gently. You temper them with pasta water first. You—"

"Just make the damn carbonara." I laugh.

"You think?"

But he's already moving, hands flying through the steps with barely contained violence. "Plate. Pepper. Done."

The whole thing takes him maybe three minutes, and he narrates each step like he's teaching a particularly slow child.

Which, culinarily speaking, I am.

"Now swirl it together. Gently," I direct, and he gives me a look. "Pretend you're not the boss of the entire world for one second, Saint."

Saint's mouth twitches, but he does as told, stirring in a slow, sensual spiral.

I catch the motion on camera, the glisten of gold, the flecks of pepper.

My breath hitches. I'm not even pretending to be in this for the content. I just want to watch him work.

"Do the thing with the pepper grinder. The one that makes you look like you're about to threaten someone with it."

He laughs, but the sound is low, and his grin is all teeth. Saint grabs the oversized grinder from the shelf, then leans his weight onto the table, bracing it with one palm while he twists. The pepper rains down in heavy, abrupt bursts. I film the motion, tight on his hands, then pan out to catch the muscles bunching under his forearm because I just can't help it.

Noticing what I'm doing, he leans out of the shot. "Is this for your followers, or for you?"

"Both," I admit.

"How many followers do you have again?"

"About two million."

"Jesus fucking Christ. And they just watch you … live your life?"

"I give them advice," I correct, taking a forkful.

When I take a bite, the moan I make is indecent.

His eyes darken. "Keep making sounds like that and we're going to have a different kind of video on our hands."

"Saint!" I laugh, but my cheeks burn.

He picks up my phone, still recording, and pans onto my face. "You missed the best part. Do it again."

"What? Why?"

"So I can show you what it's like to watch you fucking that fork."

I nearly choke.

Saint sets my phone down and moves behind me. His hand covers mine on the utensil and guides it into the mound of pasta, swirling another bite onto the tines. "Open."

He brings the loaded fork to my lips, but doesn't feed me right away. Instead, he hovers it just out of reach, making me chase the taste. When I lean forward, he draws back, a smug tilt to his mouth.

"Beg," he says.

I roll my eyes, but play along. "Please, Chef."

That's all it takes. He slides the fork between my lips.

"Chew," he orders.

I do.

"Swallow."

Saint watches me with a fire that liquefies my insides. I want to say something clever, but my brain's been replaced with a tangle of hormones and the word *yes*. I can't help it. Another soft moan escapes.

"There it is." His eyes eat me alive. "That's what two million people want to see. Not me. You."

"That's not—"

"True?" He takes the fork, loads it again, and holds it just out of reach. "Tell me you don't know exactly what you're doing."

I reach for the fork, but he pulls it back.

"Say please."

"You're being ridiculous."

"And you're being filmed." He nods at my phone, still recording. "So what's it going to be, Wrenley? You going to be good for me?"

The question shoots straight into my underwear. "Please."

He feeds me slowly, deliberately, making me work for every bite while his other hand rests on my hip, thumb stroking bare skin where my shirt's ridden up.

"Ivy's at Noa and Stone's tonight," he says against my ear. "Sleepover."

I swallow hard. "And?"

"And nothing." He sets the fork down and reaches around me to stop the recording. "Just information."

But his hand is still on my hip, and I can feel how hard he is pressed against my back.

The kitchen door slams open. "Chef, we need—"

"Out." Saint doesn't move, doesn't even look. "Now."

The door swings shut immediately.

"You're terrorizing your staff," I say.

"They'll survive." He spins me on the stool to face him. "Nine o'clock. My place."

It's not a question.

"I don't know. I have to edit your very talented hands and post this by tonight."

"Nine. O'clock." His thumb traces my bottom lip. When he pulls back, it's slick with olive oil. "Don't make me come get you."

Then he's gone, leaving me sitting there with sore thighs, wet underwear, and my phone now containing food sex footage I'll never post, already counting the hours until nine.

"Cover the pass," I tell Eddie, untying my apron at 8:45. On a Friday night. During the dinner rush.

He nearly drops his tongs. "Chef?"

"You heard me."

"But we've got three eight-tops coming in fifteen minutes."

"Did I fucking stutter?"

Eddie's mouth snaps shut. The entire line falls silent, pretending to be fascinated by their stations while exchanging glances with each other.

I never leave early. Not unless Ivy's sick or there's an emergency. And I sure as hell don't leave during Friday service.

"Yes, Chef," Eddie says.

I grab my keys from the office, ignoring the weight of their stares. Let them talk. Let them wonder why their head chef is abandoning ship for the first time in three years.

The drive home takes twelve minutes. I make it in eight.

My personal kitchen is too quiet after the cacophony of

service. I should feel guilty about leaving Eddie in charge, but all I can think about is the way Wrenley looked at me this afternoon, lips shining, making those sounds over my fucking pasta.

Everything's already prepped. I did it this morning before Ivy woke up, telling myself I was just being efficient, not that I'd been planning this since the moment my eyes popped open at dawn, before I'd even asked Wrenley.

Ingredients lined up on the marble island. Knives honed to surgical sharpness. A Barolo breathing on the counter that costs more than most people's car payments.

8:57.

Through the kitchen window, I catch the sweep of headlights.

She parks crooked, then has to reverse and try again. I watch her check her reflection in the rearview mirror three times before getting out.

When I open the door, she's holding a bottle of wine and looking everywhere but at me.

"Hi," she says.

"You brought wine."

"Seemed rude not to." She finally settles on my face. "Plus, I wasn't sure if this was a social visit or if you were going to lecture me about pasta water again."

"Depends. You still think pasta goes in cold water?"

"I think pasta goes wherever you tell me to put it."

The corners of my lips twitch. "Good girl."

I take her coat, allowing my fingers to brush her shoulders. "Nice choice on the wine."

"The guy at the store helped. I told him I needed something for dinner with a chef who would throw a fit at the wrong wine pairing."

I cock a brow, utterly insulted. "I don't throw fits. I have justified reactions to incompetence."

She laughs, and the sound tips my heart sideways. I want to taste that laughter to see if it's as bright on my tongue as it is in the air.

Wrenley toes off her boots and follows me into the kitchen, stopping short when she notices the island set up with ingredients. "What's all this?"

"Your education." I put her bottle of wine to the side and pour her a glass of the Barolo. "We're making risotto."

"We?"

"You. I'm supervising."

Her facial muscles do a complicated dance as she mulls this over. "You want me to cook for you."

"I do."

She surveys the *mis en place*, then me. "I have zero idea how to make risotto."

"Good. We'll start from zero. Apron." I toss her a spare from the hook by the pantry. She catches it, tying it around her waist with the kind of confidence that makes me want to see her in nothing but that.

She reads my mind, grinning. "You have that look. Like you're about to criticize my knife skills and then bend me over the prep table."

"Only if you're lucky."

Her cheeks color, but she holds my gaze.

And to my insane delight, she unties the apron and begins peeling off her clothes underneath.

My hand freezes on the wineglass, watching as she pulls her sweater over her head. She's not wearing a bra, just a thin camisole that clings to her curves like a second skin. The kitchen light catches on the lines marking her shoulders, thin white scars forming a crosshatch pattern along one side of her collar-bone. They gleam like silver threads, some older and faded to white, while others are newer with the faintest blush of pink.

They tell a story I've heard in fragments, one I wish I could erase.

I've seen them before, kissed them multiple times, and traced them with my tongue, but the sight of them always awakens the beast nestled inside me. Knowing she did this to herself, that she carved her pain into her own flesh when there was no one to protect her, makes my throat constrict.

I'd like to find every person who made her feel this was necessary. Her attacker, the police, the commenters, and the detective who suggested she invited it, and tear them apart with my bare hands.

Wrenley's eyes flick down to where my attention is fixed, then back to my face. She doesn't cover her scars or look away. Rather, she lowers the straps and slips out of the camisole, too.

Silence turns out to be a hidden talent of mine, because I'm able to remain still and quiet as she takes off her pants and underwear, then re-ties the apron, covering just enough to make me want to tear it off with my teeth.

I stay exactly where I am, a predator's reaction to unex-pected movement.

Her voice in that video swirls inside my skull, hoarse and shredded. *When I can't breathe, I dig my nails in until skin splits. That's from reading comments about how I should be grateful he didn't do worse...*

The memory makes my jaw clench so hard my teeth might crack. Wrenley's standing before me now, vulnerable and brave in nothing but my kitchen apron, and I'll stop at nothing to build walls around her so no one can hurt her again.

"You're staring again," she says quietly.

I force myself to exhale. "I'm appreciating."

"Appreciating what, exactly?" Wrenley adjusts her apron strings.

I set down my wineglass and circle the island, keeping a deliberate distance. "Your courage."

A half smile plays on her lips. "This isn't courage. It's impatience. I really want you to fuck me again."

"Is that right?" I reach for the olive oil, pouring a shallow pool into the pan without taking my eyes off her. "Hands."

She extends them, palms up, just like a kid doing as she's told.

I take them in mine, positioning her fingers around the wooden spoon, and she moans in disappointment.

"First rule of risotto: constant motion." I guide her hand to the pan, standing close enough that she can feel my breath on her neck but not touching her anywhere else. "Like this."

The burner ignites with a soft whoosh. I place the pan over the flame and add a knob of butter, watching it melt and bubble alongside the oil, then reach around her to add minced shallots. "Stir until translucent."

Wrenley obeys, the wooden spoon making lazy circles. The kitchen fills with the sweet, sharp scent similar to garlic, onions, and butter.

"Stir from the center," I instruct, purposely keeping my body just far enough away that she can feel my body heat, but not my touch.

Her shoulders tense as she concentrates, the muscles in her back shifting under smooth skin where the apron ties leave most of it exposed. A flush creeps up her neck.

"Am I doing it right?" she asks, her voice pitched lower than normal.

"Slower," I murmur near her ear. "Cooking isn't a race."

She shivers.

"Now the rice."

My arm brushes against her bare side when I reach for the Arborio rice, and she gives a sharp inhale.

"Keep stirring," I remind her. "The rice needs to be coated in fat before we add any liquid."

"Coated in fat," she repeats, a hint of a smirk playing at her lips. "Sounds filthy."

"Cooking can get dirty." I allow my chest to press against her back for just a moment before retreating. "It's about heat and moisture and knowing when something's ready to be devoured."

Her breath catches. The wooden spoon falters in its circles.

"Don't stop," I warn.

Wrenley nods, leaning back so she's pressed against my chest. I step away, denying her the contact.

She follows my retreat with a frown. "You know, most men would be a little more enthusiastic about a naked woman in their kitchen."

I stare at her, *really* focus on her without blinking so she knows exactly what I plan to do to her, while I pour a measured splash of wine into the pan, watching it sizzle and evaporate. "My kitchen. My rules."

Wrenley bites her lip, reading my intent flawlessly, and shifts her weight, the apron sliding against her breasts in a way that makes my cock throb.

I correct her grip on the spoon. She tries to lean into me, but I move away, letting her chase the scent of my skin and the scrape of my voice instead.

She's trembling and furious about it, and I'm fucking obsessed with it.

I say, "You're too tense. Loosen your wrist," and she does, but not before shooting me a look that's all challenge.

I correct her again. "You're doing it wrong."

Then I brush her hip, just barely, a reward for good behavior. She flushes, then smirks, then flushes deeper when she realizes she's playing right into my hands.

I make her stir and stir until her arms ache and the air between us is thick enough to scrape with a knife. I let her sweat it out. The kitchen is a crucible, and I want her melted by the time I'm done.

She tries to needle me. "You know, I could just take the apron off and—"

"Keep stirring."

Her eyes flick up, golden and furious and wanting. She wants me to break, wants me to lose the control I've spent years perfecting.

Fine. I let her think she's getting close.

I move in, pinning her between the island and my body, but I don't touch her anywhere except the back of her hand, guiding it in slow, torturous circles.

The silence spools out, punctuated only by the scrape of spoon on steel and the tiny, involuntary sounds that slip from her lips every time my hand covers hers. She's about to crack, but I want the tension to distill until she's blinking back tears, not sure if it's the onions or the fact that I haven't even kissed her yet.

She tries to break it.

"What happens if I let go?"

I lean in, breath grazing the shell of her ear. "Then I'll have to take over. Is that what you want?"

Her eyes close like she's bracing for impact. She doesn't answer, but her wrist flicks just enough to send a fleck of rice over the side of the pan. I say nothing, but let my hand close over hers, guiding her through the motion.

She's biting her lip now, fighting the urge to fucking climb me.

I want her to beg. I want her to admit that she's as ruined by this as I am.

My mouth hovers just above her shoulder, not quite touching. "You're shaking."

She laughs, but it's a broken thing. "You're a sadist."

"Only with you." My fingers graze the inside of her elbow, then fall away again.

She stirs, and stirs, and stirs. I add liquid a ladle at a time, and every time I do, I make her wait for it.

Her breathing picks up. She's so close to coming apart.

The risotto thickens. So does my dick.

Coming up behind her again, I press my hips into her bare ass so she can at last feel how hard she's made me, giving her just enough friction to make her gasp.

The muscles in her arms go slack for a second, and she almost drops the spoon. I force her to keep going.

She's trembling now. The straps of her apron are barely holding, and I can see the curve of her breast where the fabric gapes. I resist biting the soft, perfect flesh. With time, I'll mark her everywhere that's already been marked, so the next time she looks in the mirror, she'll only think of me.

"Why aren't you touching me?" she hisses, not even trying to keep her composure anymore.

"Because you're not finished," I say and kiss the back of her neck, tasting salt, heat, and the faintest trace of her perfume.

She whimpers. I know Wrenley hates that she made that sound, but she doesn't stop. I take the wooden spoon from her hand and toss it in the sink, then spin her to face me.

Wrenley's breathless. Her pupils swallow the gold.

She's panting, eyes flicking between my mouth and my

eyes. Wrenley Morgan wants to tackle me onto the tile, claw at my shirt, and rip me open, but she's holding herself together by a frayed thread.

Time to snap it.

I palm her jaw, thumb pressing just hard enough to make her mouth open.

"On your knees, Wrenley."

She sinks down slowly.

The tile is cold, her knees are bare, and the air is electric. I stand above her, hands steady at my sides, and wait.

Wrenley looks up, eyes wild and wet.

"Now what?" she asks, her voice as fragile as new skin.

I brush a strand of hair from her face.

"You want to touch me?" I ask.

She nods, desperate.

"Not yet."

I stand and unbutton my shirt, slow enough that her hands twitch toward me before she thinks better of it. I let my fingers run down the line of buttons, then shrug it off. Her gaze follows every move, starved.

"You can look," I say. "But you don't get to touch until I say."

She licks her lips, chest rising and falling so fast I worry she might hyperventilate.

I reach for her chin and tilt her head back. "Open."

She obeys. I slide two fingers between her lips, not gentle. She moans and bites down, just a little, then sucks. I leave them there, watching her eyes go glassy.

"Good," I say. "You're learning."

I withdraw, tracing her mouth with my wet thumb, and she makes a noise that's half protest, half plea.

I step out of my pants, kicking off my briefs and allowing my cock to spring free.

Her mouth parts wider, her tongue wetting her lower lip.

"Want it?" I ask, my voice a rasp.

She nods, not taking her eyes off my dick.

I take myself in hand and stroke, slow, letting her see what she's been yearning for.

"Please," she whispers. "Please, Saint. Let me take you into my mouth."

"That's a start." I bring the head of my cock to her lips, and she takes it, tongue swirling before I'm even all the way in. Her eyes flutter shut, and when I push deeper, she moans like it's relief. She's greedy, hungry, and I have to brace a hand on the counter to keep from buckling when she hollows her cheeks and sucks.

I grip her hair, guiding her pace, and she lets me. Christ, she wants me to control it, wants to be used and cherished at the same time. I hold her there, hips rolling, until the heat builds so fast I have to pull back or lose it right then.

She gasps for air, eyes hazy, mouth soaked. "Don't stop."

With a pained grunt, I let her take me again, slower this time. I grip the edge of the counter, refusing to touch her, refusing to give her the satisfaction of control. I want to see how far she'll go before I can't be the one who holds the power anymore.

Because this girl, this fragile, hopeful, brilliant woman, is determined to tame me.

Her hands slide up my thighs. She pulls me deeper and hums, the vibration short-circuiting my brain. Her eyes never leave mine. She's daring me to flinch, to look away, to admit that I want her so badly I'd burn down the whole goddamn world just to keep her in this kitchen, on her knees, forever.

She pulls off, dragging her tongue along the underside, then whispers, "How am I doing?"

I can't answer. I can only watch as she licks me again,

slower this time, using her hand to stroke what her mouth can't reach.

It's too much. I clench the counter until my knuckles ache, then catch her chin in my hand and pull her off with a wet pop. She grins, flushed and triumphant, licking her lower lip as she kneels at my feet.

"Stand up," I say.

She rises, the apron gaping at the sides to show every inch of pale skin.

I back her up against the marble island, gripping her waist so hard she gasps. The knot of the apron is a single tug away from coming loose, but I leave it for now, sliding my hand under the hem to palm her bare ass. My fingers find the heat between her legs, and she shudders, moaning into my mouth when I kiss her, deep and bruising.

"You're dripping," I say, letting my fingers slide through the slick mess she's made of herself.

"For you," she says, and the words are a dare.

I hike her onto the counter, shoving aside the risotto and the wine. The apron barely covers her, and I push it up, exposing her thighs, her pussy glistening and swollen.

I spread her legs wide, stepping between them, and slide two fingers inside her.

"You're going to make a mess on my counter," I say, working her open with slow, curling strokes.

She tries to grind down on my hand, but I hold her in place, thumb circling her clit in tight circles until she's gasping, hands splayed behind her on the marble.

"You're going to make me—"

I clamp my hand around her thigh and fuck her with my fingers, slow and deep, until her head falls back and she whimpers. The sound is pure, unvarnished need. She grabs my wrist, needing something to anchor her, but I don't slow.

She shatters, legs trembling around my waist, her whole body arching off the counter as she comes on my hand. Her eyes roll up, her mouth open, and I watch every second of it, greedy for the way her body gives in to me.

While she's still pulsing around my fingers, I pull her forward, so the apron bunches at her ribs, and bury my cock inside her.

She's so wet I slide in to the hilt without resistance. Heat, muscle, velvet—she clamps around me, body still quaking from her orgasm. Her eyes flutter, her lips part, and there's a little catch in her throat as she tries to say my name and fails.

I fuck her slow at first, just to hear her gasp at the stretch, and then pick up the pace.

Her ass scoots on the marble, hands scrambling for purchase on the slick surface. I grab her wrists and pin them behind her, forcing her chest up and her body open, arching her back.

Wrenley wants to move, to take control, but I'm not ready to relinquish it yet. I keep her pinned, helpless, at my mercy. Each time I bottom out, she shudders, eyes rolling back, thighs tightening around my waist. I want to make her come again. I'd love to see how many times I can shatter her before she taps out.

"Fuck," she gasps, voice gone thin and wild. "You're … fuck, Saint—"

"That's right," I say, pulling out just enough to make her whimper, then slamming back in, harder. "Say my fucking name."

I fuck her slow, then hard, then slow again, never letting her settle, never giving her the rhythm she wants. It drives her insane. She's panting, gasping, a string of curses and pleas leaking out between the shattered moans.

Her heart pounds so hard I can see it through her skin.

Her nipples are dark and hard, the edge of the apron barely grazing them. I bend my mouth to one, biting just shy of pain, and she jerks like I've electrocuted her.

"Saint, please—"

"Please what?" I ask, but I don't stop. I circle her clit with my thumb while my cock stirs her up from the inside. She's so tight around me I worry I'll lose it too soon.

"Please, I need—"

I let go of her wrists just to see what she'll do. Wrenley doesn't even try to fight me. Instead, she wraps her arms around my neck and pulls me in, nails clawing, teeth scraping my jaw. She's feral, all instinct and need.

She claws at my shoulders, nails raking down my arms, dragging me closer. I feel the sting and welcome it, want her to mark me the way I'm marking her. I want her to carry this everywhere, in every step, every breath, every goddamn day she tries to pretend she's not mine.

"Why—" she gasps. "Why are you—"

"Because I can." My lips scrape against her ear. "Because you like it when I make you wait."

I kiss her hard. Then I grab her ass, lifting her so I can fuck her at the perfect angle, the head of my cock stroking just right, over and over.

Wrenley comes apart in seconds, clinging to me, her body shuddering so violently I have to hold her up. Her nails rake my back, and she clamps her legs around me and rides my cock. I let her have it, let her fuck herself sick, and it's almost enough to break my composure.

I'd love it if I could last longer and draw this out, but she's too tight, too hot, and her moans are like a goddamn metronome counting down to my surrender.

I let myself come, holding her through the aftershocks, biting her shoulder as I spill inside her, filling her until it leaks down her thighs and onto the marble. I don't pull out, not yet. I want her to feel me, want her to remember this every time she sits down at my counter to eat her morning yogurt.

We stay wound together, sweaty and sticky, her cheek pressed to my chest, my hand wrapped around the back of her neck. I wait for the world to return to a normal rhythm, for the pounding in my head to subside enough that I can string sentences together. When I finally look down, she's got a lazy, blissed-out smile, eyes half lidded and glazed.

She swallows, then says, "You didn't even let me try the risotto."

For the first time in a long while, I respond with a full laugh.

TWENTY-SIX
WRENLEY

The risotto is perfect. Because of course it is.

I'm sitting at Saint's counter in one of his faded, button-up plaid shirts, legs dangling, watching him move around his kitchen like he hasn't just taken me apart one hundred different ways. He's wearing gray sweatpants that ride low, nothing else, and his hair is still mussed from my hands. When I spot the marks I left on his shoulder when I bit down to keep from screaming, I look down and blush.

"More?"

He offers me a forkful.

"I'll devour the entire bowl if you let me."

The risotto melts on my tongue, creamy and rich, with just enough bite.

"Better than the carbonara?"

"Nothing's better than that carbonara." I steal the fork from him, take another bite. "But this is close."

He leans against the opposite counter, watching me eat his food in his kitchen wearing his shirt, and his usual stone expression shifts. Softer. Dangerous.

"How does someone who can't cook end up with two million followers?"

The question makes me snort, and I laugh over a mouthful.

Swallowing, I reply, "My channel isn't just about cooking."

"What's it about?"

I take another bite, buying time to absorb the fact that Saint wants to know more about me. That a starred chef who is hot, infamous, and successful is actually *interested* in my life.

"I was a digital media major at UT. Spent most of college hiding in the design lab editing other people's projects because it meant I didn't have to present them myself." I hand him the fork. "My roommate Emma was obsessed with this new app where people posted short videos. I helped her edit hers sometimes."

"But never made your own?" He takes his own bite.

"God, no. The thought of people watching me made me want to throw up." I watch him eat, precise even now. "Then Emma bet me fifty bucks I couldn't post one video. Just one. Said I was wasting my editing skills being behind the scenes and that I needed to embrace the future."

Saint raises an eyebrow. "Fifty whole dollars?"

I grin at him. "Rent was due. I was desperate. I filmed myself organizing my entire desk at 3 a.m. because I couldn't sleep. Seven takes because I kept thinking my hand was too close to the lens or my breathing was too loud. Finally posted it with no caption, no hashtags, nothing."

"And?"

"Woke up to twenty thousand views and hundreds of comments from other insomniacs who organize things when they can't sleep. People asking what label maker I used, where I got my drawer dividers, if I had tips for color-coding schedules." I shake my head. "It was like finding out there were thousands of people whose brains worked just like mine."

"So you kept going."

"I posted this video of me trying to parallel park for literally twelve minutes. Just me, sweating, restarting eighteen times, with text overlays like 'Why did I say yes to downtown dinner' and 'This is my villain origin story.' I almost deleted it because who wants to watch someone fail at basic adult tasks?"

"Let me guess, it went viral?"

"Eight million views. The comments were all 'I've been driving for ten years and same' or 'This is why I exclusively Uber.' Suddenly, brands wanted to sponsor me because I was 'refreshingly honest.'" I make air quotes. "Like being bad at parking was a personality trait they could monetize."

"Anything can make money if you market it right." He takes the empty bowl to the sink, and I wish I were quicker because I would lick it clean. "I once worked for a chef who built his entire brand on being an asshole. Threw plates, screamed at servers. Reservations booked solid for two years."

"Don't you throw plates?"

"I throw knives. Much more efficient." He glances back at me and winks. "Kidding. Mostly."

"The weird part is how addictive it got. Every mundane disaster became content. Locked myself out? Film it. Tried to cook and set off the smoke alarm? Film it. Anxiety spiral at Target because they moved the shampoo aisle? *Definitely* film it." I pause to take a sip of wine. "Honestly, that one helped me laugh about it instead of crying in my car after."

"Profitable therapy."

I laugh into my glass. "Cheaper than actual therapy. Well, in addition to actual therapy." I watch him move around his kitchen. "My Amazon storefront alone makes more than my parents make in a year. Dad still doesn't understand how linking products counts as a job."

"Because you film yourself shopping?"

"Because I show people the exact label maker that helped me get my life together when I couldn't remember which pills to take when. The drawer organizers that made it possible to find matching socks during a depressive episode. The—" I stop. "Sorry. I sound like a commercial."

"You sound like someone who figured out how to help people while helping yourself." He comes back to stand in front of me. "Nothing wrong with getting paid for it."

"Tell that to the messages saying I'm making anxiety trendy. Or that I make people feel worse because my breakdowns have better lighting than theirs."

"Fuck those people."

His casual dismissal shouldn't surprise me, but it does. "Excuse me?"

"You heard me. Someone's always going to be angry that you're succeeding." His hands find my knees. "Trust me on that."

There's definitely a story there. "Speaking from experience?"

"We're not done with you yet." He squeezes gently. "These videos of yours. Show me."

I pull out my phone, suddenly self-conscious. "You must've researched me before you had me watch Ivy and seen my videos."

"Only enough to know you weren't a serial killer." He points at the phone in my hand. "Show me your favorite one."

I think about it, sticking my tongue in my cheek. "Okay, but you can't judge me. This is a recent one from last week."

The video shows me attempting a "productive morning routine," but I'm clearly dead inside instead of fully awake.

I make coffee, miss the mug entirely, and just stand there watching it pour onto the counter. Text overlay: **Morning routine but make it honest.**

I don't even clean it up, just put the mug under the stream and then drink.

Saint scrolls to the comments, reading aloud. "'The way you didn't even flinch when you missed the mug.' 'This is the most relatable thing I've ever seen at 6 a.m.' 'Finally someone who doesn't pretend mornings are magical.'"

I grab the phone. "No, go to the good ones."

He scrolls further. "'Your last fuck flew away and you didn't even wave goodbye.'"

"That one's my favorite." I grin.

Saint looks at me. "Two million people watched you fail at coffee?"

"Someone commented 'This video made me feel better about eating cereal with a fork because I'm too lazy to wash spoons,' and honestly, that's my target audience."

He hands my phone back. "This is what made you famous?"

"Being a disaster? Yeah, basically." I set the phone aside.

"Your followers get you," Saint says quietly.

He reaches out to tuck the pink strand of hair behind my ear. The gesture is so gentle it makes my eyes burn.

"What changed your mind about returning to social media after what happened in Miami?" he asks, stroking my temple.

Instead of answering right away, I study the rim of my empty wineglass, gathering courage. I've been waiting for this question since the bathroom panic attack. Since he picked up my phone and saw the comments that sent me spiraling.

"When I went into hiding after the attack, I got this email from a girl in Wisconsin. She'd been following me for years. Said she recognized the signs when I disappeared because she'd gone through something similar." I take a deep breath. "She told me that watching me struggle with anxiety made her feel less alone. That my videos were sometimes the only thing that got her out of bed."

Saint drops his hand from my temple, giving me the space to continue.

"At first, I thought, *great, more pressure*. Another person I'll disappoint when I inevitably break down again." I laugh, but it's humorless. "But then I realized, maybe that's exactly why I should keep going. Not to pretend everything's perfect, but to show that it's ... survivable. He took enough from me already. My safety. My privacy. My ability to sleep through the night. I refused to let him take my career, too."

I wait for Saint's judgment and the inevitable lecture about priorities, but he does none of those things. He refills my glass without asking, and keeps listening.

"My therapist calls it reclamation," I continue. "Taking back what was stolen. For some people, that means never going online again. For me, it meant refusing to be silenced."

Saint drinks from his glass, standing close enough to become a pillar of strength, and I resist leaning into it.

"Your turn," I manage. "How does someone like you end up here? You could be running kitchens in New York, Miami, anywhere. Instead, you're in Falcon Haven feeding risotto to a girl who thought pasta water should be cold and dents your fancy cars."

Saint steps forward, bracing his hands on either side of my hips. "Someone like me?"

"Talented. Trained. Probably have your Michelin stars somewhere in your pocket." I wave vaguely at his setup. "This kitchen alone costs more than most people's houses. You're not some small-town chef who got lucky."

"You googled me."

"I tried. You're a ghost online."

Which had driven me crazy for weeks.

"Good," he says.

"Why is that good?"

He's quiet for long enough that I think he won't answer. "You're not the only one who came here to hide, Wrenley."

I want to ask more, but I recognize the look written all over his face. It's the same one I get when people ask why I moved here, why I don't do meetups anymore, why I flinch when delivery drivers knock too loud.

"Ivy's mother?" I guess softly.

He squints at something over my shoulder. "Part of it."

I reach out before I can stop myself, hand finding his cheek. He turns into the touch, eyes closing briefly, and I realize I'm not the only flawed person in this kitchen.

"You don't have to tell me," I whisper.

"I know." He opens his eyes. "But I want to."

He straightens, and I think he's about to start pacing until he pulls at the neighboring stool and sits beside me.

"Celine hated the city. She hated the hours, hated the way I smelled like grease and cigarettes even after I showered. But she tried to make it work because she thought that's what you do when you get married."

I stay silent, my turn to be the listener.

"After Ivy was born, it got worse. I'd leave for work before sunrise and come home after she was asleep. I could tell you the exact number of times I was home for dinner Ivy's first year. Four. We fought about it, but I kept telling myself I was building something for us. For her. That the time apart would be worth it, eventually."

His hands knot together, ink tangling.

"When she died, I stopped being able to cook. Not wouldn't. *Couldn't.* My hands would shake every time I picked up a knife. It was the longest eight months of my life. I'd stand in the kitchen at four in the morning, trying to do basic prep. Brunoise. Julienne. Things I'd been doing since I was sixteen. Nothing worked."

My hand finds his, covering the lattice of his knuckles, the blue of his veins, and the black of his ink with all the warmth I can give. His expression doesn't change, but the tension in his fingers gives him away, how he wants to clench and squeeze and break and pull away all at the same time.

"I thought I'd use my savings to stay home with Ivy, maybe start a fucking food truck. Something small." He huffs a laugh, but it's only air. "But I didn't know how to be alone with her. I didn't know what to do with a two-year-old who only wanted her mother. Ivy stopped talking for almost a year after Celine died. At first, I thought it was normal. Kids regress. Sometimes she'd go completely silent except for screaming at night. No words, just noise. Then I did the unthinkable."

Saint's expression wrenches with agony.

"I gave her to Celeste and ... left her. I told myself it was temporary. Gave myself permission to fall apart completely. I'd work a dish washing shift at whatever kitchen would take me, drink until closing, find someone willing to take me home. Sometimes two someones. Started drinking at noon, stopped when I passed out. Some nights I'd wake up with no memory of where I'd been or who I'd been with."

I trace circles on his wrist, encouraging him to continue.

"Then one morning, I woke up in Ivy's nursery at

Celeste's apartment. Ivy was peering at me over her crib's railing, and her eyes were just like Celine's. Not the color, but the *love*. That little girl saw me at my worst, and it was like Celine was telling me not to leave this gorgeous girl again. So I called my father, who was retiring and had a restaurant in a small town in America. He and Celeste talked, and said the one chance I had with Ivy was to clean myself up, move here, and run it." Saint snorts, looks up at the ceiling. "I told him owning a restaurant, even in a town with a population of a thousand, wasn't going to be easy. He said he needed my help. But I told him I wasn't looking for a kitchen in the middle of nowhere and to just sell the place."

"But you came, anyway."

"I owed it to Ivy. I didn't want to fail her, too. So I came to look. Just to humor the old man." His mouth quirks in one corner. "Ivy was barely two and a half. Still asking for her mama every night. I was running on fumes and antidepressants."

I can picture it so clearly. Saint, empty-eyed and weary down to the bone with a toddler who couldn't understand why her world was upside-down.

"When we drove into town, Ivy fell asleep in her car seat. First time in weeks she'd slept without screaming." His voice cracks slightly. "I pulled over by the lake and just sat there, watching her. It was the first time I'd felt anything close to peace since Celine died."

The urge to pull him into my arms and bury my face in his neck is strong, but something in his posture tells me he needs to finish this without interruption.

"My father showed me the restaurant the next day. It was a disaster. Leaky roof, ancient equipment, peeling wallpaper and outdated furniture. But there was this moment when I walked into the kitchen. I picked up a knife without thinking and started chopping onions. My hands didn't hesitate. The skill was still there."

"So you stayed," I say.

"I stayed." His eyes find mine. "I gutted the place, rebuilt it from scratch. Named it after Ivy. C'est Trois means 'it's three.' Just me, her, and the restaurant."

The simplicity of it breaks my heart.

"I'm sorry about Celine," I say.

"I'm not the man she married anymore." His voice is flat, stripped of emotion. "Maybe that's a good thing."

I slide off the stool and step between his knees. His hands find my hips automatically, steadying me. I cup his face, thumbs brushing along his stubbled jaw.

"I like this version of you."

Saint lowers his eyelids to half-mast. "Even when I'm an asshole?"

"Especially then." I lean in, resting my forehead against his.

Our lips meet in a kiss that's softer than anything we've shared before. His hands slip under the borrowed shirt to rest against my bare skin, warm and solid.

"You shouldn't," he murmurs against my lips.

"Shouldn't what?"

"Like me. Any version of me."

I pull back just enough to see his face, the shadows under his eyes, his gorgeous bone structure, the tension in his jaw. "Too late."

"Stay," he murmurs.

Saint stands, lifting me effortlessly. I wrap my legs around his waist as he carries me toward the bedroom.

"Ivy will be thrilled to find you at breakfast when she gets dropped off tomorrow morning," he says between crushing our mouths together.

"I'd like that."

He kicks his bedroom door shut behind us, both of us pretending this is just about convenience, about not wanting to drive home late, about Ivy's happiness in the morning.

Both of us knowing it's something else entirely.

TWENTY-SEVEN
WRENLEY

wake up to the sound of someone pounding on Saint's front door like they're trying to break it down.

Saint's arm tightens around my waist, his body going rigid beside me. The digital clock on his nightstand glows 7:23 a.m. Ivy won't be back from her sleepover until ten.

"Expecting someone?" I whisper.

"No." His voice is rough with sleep and something sharper. Suspicion.

The pounding continues, followed by a voice that makes the blood freeze in my veins.

"Wrenley! I know you're in there! Your car's in the driveway!"

Brenda.

I bolt upright, clutching the sheet to my chest. "Oh god. Oh no. This is bad. This is so fucking bad."

Saint sits up, instantly alert. "Who is that?"

"My agent. My manager." I scramble out of bed, searching for my clothes from last night. "Shit, I never gave her my new address above the bookstore. She wasn't supposed to be here until next week!"

The pounding intensifies. "Wren! Open the door! We need to talk!"

Saint moves, pulling on sweatpants. "Stay here."

"No, wait for me!"

But he's already heading for the bedroom door.

I throw on his shirt from last night and race after him, my bare feet silent on the hardwood. Through the living room window, I catch a glimpse of Brenda's rental car, a gleaming white BMW.

Saint doesn't see me coming.

I leap onto his back, scrabbling against his neck as he chokes out a "What the fuck—" and stumbles away from the door with one hand still reaching for the doorknob.

"She can't see you!" I hiss into his ear. "Not like this!"

"Why not?" Saint growls, but he stays in place and doesn't try for the door again.

I cling tighter, wrapping my legs around his waist like a deranged koala. "Because she'll make this into a PR nightmare."

The front door rattles again. "I can hear you in there!" Brenda's voice cuts through the wood. "Open up before I call the police!"

"She would," I warn, keeping my spot as Saint's new spider-monkey. "She's the type to call the fire department, too. Report me missing. Make a scene."

"Fucking hell," Saint mutters, reaching behind to grab my thigh.

"Promise you'll hide."

"In my own fucking house?"

"Please," I whisper, my lips brushing his ear. "She can't know about us."

Something in my voice must get through to him because he stops trying to pry me off. "Fine."

I slide down his back, my bare feet hitting the floor with a soft thud. Saint turns to face me, surveying my disheveled hair, his oversized shirt down to my knees, and the obvious fact that I'm wearing nothing underneath.

He cocks a brow. "I don't think my presence or not will make a lick of difference."

I've resorted to pushing against his pecs.

"Go. Bedroom. Now." I shove at his chest, but it's like trying to move an inked-up mountain.

Saint's mouth quirks in what might be amusement if I weren't having a complete breakdown. "You realize I'm six-four and covered in tattoos. I don't exactly blend into furniture."

The pounding stops abruptly, replaced by the unmistakable sound of a key turning in a lock.

We both freeze.

"She has a fucking key?" Saint's voice drops to a deadly whisper.

"No." My blood turns to ice. "She picked the lock. Oh god, she actually picked the lock."

The front door swings open with a theatrical flourish, and Brenda Chu waltzes in. She's perfectly put together despite the early hour in a designer blazer, red lipstick, and a blowout that doesn't move despite the autumn wind following her.

Brenda's eyes land on me first, then slide to Saint's bare chest with the pause of someone who did not expect to see a glorious rack of muscles under tanned skin and multicolor ink before 8 a.m.

"Well." She blinks, tucking what looks suspiciously like a

lock pick into her purse. "You must be the owner of the guest-house Wrenley's been staying in."

Saint crosses his arms, forearm muscles flexing. "Yeah, I'm Saint."

"Brenda Chu." She extends a manicured hand that Saint takes. I am beyond thankful when her expression doesn't give away her likely realization that this is *the* reclusive, hot chef she'd been pushing me toward from the beginning. "Pleasure."

Thank god for professionalism.

"Brenda!" I jump in. "What are you doing here? You said next week."

Brenda releases Saint's hand and turns to me with a genuine smile. "That was before your last video went viral and Vita-Beauty wanted to move up the timeline of their offer."

For reasons I can't explain, heat spreads up my neck at her blunt explanation of my success in front of Saint. I don't know why. He's never given any indication that he looks down on my profession, but I can't shake the feeling of inadequacy in front of his sheer charisma and talent, even when he's not in the kitchen.

"Did it? I haven't checked the numbers lately."

"I figured. That's why I'm here." Brenda wraps me in a fragrant hug, and as one of the only people I've truly connected with during the rise of my career, I relax in her embrace and return it fully.

She says over my shoulder, "Would you mind if I borrowed her for a bit? Girl talk."

"Sure thing. I have to go pick up my kid, anyway."

Brenda and I pull apart in time for Saint and me to exchange a quick, loaded look with each other before he disappears into the the hallway.

Brenda immediately grabs my arm, yanking my attention away from his perfect ass and back to her.

"Jesus, Wren," she whispers, eyes wide. "When you said you were staying in someone's guesthouse, you didn't mention it was attached to six feet of walking tattoo art with the face of a dark fae lord."

"Yeah, I might've left that out…"

Brenda pushes her lips to the side and squints at me. "You've been hiding shit from me, and that's okay, but now you need to *confess*, girl."

"At least let me do it with pants on."

"Fine. I'll let you collect yourself. I noticed a cute café on the way to this gorgeous place. Lucy something?"

"Libby Jude's."

"Yes, that! I'll meet you there in…" She looks me up and down. "An hour? I think you need an hour."

"An hour would be great," I say, relieved. "I should probably shower."

"And remove the evidence of fucking that man senseless?" Brenda's perfect eyebrow arches at the same time my mouth opens in horror. "Honey, your neck looks like that man turns into a sexy vampire at night."

My hand flies to my throat.

"Save it for brunch." She spins, hips swaying toward the door. "I want all the dirty details over mimosas. And you're paying since you've been holding out on me. Oh, and bring that the raw footage of your chef's hands. I want to see what's got our engagement rates through the roof."

After she leaves, I sink against the wall, exhaling slowly. Saint emerges from the hallway, now fully dressed in jeans and a T-shirt that hugs his chest in ways that should be illegal before noon.

"So that's your agent," he says, voice carefully neutral.

"That's Brenda." I run a hand through my tangled hair. "Professional bulldozer, expert manipulator, lover of spicy fantasy novels, and apparently an amateur locksmith."

"You two seem close."

"She's been with me since the beginning. Stuck around when a lot of others bailed." I glance at the front door. "Though I might reconsider our relationship now that I know she can break into houses."

Saint's mouth curves. "Your friend's got skills."

"Oh please. You're just impressed because she didn't flinch when faced with your morning scowl."

Saint offers me a wry look.

"It's because she doesn't have a soul," I add. "She once made a venture capitalist cry during a contract negotiation. With just her eyebrows."

Saint's mouth curls into a genuine smile. "I like her already."

I push off the wall. "I should get ready."

Saint crosses to me, his hand resting possessively on the small of my back. "Want me to come with you?"

"Absolutely not. Brenda would eat you alive and then use your bones to pick her teeth while negotiating a cookbook deal."

He laughs, a rare sound that still sends warmth cascading through me. "I've faced worse critics."

"No, you haven't." I stretch up on tiptoes and kiss him quickly. "Trust me on this."

Forty-seven minutes later, I'm dressed in yesterday's clothes, smelling like Saint's soap, and sliding into a booth across from Brenda at Libby Jude's. She's already ordered mimosas and is typing furiously on her phone, pausing only to take a sip of her drink.

"This place is very cottagecore, don't you think? Too bad

their socials are abysmal. Missed opportunity, in my opinion."

I give Brenda an indulgent smile before taking a sip of my drink. "This town isn't too interested in leveraging social media."

Brenda's eyes widen as she sets down her phone, giving me her full attention, an honor usually reserved for seven-figure deals. "Good lord, it's like I've entered a time warp. Next you'll tell me people here still use landlines and write letters."

"Some do, actually."

"That's the problem with these adorable 'burgs. All charm, zero hustle. Do you know the owner hasn't even claimed her Google Business listing? It's criminal."

"Not everyone wants to be found, Bren."

"Like you?" She gives me a pointed look over her mimosa. "Speaking of which, I'd like to discuss that mountain of sex appeal you've been climbing. The one with the hands."

I nearly choke on my drink. "Can we not?"

"Oh, we absolutely can and will." She leans forward, eyes gleaming. "Wrenley Morgan, you little minx. You've been holding out on me. That video of him making the pasta dish? Because it has to be him, right? Pure genius. The engagement metrics are insane."

"It was just one video," I mutter, a curious sinking feeling forming in my gut. "And I promised him it would be anonymous."

"Sure, for anyone who's never met him, but I am no longer that woman. It was food porn of the highest caliber. The way he handled that knife? The tension in his forearms when he kneaded the dough? And don't get me started on how he handled those fresh-made noodles." She fans herself dramatically. "I nearly combusted when he burst the egg yolk between his fingers. It was indecent."

"Brenda!"

"What? I'm just saying what two million women are thinking." She takes a delicate sip of her mimosa. "The algorithm doesn't lie, darling. People are thirsting for your mystery chef. And that means they're going to start sleuthing."

My pulse quickens. "It was just his hands. And he doesn't have unique tattoos on his fingers."

"Oh, honey." Brenda leans back, crossing her arms with the confidence of someone who's seen the internet unmask anonymous celebrities based on a single nostril in a blurry photo. "Those aren't just any hands. Those are the hands of a man who knows exactly what he's doing with them. Trust me, your followers are already freeze-framing that video looking for identifying marks. Some are playing detective in the comments."

My stomach drops.

Brenda slides her phone across the table. "See for yourself."

I scroll through the comments section, my heart racing faster with each one:

@thighnoodles: if you don't tell us who he is i'm gonna start knocking on restaurant back doors like a divorced wife in a Hallmark movie

@egirlscancooktoo: i showed this to my mom and she just sighed and said "that's a provider." what does that MEAN

@user000deadinside: you think we won't recognize those hands when you try to soft launch him in the background again??? girl we're IN THE WALLS

@moth4hire: wrenley i am two frames away from losing my job over this. give us a *single* clue. even just the damn state.

@mosswife: this is not a cooking video this is a relationship reveal and we're all pretending it's not

@rejectedpesto: i'm not saying i screenshotted the cutting board to reverse search the wood grain but i did and i'm ashamed

@babygirlofgrief: the comment section is fighting for its life rn. WHO IS HE

@griefpizza: girl if you don't tell us who he is we're gonna start calling him "chef daddy" and you're gonna hate it

@gothwheatthin: his wrists say "therapy," his knuckles say "i never went"

@kneadtoknow: ho is you letting him season you like that

@beepboopoven: anyone recognize the ink? I reverse image searched and got NOTHING

"Okay, so they're not in not full dox-mode. They're buzzing, but not feral yet." My voice rises the more I try to reason with myself. "I didn't think it would blow up *this much*, though. I mean, yeah, his sexiness can be spotted literally in his fingertips, but it's not like I showed his face. Or said his name. The finger tattoos are basic enough. One little flame, some Roman numerals, and that half-faded X on his ring finger that lots of people do instead of wedding rings now. I've seen at least four baristas with the same one!"

"Okay, Wren, calm down. Would it be so bad if he's identified? I told you that bringing this reclusive, hot chef into your world would work wonders for improving your rep online. And look, it's working!"

I spin the stem of my mimosa, the drink souring in my stomach. "I should take it down."

"Seventy-two thousand saves. Two hundred brands flagged it as high engagement. You didn't even tag a product, and your click-throughs tripled. If you take this down, I will throw myself into your ring light and haunt you forever."

"It wasn't..." I pause because I can hear how defensive I sound. "He didn't want to be part of my online persona. I promised."

Brenda raises a perfectly groomed brow. "You really want to pretend you didn't launch a whole man last week?"

I half-laugh, half-die. "It wasn't supposed to be anything. It was just nice to do with him. Quiet. Safe."

"Baby," Brenda says, gently now, "quiet doesn't trend."

"This doesn't work for him," I say firmly.

Brenda blinks.

"Returning to social media was my choice because I love the community I built and that I'm a part of. This is my comeback. My second chance. Saint didn't ask for any of it."

Brenda softens, just a little. "You can't fault yourself for being so damn good at making content."

I stare at the screen again, taking in all the comments, the freeze-frames, and the zoom-ins. They love him. And they don't even know who he is.

Which means the second they find out ... they'll eat him alive.

And he'll know it was me who fed them.

TWENTY-EIGHT
SAINT

vy's back from her sleepover and crunches through cereal next to me, using one of the good mugs again because she says it makes the flakes taste better. I told her that made no sense. She said I was old.

She's in a talking mood this morning. Humming something under her breath, tapping her spoon against the rim like it's a drum. I should tell her to stop before she chips the porcelain, but I don't. I like the sound of her in the kitchen.

It used to be a quiet house. I thought I liked that.

Now, when it's silent, I notice what's missing.

Ivy grabs my attention again when she drapes herself over the counter like she's melting. Crumbs from her cereal cling to the sleeve of her unicorn onesie.

"I'm so full," she groans, then unspools off the stool and toward the cushioned bench in the breakfast nook.

"Almost like I warned you," I say, handing her the small blanket she always insists she's too old for until she's tired.

She mumbles something about needing lots of stomachs like cows, then curls up without further complaint.

I refresh my coffee and lean against the counter, staring out of the bay windows above Ivy and into our wooded backyard. There's no rush to do anything today. It's one of the rare mornings when the house doesn't need anything from me. No prep list. No kid meltdown. No mess in the sink.

But my phone's in my hand, anyway.

I tell myself it's out of habit. Emails. Schedules. Maybe a shipment delay. That's the excuse I've been using every morning for the past three weeks, ever since Wrenley started posting again. It's not a habit I'm proud of. Not something I admit. At first, it was curiosity. Then concern after becoming aware that she had a seriously unhinged, dangerous fan and someone needed to be on her page to protect her. Now it's something I can't name.

I tell myself it's just to make sure she's safe. That after what happened in my restaurant bathroom, I have a responsibility to check on her. That it's not pathetic at all to be thirty-four years old and watching a woman talk about her morning routine.

I open Instagram. The handle my agent chose—@Salty-Saint—flashes across the top. It's absurd. I didn't pick it. My former agent grabbed a handle for me on all social media accounts despite my severe hatred of all things online. I'll never thank her, but it did make it a lot easier to find Wrenley by having an existing account.

Her latest video appeared twenty minutes ago. I haven't watched it yet, which feels like a personal failure.

Wrenley stands in her tiny kitchen, explaining how to make a smoothie recipe I taught her that she swears doesn't taste like "lawn clippings and regret."

I'll take that as a compliment, I suppose.

Her hair is piled on top of her head, that pink streak escaping to brush her cheek. She's wearing a sweater that's too big for her frame, one I recognize because it's mine. She stole it last week. And I didn't ask for it back.

My breathing slows at the sight of her smile. This is a genuine one, not the polished, closed-mouthed tilt she started off using when she recorded herself again. I've cataloged her smiles. I know which ones reach her eyes.

I scroll to her previous post from a few days ago with her at the lake, wind ruffling her hair, explaining why she's been quieter than usual online. I've watched it multiple times, noting how her voice changed when she mentioned finding peace in unexpected places.

Am I that peace?

Do I even want to be her happy place?

Ivy snores softly, the blanket pulled to her chin despite her insistence that she's "practically a teenager." I lower the volume and tap on Wrenley's profile, scrolling back through the last week of content. Each thumbnail is a moment I wasn't with her, a glimpse into the parts of her life that exist outside of what she shares with me because I've asked that Ivy and I not be included in her content, and she's respected that.

I can't name this restlessness, this need to see what she's doing when she's not with me. It's not surveillance. It's not obsession. It's just ... checking.

She's fine. She's happy. She's wearing my clothes like it's the most natural thing in the world, and I'm watching her like some kid with his first crush.

So, like the glutton for punishment that I am, I read the comments.

GIRL, you are THRIVING lately!

    ma'am that is a MAN's sweater and we see you

who else is zooming in on the background for clues about chef daddy?

Chef Daddy? My brows furrow.

The nickname hits like a slap of cold water.

The comments on her videos used to be about her. Wrenley's smile, what products she uses, her progress. Now they're filled with questions about someone else.

Holy fuck. About me.

I click on a comment that's gathered hundreds of replies.

Okay but we need to talk about those sex hands in the pasta video. Criminal that we don't have a face to match.

The pasta video. My mind stutters over the phrase. The one I let her film of just my hands and the counter because she asked so sweetly, and we'd both just finished a thorough fuck.

No face. No name. No identifying information except—

I tap on Wrenley's profile and scroll frantically, looking for it. The thumbnail appears halfway down her feed: a close-up of a cutting board, a knife, with my tattooed forearm just visible at the edge of the frame.

Four hundred thousand likes.

Holy fuck.

I tap on the video, first noticing the caption: *This carbonara made me believe in emotional support carbs again.* I'd watched the video when she first posted it, when it was at something like two hundred views, and I was forced to admit that she is one savvy creator who knows how to trigger views without being obvious.

This time, though, I head straight to the comments.

My coffee mug freezes halfway to my mouth. I scroll through, a sinking feeling spreading through my chest.

Anyone notice the knife technique? That's professional level.

Those forearms are making me feel things I shouldn't before 9 a.m.

Did anyone else catch the tiny burn scar on his left wrist? Classic chef mark.

That's a $300 Japanese knife. This isn't some rando boyfriend.

I work in a restaurant and THOSE ARE MICHELIN HANDS. I'd bet my entire paycheck.

I'm comparing the tattoos to every chef in the northeast with ink. Will report back.

I scroll faster, my heartbeat rising to a staggering level.

After closing the app, I set my phone face down on the counter, breathing through my nose.

They know.

Fuck me, they're going to know.

The hot coffee in my hand suddenly feels like acid, burning through my palm. I set it down before I lob it through the window.

Michelin hands. Chef Daddy. Four hundred thousand people analyzing my fucking wrist bones.

I rub my thumb over the burn scar they'd noticed, a souvenir from my first job when I was sixteen and thought I was invincible. Now it's a beacon for internet sleuths with too much time on their hands.

It suddenly dawns on me how Wrenley directed me that day. *Go slower, let me see the knife, hold the yolk between your fingers.* At the time, I thought her taking control was sexy and irresistible, but it's taking on a different meaning now. She'd said people loved food prep videos. That was her reasoning. Not "I want to use your chef credentials to boost my engagement," even though, clearly, that's what she's done.

Wrenley wasn't just capturing a moment. She was *curating* me.

And then, my worst nightmare comes true. A new comment appears at the top.

Wait, isn't she in that town where Bernard Toussaint opened his restaurant? The chef who disappeared from France after his wife died?

My stomach drops through the goddamn floor.

I scroll frantically through the thread, watching as the speculation builds in real time. Someone's already replied with a link to an old *New York Times* profile. Another is posting screenshots from C'est Trois's website, which doesn't even have pictures of me, just the restaurant interior.

The walls are closing in. I tap on Wrenley's profile again, noticing things I missed before. She never tags the town and carefully crops her backgrounds so that there are no identifying landmarks, but occasionally slips, leaving just enough for a dogged viewer to figure out where she is. The dock by the lake or the bookstore's window reflecting Main Street, though it's blurred.

Little breadcrumbs. Little clues.

Ivy stirs on the bench, mumbling something about rainbows before settling back to sleep. I look at her peaceful face, at the dark hair that's so like mine, at the innocence I've fought tooth and nail to protect.

Three years of careful obscurity. Three years of building a life of privacy and safety for Ivy, so she could grow up without the dark cloud of her mother's death, of the interest of the press, and the over-glorified fame of her father.

I just became Saint, the grumpy chef with the spirited daughter who runs that French place on Main.

All of it unraveling because I let someone in.

My phone buzzes with a text.

Wrenley: Thinking about you. Brenda's dragging me through meetings, but I really need to talk to you. Are we still on for dinner tonight?

I said yes to being filmed. She asked, and I agreed.

But I didn't expect the video to look like that. I didn't expect people to start pulling it apart.

Wrenley knew. She must have known what she was doing. The angles, the lighting, the way she made everything I did look like sexual foreplay. The careful framing showed just enough ink and just enough technique to make her followers curious. She's too skilled not to have calculated this.

Fuck, I'm an idiot. She used the perfect recipe for viral content: seduction, skill, and the hint of something forbidden.

My phone buzzes again.

Wrenley: You ok? Brenda's pitching a beauty brand collab but I'd rather be making that risotto with you again...

. . .

The domesticity in her message makes my jaw lock. Like we're some normal couple sharing inside jokes. Like she hasn't just turned my life into content.

"Papa?" Ivy's voice pulls me back. She's sitting up on the bench, hair sticking in seventeen directions. "You look mad."

She squints at me, much too perceptive for her age.

"Keep sleeping, *mon trésor*. Everything's okay."

I can't stop fucking looking at the comments.

I used to stage at his restaurant in Paris. Absolute legend. If that's him...

Falcon Haven.. Found it. It's the only town within 50 miles with a restaurant called C'est Trois.

Someone needs to go there and confirm it's him!!

I should've said no. I should've told Wrenley no cameras, no content, not even a blurry photo of the pasta we made. My face isn't even in the frame, and still they're building a fucking dossier on me.

Ivy's already been through one public mess that cracked her world wide open. I won't let her live through another. I'll destroy the entire internet myself before that happens.

Yet Wrenley's message is still open. My thumb hovers over the screen, the reply box waiting.

Don't say anything you can't walk back.

Randomly, I don't hear Wrenley's voice in my head after that thought. I hear her agent's, that kind of PR-fueled, sharp-edged truth someone like her would throw at me if I texted my displeasure at this whole shit show.

I'm no publicity virgin. I've been in the media before and know how this works. But that doesn't make this any less infuriating.

I back out of the message screen and open the video again, trying to figure out what, exactly, made this thing blow up. It's not flashy. There are a thousand videos just like it. Hands chopping herbs. Hands stirring pasta. A few tattoos. A decent knife.

So why this one?

I watch it again, slower this time, and the answer slips in quietly.

It's not the food, or the way the yolk breaks so cleanly in my hands.

It's *her*. Wrenley.

She's used a voice-over instead of our sexy banter while filming, but there's a tone shift I didn't notice the first time. Wrenley isn't teaching. She isn't performing. Even though I'm not on screen, even though she's cut my voice entirely, the warmth in her voice as she discusses what I'm doing says everything.

One shot lingers on my hands, not with the clinical skill of a cooking tutorial, but with awe. She zooms in when I crush the herbs, catching the way my knuckles flex, holding the shot longer than necessary.

Her breath catches audibly in the voice-over. The microphone picks up the smallest inhale, a sound I recognize from when she watches me in the kitchen, from when I'm inside her.

And her laughter. She laughs at something she remembered I said, quiet and breathy, the sound you make when you truly like someone, and you can hear her smiling even though she's just recording her voice. That one-sided banter of hers that she keeps in, the way her voice tilts when she's talking to me instead of her audience ... it's all there.

Goddammit. This isn't curated content. This is a confession.

Which means the comments themselves aren't the problem. The problem is that two million people can sense exactly how she feels about me. This video didn't go viral because of my knife skills.

It's because Wrenley is in love with me. This is a love letter she didn't know she was writing.

That's why people are responding the way they are. They feel it. The intimacy. The way she sees me. Not as some mysterious chef or potential brand partner, but as something real. Someone she wants.

And it scares the shit out of me because I want her, too, and I don't know how to want her without ruining the life I built to protect Ivy.

Apparently summoned by my thoughts alone, Ivy pads over, dragging the blanket behind her, thumb stuck in the collar of her onesie.

"Papa, can I have your phone?"

She always says it like that. Can I have your phone. Never, can I play a game. Can I watch a show. Just the phone. Like it's a portal to a grown-up world she's desperate to be a part of.

I hesitate. "Not right now."

She tilts her head. "I want to watch the egg video."

I peel my gaze off the phone and stare down at her, my spine straightening. "Egg video?"

She shrugs. "The one where you break the yellow part. Auntie Noa was talking to Uncle Stone about it last night."

Fuck.

Wrenley didn't mean for this to happen. But she filmed it.

Edited it. Posted it. And she knew what she was doing. Maybe not all the way, maybe not with malice, but enough.

And I let her.

Ivy stares up at me with big, innocent eyes, waiting for my answer. Her gaze is free from the multiple sucks this world has to offer her once she's old enough.

"Not today, *mon trésor*," I say, keeping my voice even. "We'll find something better to watch."

She accepts it without question, running into the den where our television is, shouting, "With popcorn!" before she disappears around the corner.

I set the phone down and rinse my mug out at the sink, slow and methodical, the way I handle most breakable things.

Because dinner's off.

And if Wrenley doesn't know it yet, she will soon enough.

TWENTY-NINE
WRENLEY

'm setting the table for a dinner that might not happen, arranging silverware with the attentiveness of someone who's lost her mind.

Fork on the left. Knife on the right. Blade facing inward because that's what civilized people do, even when their world is imploding in real time.

My phone sits face down on the small kitchenette counter of my apartment, silent since I texted Saint this morning. The one when I said I was looking forward to tonight. Before the comments started rolling in. Before his anonymity became a group project for millions of strangers.

I smooth the napkin for the third time, then catch myself rubbing the front of my shoulder raw. The skin is already pink from my nervous scratching. I pull my hand away, tucking it under my arm before I do more damage.

The pasta water bubbles on the stove, ready for the spaghetti I bought because Saint mentioned it was Ivy's favorite. I'd planned to make something simple. Something that wouldn't require his help, so he could just relax, and I could cook for him for once.

Now I'm not sure if he's coming at all.

I flip my phone over. Still nothing.

The comments are probably worse now. They always get worse as the day progresses, as more people discover the video, and as the algorithm pushes it to a broader audience. I haven't looked since this morning, but I can feel them multiplying like bacteria in a petri dish.

I meant to delete it. After Brenda left, after I saw how far the speculation had gone, I meant to take it down. But every time I clicked on my account, I found myself watching it instead. Watching Saint's hands move with that impossible grace, remembering how those same hands felt on my skin just minutes before I filmed him.

I love the way he cooks, and the respect and care he takes, like he's coaxing a miracle into fruition. That's all I meant to show.

It was about sharing something beautiful. Something that made me happy after months of fear and self-sabotage.

I dump the pasta into the water with more force than necessary, then wipe my hands on a dish towel. The sauce simmers quietly, a simple marinara because I'd be too nervous to attempt something more complex on a good day, never mind an evening with him.

A knock on the door nearly sends me jumping out of my skin.

For one suspended moment, I can't move. Then I'm rushing toward it with my heart in my throat, smoothing my hair and tugging at my dress before I swing it open.

Saint's standing there, rain dripping from his hair onto his shoulders. I don't know when it started to storm, but it suddenly floods my senses—the damp smell, the sound of it beating against the tin roof, the sight of his dark strands plastered against his forehead.

His jaw is set in a hard line, eyes focused somewhere over my shoulder. The collar of his black jacket is soaked, rivulets trailing down his broad shoulders.

"You came," I breathe, relief washing through me.

His eyes finally meet mine, as cold and distant as winter lakes. No warmth. No crinkle at the corners. Nothing of the man who'd fucked me against the wall a few days ago.

Saint holds out a bottle of wine without a word.

"Thank you," I say, reaching for it. Our fingers brush during the exchange, and I feel the familiar spark that always ignites between us when we touch.

But Saint simply lets go.

"Come in. I was worried when you didn't answer my texts," I say, stepping aside.

Saint's boots leave wet ghosts on my tile. He stands in the entryway, rain dripping from his cuffs, and surveys my quaint apartment with a look I can't read. The silence swells until the only sound is the hiss of my pasta boiling over.

I rush to the stove, cursing under my breath, and kill the heat. Saint's behind me before I can process his movement, reaching for a clean dish towel and mopping up the starchy water spreading across the stove.

"Sorry," I say, my voice smaller than I intend. I hate how needy I sound. "I got distracted."

"Did you burn yourself?" Saint tosses the towel over the edge of my sink and holds up one of my hands, inspecting it.

The electricity is instant, like he brought lightning inside with him as well as the sudden storm. It flashes outside the window above my sink as if punctuating the feel of his touch.

Something in his voice is off, though. Less rasp, more empty. I want to reach for him the way I always do, but I know better than to do any sudden movements in front of an unpredictable animal.

I clear my throat, pulling out of his hold. "I'm fine. Um, I was just going to make spaghetti and salad. Ivy told me it's one of her favorites. I hope that's okay."

"She's at Noa's again tonight," Saint says, grabbing the pot with his bare hands and pouring the pasta into a colander in the sink. "Last-minute sleepover."

"Oh." I back away into the main area where I've set the small, circular table. "Should I reschedule?"

He just incorporates the pasta into the sauce, water flying off his hair and forearms in small arcs. "We're good. I'm here now."

I set the wine on the table. My hands are shaking so badly I nearly tip it over. Every motion of mine feels like performance art for an audience who won't clap.

He scoops the spaghetti into two bowls, sprinkles cheese, and brings them to the table. Though my stomach is the size of a pebble, I sit down to eat. He watches my every movement, even when I fold my hands onto my lap and pretend I'm not vibrating out of my skin.

When Saint sits across from me, I think he's going to be the first to speak, maybe ask about the video, or the comments, or the fact that he's been found out.

But he doesn't. He says, "How was your day?"

The question is so unexpected, so dissonant, that I almost laugh. "Good. Brenda's still here. She's at the bed-and-breakfast, discovering the local wines."

Saint stares at his steaming bowl. "She's good at her job."

I nod, because it's true.

I open the wine, pouring him a glass, then me, the silence stretching out until it's as taut as the line he drew between us.

He finally picks up his fork, twirling pasta with the same arrogant ease he gives to every task.

I take a sip of wine, and it burns all the way down.

Noticing my eyes on him, he says, "You're making me nervous."

I force a laugh, but it sounds like something dying. "Sorry. I've never cooked for you before. It's like trying to paint for Picasso."

Saint finishes twirling the spaghetti, chews, swallows. "It's good."

I almost start crying right there, because it's not good. It's overcooked, and the sauce is too thin, and I forgot to salt the water. But he keeps eating, forkful after forkful, like it's his job to get through this meal.

Our mutual silence starts to grow teeth.

Saint's face is blank. I can't find him anywhere in there. Not the man who called me *cherie* and fucked me with enough care to make me believe I could withstand the worst and still be strong, not the one who made me risotto bare-chested or let me sleep with my head on his chest and his arm wrapped around me.

I feel the panic coming before it even starts. The prickling at the back of my scalp, the way my chest hollows out. I take two slow breaths, then three. All I want to do is pick at my shoulder or twirl a piece of hair around my finger and yank until it comes clean out of my scalp, yearning for that addictive sting.

My focus shifts to my fork, the wedge of Parmesan cheese, the scent of tomato and basil and the rain.

None of it helps.

I raise my eyes. "Saint."

He doesn't answer.

"Saint, please." My voice is so thin I barely hear it myself.

He sets his fork down.

"I saw the comments," he murmurs.

He meets my gaze, and it's like staring down a sniper scope. The look on his face is so sharp, so targeted, that I flinch.

"They found me. Which means they also found Ivy."

I want to mount a defense and tell him that he's being paranoid, that his name isn't even attached, that it's not like I posted his address or Ivy's school. But I can't.

Because I know. I know how the internet works. I know how quickly interest turns into obsession.

"I knew it would get views," I say quietly. "I just didn't think it would get *you*."

Saint doesn't speak, but the shift in his jaw is answer enough.

"I filmed you because you're beautiful to me."

He doesn't move. Doesn't speak. Just watches me, and it's worse than yelling.

My fingers tremble as I press the napkin into my lap, grounding myself.

"You didn't know it at the time, and maybe you still don't, but you pay attention to me like I matter, like I'm not broken or needy or some volcano about to overflow. That morning … you made me feel good. Wanted. Human again. I posted it because I wanted to hold on to that, not because I wanted people to find you."

I look down at my hands. There's a red crescent forming on my wrist where I've been digging my nails in.

"But I didn't stop to think about what it would mean for you. Or for Ivy. I was selfish. Not for views or content, but because you've been the only thing that makes me feel real lately. And I didn't want to let that go."

He pushes back from the table.

The scrape of his chair is gentle, almost polite, but it hits my eardrums like a slammed door.

My entire body reacts in that prey-like way I thought I'd trained myself out of. Saint's not angry, or loud, or cruel, but I feel the pressure drop.

Saint walks to the window, the one that overlooks Main Street, and drags a hand through his damp hair. His back is to me, broad and silent. Droplets cling to the curls at the base of his neck.

"I can't afford this," he says finally, and his voice is quiet, wrecked. "I can't afford to want you the way I do."

The world tilts, just slightly.

"You think I don't know what this is doing to me?" he goes on, still not turning around. "You think I don't feel it, every time I look at you? Every time I have to tell myself not to touch you, not to fall in deeper?"

He shakes his head once, hard.

"You were supposed to be temporary. A blur. A soft-landing nanny gig for a kid who needed warmth."

Saint turns now, and the look in his eyes isn't cold.

It's worse.

It's heartbreak.

"You're not temporary," he says. "You got under my skin. Into my house. Into my child's heart."

His gaze drops to the wineglass he never touched. "And now you've made me visible again."

I rise slowly from my chair, fighting the ringing in my ears. "I never meant to do that."

He doesn't answer.

"Saint." I step toward him, but he backs up half a pace. Not much. Just enough to make it feel like a rejection.

"I'm not mad," he says, voice hoarse. "I'm not even blaming you. I just... I can't think around you, Wrenley. And that used to be a good thing." His throat bobs. "But now it's dangerous."

My fingers twitch at my sides, the way they always do before I scratch, and I clench them into fists.

Saint sees. Of course he sees.

And that's what finally makes him soften. Crestfallen, he steps toward me before he can stop himself.

"Don't," he murmurs, gently covering my hands with his. They eclipse mine, warm despite the rain that's soaked him through. "Don't scratch."

His gentle tone makes my chest ache. I wish I could collapse into him, press my face against his skin and feel his heartbeat, but I can't move.

"I'll take it down," I whisper. "I'll delete it right now."

Saint's thumbs trace small circles on my wrists. "It won't matter."

"I can make a statement. Tell them they're wrong. That it's not you."

"Lying won't help." His voice is soft but final. "The internet is like an ant colony. Once they pick up the scent, they'll follow it all the way home."

I know he's right. I've seen it happen countless times. The collective obsession, the thrill of the hunt, the rush of discovery. They'll keep digging until they unearth every detail.

"I'm sorry," I say, the words pathetically inadequate.

"I know." His hands slide up my arms, coming to rest on my shoulders. "That's what scares me."

My pasta grows cold on the table. Outside, lightning flashes, illuminating the stark angles of Saint's face.

"When Celine died, there were photographers at the funeral. They wanted grief porn. The widowed, millionaire chef, barely thirty. The tragic accident. They camped outside our apartment for weeks, following me to the grocery store, to Ivy's daycare. One asshole actually asked me to comment on whether I blamed myself for her death while I was buying diapers."

My stomach turns.

"That's when I realized fame isn't something you can turn on and off. It's a parasite. It feeds on everything you try to keep private." He squeezes my shoulders. "I spent three years building walls around us and making sure Ivy could grow up without cameras in her face and strangers knowing her business."

Thunder rumbles overhead, shaking the windows.

"And now they know where we live. They know what school she goes to, what restaurant I own, probably what fucking cereal she eats for breakfast. I've spent three *fucking* years making sure Ivy could grow up without that circus following her around."

"And I just let them back in."

Saint's silence is answer enough.

The weight of what I've done settles over me like concrete. I think of Ivy's bright eyes, her fierce independence, the way she trusts so selectively. How many photos of her are already circulating in comment threads? How many strangers are analyzing her face, looking for resemblances, building theories about her mother's death?

"I'll fix this," I say desperately. "I'll make them stop."

Thunder rumbles overhead, closer now. The storm is moving in fast. Rain pelts the windows harder, drumming against the glass like impatient fingers.

"They'll come," he says matter-of-factly. "Food bloggers. Journalists. People with cameras looking for the tragic chef who vanished after his wife's death. They'll want the comeback story. About why I left and whether I've moved on with the pretty influencer who makes videos in my kitchen."

The room spins. I grip his forearms to steady myself. "Saint, what are you saying?"

His muscles tense underneath my palms. Saint's still here, still solid, but that part of him I've been slowly earning starts to slip out of my grasp.

"I'm saying I don't know how to protect you and Ivy at the same time."

I blink, the words slow to land.

"I never asked you to protect me," I say.

"No." His voice is rough. "But you made me want to."

His gaze drops to where I'm still holding him. Like it hurts and he needs to peel me off. Like he never wants me to let go. Like he can't decide which it is.

"You said you felt real with me," he murmurs. "I haven't felt real since the day Celine died."

I can barely breathe.

"That night, when I first met you, I forgot about all of it. The grief, the guilt, the need to stay hidden. I'm not supposed to have this. You. Any of it."

I shake my head, confused. "You're allowed to move on."

"That's not what this is," he says, eyes flicking up to meet mine. "This isn't moving on. This is falling. Blindly. Recklessly. Like I don't have a child who depends on me."

His hands lift and cup my face. Saint doesn't pull me in. Just touches. As if it's the last time he'll let himself do it.

"You said I made you feel real, too," I whisper, fighting the burn behind my eyes.

"You did," he says, so quietly it feels sacred. "You still do."

His brow presses against mine. His breath warms my cheek. I don't close the gap between us. I don't move.

I wait.

He inhales slowly. Holds it.

"I can't stay."

I press my lips together to keep the sob in my throat from escaping. I don't beg, and I don't chase.

But I don't let go, either.

"I want to," he says. "Fuck, Wrenley, I want to stay. I want to sit at your table and eat your overcooked pasta and hold you while it storms."

His thumbs brush along my cheekbones, catching the tears that have started falling without my permission.

"I want to wake up next to you every morning and teach you how to make proper coffee. I want to watch you film your ridiculous videos and pretend I'm annoyed when you steal my clothes."

The memories are torture, each one dying a small death.

"But wanting something and being able to have it are two different things."

When he pulls back, his hands fall away from my face.

"I have to think about Ivy first. Always."

I nod because I understand, even as it destroys me.

"I'm sorry," he says, and his voice breaks like bone.

He reaches past me and grabs the jacket from the back of his chair. Then he walks out.

No slammed door. No harsh goodbye.

Just the soft snick of the latch.

And silence.

THIRTY
WRENLEY

read every single comment on the video before deleting it.

That's the kind of masochist I am. I scroll and scroll, absorbing the theories, the threats, the couch sleuths. I read the ones that call me a liar, a manipulator, a social climber. Some call me a tragedy tourist, others a whore who goes after dead wives' husbands. The worst part is how none of it surprises me. The internet is a lever that pries your ribs apart and counts every bone inside, and I have been doing this long enough to know how the machine works.

I delete the video from my profile, my phone, and my head, but the last one doesn't take.

Brenda texts me ten times in the hour after I take down the post. She's already in damage control mode, drafting statements and contingency plans in her head. I don't answer. There's nothing I can say to her that won't make me sound like a child who's dropped her ice cream on the sidewalk and is now blaming the cone.

Instead, I clean. I scrub the stovetop until it gleams, empty the fridge of everything that smells even faintly like leftovers, and dismantle the ring light in my kitchenette. I vacuum the living room and try not to spiral. I do all the things Brenda, Dr. Hollis, and the nicer part of the internet have suggested I do.

I put on real clothes and brush my hair and film a morning routine video even though every cell in my body wants to crawl back to bed. In the week after Saint leaves, my rented apartment looks like a Gen Z showpiece. The wine bottle he brought is the only thing gathering dust, half drunk in the corner of my counter.

Despite all this, my numbers keep climbing. My followers, my engagement, the offers in my inbox. It's all supposed to make me feel better, but it doesn't. I take the brand deals anyway. I film a segment for a teeth whitening pen, careful with my angles so the pink in my hair says "quirky" rather than "unraveling." I do a #sponsored post for a weighted blanket, pretending it's not just a shroud for adult sadness.

The more I act like everything's fine, the more convincing I become, even to myself.

And I *am* fine. If this had happened to me six months ago, I wouldn't have been okay. But I've done a lot of work on myself since then. I've ghosted my followers once, and I don't plan on regressing. I've regained confidence, created a safe space, and found a town where I can be happy. I'm more careful online than I've ever been and still doing what I love, and it shows.

I'm not going to vanish this time, but what I need to do is show up with intention.

Brenda's call comes as I'm halfway through a shoot for a sponsored collagen powder. She tells me she's downstairs waiting for me in the bookstore, which is impressive, considering she was supposed to have left town last week.

By the time I get down there, she's sitting on a padded bench by the window aggressively untangling a string of beads hanging from her phone case, radiating the sort of energy that makes entire Starbucks lines part like the Red Sea.

"Brenda!" I put on my most chipper voice. "Good to see you."

Brenda glances over as I slide onto the bench next to her, her red lips twisted into a tight smile. "I've canceled two flights and don't plan on canceling the one this afternoon, so I came here to say that you're numbers are great. Better than that, actually. However, the problem is that everybody else is using your content for clout because you've given them no alternative. You took the video down!"

She gives up on untangling and shows me her screen, scrolling through a list of notifications that contain Chef Daddy conspiracy threads, screenshots, and open calls for anyone who has eaten at C'est Trois to weigh in.

"They're not letting it go, Wren."

I watch a short clip of a woman doing a side-by-side breakdown of my deleted video and a grainy chef's interview of Saint from years ago.

"People have always been ravenous," I say.

Brenda sighs, the kind of sigh that means she's about to say something she knows I won't like. "They're contacting the restaurant. Someone tried to book a table by pretending to be your cousin."

My stomach sinks when I picture Saint having to dodge these types of calls, but I read between Brenda's lines and say, "I'm not making a statement. That would just restart the whole thing."

"You need to at least give your audience a reason even if it's a lie. 'We're just friends,' or 'he's not comfortable with social media' or 'I made it up for engagement.' Anything."

"I'm not going to throw him under the bus for content. Or Ivy. That's nonnegotiable."

Brenda's knuckles blanch white as she scrolls. "You're not seeing the play here. If you don't control the narrative, the internet will. And it won't be nice."

"I'd rather be called a liar than use someone else's pain for a redemption arc. Let them speculate." I reach for the beads, untangling them with more patience than she could ever muster.

She stares at me for a long time, eyes narrowing. "You're sure about that?"

I nod. "I'm sure."

Brenda leans back, crossing her arms high and tight, like she's physically holding back a monologue. The urge to fill the silence is strong, but I resist. She's always been at her most dangerous when quiet.

"Fine," she says after a minute, voice clipped. "But you know what's going to happen, right? They won't stop until you give them a narrative. If you don't, they'll write their own, and it's never the one you want."

I stifle the habitual reaction of panic, choosing to use the mental tools at my disposal instead. "Maybe they'll get bored. The internet has the attention span of a toddler with a sugar IV."

I hand her phone back and catch her gaze before she can look away. "I'm not going to fan the flames and make Ivy a trending topic."

Brenda softens just enough that I can see the real reason she's here. "You love him."

It isn't a question. Not from her. Not from me, either.

I lean my back against the cold windowpanes. I've never said it out loud, but it's been obvious from the beginning. How nervous Saint made me, how I became so clumsy in his presence that I literally fell into the bushes in front of his restaurant. Every time I was near him, the only thing that mattered was the next thing he'd say.

I think about the first time I really saw him. Not the first time we met, when he barely looked at me, or the first time he called me by my name instead of "you." Not even the first time he touched me.

It was when I felt the weight of his palm on the back of my neck, steadying me during a panic attack I'd tried to hide, the way he didn't say a word about it but just stood there, a tree in a hurricane, until my breathing came back. I'd let him see me at my worst: unwashed, trembling, a bundle of nerves with a brain that trips every anxiety wire in my mental house, yet he accepted every flaw of mine without question. Without judgment.

The grumpiest man in Falcon Haven, so cranky that his moods could color the entire town from the inside out, never made me feel small.

"I love them," I correct Brenda, worrying the edge of my sleeve and thinking about the sweet, mouthy little girl who stands her artistic ground. It's not possible for Saint to raise anything less. "That's why I'm not going to make this worse."

Brenda nods, but there's a sadness in her eyes, a kind of fatigue. "You know, you used to be a lot more selfish. I kind of miss it."

I snort. "You only liked it because it made your job easier."

"You really think you can just hide out in this town and not let the world in?"

I glance around the bookstore, at the quiet shelves and the hand-painted signs and at Marcus behind the register who's been wearing the same argyle sweater since September.

"I think I can try to find a balance. I owe that to myself."

Brenda's eyes flick over me, searching for cracks.

"You know what I don't get?" she says. "You built this entire thing, this weird little empire of honest failure, and now you're just going to … what? Be a person? With a ho-hum day and a coffee order and a favorite park bench?"

Brenda's the only one who knows what I looked like at my lowest, when the only thing I could do was lie on the kitchen floor and let the tile cool my skin while I wondered if I'd ever be worth anything again. She's seen the screenshots, the threats, the humiliations that come with being a woman who posts her life for a living. She's been the first to call me after every disaster, even the ones she caused.

I look out the window at the town square, where the leaves are just starting to turn. It's beautiful here. I'm *happy* here.

Even if I have to learn to find contentment without Saint and Ivy.

"I was a mess then," I say, and it's not even an apology. "But I'm not a mess anymore."

Brenda stares at me for a long beat, then laughs. "You're the weirdest success story I've ever managed."

She stands, smoothing her bright blue skirt with the kind of violence that could iron out steel and slings her bag over one shoulder.

"I'm not saying you're right, but I am saying you're not wrong. Don't go all withering Midwesterner on me, though. If you start saying things like 'it is what it is,' I'll have to stage an intervention."

"Duly noted," I say, and mean it.

Brenda leaves me with a brisk hug and a business card for a lawyer who specializes in "online privacy reclamations." I doubt I'll ever call, but the gesture matters. She's always been better at armor piercing than damage repair, but maybe that's why she's the only one I ever let in.

I spend the next hour shelving books for Marcus, who claims his back is "made of antique glass." He tells me I have a librarian's soul and that I should apply for a permanent job once my "influencing days" are over. I thank him, but tell him I'm happy doing what I'm doing for now, then wonder if that's too close to the phrase Brenda banned and if she's going to show up with a canceled flight and a pitchfork.

Before heading upstairs, I decide to go for a walk, studying the glowing Halloween window displays and trying to picture what my life will look like tomorrow. It's not a panic spiral. It's more like a question posed by a teacher who genuinely wants you to get the answer right.

I take the long way around, up Main Street and around the square (notably away from Saint's restaurant), past the bakery and spinning barber poles.

The town is quiet, but the air is different from last week. People glance my way, but there's no edge to it. Not yet. Maybe they're just used to me by now, or perhaps they see what Brenda sees: a girl who's finally decided to take her own advice and just exist.

Back in my apartment, I open the windows to let in the crisp air, and I film a new video. Not a makeup tutorial, not a hack, not even a pretty flatlay. Just me, pouring the last glass of red from Saint's bottle, cooking pasta for one. No music, no voice-over.

The incoming comments are gentle. Some ask if I'm okay, if I need support, or if there's anything they can do to get me to post more. A few trolls show up, but nothing that stings.

Mostly, they just miss me.

Once finished, I turn off my phone, then set down my fork

and stare at the empty chair across from me, and the ache of missing him is so sharp I can't breathe.

THIRTY-ONE
SAINT

know I've fucked up when the bread won't rise. The dough sits there like a lump of regret, refusing to stretch or climb. I poke it, and it sighs back at me with disappointment.

This isn't my job. Prepping and baking are usually reserved for our boulanger and station chefs, but I can't sleep. I should be organizing and delegating for the Thursday dinner rush, but instead, I'm chained to someone else's workstation, staring at a failed starter with the haunted zeal of a man seeing his own future in a glass bowl.

"You brooding or proofing?" Rome asks, coming around the prep table with a crate of apples balanced on his shoulder, cowboy hat in place, and worn jeans and boots dragging dirt across the floor.

I glare at him. "Do you see any movement?"

Rome sets the crates down, cracks his neck, and squints at the dough. "You used the right yeast?"

Rome likes to think, since he helps out by providing local produce on his farm, that he's an honorary sous chef.

"Of course I used the right fucking yeast." I press my palms into the counter, willing the dough to rise by intimidation alone.

Rome grins. "Chill, Chef. It's just bread."

"It's not just bread," I snap, but then I see the glint in his eye. He's baiting me on purpose, trying to get a rise out of me since the dough can't manage it.

He waits for the next blowup, but when it doesn't come, he frowns. "Where's the hurricane?"

"What?"

"The hurricane. You know, the thing where you go berserk over a garnish being one-sixteenth of an inch too wide and then the whole staff cowers for the rest of the night."

"It's five in the morning," I say, aware of how tired I sound.

"You look like shit."

"Thanks."

"All right, well, the good news is I have all morning to pick apart your mood."

Rome bites into an apple with vigor, juice splattering the stainless. I glare at him. The prep cook, a string bean named Lyle, keeps shooting nervous glances between us like he expects a knife fight.

I want to tell him he's not wrong.

Rome finishes his apple, tossing the core in the trash. "You know what I heard? That video of yours hit ten million views before she deleted it."

I go still. "Wrenley deleted it?"

"Yesterday afternoon. Poof. Gone. Like it never existed."

There's a small, tectonic movement inside my chest. I haven't looked at the video since finding it. Watching the comments multiply within five minutes was enough.

"I didn't know," I answer Rome.

"Interesting." Rome leans against the counter, crossing his arms. "So you're telling me she took down a viral video with millions of views that was probably worth serious money in sponsorships ... and you didn't even notice?"

I scrape the failed dough into the trash. "I've been busy."

"Too busy to notice the woman who's got you baking bread at dawn like some Victorian widower?"

"Fuck off, Rome."

"That's more like it." He grins, unperturbed. "Brother, if you don't fix this, I will."

"What the fuck are you on about now?"

"That girl deserves someone who knows her worth."

I turn to him. Slowly. "You wouldn't."

"Try me. I have a thing for complicated women who've been hurt by stupid men."

I'm around the prep table before I can think, getting in his face. Rome doesn't back down. He never does.

"She's not some conquest for you to add to your collection," I growl.

"No," Rome says, voice dropping to match mine. "But she's also not some girl you get to know and then abandon when things get complicated, either."

"You don't know shit about what went on between us."

"Don't I?" He shifts, and I catch the scent of hay and leather that follows him everywhere. "I know you've been in here every morning this week, destroying perfectly good ingredients because you can't sleep. I know you've been snapping at your staff like they personally killed your dog. And I know that woman deleted a video worth more money than most people make in a year to protect you."

"She made her choice," I say, but it sounds hollow even to me.

"Bullshit." Rome steps closer, hat shadowing his eyes. "She made a sacrifice. There's a difference."

Lyle clears his throat from across the kitchen. "Should I ... should I come back later?"

"No," I bark, not taking my eyes off Rome.

"Stay," Rome says, giving Lyle a reassuring nod. "I'm done here, anyway."

Rome grabs another apple, polishes it on his shirt, and tosses it to me. I catch it reflexively.

"You know what your problem is?" He adjusts his hat, stepping back. "You think you're doing her a favor. But what you're really doing is only protecting yourself."

"And what do you know about it? You've met her *once*."

Rome shrugs. "It was enough to like her. And I was there all day with you two. I can't unsee what I saw, and that was two people who were happy together." He hooks his thumbs in the pockets of his jeans, voice softening. "Look, I get it. You built walls for a reason. But those walls aren't just keeping people out anymore. They're keeping you trapped."

I respond with a dismissive grunt. "You don't have a child. You don't know what it's like."

"Maybe not." He straightens, gathering his invoices. "But I know what loneliness looks like. And it's staring back at me right now."

Rome turns to leave, pausing at the kitchen door. "For what it's worth, she didn't just delete that video for you. You know she did it for Ivy, too."

He walks out, boots scuffing against the tile, leaving me with an apple in my hand and a sour taste in my mouth.

I spend the rest of the morning in a fog, delegating tasks with minimal words and maximum intensity. The staff scatters when I approach, a choreography of avoidance I've perfected over the years. Usually, it satisfies me. Today, it just annoys me.

By six o'clock, the dining room is at capacity. Every table is full, and the waitlist is thirty names deep. The servers weave through the dining room with trained professionalism, but their faces are tight with strain.

I turn my attention to the plate in front of me, wiping a smudge of sauce from the rim with a towel. Something feels off tonight. The energy is wrong. Too many cell phones out, too many heads turning toward the kitchen instead of focusing on their food.

"Table twelve wants to know if you'll come out and talk to them," Mags says, sliding a ticket to the expediter. "They specifically asked for the chef."

I stop the expediter with a hand up before he can read out the order.

"I'm busy," I reply, not looking up from the plate. "Tell them I'm in the middle of service."

"They said they're food vloggers from New York. They want to discuss a feature."

I set down my spoon. "I don't do features."

Mags hesitates. "They're being persistent."

"Then tell them I am persistently unavailable."

She nods and retreats. I return to plating, but my concentration is fucked. Food vloggers. From New York. And I thought it was bad when it was just random fans wanting to see a dish "made by the hands."

The kitchen suddenly feels too hot, too crowded. I scan the dining room again, noticing how many phones are pointed in my direction, how many eyes flick toward the pass when they think I'm not looking.

"Table nine wants to know if you'll come out and take a

picture with them," Eddie pipes up from the pass. "And table twelve is asking if we have merchandise."

I stare at him. "Merchandise?"

"T-shirts. Mugs." Eddie shifts uncomfortably. "Something about 'Chef Daddy.'"

"Chef what?" The words leave my mouth so slowly they might as well be crawling across the floor.

Eddie's ears turn the color of the beet puree we serve with the duck. "Chef ... Daddy. That's what they're calling you online. And you've gained two hundred thousand followers."

I stare at him so long that he actually takes a step back, bumping into Lyle, who drops a stack of plates. The crash echoes through the kitchen like a gunshot.

Eddie holds up his hands in surrender. "Their words, not mine. Though I did see someone wearing a T-shirt with 'The Hands' written across it when I came in."

My responding laughter makes him freeze. It's such an unexpected sound that three other line cooks flinch.

Eddie hesitates. "So that's a no on the merch?"

"That's a fuck no. And we have a dress code. If anyone doesn't follow it, they're out on their ass."

"Got it, Chef." He scurries back to the dining room, leaving me to stare blindly. The expo shouts out orders that are piling up. These are dishes I could prepare in my sleep, but right now, it feels like he's shouting in a foreign language.

One of our new servers approaches with her phone out. "Chef, do you mind if I—"

"Put that away before I toss it in the fryer."

She blanches and backs away.

I return to plating, but my hands aren't steady anymore. The quenelle of crème fraîche slides off-center. The microgreens scatter unevenly. Everything is just slightly wrong, like a painting tilted two degrees.

"Refire on table seven," Mags calls out. "They said the duck is too pink."

I look at the returned plate. The duck is perfect. Pink in the center, crispy skin, sauce pooled exactly where it should be. But they're not actually complaining about the food.

They want to see me.

"Table seven can go fuck themselves," I mutter, but I start preparing a new duck anyway. Because that's what you do. You cook. You serve. You don't let the circus distract from the craft.

Unfortunately, the circus has already set up camp in my dining room.

"Chef." Eddie appears at my elbow again. "There's a woman at table fifteen who says she knows you. Says her name is Brenda Chu?"

My knife stills against the cutting board.

Brenda. Wrenley's agent. The woman who picked my lock and sized me up like livestock at a cattle auction.

"What does she want?"

"She ordered the tasting menu and asked me to tell you she's here on business. Not pleasure." Eddie pauses. "She also said to tell you she doesn't bite unless provoked."

I set the knife down, wiping my hands on my apron. Through the kitchen window, I can see table fifteen. Brenda sits alone, perfectly composed in a royal blue blazer, scrolling through her phone with the casual indifference of someone who's never doubted her place in the world.

She's not here for the food.

"Take over the pass," I tell Eddie.

Eddie's eyebrows lift halfway to his hairline, but he nods and takes my place. The kitchen's rhythm doesn't falter as I untie my apron and fold it.

I'm through the doors before I can change my mind. The

dining room's ambient chatter dips as I emerge. Phones discreetly angle in my direction, catching the rare sighting.

Brenda doesn't look up as I approach, her manicured finger scrolling through something on her screen. Only when my shadow falls across her table does she finally acknowledge me.

"Chef Toussaint." She sets her phone face down. "Your duck is extraordinary."

"What do you want, Ms. Chu?"

She gestures to the empty chair across from her. "Five minutes of your time."

I remain standing. "I'm in the middle of service."

"Yet here you are." She takes a deliberate sip of wine. "You should know I'm not typically this accommodating. I canceled my flight to be here."

"Is there a point to this conversation?"

Brenda studies me with the skillful eye of someone who assesses value for a living. "She deleted the video."

"Yeah, I heard."

"Do you know what that cost her?" She leans forward, voice dropping. "Three brand deals worth five figures. A cookbook offer. And about ten thousand followers who think she's ghosting them again."

My gut twists. "And?"

"And she's miserable."

Brenda's smile drops, revealing genuine concern beneath her polished exterior.

"She's not the only one," I mutter, then immediately regret the admission.

Brenda's eyes sharpen like she's just spotted prey in tall grass. "Interesting."

She pulls her phone back up, taps the screen a few times, then slides it across the table. "Look at this."

I exhale loudly, then end up taking the seat across from her and reaching for the phone.

Reluctantly, my gaze lands on a video of Wrenley in her kitchen. She's laughing, sunlight catching in her hair as she holds up a mug that says "I'd rather be sleeping." The caption comically reads: *How to pretend you're a morning person when you're actually dead inside.*

Yet she looks radiant. Healthy. Happy.

I swipe to the next video. Wrenley at the lake, skipping stones with perfect form. Her wide smile is genuine as she celebrates a five-skip throw. The comments below are filled with heart emoji and variations of **she's back!**

"She seems fine to me," I say, handing the phone back.

Brenda keeps her phone raised, the paused video of Wrenley jumping in triumph angled at me. "That's because she's exceptionally good at her job. Millions of people think she's thriving. The magic of good content creation."

I clench, then unclench my jaw. "Why are you telling me this?"

"Do you know what she does before filming these?" Brenda asks, voice deceptively casual.

I don't answer.

"She sits on her bathroom floor for twenty minutes, practicing her smile in the mirror." Brenda leans forward, her free hand tapping against the stem of her wineglass.

The revelation punches through me like a fist. I picture Wrenley, my vibrant, chaotic Wrenley, rehearsing happiness in a mirror.

"She used to get up, film, edit, and post, all by 8 a.m.," Brenda continues, swirling her wine. "When she was in LA, New York, anywhere with a decent following. Now she spends hours on a single video. She keeps deleting takes because her smile doesn't look genuine."

"You think that's my fault?" I ask, my voice scraping against my vocal cords.

She takes a sip, then sets down her glass. "I think you both made choices. But I also think you should know something about her that you clearly don't understand."

Brenda leans forward. "I've been her agent for two years. I've seen her through stalkers, death threats, breakdowns, you name it. But I've never seen her quit. Not once. And after what happened with her attacker, most people would've disappeared forever. But after taking time to mentally recover, Wrenley refused. Said her community mattered too much."

I shift uncomfortably, eyes darting toward the kitchen where Eddie's watching me like I've grown a second head, because there's no way I'm still entertaining someone in the dining room when I'd usually drop a curt reply and then dip.

"She was doing well before Falcon Haven, I won't lie," Brenda continues. "But thriving? Not until she came here."

"If this is some kind of guilt trip—"

"This isn't about guilt." Brenda cuts a perfect bite of duck and chews thoughtfully before swallowing. "She started sleeping through the night. Cooking actual meals instead of eating protein bars. Making friends outside of social media."

Brenda pins me with her gaze.

"And I've read about you, too, Chef Daddy. I know the recluse you claim to be, yet you let her into your home, put your daughter in her care, and your restaurant's ratings are up fifteen percent since she came into the picture."

I narrow my eyes. "If you've researched me the way you say you have, you'd know I don't give a shit about ratings. It's why I'm in a town with a population below one thousand."

"Yet your C'est Trois is humming again. Your staff says

you were almost pleasant for the last few weeks there." Brenda plays with her fork. "Funny coincidence, that timeline."

"Then I'll fire them all tomorrow."

Brenda laughs. "You're not actually the tyrant you claim to be. Look at them."

I do. My team works in perfect synchronicity, even without my hovering. Eddie's assisting the expo calling orders with confidence, the line cooks responding with their expert training (mine). But they're fine without me. Better, maybe.

"She helped you, too," Brenda says beside me. "That's what no one's talking about. Everyone's so focused on how you affect her that they're missing how she affects you."

I'm too stubborn to reply, so I grunt a noncommital response instead.

"Right." Brenda laughs under her breath. "It's pure luck that you're no longer pale with bags under your eyes and your restaurant is currently filled with people who came to see the man behind the viral hands."

"That's not why I cook," I snap, unable to stop myself. "I don't do this for views or likes or whatever the fuck else drives people to document their entire existence online."

"No?" Brenda raises a perfectly shaped eyebrow. "You do it because you love it. And when was the last time you *actually* loved it, Chef, rather than going through the motions? Before or after Wrenley?"

Her question hits me like a pan to the face.

My resulting silence must be answer enough, because Brenda's expression relaxes into something almost sympathetic.

"Look, I'm not here to play therapist. I'm here because I care about my client, and because, against my better professional judgment, I think you two might actually be good for each other."

"It's not that simple."

"It never is." She dabs her napkin at the corner of her mouth. "But here's what I know about Wrenley Morgan. She was falling apart before she came here. Completely unraveling. And then she met you and your daughter, and suddenly, she didn't feel like she needed to cling to her platform so hard. She started living outside of it and finding true happiness. Now, that's not necessarily good for *me*, but I love that girl, and I love that she found her place in this world. I wouldn't even ask her to monetize it, which goes against all my principles. It would be hers alone. I understand that about her now."

I'm listening to Brenda's every word, but I'm staring through the small windows of the kitchen doors, where Eddie is expediting with surprising competence. "I have to protect Ivy."

"From what, exactly? Being happy? Having someone who cares about her?" Brenda shrugs. "From what I've seen, Wrenley loves that little girl almost as much as she loves you."

Brenda's phone vibrates on the table, a string of notifications lighting up the screen. "Listen, I have to actually make my flight this time because I have plenty of other stubborn-ass clients to talk off cliffs."

She rises, hooking her designer purse. "Wrenley's not a risk, Saint. She's a choice. And you're allowed to choose her."

With that, Brenda throws a wad of hundreds on the table and winks. "Keep the change. And the advice."

I bite down on the inside of my cheek, preventing the annoyed growl from breathing fire through my nostrils, and watch her leave until I start to feel stupid just sitting in the middle of my dining room, scowling.

Back in the kitchen, I work like a man possessed. The staff leaves me alone, either out of respect or fear. I send out the last orders myself, wipe down every surface, then keep going, starting with breaking down boxes, scrubbing out the walk-in, and reorganizing the dry goods until my hands are slick with sweat and the sting of lemon degreaser.

When it's finally quiet, I stand in the middle of the kitchen and try to remember what it felt like to care about anything other than keeping my head above water.

The answer is, I can't remember. It's buried under years of making sure Ivy had a father who didn't fall apart every time she scraped her knee or woke up screaming in the dark. I built my life like a bomb shelter, every wall reinforced, every entrance and exit accounted for.

I thought I was doing it for her, but the longer I stand in the silent kitchen, the more I wonder if I was ever protecting anyone but myself.

THIRTY-TWO
SAINT

vy is asleep when I get home, her arms thrown wide and mouth open in a way that makes her look much younger than five. I hover in her doorway for a while, watching her chest rise and fall, feeling the ache of everything I'm supposed to give her. For years, I told myself that keeping her safe was the same as keeping myself safe, that if I just kept turmoil out, the world would never cut into her.

But what if I was just using her as a shield? What if I was so afraid of wanting anything for myself that I hid behind her and let Ivy become the reason I never had to take a risk?

When I finally head downstairs, I find Erin curled up on my couch with a glass of my wine, scrolling through her phone. She's changed out of her professional clothing and into an oversized sweatshirt and leggings, which I understand because it's past 3 a.m....

... until I notice what sweatshirt she's wearing.

It's one of mine, a lived-in, gray one with a flying unicorn pulling a rainbow banner saying "GIRL DAD" that Ivy chose for me a while ago. It's also the one Wrenley stole every morning because she said it had the perfect mix of softness, Ivy-ness, and Saint-ness.

"Make yourself at home," I say dryly, also noticing the fire she's lit in the hearth.

She looks up with a smile that's nothing like the professional mask she wears at school or with my daughter. "I hope you don't mind. I found the wine in your pantry, and Ivy was asking about the fireplace earlier. Thought it might help her sleep better."

My gaze lands on the wine bottle next to her glass. A 2015 Pauillac I brought back from France last year.

"That's a two-hundred-dollar bottle, Erin."

"Is it?" She takes another sip, completely unbothered. "It's delicious. You have excellent taste."

I run a hand through my hair, then move to the kitchen. Bourbon would be preferable, but since I'll be seeing Ivy in a few hours, coffee it is.

Erin gets to her feet and follows, wineglass in hand.

"So," she says, leaning against the doorframe. "I saw the video before Wrenley deleted it."

My hands still on the coffee maker. I've accepted I won't be sleeping tonight. "And?"

"I have to say, I was surprised. You don't strike me as the type to let someone film you."

There's a subtext to her tone that makes my shoulders tense. "It wasn't planned."

"No, I imagine it wasn't." She moves closer, wineglass dangling from her fingers. "But I can see why it went viral."

I can no longer keep my back turned on her. "What's your point, Erin?"

"My point is that I've been watching you for months, Saint. Watching you hold everyone at arm's length, including me." She sets the wineglass on the counter at my elbow. "But you let her in after what, a week?"

Erin's crowding my space enough that I can smell her perfume, spicy and musky, nothing like Wrenley's tropics and flowers.

I lean back against the counter, arms crossed.

She rests a hand on my forearm. "I don't mean to sound ungrateful. Ivy's the best kid I've ever worked with, and you pay me more than I make teaching, but we both know why you hired me, and it's not for my lesson plans."

I stay where I am, a cold curiosity blooming. "Why do you think I hired you?"

She shrugs, rubbing her thumb back and forth against my arm. "Because I'm a safe bet. I'm someone who can handle your daughter without getting attached or messy. I'm not going to fall in love with you, Saint. I'm not going to try to be her mother. I'm not the type to get my heart broken."

Erin lifts her wine with her free hand, takes a sip, then sets it back down, all while keeping her unwavering gaze locked on mine. "Tonight, Ivy woke up twice. She kept calling for Wrenley, even though she wasn't here. She said she dreamed Wrenley was lost at the bottom of the lake."

I flinch, both at the fact that Ivy's having nightmares again, and that Erin's hitting much too close to the truth.

Erin sees it, inching closer until her breasts press against my crossed arms.

"You know," Erin murmurs, sliding her hand up my arm, "I could help you forget about her."

I don't move as her fingers trace the tattoo peeking from beneath my sleeve.

"I'm not looking for that," I say, tone flat.

"Aren't you?" She presses closer, her body warm under my sweatshirt. "You used to be. Before her."

My hands find her shoulders, creating distance between us. "Erin—"

"I've heard the stories, Saint." Her fingers trail down my chest, stopping at the hem of my chef's jacket. "The chef who worked hard and played harder. The man who never spent two nights with the same woman."

She flexes her hand, her fingers brushing against my cock.

When she goes under my shirt, palm flat against my clenched stomach, I let her.

"We could be good together," she murmers, leaning in and tilting her head up until our mouths nearly touch. "No complications. No feelings. Just this."

For a split second, I fall into the old version of myself, the one who would've taken this offer without hesitation and bent her over the counter and fucked away the emptiness while replacing it with fleeting pleasure.

But the image leaves me cold. And flaccid.

"Stop."

I catch her wrist before she can go lower.

"You don't mean that," Erin says with a disbelieving smile.

I drop her wrist, but she doesn't back away. Instead, she takes my rejection as a challenge, pressing forward until her body aligns with mine. The familiar weight of a woman against me triggers nothing—no heat, no desire, no distraction from the hollow ache in my chest.

"Ivy's upstairs," I remind her.

Not that it ever stopped me from taking my time with Wrenley and making her see stars.

"She's sound asleep. I checked twice." Erin slides her hands up my chest again, this time with more purpose.

Her lips brush against my jaw, and I feel ... nothing. Not

even a flicker of the old hunger that used to drive me from bed to bed, body to body.

She tilts her head, studying me with a calculating gaze. "Fuck me, Saint."

I gently pry her off and step to the side, the kitchen feeling too small, too intimate.

Erin follows, undeterred.

"Saint."

Erin's voice drops to a silky purr. She plays with the hem of the sweatshirt, then, with calculated ease, she pulls it over her head, revealing her bare breasts, nipples hardening.

"No strings," she says, reaching for my hand. "No complications. God, I've wanted you for so long."

She guides my palm to her breast, warm and full.

My body should respond. It's a familiar dance, the late-night encounter, the willing woman, the promise of forgetting everything in a haze of sweat and skin. I've choreographed this a hundred times before.

But my hand feels wrong and alien, like I'm watching someone else's hand attached to someone else's arm.

Erin reads the hesitation and leans in, pressing her lips against my mouth, arching into my hand and hoping for friction, reaction, anything.

I almost laugh. The irony is that with Wrenley, I never had to try. She was nervous and shy, but when I put my mouth on her, it was like I released a kraken. She couldn't get enough of me, and I hunted and marked her despite the very real risk that she could rip my heart out of my chest and eat me alive.

With Erin, I wait for that spark, for the heat to simmer into an explosion, for some knee-jerk reaction of who I used to be.

Nothing.

I pull back but Erin chases me down, catching my mouth harder this time, her teeth dragging, tongue insistent.

When I can't take the desperation anymore, I gently break the kiss.

Her breath comes fast, chest rising and falling. She straightens, anger flickering behind her lashes.

"Is it because of her?" Erin asks.

I don't answer.

Erin retreats but doesn't bother to cover up, her shoulders squared and her chin high. "You really can't do it, can you? She's not coming back to you. She's going to move on, leave this town, and live some fake life in a city like LA or New York. Wrenley's the complete *opposite* of you, Saint! She's the exact type of person you want nothing to do with."

I scrub a hand over my jaw and let the silence stretch until it starts to sweat.

"You done?" I ask.

Erin blinks, momentarily thrown. "Excuse me?"

"I said"—I take a step closer, dropping my voice into that low, razor-lined register that used to make line cooks cry—" are you fucking done?"

She folds her arms over her bare chest. "I'm just trying to make you see reason. Wrenley doesn't belong here. She doesn't belong with you."

"And you do?" I laugh, and it's not a nice sound. "You think because you slipped on a sweatshirt and drank my wine that makes you part of my life?"

Her face hardens. "You're being an asshole."

"Yeah, well, congratulations. You finally met me." I step around her and reach for the sweatshirt still puddled on the floor. "You don't get to use my daughter's nightmares as leverage. You don't get to wear Wrenley's sweatshirt and crawl into her spot like you're auditioning to replace her. And you sure as shit don't get to decide who belongs in my life."

Erin stiffens. "So what—you're in love with her?"

I toss the sweatshirt onto the couch. "I was a fucking idiot for letting her go. That's all you need to know."

Erin says, voice tight, "You really think a girl like that is sitting in that apartment dreaming about playing house with a moody chef and his five-year-old? She has millions of fans. You have an awkward kid who draws on your walls."

I grab the wineglass she left behind, overcoming the urge to throw it at the wall to watch it scare the shit out of Erin, the least she deserves after insulting my daughter. I dump it in the sink instead and say, in a deadly tone, "I don't know what I think, but I'll take not knowing over wasting another second pretending anyone else was ever going to measure up."

Erin sputters. "If you want to chase some influencer who's allergic to real life, then fine."

When I turn around, Erin's shoving her arms through her blouse, then grabbing her bag. Her cheeks are red, her expression tight with wounded pride.

"You need to find another nanny," she snaps.

I nod once. "Yep. Figured."

She hesitates like she wants to say something else, but the door slams before she can decide.

The kitchen smells like her perfume and smoke. I open a window, then finish making the coffee. With a steaming mug in my hands, I take a seat at the kitchen island and drink it black, watching the fire in the living room burn down to coals.

THIRTY-THREE
WRENLEY

Wine is the first to go into my cart because it's the only item on my to-do list that makes sense.

The Merc on Main Street has six aisles and a few shelves of local wine, most of them with hand-drawn labels and names like "Blushing Falcon." I pick that bottle and head to the counter. An elderly lady with bright purple nails, a puff of white hair, and neon pink lipstick rings me up.

"That'll be sixteen dollars," the woman says, her voice so surprisingly booming that I nearly drop the bottle. "Blushing Falcon's our best seller. Though I'd have gone with the Midnight Wing whiskey myself. Has a kick that'll knock your socks clean off."

"I'll keep that in mind for next time," I say with a smile, digging through my purse.

"You're that internet girl, aren't you?" She leans over the counter, squinting at me through rhinestone-studded reading glasses that hang from a beaded chain. "The one staying above Cornerstone?"

"That's me. Wrenley Morgan." I extend my hand, which she shakes with surprising strength.

"Maisy. Been running this merc since Nixon was president." She eyes me up and down. "You're prettier in person than on that phone screen. Less shiny."

"Um, thank you?"

The bell above the door jingles as three leather-clad men enter, their motorcycles rumbling to silence outside. They're massive, bearded, and covered in tattoos, the kind of men who'd make most people nervous.

Maisy doesn't even glance their way. "You boys better have wiped those boots. I just mopped. Last time you were in here, you left mud all over my clean floor and scared Mrs. Hemsworth so badly she dropped a dozen eggs."

The largest one, easily six-foot-five with a wild gray beard, looks sheepishly at his feet. "Yes, ma'am."

"You filmed our Saint's hands."

Maisy jarring subject change almost makes me do a double take. I freeze, my credit card hovering between us. "Yes. That was me."

"You've caused quite the stir around here. Not that I mind. It's been a while since we've had a decent scandal. I was starting to get bored."

One of the bikers chuckles, approaching the counter with a bag of beef jerky. "Miss Maisy loves her gossip more than her morning coffee."

"Hush, Tank." Maisy waves him off without looking away from me. "Saint's been moping around town like a kicked dog for well over a week. Haven't seen him this worked up since he first moved here."

My stomach drops. "He's moping?"

"Honey, that man's been ordering his groceries for pickup instead of coming in here himself. That's not normal behavior for someone who used to argue with me about the ripeness of my tomatoes twice a week."

"I didn't mean to cause any trouble," I say.

Macy accepts my card and swipes it. "Trouble? That man's been walking around like a storm cloud for three years. First time I've seen him smile was when you came into town."

Another one of the bikers steps forward, his leather vest creaking. "You're the one who made the pasta video?"

I nod cautiously.

"My old lady made me watch it six times." He grins, revealing very white teeth. "Name's Diesel. You've met Tank, and this here's Crow."

The third one nods, all three suddenly seeming less intimidating and more like overgrown teddy bears in leather.

"Nice to meet you," I say.

"Saint's good people," Tank continues, grabbing another bag of beef jerky from the counter display. "Helped my nephew get a job at the restaurant when he was going through a rough patch. Kid's doing real good now."

Maisy hands me my receipt. "What Tank's trying to say, in his roundabout way, is that Saint's been alone too long. The man needs someone to ruffle his feathers."

"I don't think I'm the right person to ruffle anyone's feathers," I say, tucking the wine bottle under my arm. "I seem to cause more problems than I solve."

Diesel snorts. "Lady, you got that man cooking again. Actually cooking, not just going through the motions. My buddy works the line at C'est Trois. Says Saint's been whistling while he preps. Whistling."

I have trouble picturing a Saint humming out a tune while using his sharp knives.

"Saint doesn't whistle," all four of them confirm in unison, Maisy included.

Tank leans against the counter, his massive frame making the wooden structure creak. "You know what he did last week? Sent the whole kitchen staff home early because they'd had a good service. Gave them all a bonus."

"Again, not normal," Crow adds, speaking for the first time. His voice is surprisingly soft for someone who looks like he could bench press a motorcycle.

Maisy adjusts her rhinestone glasses. "Then you posted that video, and *poof*. Back to grocery pickup and scowling at anyone who looks at him sideways."

My chest tightens. "I took the video down."

"We know, honey." Maisy's expression softens. "But it looks like you took his heart at the same time."

I scoff, but my cheeks are starting to match my Blushing Falcon.

"Question is," Tank says, "what are you gonna do about it?"

"There's nothing to do," I reply. "He made it clear we're not compatible."

"Did he now?" Maisy's eyebrows shoot up toward her white hair.

I shift the wine bottle, suddenly feeling like I'm being judged by the world's most unlikely jury. "It's complicated."

"Love usually is," Maisy says, ringing up the bikers' purchases. "But that doesn't mean you give up on it."

"Who said anything about love?"

The question comes out more panicked than I intended.

All four of them exchange glances, and I realize I've just confirmed everything they suspected.

"Sweetheart," Maisy says, leaning across the counter again, "I've been watching people fall in love in this town for fifty years. I know the signs."

The bell jingles again as another customer enters. I take that as my sign to find an escape hatch.

"We're rooting for you!" Tank shouts. His two other friends pump the air and heartily agree.

Cheeks burning, I scamper away after giving an awkward wave.

Outside the Merc, I clutch my wine bottle and take a steadying breath. The whole town knows. Of course they do. Small towns often have information systems in place that are more efficient than those of the Pentagon.

I start walking back toward my apartment, trying to ignore the flutter in my chest at Tank's words. Saint, whistling in the kitchen? It doesn't sound like the grumpy chef I know, yet I want it to be true so badly it hurts.

My phone vibrates in my pocket. I figure it's Brenda with another brand deal, but check it anyway as I walk under a canopy of red, yellow, and orange leaves, my boots crunching on the ones that have fallen.

But when I pull it out, the notification halts me mid-step.

@SaltySaint has posted for the first time in 1,325 days.

My thumb hovers over the screen, ready to swipe but also *not*. It has to be the sun's rays dappling through the spaces between the leaves, obscuring my screen to the point that I'm not reading it correctly. There's no way Saint would post. Saint only uses his phone to keep tabs on Ivy. I don't think I've ever received a text from him, but because I am who I am and have a whole life on social media, of course I found him and followed him, no matter how dead his account was.

It's not dead, anymore.

I swipe, opening to the post.

When his post loads, there's no music, no caption, just a shaky, poorly lit shot of the weathered garden bench under an oak tree where Ivy and I used to sit for hours. The camera jerks as whoever's filming—Saint, it has to be Saint—struggles to keep it steady. A thumb briefly obscures the corner of the frame, prompting a smile from me, before disappearing.

The focus shifts to a small, dented tin bucket on the bench, the one where Ivy keeps her painted rocks, and a single new rock is placed prominently at the top.

My breathing hitches when I see it: a child's rendering of a red heart with a heavy black outline and a jagged lightning bolt cutting through the center.

A broken heart.

His video lasts only twelve seconds, ending with what sounds like a curse, then a frustrated exhale as the camera cuts off abruptly.

I replay it three times.

My legs feel unsteady, so I sit down on the curb right there on Main Street, clutching my phone and the wine bottle like anchors. The broken heart rock is Ivy's work, obviously. Saint's not one to paint rocks. But the message is unmistakably his.

I notice one comment below the video and tap it open. It's Saint, who's instead of making a caption, accidentally turned it into a comment. Typical, and another smile pulls at my lips until I read it.

Yours if you want it.

Four words that make my chest cavity feel like it's expanding and contracting at the same time. I screenshot the comment before I can think about why, then stare at the image until my eyes water.

No explanation, no context for anyone who doesn't know about Ivy's rock collection. But I know.

I know that Ivy painted this after Saint told her we couldn't see each other anymore. I know she's been asking for me, according to what I've heard around town. And I know that Saint, who hasn't posted on social media in over three years, just put himself out there in the most vulnerable way possible.

For me, after ripping my heart out and stomping on it.

I don't even remember standing up and walking back to my apartment, but suddenly I'm there, setting the wine on my counter. My reflection in the wall mirror shows wild hair and flushed cheeks, like I've been running instead of having an existential crisis on a public street.

I don't overthink it. I can't. If I stop to analyze, I'll talk myself out of going.

The wine stays unopened. My phone gets tossed onto the couch. I grab my keys from the hook by the door and rush out, not bothering with a jacket despite the autumn chill.

My car starts with a reluctant whine, and I'm backing out of my spot before I can second-guess myself. The fifteen-minute drive to Saint's property stretches like pulled taffy, each familiar turn both too slow and too fast. My heartbeat matches the rhythm of the windshield wipers as they sweep away the light mist that's started to fall.

When I pull into his gravel driveway, I don't head toward the main house. Instead, I follow the stone path around the side, past the kitchen garden with its neat rows of herbs and through the small wooden gate that always sticks unless you lift it slightly while pushing.

And there he is.

Saint sits on the same bench I did when I first got here, elbows on his knees and head bowed. He's wearing a black, long-sleeved shirt that stretches across his shoulders, jeans worn down at the knees, and his favorite scuffed boots.

"That was a dirty move."

My voice shakes as I say it, betraying the whirlwind inside me.

Saint's head snaps up. His eyes find mine, blue and bottomless as Falcon Haven's lake in winter. He doesn't smile, doesn't stand or reach for me. He just watches me like one of Rome's horses, like I might spook if he moves too quickly.

"I know," he finally says.

I take three steps closer, leaves crunching under my boots. "Using social media? You hate that place."

"Turns out I'm an expert at that. Hating on things that could be good for me."

Ivy's bucket of rocks sits beside him, the pile inside askew. I itch to reach inside and find the broken heart Ivy painted, but I stay rooted in place.

"Where's Ivy?" I ask, well aware of how quiet the garden is without her presence.

"School." He shifts on the bench, making room beside him. "She doesn't know you're here."

I don't take the offered seat. Not yet. "And if I hadn't come?"

"I would've waited."

The mist is heavier now, darkening the shoulders of his shirt and catching in his eyelashes.

"How long would you have waited?" I ask, aware that I'm pushing it, but unable to stop. I've been miserable these last few weeks. *Miserable.*

Saint leans back against the bench, moisture collecting in the hollow of his throat. "As long as it took."

His sincerity sinks into me like a nutrient I've been denying my body for much too long. I take another step, close enough now that I could drag my finger along his jawline if I dared.

Saint doesn't rise. He stays exactly where he is, allowing me the rare vantage point of looking down at such a tall, commanding man.

"You pushed me away," I say. "You said we couldn't do this without putting Ivy in harm's way."

"I was wrong." He keeps his eyes on mine, but his sentence sounds like he dragged it over gravel first. "I thought I was protecting her and shielding myself."

I cross my arms, hugging my own body against the growing chill. "And now?"

"Now I know what it costs to keep you out." His jaw works, the muscle there jumping. "It didn't protect Ivy. It just taught her that love is something you run from."

The rain picks up, gentle but insistent. Droplets catch in my hair and run down my neck. I should be cold, but now I'm burning from the inside.

"You can't just decide that." I fight to keep steady. "You can't just wake up one morning and change your mind about me being worth the risk."

Saint stands then, slow and deliberate. The bench creaks as he rises to his full height and brings us closer.

"It wasn't one day." His voice drops as I lift my chin to keep my gaze on him. "It was every day. Every fucking day without you."

The rain slides between us, a curtain of silver that does nothing to dilute the beauty of his eyes. I want to surrender to him, but the memory of his rejection still stings like a fresh stab wound.

The honesty in his voice makes it hurt to breathe. This isn't the Saint I've come to know, the man who guards his words like they're made of gold and communicates in grunts and nods and rare, precious smiles.

"I need more than that," I whisper. "I need to know this isn't temporary. That the next time someone recognizes you or asks about us, you won't shut down. I would never put Ivy in danger. *Ever.*"

"I had a nanny problem," Saint says quietly.

I'm taken aback. "What?"

"That's what started all of this." Saint runs his hand through his mist-dampened hair. "I needed someone to watch Ivy, and the universe sent you instead."

"I'm not sure whether to be flattered or insulted."

"I'm saying you were the opposite of convenient." A flicker of a smile crosses his face. "You were the least convenient person who could have walked into my life."

"I was temporary," I say, bristling. "And helping you out of a bind."

"Fuck, I'm not saying this right." Saint spins on his heel, then comes back. "You were never temporary. You were a fucking wildfire that burned down every wall I built. And then when I saw how much Ivy loved you, how much I—" He stops. "I panicked."

My heart keeps hammering. "What about my job? The publicity? The comments? The risk to your privacy?"

"Let them try." A raindrop slides down his temple, along the sharp line of his jaw. "I spent three years teaching my daughter to be brave. Then I met you and forgot how to prove it. I was wrong, Wrenley. The thing that hurt us the most was me pushing you away."

The rain picks up, but neither of us moves. Saint reaches into Ivy's bucket, pulling out the broken heart rock. He holds it between us.

"She painted this the night after you left. Asked me why I 'broke' Miss Wrenley." His thumb traces the jagged lightning bolt splitting the red heart. "I told her adults sometimes make mistakes. She said that was stupid because mistakes can be fixed."

My throat closes.

"She's been setting three plates at the table every night,"

he continues. "Keeps asking when you're coming home. Not if. When."

Saint clasps both my hands in his with Ivy's heart rock in between. "What kind of father does this make me?"

Our combined hands blur through my tears. "One who's learning."

"I don't deserve your forgiveness." Saint is close enough that I have to tilt my head back to see his face. Rain streams down his cheeks. "But Ivy does. She's been asking me every day if I scared you away forever."

"And what do you tell her?"

"That I'm trying to fix my mistake." His hands release mine to frame my face, thumbs brushing away rain and tears. "She said I better grovel really, really good because you're worth it."

A laugh breaks through my sob. "She said grovel?"

"Her exact words. Apparently she learned it from that princess movie where the prince has to win back the girl." His mouth quirks in the ghost of a smile. "She also said I'm supposed to get on my knees."

Oh my God. "Saint, you don't have to—"

He gets down on both knees, getting soaked in the growing puddles. This proud, intimidating man who commands a kitchen and makes grown servers shrivel is kneeling in the rain, looking up at me like I hold his entire world in my hands.

Or his broken heart in the form of a rock made by his daughter.

"I don't care if they camp outside the restaurant," he says, voice strong despite the vulnerable position. "I don't care if they follow us to the grocery store or turn our lives into a circus. I care that my daughter painted a broken heart because the woman she loves disappeared from her life."

His hand squeeze mine, the stone heart warming within my palm.

"I can't control what goes viral," I whisper, "And I don't want to give up what I do, but I wouldn't ever show Ivy."

His eyes never leave mine. "I've already told my staff, no photos in the restaurant. Had my lawyer send cease-and-desist letters to the food vloggers who've been calling. Changed all my social media settings." He pauses. "Well, Noa changed them. I'm still terrible with that stuff."

Despite everything, I smile. "You made a video."

"Took me forty-seven tries. Ivy had to show me how to work the camera." His thumb strokes across my knuckles. "But I would've figured out TikTok if that's what it took to get you back."

The image of Saint struggling with TikTok makes me laugh through my tears. "I don't think you're ready for TikTok."

"I'm ready for whatever comes with loving you," he says simply. "The comments, the attention, the people who think they know our story. None of it matters without you here."

I gasp, heart swelling into my throat. "What did you just say? The first part, I mean, the part about—"

"Being in love with you? Yeah. I mean it. I fell for you the night you broke into my property and threatened me with my own cast iron skillet. I've been falling ever since."

The broken heart rock stays warm and dry in my palm, Ivy's childish artwork suddenly the most precious thing I've ever held.

"Ivy's been teaching me about second chances," Saint continues, his voice soft as the rain. "Apparently I'm a slow learner."

"The slowest," I agree, pulling him to a stand.

His arms come around me, solid and sure, holding me

against his chest where I can hear his heart racing. "Is that a yes?"

I think about Maisy and the bikers rooting for us. About Ivy setting three plates every night. About the way this man gives me the courage to want things I thought I could never have in the real world.

"Ask me properly," I whisper against his throat.

"Wrenley Morgan," Saint says, his voice low and rough against my ear, "will you come home with me?"

"Yes," I breathe into his skin.

Saint's eyes darken, and he guides my mouth to his with a crooked finger under my chin. He takes my breath, obliterates my mind, and tastes like heaven. He cradles my head, deepening the kiss, a groan rising from deep within his chest.

"Your post," I murmur against his lips. "It's probably going viral since you haven't uploaded a thing in years. Everyone was waiting."

Saint's roaming hands pause at my waist. "Let it. I want the whole world to know I'm the idiot who almost lost you and now I'm the lucky bastard who gets to keep you. Think your followers would approve?"

I laugh, pulling him closer as the rain soaks through our clothes. "Oh, they're going to *lose their minds*."

"Good," he growls, and kisses me again. "About time Chef Daddy lived up to his name."

THIRTY-FOUR
WRENLEY

We're both soaked through when we step back inside the house. The rain ticks against the windows, soft and steady like it's trying not to interrupt.

Saint shuts the door behind us and shrugs off his wet shirt, then nods toward the hallway. "I'll grab you something dry."

Swallowing loudly while staring at all that carved, toned muscle under his ink, I trail behind him toward the bedroom. The air inside is warmer, but it's not the heater. It's the way he keeps glancing over his shoulder at me with twin flames in his eyes.

With his bare, rippling back to me, he goes to his drawers and pulls out one of his old tees, triple-washed, gray, over-sized. I take it without a word and disappear into the bathroom.

By the time I return, he's changed into low-rise sweats. His hair is damp, pushed back, and the fire in his eyes has turned into a damned inferno.

The sight of him like this, his skin glistening from leftover rain, the carved V of his muscles disappearing into his sweats and his hair slicked back, makes my knees go weak.

Saint's gaze moves down to my bare thighs, then back up to my face and stays there.

"You okay?" he asks, but there's nothing casual about the question. He's looking for signs of retreat, of second thoughts, of any reason to stop what's about to happen.

I nod. Words are beyond me.

He crosses the floor in three strides.

The scent of him—rain, grass, cologne—fills my lungs. He stops just short of touching me.

I'm drawn to him like a magnet, sliding my palms up his chest, feeling the heat of his skin, the wild stutter of his heart. I tip my chin up, and he bends down, mouth finding mine with a hunger that's almost violent. Tasting him again is so dizzying that I can't decide which way is up.

Saint's hands slide down to the back of my thighs, and in one motion he lifts me into his arms, holding me there like there's nowhere else I could possibly belong. He carries me to the dresser, setting me on it and I almost laugh, because of course he chooses the dresser over the comfort of a bed, but the look in his eyes swallows the sound.

Saint kneels between my knees, palms braced on either side of my hips, and just looks at me. His breathing is short when he drags his knuckles up my thigh and goose bumps bloom in their wake.

My fingers tangle in his damp hair, tugging gently, urging him closer. Saint doesn't need much encouragement. His mouth finds the sensitive skin of my inner thigh, and a shiver racks through me. His tongue traces a hot path upward, my hands fisting in his hair, gluing him to me as the pleasure builds, tight and hot in my belly.

Saint captures my gaze while sucking on my clit, and I nearly come apart by that alone.

He releases his lips long enough to rumble against my swollen folds, "You taste like mine," before diving back in.

My world narrows to the feel of his mouth, the rough scrape of his stubble against my thighs, the insistent pressure of his tongue. I cry out as the first wave hits me, sharp and overwhelming.

Saint doesn't stop. He pushes me higher, gripping my hips to pull me closer, holding me steady as I come apart.

Before the shudders fully subside, he's standing, his hands at the hem of my borrowed T-shirt. He pulls it over my head, tossing it aside without a glance. His eyes roam over my bare breasts, lingering on my hardened nipples.

"Beautiful," he says in a thick voice, his lips shining.

Saint lifts me again, my legs wrapping around his waist instinctively, but he still doesn't carry me to the bed. Saint chooses the wall, his erection hot and hard against my entrance.

He kisses me then, deep and flavorful, his tongue tangling with mine when he enters me in one smooth, easy thrust.

I gasp into his mouth at the sensation of being filled by him again, the friction just right, the angle so deep I see white behind my eyelids.

Saint's rhythm is urgent, desperate, each thrust a claiming.

This isn't just sex. It's our reunion, our *re*claiming, a collision of two people who were starved for each other.

I brokenly say his name against his mouth, over and over, as he keeps driving into me.

He bites my lower lip, grinning when I whine, then slides his hand behind my head to cradle it, his other arm braced under my thigh, holding me against the wall as if I weigh nothing. I'm so high up I'd fall if he let go, but he never does.

Saint has always been the only man to make me feel weightless and pinned down at the same time.

Saint pulls out, just enough to make me mewl in protest, then lifts me higher against the wall. He's strong enough to manhandle me like I'm nothing, and for once, I want to let myself become just sensation and heat.

He shifts his grip, cupping my ass. There's a glint in his eyes, a dare, and then he does something I don't expect.

Saint rocks his hips in a slow, rolling grind, then dips his head and sucks my nipple into his mouth, hard and greedy, while still circling inside me.

The sudden, sharp pull makes my toes curl. I clutch at his shoulders, nails raking the wet, hot skin, clinging as he slides in and out, slow at first but with growing, premeditated intent.

I can't get enough of him, his hands, his mouth, the way he fills me completely. Saint releases my nipple with a wet pop and braces my back with one arm, bending his knees so he can fuck me up, not just in. It's an angle I've never felt before, and the sensation is so intense and precise that I can't even moan, I just gulp at the air, my body clenching around him, his cock hitting the same spot inside me until I'm whimpering.

I'm not just coming; I'm unraveling, every muscle in my body seizing, my mouth frozen open in a silent scream.

"You feel that?" he rasps, voice wrecked. "That's me. All fucking me."

I nod, the words lost, and he rewards me with a slow, devastating thrust that drags the ridge of his cock so deep I see into space.

Saint's eyes are narrow slits, blue turning almost black. His lips bracket my jaw, teeth scraping as he mutters, "I'm never fucking leaving, you hear me?"

I want to answer, but my brain is too busy detonating behind my eyes. All I can do is nod, pulling at his hair, needing him closer, needing him to finish what he started. Saint reads my mind, one hand leaving my ass to slip between our bodies, thumb circling my clit.

I come again, raw and bright and so sudden it nearly hurts. My body pins itself to the wall, Saint's arm the only thing holding me together. He groans, shudders, then comes with a force that makes me feel drunk, dizzy, completely gone. His hips piston through the aftershocks, wringing every last drop until he's spent and I'm boneless … and stuck onto him like a sticker.

While still inside me, he spins us, this time carrying me to the bed. Saint lays me down, sliding out. Then he crawls over me, kissing up my stomach, my chest, my collarbone, until he reaches my lips.

We kiss until he settles beside me with a contented sigh. The Saint who never lets anyone see him soft is gone, at least for me.

"Are you real?" I mumble, burrowing into the pillow to escape the possessiveness of his stare. I don't think it will ever fully sink in how important he thinks I am—that I matter.

He laughs, soft and easy. "I'm not going anywhere, if that's what you're asking."

I roll onto my back, searching his face for any trace of the old Saint, the one who would push me away the second things got too close. I find none.

"Ivy will be home soon," he says, then runs his palm down my bare arm. "You want to stay for dinner?"

I smile. "Only if you're cooking."

Saint's mouth quirks. "I'll do you one better."

He leans over, grabs his phone from the nightstand, and starts typing, then hands it to me with a sly grin.

On the screen is a reservation confirmation. For three. At 7:00.

"Ivy's favorite," he says. "There's a new dessert on the menu. She's been talking about it for a week."

My face splits into a smile so uncontrolled that I have to hide it behind both hands. "You made a reservation at your own restaurant?"

He shrugs, grinning for real now. "Never done that before. Figured you should be my first."

"Saint…" It finally hits me that it's a reservation for three. The rest of my sentence dissolves.

He sits up, elbows on his knees. "You don't have to come if you don't want to. If you're not ready. But I want her to see that I'm not hiding. That you're…" He shakes his head, at a loss for words.

"That you want me to stay," I finish.

He doesn't answer, just pulls me onto his lap. I brace for another round, but instead, Saint wraps my legs around his waist and holds me so tight, my bones fuse to his.

Saint rests his chin on my shoulder, breath cooling the heat he'd just set off, and murmurs, "Ivy's been making a list of her favorite dinners. Every night, she asks if I think you'd like them, too." He buries his nose in my neck, voice muffled. "The way she says your name. You should hear it."

I should. I want to. I want everything. Dinners, lists, the slow creep of new traditions. The thought makes my eyes sting.

He must sense the shift because he kisses my jaw and says, "We can start over. Tonight, if you want."

Start over. As if this is a story that could ever loop back to the beginning.

"I don't want to start over," I say, twisting a little so I can see his face. "I want more of this. Messy, complicated, all of it."

Saint's eyes crinkle at the edges. "Good. Because this is about as neat as I get."

He stands, still holding me, and deposits me on the bed, then disappears into the bathroom and turns the shower on.

I'm too busy admiring his bare ass to notice when he glances over his shoulder and crooks a finger. "You coming?"

THIRTY-FIVE
WRENLEY

By the time Saint and I make it out of his house and to C'est Trois, Ivy's sitting at a corner table in the crowded restaurant, a line of Barbies placed on the pristine linen and a single pink shoe half on, half off her foot. She doesn't look up when we come in, much too focused, her tongue poking from the corner of her mouth as she positions each doll in perfect rows while Noa looks on.

But the second she hears my voice, just a soft "Hey, bug," she drops everything and barrels into me like a heat-seeking missile.

She hits me hard enough that I stumble, laugh, and crouch down to hold her close.

"You came back," she says into my shoulder.

I press my face into her hair.

"I did. Couldn't stay away from you."

Ivy's arms squeeze tighter, little hands digging into my back.

Saint stands above us, watching with a look I've never seen him wear in public, unguarded and proud.

Noa elbows him, not delicately, and jerks her head toward me and Ivy as if to say, *See? The world didn't end.*

Ivy pulls back, her nose inches from mine. "Can we eat yet?"

"Absolutely," I say with a laugh.

Saint pulls out a chair for me, his hand a heavy, sure presence at my waist. The restaurant is packed, louder than I've ever seen it, the energy rolling off the walls in a way that would have made me twitchy a month ago.

But tonight, I feel curiously steady, like the three of us could hold against any noise the world throws at us.

The host brings menus, but Saint waves them off.

"We're getting the chef's menu," he tells Ivy, who grins, because she knows that means tiny plates of everything and at least three kinds of bread.

Noa slides her purse over her shoulder and grins at us. "You know what? Now that you're officially together, Stone and I should totally double-date with you two. We could go mini golfing. Saint would love that."

Saint's face goes carefully blank. "Absolutely not."

"Oh come on, it'll be fun. We can get matching T-shirts. Maybe do one of those escape rooms where you have to work together as a team." Noa's eyes gleam with mischief. "Stone's really into trust exercises."

"Noa."

"What? I'm just saying, now that you're all domesticated and posting feelings on the internet, you might as well lean into it." She winks at me. "Fair warning, Saint gets really competitive at mini golf. Like, scary competitive."

Saint's jaw ticks. "Get out of my restaurant."

"Already leaving!" Noa calls over her shoulder, blowing Ivy a kiss before she heads for the door.

Ivy looks up from arranging her Barbies, and when she

sees me really looking at her, she sets down the doll in her hand.

"Miss Wrenley," she says quietly, "I missed you."

The simplicity of it hits me harder than any elaborate explanation could. "I missed you too, Ivy."

"Are you going to go away again?"

"Not if I can help it," Saint says, using his protective expression on us both.

"Good." She picks up one of her dolls again.

"And you know what?" I say to her. "You don't have to call me Miss Wrenley anymore. Just Wrenley is fine."

Her eyes go wide. "Really?"

"Really."

"Just Wrenley." She tests the name out, smiling with her entire face. "I like that better. I'm only allowed to call adults who are family without mister or missus."

"I like that better, too."

Saint goes very still, his fingers tightening around his water glass. When I meet his eyes, his expression is careful, but there's a warmth there. He clears his throat and takes a drink, as if he's trying not to show too much emotion but failing.

The first course arrives: small plates of seared scallops with pea puree, which makes Ivy scrunch her nose before asking for more. Saint explains each dish as it comes, but I'm only half listening, distracted by the low rumble of his voice and the patient cadence he reserves just for his daughter. I can't believe that I'm sitting here. That I'm a part of this. It's like a dream, but I get to live it without filters, ring lights, or heavy editing. I'm not thinking in captions or engagement metrics or how I'll frame this moment for my audience. I'm just here, present, drinking in the clatter of forks and the way Ivy dips her bread in sauce and how Saint's attention lingers on me, like he can't decide if he wants to devour the food or me first.

I'll always love what I do, but there is something to be said about finding yourself outside of your online persona.

The truth is, I've always been good at performing. Not in a fake way. If anything, I've built my whole following on being a little too honest and vulnerable. But the idea of fitting into a room like this, where everything is tangible and unscripted, used to terrify me. I never knew how to belong in a place unless I could crop out the awkward parts, mute the noise, or delete the whole experience if it got too uncomfortable.

Here, with Ivy's voice pinging above everyone else's in the room and Saint's hand finding mine under the table and rubbing the inside of my wrist, I don't want to edit anything out.

I want every minute, every awkward silence, every too loud laugh. I want to watch Ivy eat a bread roll in three bites and listen to Saint complain about the wine list even though he picked it himself.

I want the real version of this life, not the highlight reel.

Saint keeps catching me staring. The first few times, he just quirks an eyebrow, but eventually, he leans in and murmurs against my ear, "You're making it very hard to focus on the food."

I flush, which only makes him smirk.

"Sorry," I whisper. "I just—"

"I know." He bites his lower lip without breaking our stare, and I nearly soak the chair. "Same."

Ivy, oblivious to the electrical currents passing between us, pipes up with, "Is it true that if you eat too much bread, you turn into a duck?"

Saint coughs and leans back.

I laugh. "I think if you eat enough bread, you'll have to waddle home, which is almost the same thing."

Ivy chews on her bread, then says, "Miss—I mean, Wrenley, do you like it here? Or are you just visiting?"

The words are so blunt and childlike that it takes me a second to realize what she's really asking. Saint freezes, too, the fork paused halfway to his mouth.

I set my fork down. "I like it here. A lot."

Ivy doesn't seem satisfied with my answer. She keeps watching me. Waiting.

I shift in my chair, feeling the heat of Saint's leg pressed against mine.

"I'm not going anywhere if you don't want me to," I amend.

She considers this, then says, "Papa says nobody stays forever."

"That's not what I said."

Saint's voice is gentle, but firm.

"You said nothing lasts. Even bread gets moldy."

Saint closes his eyes, the regret obvious in the lines of his face.

"Some things last," he says, opening them again, "if you take care of them."

The next course arrives, and Ivy eats it with both hands, noodles smearing across her cheeks. I watch her, and I watch Saint, and I realize I want this more than any brand deal or viral video or blue checkmark. I want to sit at this table, in this restaurant, with these two, every single night until the world ends.

I lose track of how many times Saint's hand finds my knee, or how many times Ivy brings the conversation back to whether I am coming over for breakfast tomorrow, or the next day, or ever again. She's as subtle as a sledgehammer, but I don't mind.

After dessert, which Ivy pronounces "illegal" in its deliciousness, she's nearly asleep at the table, her head lolling.

We finish, and Saint scoops Ivy into his arms, her dolls tucked into the crook of his elbow. She's half asleep, blinking in slow motion, content to rest her head on his shoulder while holding out her hand for me. I clasp onto it and follow as he weaves us through the tables.

In the kitchen, the staff see me and erupt into cheers and clapping, the kind of rowdy, unfiltered affection that would have horrified me before. But now, I just smile and duck my head, letting the sound of it soak in while Saint barks at them to shut up or get fired if they wake his daughter.

Outside, the rain has stopped. The air is sharp and clean, and the sky above the parking lot is bruised purple, the moon pressed like a thumbprint through the clouds. Ivy is mostly asleep, but she's holding on to my hand so tight that I have to walk at an awkward angle to keep pace with Saint's long strides.

We don't talk as we load Ivy into her car seat, Saint buckling her in while I brush the hair out of her eyes.

She stirs, blinking up at me.

"Don't go away," she mumbles, then drifts off again.

Saint catches my hand as we both straighten. "She's not the only one who means that."

He releases my hand only long enough to pull his key ring from his pocket. It's heavy and battered, and he slides off a single brass key and holds it out to me, palm up.

I stare at it.

The town itself feels like it's holding its breath, waiting for me to interpret the gesture.

"My house has a heavy security system," Saint says.

"Even if Ivy manages to dodge it every now and again. I think it's time you had a way in, too."

His joke is light, but there's nothing casual about Saint handing over this key, not with Ivy's sleep-slackened face glowing in the back seat, not with the memory of every time he's ever shut a door between us.

I lift my gaze to his. "Are you sure?"

Saint's mouth quirks, but there's nothing sarcastic about the gesture. "I don't give these out. You're the only one."

I take the key. It's warm from his hand and heavier than it looks. My throat threatens to close, but I croak out, "I won't lose it."

He leans in, close enough that his breath stirs the hair at my temple.

"If you do," he murmurs, "I'll give you another. And another. And another."

"Saint."

He leans back at my tone, studying my face.

"I need you to know something." I shift my balance, finding my footing. "I choose this. I choose you."

His expression shifts from concern to affection.

"Good," he says simply. "Because I wasn't planning on making it easy for you to leave again."

"Is that a threat, Toussaint?"

"It's a promise."

He backs me against the car, and when his mouth swoops down, my lips are already parted for him.

Saint kisses like he cooks, with complete focus and zero apology for what he wants. His hands span my waist, holding me exactly where he needs me, and I arch into him because I've missed this, missed him taking what's his.

A little squeak from inside the car makes us break apart,

and I peek through the window to see Ivy blinking drowsily at us, a sleepy smile spreading across her face.

"Papa," she mumbles, "are you kissing Just Wrenley?"

Saint's laugh vibrates through his chest and into mine. "Yes, *mon trésor*. I am."

We stay in each other's arms, and I think about how this is what happily ever after actually looks like, quiet moments where love is found in the everyday spaces, where home is wherever the three of us are together.

"I love you, Wrenley."

It's the second time he's said it, and it lands like a dream come true, like a vow, like the beginning of everything we're going to build together.

"I love you, too, Saint."

The declaration flows from me like it's been waiting its entire life to find him.

"Both of you," I add.

Saint smiles as he tilts my face up and our lips meet.

Welcome to your fresh start, Wren.

This time, I think I'll stay for the whole thing.

EPILOGUE – WRENLEY

Saint's golf ball hits the clown's nose. The colorful statue lets out a wheezy honk and spits a jet of water directly into Saint's face.

"That's it," he says flatly. "I'm burning this place to the ground."

I bite the inside of my cheek, holding back a laugh, but then he drags the hem of his shirt up to wipe his face, and I'm gifted with his inked, washboard abs.

"Exhibitionism isn't going to improve your score," Rome drawls from behind us, tipping his cowboy hat. "Though I appreciate the show."

"You can't arson your way out of losing," I add, lips twitching as I wind my arms around Saint's waist and tip my head up.

"I absolutely can." He presses our chests together, hands bracketing my hips. "But are you going to keep looking at me like that every time I embarrass myself in public?"

"Only if you keep letting me win."

"*Cherie*, I have never let you win."

"Liar."

"Ask anyone," he says, pressing his mouth to my temple. "I'm pathologically competitive. Except with you. With you, I'd lose on purpose if it meant you'd smile like that again."

Noa wolf-whistles from the next hole.

"Oh, good," she calls. "I was worried this date wasn't going to include a strip show."

"Keep talking," Saint says without looking at her. "You'll be next in line when the clown catches fire."

"I *live* for threats," Noa retorts with a grin, tossing her ball into the mouth of a giant plastic shark while Stone stands beside her pretending this is normal. He flew in an hour ago and is still dressed in his designer suit.

Stone takes his first swing, sending the ball careening off the edge of the pirate ship. It ricochets, misses the green entirely, and lands in a decorative moat. He regards the situation with folded arms.

"That tracks," he says.

Noa hooks her arm through his and kisses his cheek, and both of them appear genuinely delighted with each other.

While they're canoodling, Rome steps onto the last green, lines up, and taps the ball in without breaking stride.

He turns, stretches his arms over his head, and says, "I'm done. Someone hand me a drink."

"You're not even going to ask your score?" Noa asks.

"I already know I won," Rome replies, grabbing the beer Stone hands him and taking a long pull.

Saint mutters next to me, "God help the woman who ends up with that one."

I laugh and elbow him playfully. "That can be said about all three of you men."

Rome's date finally emerges from the snack bar, all legs and sequined top that catches the mini golf course's carnival lights. She's his third this month. Or maybe fourth, I've lost count.

She munches on popcorn while pressing herself against his side.

"Anyone keeping score?" she asks.

"Only the losers," Rome says with a wink, his arm sliding around her waist. "Winners focus on more important things." His fingers brush against the exposed skin of her midriff, and she giggles.

Saint rolls his eyes. "You're insufferable."

"And you're drenched," Rome counters. "Seems like the clown made its choice."

I grab Saint's putter before he can weaponize it. "How about we finish this round and head to dinner? I'm starving."

"Good idea," Noa says, hooking her arm through Stone's. "Stone's jet lag is hitting, and I promised him decent food if he went on this triple-date."

I stifle another smile. Noa took her double-date threat and multiplied it, adding Rome and his flavor of the week solely to irritate Saint. She got my stamp of approval because Saint's grumpiness is my favorite kind of foreplay.

I lean into Saint's side, savoring his warmth in the cool evening air on the last day of fall. It hits me that I have no plans to move back to the city. Falcon Haven is my home. This is my new life, surrounded by real friends and loved by a man who once scowled at the very idea of a happily ever after. I don't think I've grinned around a bunch of people as much as I have with this group, and while my cheek muscles ache, I love every minute of it.

We'd taken Ivy to the yearly carnival earlier in the day, then decided to come back at night for some adult time. About a month ago, we found and hired a new nanny, Francine. So far, she's great at handling both Ivy *and* Saint.

"I wish you could film Saint," Noa says to me as she breaks away from Stone and walks up to us. "The look on his face when that clown sprayed him would have broken the internet. Again."

"Absolutely not," Saint says, steering me toward the exit. "My humiliation is not for public consumption."

There's no real heat in his response. He's gotten used to the idea that parts of my life will end up online, though he still draws hard lines around Ivy and himself, which I respect.

"What about a cooking challenge?" Rome suggests, his date now perched on his hip like a glamorous accessory. "Saint versus Stone. Battle of the millionaires."

Stone looks horrified. "I don't cook. Ask Noa. I have people for that."

"Yes, he only joined me in the kitchen initially to get into my pants," Noa says, yelping when Stone pokes her side.

"It worked, though," he says, pulling her close and kissing the top of her head.

Rome's date giggles at their banter. I think her name is Amber? Scarlett? She pulls at his arm, pointing toward the Ferris wheel. I still can't place her name, but her bouncing breasts suggest she really wants on that ride.

"I'm starving," Stone announces, loosening his tie. "Please tell me Maisy's still running the barbecue stand."

"Same spot as always," Saint confirms.

Though he wouldn't be caught dead running a food stand at a carnival, the only reason I was able to drag him back here after dropping off Ivy was the promise of Maisy's home cooking and the line of food trucks that drive into town specifically for the carnival. He plans to taste everything on offer and I'm more than happy to sample every bite of what he wants to feed me.

I pull out my phone to check on Ivy. Francine has sent a

photo of four girls in a living room that looks like a craft store exploded. Glue sticks, construction paper, and what might be an entire bag of sequins cover every surface. Ivy's expanded her friend group in the month since Saint and I have been together, finding other kids with a passion for art. Francine encourages the mess, then makes them all clean it up. It's the best of both worlds.

"Art project or natural disaster?" Saint asks, looking over my shoulder.

"With Ivy? Both."

"Carly!"

Noa's shout cuts through the carnival noise. I turn to see a tall, beautiful woman with red hair near the entrance, phone pressed to one ear, finger in the other, trying to hear over the music. She's picking her way across the grass in a navy suit and heels that keep sinking into the earth.

Rome goes very still in my periphery.

"Is that a friend of yours?" his date asks, following his gaze.

"Something like that," he responds.

Carly pockets her phone and looks up, spotting our group. Her shoulders relax, though her eyes narrow at the sight of Rome's arm draped around his date.

"There you are," she calls, striding toward us with the confidence of someone who knows exactly how good they look in a tight-fitting pantsuit. "Sorry I'm late. Client crisis."

"Sounds traumatic," Rome drawls, but his study lingers on her, tracking her movements with interest.

From what I understand, Carly, Noa, Rome, and Stone all grew up together here in Falcon Haven. They share a history that even Saint's glare can't cut through, and they've never given us the full story of their shared childhoods.

"Never traumatic enough to affect my billable hours,"

Carly quips, stopping in front of us. "Stone. You're back from London. Still pretending to be human?"

Stone's mouth quirks. "Carly. Still pretending to be pleasant?"

"Only on special occasions." She kisses his cheek, then hugs Noa. "Thanks for the invite. I needed an excuse to escape my inbox."

Rome's date shifts, clearly sensing the change in dynamic.

"Hey, Red," Rome says. "Didn't know you were joining us."

"Last-minute edition," Carly replies. "Noa insisted I needed fresh air and fried food."

She extends a hand to Rome's date. "Carly Westbrook."

"Violet," the woman responds, shaking Carly's hand with a tight smile.

Violet removes her hand and re-wraps it around Rome's arm, her mouth now strained at the corners.

"We were just heading to get food," I say, breaking the tension before it can solidify. "Want to join?"

"Absolutely," Carly confirms, falling into step beside Noa as our group moves toward the food trucks. She leans in, her voice dropping, "I see Rome's almost done making his way through the alphabet."

Nudging her, Noa says, "Don't be mean. He's lonelier than he looks."

Carly snorts. "Oh, please."

Violet keeps tugging on Rome's sleeve, asking to ride the Ferris wheel with him, but his attention doesn't stray from Carly, who orders the brisket platter and a beer from Maisy.

"Victory meal," she explains to me as Saint places our order between asking Maisy about her latest shipment of mangoes. "Just destroyed opposing counsel in court today.

His client's paying my client's legal fees and my bonus vacation to Cabo."

"Ruthless," Stone says approvingly.

Carly catches Rome staring. "Problem?"

"Just wondering when you got so bloodthirsty."

"Law school. Turns out I'm good at making grown men cry."

"I bet you are," Rome says, but it's not with his usual easy charm.

She gives Rome the side-eye. "Why are you staring at me eating carnival food?"

"Maybe I like watching you eat."

"That's creepy, Rome."

"Everything I do is creepy to you, Red."

"Not everything." She finishes her corn dog and reaches for a funnel cake. "Your ranch expansion was smart. Risky, but smart."

"You've been paying attention to my business?"

"I pay attention to everything. It's my job. Speaking of, you might want to get a lawyer."

"Are you volunteering?"

"I don't do small-town legal work. Too boring."

"I'm not boring."

"No," Carly says, chewing slowly and then swallowing. "You're not."

The rest of us look on, our gazes ping-ponging between the two of them until Violet whines, "Can we please go, already? The Ferris wheel line is finally short."

"Your wish," Rome says, peeling his attention away from Carly to wink at his date. "Though I know another ride I'd prefer."

"We'll catch up with you later," Violet says to us, backing away and pulling Rome with her. "Save us some food?"

Rome tips his hat at us before spinning on his heel. "Don't wait up."

Carly watches them go, a chunk of brisket growing cold on her fork.

"Fifty says they don't make it past the cotton candy stand," Saint muses, and I poke him in the ribs, giving him a look that says *now is not the time.*

Saint gives me a one-sided smile that tells me he knows exactly what shit he's disturbing.

"Come on," Saint says, his hand sliding down to intertwine with mine. "I saw a Korean fusion truck. I haven't had good bulgogi in months."

I let him pull me toward the trucks, grateful for the excuse to have him to myself. He orders for both of us: bulgogi tacos, kimchi fried rice, something with gochujang that makes my mouth water just watching him negotiate with the chef about spice levels.

"Here," he says, holding a taco to my lips. "Try this."

I take a bite, and the flavors explode on my tongue—sweet, salt, spice, and citrus.

He feeds me another bite, his thumb catching a drop of sauce at the corner of my mouth. The simple touch sends heat spiraling through me.

Saint notices the way it rises into my eyes. "Time to go home."

I drag him toward the parking lot, but Saint has other plans, tugging me behind a row of game booths where the carnival lights cast bright colors across his face. He backs me against the wooden wall, caging me in with his arms.

"Did I tell you how beautiful you look tonight?" he murmurs.

"Only twice," I whisper back, winding my arms around his neck. "But I wouldn't mind hearing it again."

His lips brush against my temple. "Beautiful. Radiant. Mine."

My heart flutters as he captures my mouth, stealing my breath with a kiss that makes me forget we're in public. The world narrows to Saint's hands on my waist, his taste on my tongue, the solid warmth of him pressing me against the booth.

Saint pulls back gently, his arms sliding around my shoulders and his forehead resting against mine. "You're happy?"

"Deliriously," I say, brushing my nose against his. "Though I'm still convinced you let me win at mini golf."

He exhales against my skin, the kind of release that only happens when everything is finally okay.

"I didn't let you win," he murmurs. "You cheated. Distracted me with the way your ass looks bent over that putter."

"Then I should weaponize it more often."

"You already do."

I laugh, grabbing his hand as we step back into the carnival's glow, the hunger still curling between us, and a whole life waiting to be devoured.

MORE BOOKS FROM SK ALLISON

all in kindle unlimited

If you don't want to leave Falcen Haven just yet, read:

Still Yours (Stone and Noa's Story)

If you like your grump to be a single dad (or a dad-to-be), read:

Trust Me Deep

Rock Me Hard

Play Me Wild

If you like your men to fall in love in a small town, read:

Love Me Right

If you like your playboys with a dash of suspense, read:

Dare Me More

If you like your tattooed bad boys and morally gray heroes, read:

Hurt Me Good

Crave Me Now